1.99

Praise for Mary Daheim and her Emma Lord mysteries

THE ALPINE ADVOCATE

"An intriguing mystery novel."
—M. K. WREN

THE ALPINE BETRAYAL

"Editor-publisher Emma Lord finds out that running a small-town newspaper is worse than nutty—it's downright dangerous. Readers will take great pleasure in Mary Daheim's new mystery."
—CAROLYN G. HART

THE ALPINE CHRISTMAS

"If you like cozy mysteries, you need to try Daheim's Alpine series. . . . Recommended."
—*The Snooper*

Please turn the page for more reviews. . . .

By Mary Daheim
Published by The Ballantine Publishing Group:

THE ALPINE ADVOCATE
THE ALPINE BETRAYAL
THE ALPINE CHRISTMAS
THE ALPINE DECOY
THE ALPINE ESCAPE
THE ALPINE FURY
THE ALPINE GAMBLE
THE ALPINE HERO
THE ALPINE ICON
THE ALPINE JOURNEY
THE ALPINE KINDRED
THE ALPINE LEGACY

THE ALPINE
LEGACY

Mary Daheim

THE BALLANTINE PUBLISHING GROUP • NEW YORK

A Ballantine Book
Published by The Ballantine Publishing Group
Copyright © 1999 by Mary Daheim

All rights reserved under International and Pan-American Copyright Conventions. Published in the United States by The Ballantine Publishing Group, a division of Random House, Inc., New York, and simultaneously in Canada by Random House of Canada Limited, Toronto.

Ballantine and colophon are registered trademarks of Random House, Inc.

www.randomhouse.com/BB/

Library of Congress Catalog Card Number: 99-90323

ISBN 0-345-42123-X

Manufactured in the United States of America

First Edition: October 1999

10   9   8   7   6   5   4   3   2   1

THE
ALPINE
LEGACY

Prologue

WHERE DID EMMA Lord go wrong?

Middle-class, educated, entrepreneurial, Lord has all the qualifications for leaving her mark on Skykomish County. Instead, she's taken the easy, craven, and commercial way out by publishing the conservative, knee-jerk, reactionary Alpine Advocate.

Emma Lord would like you to believe that her editorials (mealymouthed if well-mannered essays describes them better) have helped create progress and change in Alpine.

Not so. She has been a stumbling block, a lumplike obstacle, an entrenched self-serving member of the establishment who literally sleeps with the enemy. After nine years as The Advocate's *editor-publisher, Lord has nothing to show for her tenure except (we suspect) a fat bank account.*

Let's look at the facts:

Alpine, Washington, is a small logging community of four thousand inhabitants, with perhaps another twenty-five hundred in surrounding Skykomish County. Some might even refer to our craggy corner of the Pacific Northwest as backward, isolated, and out of touch with contemporary issues and ideas.

They're right.

Alpine's Northern European—specifically, Scandinavian—heritage encourages clinging to the past and resisting the future. Founded as a logging community before World War I, the town was almost wiped out when the original mill was shut down in 1929. Fortunately, there were at least two risk-takers who saved Alpine by building a ski lodge and encouraging sports enthusiasts to take to our snow-covered slopes.

When logging was resumed during and after World War II, the town grew, even flourished. By the late Seventies, commuters from as far away as Everett moved into the area, creating a broader economic and social base. Then, when the ravagers and pillagers of the woods met their match in farsighted environmentalists, Alpine floundered once again. With only one small mill still in operation, the town began to slide back into history.

Luckily, there were a few visionaries to save Alpine again, this time with the construction of Skykomish Community College. The opening of the two-year school has not only brought much-needed life into the area, but ethnic diversity. Alas, there are too many "old-timers" who resent these newcomers whose skin is a different color and whose names don't end in "son" or "sen."

As Alpine undergoes yet another major shift in its socioeconomic configuration, nothing has really changed. Regressive thinkers still seem to be in the vanguard. Let's look at three nagging issues that have failed to be addressed despite urgent needs:

1. Shutting down all logging operations in Skykomish County. We are at the dawn of the twenty-first century. Why are we still cutting trees? What little old-growth timber is left will surely fall in the next decade. Emma Lord exudes sympathy for the loggers, patting these timber rapists on the head, and mewling about how hard it is for them to change jobs because their so-called livelihood has been handed down from father to son ad nauseam.

2. *Hiring a new doctor to replace Peyton Flake. The county commissioners have delayed decision-making, mainly because they're a trio of senile incompetents. While medical science doesn't have all the answers, health care in this county has deteriorated. So, apparently, has Lord's brain, since she makes only an occasional bleat on the editorial page about "hiring a qualified physician." Her lack of verve—not to mention nerve—is enough to make this reader sick—except that if I were, I couldn't get an appointment for six weeks.*

3. *Creating a shelter for battered and abused women. This project falls under the aegis of local church leaders, none of whom seems capable of doing anything but "praying for guidance on this matter," a direct quote from the Lutherans' Donald Nielsen. The need for a shelter has been evident for years, even before my arrival in Alpine. Reluctance to provide funding or merely to determine a site indicates the status of women in this community. The town, the county, and its environs are under the collective thumbs of a male-dominated society. Historically, the men at the helm of Skykomish County have shown a complete disregard for females, as they continue operating in a nineteenth-century time warp. They are a disgrace, and should have been removed from power thirty years ago. What is even more disturbing is that the one woman who is in a position of influence refuses to act.*

Emma Lord should put her tawdry little newspaper up for sale and get out of town. She is a blot on the community, and a pariah among her own sex.
—CRYSTAL BIRD,
editor and publisher of Crystal Clear,
an independent publication dedicated to progress and unity

Chapter One

I HADN'T BEEN SO angry since I was a freshman in high school and my brother Ben told a boy I really liked that I'd had a sex change. "Emma," Ben said to Nick Battista some thirty-five years ago, "is really a *man*." Nick ran like a scared turkey.

"Stop that!" Vida Runkel cried as I threw my coffee mug across the newsroom. "Violence doesn't become you."

I glared at my House & Home editor. "Then what should I do? Haul Crystal Bird into court and sue her for libel?"

Vida picked up her mug of hot water and eyed me from under the brim of her charcoal-gray fedora. "From what I've read, Crystal hasn't actually libeled you. Yet."

"She called me lumplike," I said, glancing down at my reasonably trim figure. "When did she see me? Where did she get the idea I was a lump?"

"A figure of speech, I'm sure," Vida said blithely. "Like sleeping with the enemy."

I stopped storming around the newsroom to see if Vida was being sarcastic. But her broad face under the tousled gray curls seemed innocent. Still, I could never be sure with my House & Home editor. Her mind travels many roads at once, and at terrific speed.

Still angry, I waved the latest copy of *Crystal Clear* at

Vida. "It's only a matter of time before she goes too far. Every issue gets more scurrilous. Last month, she criticized me for driving a Jaguar, and never mind that it's fifteen years old and falling apart. Now she's invaded my private life. What next? And why?"

Vida set the mug down and folded her sturdy arms across her equally sturdy chest. "A good question. Are you certain you don't know her from somewhere? After marrying and moving away from Alpine, Crystal spent most of her adult life in Oregon. Perhaps you crossed paths while you were living in Portland."

"If I did, I don't remember." Stopping by my ad manager's empty desk, I tried to get a rein on my temper. "If she liked Oregon so much, why didn't she stay there?"

Vida peered at me over the rims of her new red-framed glasses. "You didn't stay. You moved here. Crystal, at least, is originally from Alpine."

Even after almost nine years, the natives still considered me an outsider. Sighing, I sat down in Leo Walsh's vacant chair. "I'm tempted to contact a lawyer," I said, ignoring Vida's remark. "Every issue of *Crystal Clear* is more brutal."

"In the old days," Vida said, turning to her battered upright typewriter, "there were several independent publications around here. Cass Pidduck put out a virulent socialist newsletter urging the extermination of Alpine's class system, which didn't exist when this was a company town. Arthur Trews became a religious fanatic in some bizarre sect that promoted the worship of squirrels. And of course there was Averill Fairbanks and his UFO postings, so very peculiar, especially his sketches of what he called Jumping Jupiter Jackrabbits. No ears at all. What kind of a rabbit is that? Sometimes Marius Vandeventer would get quite up in arms," she added, referring to the previous owner of *The Alpine Advocate*.

"The woman can't write, either," I declared, poking at the four-page newsletter. "This is a turgid, pedantic bunch of crap."

"She spells better than Averill," Vida said, inserting a sheet of paper into her typewriter. "Certainly her punctuation is superior to Arthur Trews's and Cass Pidduck's. And please watch your language, Emma."

"It's still crap—or worse," I muttered, scrunching up *Crystal Clear* and tossing it into Leo's wastebasket. "Crystal worked for a bank in Oregon. Why didn't she stick to numbers instead of words?"

"I believe," Vida said in an annoyingly calm tone, "she put out the bank's newsletter before they downsized and let her go."

"In-house publications," I sneered. "They give people the idea they can actually write." I paused as my new reporter, Scott Chamoud, entered the office. "Scott," I began as he grinned a greeting at Vida and me before sitting down at the desk that had belonged to Carla Steinmetz Talliaferro until she quit to get married, "you're from Portland. Did you ever run into this Crystal Bird person?"

Vida looked up from her typewriter. "She wouldn't have been Bird then. As I understand it, she took her maiden name back only after she left Portland. She would have been Crystal Ramsey or Crystal Conley, depending upon which husband she was married to at the time."

Scott, who is so young and good-looking that he makes my eyes water, leaned way back in his swivel chair. "Portland, like Seattle, is a generic term for a forty-mile radius. I was born and raised in Gresham, a suburb. I'm afraid there are several hundred thousand people in Portland that I don't know, Mrs. Runkel."

My new recruit, who had joined the staff November 1, wisely deferred to Vida. Indeed, Scott had excellent manners, as well as brains and talent. After not quite a month with *The Advocate*, his only drawback was that he had severe difficulties meeting a deadline. I hoped that experience would cure him, but knew that Carla had never gotten the hang of the inverted pyramid concept in straight news reporting. Her whos, whats, whens, and wheres could be found scattered throughout the story, instead of in the lead paragraph. I was realistic, however. With the salaries that I could afford on a small weekly, the perfect reporter was beyond my means.

Vida sadly shook her head. "Imagine," she murmured, "living in a place where you don't know the other inhabitants. I've never understood why people choose cities over small towns."

The typewriter rattled as the keys clicked at Vida's usual two-fingered staccato pace. My wrath had waned, at least for the time being. I'd never met Crystal Bird, which made her use of me for target practice all the more puzzling. Luckily, she published *Crystal Clear* on an erratic schedule. She had moved back to the area in April, and brought out her first edition in June. So far, there had been seven issues in Volume One. Since this was the Friday after Thanksgiving, I hoped I'd be free of her harangues until New Year's. Otherwise, Advent was going to be a spiritual bust.

I was off to a bad start anyway. Having missed a full day of work, we had some catching up to do to make our Tuesday deadline. With Scott still easing his way into the job as well as the community, I had to handle more of the hard news until he became assimilated.

Bringing up my editorial format on the computer screen, I uttered a sigh of resignation. The second bridge over the Skykomish River was in the news again, after four years of false starts. The three old duffers who made up the county commissioners had finally yielded to pressure from the community college to change the original site. I was duty-bound to praise them and had written the first two sentences of my editorial when my old friend Paula Rubens came into the cubbyhole I call an office.

"I have my hand out," Paula announced, easing her full figure into one of my twin visitors' chairs. "Literally." She reached into her briefcase and passed a single typewritten page across the desk.

I scanned the sheet, which displayed the logo of Skykomish Community College. "Is all the stained glass your doing?" I asked, referring to the announcement of an upcoming exhibit at the student union building.

"In a way," Paula replied with a wry expression. "This is only the second quarter that I've taught glass-making at the college. Let's just say that the students who are taking part in the show have had a lot of help. And," she added, with no attempt at false modesty, "the really good stuff is mine."

I grinned at Paula, who had the power to lift my spirits. "So the glass show starts next Friday in the RUB," I said, using the acronym for the college's Rasmussen Union Building. "Why so late? Aren't finals coming up?"

"Not until December tenth," Paula replied, untangling the strands of glass beads that cascaded over her handsome bosom. "Assuming we get that far. Wouldn't you know it, my second quarter on campus, and we've got a threat of sexual harassment, two cases of date rape, and a poli-sci professor who showed up in class wearing only his mackinaw."

My eyes bulged. "How come I don't know anything about this stuff?"

Paula sighed. "Because none of it has gone public. I should have kept my mouth shut. Sometimes I forget you're the press." She laughed and gestured at my cubbyhole with a dimpled hand. "All this power in one tiny room."

"Ha." My spirits dropped a notch. "Have you seen this week's copy of *Crystal Clear*?"

Paula laughed, a hearty, rich sound that seemed to make my plywood walls shake. "Not yet. But I've seen the earlier issues. Is Crystal still trying to run you out of town?"

I nodded. "Why has she got it in for me, Paula? You mentioned that you knew her. Has she ever told you why she hates me?"

The Burlington Northern Santa Fe whistled as it slowed on its approach to Alpine. A fresh snowfall the previous night had required crews to plow the stretch of tracks between Alpine and the Cascade Tunnel.

Paula shrugged. "Don't editors need a target? You're a major one for Crystal. Who else can she pick on?"

I admitted I wasn't the only victim. She'd attacked Sheriff Dodge, Mayor Baugh, the county commissioners, the U.S. Forest Service, the state department of wildlife, the local clergy—just about everybody, and all in less than six months. "My complaint," I said to Paula, "is that when it comes to me, she gets personal. Last month she jumped me for using the term *Pilgrim Fathers* in an article on Thanksgiving, and before that, she pitched a five-star fit because Vida had written *ladies* instead of *women* in a piece about the Burl Creek Thimble Club."

Paula shrugged again, then rose from her chair. "Crystal's always been big on women's issues, and I don't blame her. Don't sweat it, Emma, she's not evil, just a little off center. She might move on to somebody else eventually."

"I hope so," I said, also getting to my feet. "Frankly, I'm so pissed I could strangle her."

"Relax," Paula soothed. "Crystal's had kind of a strange

life. Maybe she's—I hate to say it, it's such a stereotype—but maybe she's going through menopause."

"Who isn't?" I snapped, then felt chagrined. "Sorry. I'm still waiting for Doc Dewey to find the right hormone dosage before I really do go out and kill somebody."

Laughing as she put the hood of her car coat over her dark red hair, Paula headed for the door. " 'Women of a certain age,' huh? Aren't we all?"

She was right. Paula was a few years older than I, a woman of the world who appeared to have found contentment in a refurbished farmhouse down the road at Gold Bar.

"Hold it," I called after her. "You have to fill me in on those simmering stories at the college. You know I won't print any of it until charges are filed."

Paula grimaced. "I hate to be a snitch."

Making a clucking sound with my tongue, I reminded her that she couldn't wiggle off the hook so easily. "I need background," I told her. "When you work with deadlines, you snatch up all the preparation you can get."

Paula sighed and leaned an elbow against the doorjamb. "Okay. I have no names of the students involved in the date rape, but they were two separate incidents, four different kids, all off-campus. Or so President Cardenas insists. The sexual-harassment charge stems from a nineteen-year-old male who is charging his female instructor with 'excessive fondling,' whatever that means. Again, I don't know the student's name, but I *think* the teacher involved is Holly St. Sebastien in botany."

I ran Holly through my memory bank: single, mid-thirties, on the plumpish side, pretty if she tried harder, given to giggle fits. "What about the Naked Professor?"

"Sad case," Paula murmured. "It's Earl Havlik, one of the original faculty members when the college started out in the high school."

I nodded. I recalled Earl as a tall, spare man with glasses and a rather large nose.

"Earl's wife moved to Alpine with him, but she hated it," Paula continued. "Mrs. P.—I think her name is Margaret— left him about a year ago. He hasn't been the same since. Maybe you know he boarded up all the windows in his house out on the Burl Creek Road."

I had heard someone mention it—probably Vida—but didn't make the connection with Earl Havlik until now. "Poor guy," I remarked. "Hasn't Nat Cardenas or some- body else at the college tried to get him into counseling?"

"That I don't know," Paula replied. "I'll keep you posted." She exited with a wave, and I heard her greet Vida and Scott in a breezy manner. Scott was cheerful and polite; Vida grunted a goodbye. Sometimes my House & Home editor is possessive of me when it comes to my other female acquaintances.

As soon as Paula had left the newsroom, I informed Scott about the alleged—my favorite journalistic insur- ance word—activity at Skykomish Community College. As Carla's replacement, my new reporter had inherited the campus beat.

"Tame," Scott commented. "You should have heard the weirdo stuff that went on at U of O."

I nodded. "I graduated from Oregon, remember? I was there in the late Sixties. It wasn't Berkeley, but there was action."

"Such a silly time," Vida declared, pulling a sheet of foolscap from her typewriter. "We had our share of pro- testers here, too. Some of the loggers put an end to that nonsense."

Since even in more peaceable eras, the loggers— particularly those who were unemployed—spent their leisure hours pitching each other through the windows of the Icicle Creek Tavern, I didn't doubt Vida's statement.

"It was chaotic," I allowed, remembering anti–Vietnam War protests, equal-rights marches for blacks and women, and the violence that had gone along with what basically were just causes. "It changed the face of America, for better or for worse."

Vida made a tsk-tsk noise. "The women. So ridiculous, demanding equality with men. Why lower yourself?"

Scott stifled a laugh as Leo Walsh entered the office, dusting snow off his dark green parka. "It's started again," my ad manager said in disgust. "I'm used to the rain, but this damned snow for five months a year makes me wonder why I ever left California."

Leo, who had spent much of his life in the L.A. area, never seemed to get the knack of driving in snow. When the first flurries hit in late October, he totaled his Toyota by skidding into a mail truck parked by the Alpine Medical Clinic. Fortunately, Leo hadn't been hurt, and the car had been replaced by a newer model, but his insurance premium had jumped.

Vida was regarding Leo with her gimlet eye. "What point is there in living where the weather never changes? How do you know if it's April or November? Honestly, I'd go quite mad."

Leo chuckled, albeit grimly. "The weatherman in Southern California has the easiest job in the world, Duchess," he said, using the nickname that Vida despised. " 'Sunny today with highs in the seventies and lows in the fifties.' Those guys—and gals, nowadays—can't go wrong."

"They already went wrong," Vida retorted, "by living in California." She inserted another sheet of paper and began tap-tap-tapping away.

I was headed back into my office when Leo called to me. "I just saw Paula Rubens leaving *The Advocate*," he said, placing his parka on the back of his chair and lowering his voice. "Tell me, Emma, am I uglier than I thought I was?"

Leo wasn't ugly at all, in my opinion. A trifle homely, perhaps, but in an attractive, careworn way. "Why do you ask?" I inquired with a quirky smile.

My ad manager ran a freckled hand through his graying auburn hair. "Paula and I went to dinner about a month ago, Café Flore out on the highway, fine food, fine wines, fine conversation. Or so I thought. I've asked her out a couple of other times, but she's always got some excuse. You know her. What do you think?"

"I think," I said honestly, "that she's extremely busy. Paula was only supposed to be part-time at the college with her glass-making class, but they've got her teaching introductory art as well, and right now she's putting an exhibit together. Not to mention that she has her private clients. Christmas is coming, it's a hectic time of year for her."

Leo tipped his head to one side, apparently considering my rationale. "I suppose. But I'm beginning to think Rejection is my middle name." His soulful brown eyes rested on my face.

I winced. Leo and I did things together, but none of them included sex. His off-and-on-again romance with Delphine Corson, the local florist, had come to a dead end several months earlier. I knew—and Leo knew I knew—that he'd always hoped we might have some kind of future, or at least a fling. He also knew why that wasn't likely.

"Try her again after fall quarter is over," I suggested. "Paula's a very focused person."

Leo made a self-deprecating face. "Okay, why not? Or," he asked, his voice now down to a whisper, "how about dinner tonight?"

He'd caught me off guard. "Sure. What time?"

Leo was looking surprised. "Seven?"

I nodded. "Sounds good."

He broke into a grin. "You drive?"

I grinned back. "My pleasure."

Leo sobered. "I wish."

Glancing at my other staff members to make sure they hadn't overheard, I tried to keep smiling. Scott was on the phone. At the typewriter, Vida never broke stride.

But I knew she'd heard us. Vida hears everything.

I was on my way to the courthouse to pick up a copy of the county commissioners' statement on the bridge proposal when Sheriff Milo Dodge loped out of his headquarters, shouting my name. I stopped in front of the Clemans Building and waited for Milo to cross Front Street.

"You see *Crystal Clear* yet?" he asked, pulling up the collar on his brown regulation jacket.

"Yes." I bit off the word. "Are you as annoyed as I am?"

Milo's long face contorted slightly. "Hell, I don't know. Should I be?"

My shoulders slumped in disbelief. "Doesn't it bother you to have our private life in print?"

The sheriff wasn't looking at me, but somewhere over the top of my head, through the snow, toward the brown brick bulk of the courthouse. "Well . . . I wasn't sure that Crystal was talking about me."

"What?" I shrieked. "How many so-called enemies do you think I've slept with?"

Amer Wasco, whose cobbler shop was in the next block, shot me a startled look and decided not to stop for a chat. Head down, he hurried past Milo and me without so much as a murmur.

Nor did Milo lower his eyes to meet mine. "That's not what I meant," he mumbled. "I mean, who *is* the enemy?"

"Anyone in authority. Public officials. Men. And," I added with a touch of bitterness, "me."

Finally, Milo's gaze made contact. "Oh. I figured *sleeping with the enemy* was just a term. You know—a slogan or something."

Milo Dodge is not stupid. But he can be slow, or, to put it more kindly, deliberate. "Unless I'm the one who's dense," I said between gritted teeth, "Crystal Bird used the word *literally*, and was referring to you. To us, I should say, and our former relationship."

Six months ago, perhaps even six weeks ago, I could not have been so blunt without raising Milo's hackles. But after a long and painful cooling-off period, we seemed to have recaptured some of the friendship that had existed between us before we became lovers.

Milo wiped at some snowflakes that had plastered his nose and cheeks. "I don't know about that. I still think maybe Crystal was just playing with words. A metaphor, that's the word I was thinking of." He looked vaguely pleased with himself.

Maybe Milo wasn't stupid, but he was certainly being obtuse. "Okay." I sighed. "Have it your way. Let's hope the rest of Skykomish County will have the same reaction. Personally, I like keeping my reputation as unsullied as possible. Which, I might add, is no mean feat when you're the local newspaper publisher. You won't believe the calls and letters I'm going to get on this issue of *Crystal Clear*. Last issue, when she implied that I was a nincompoop, twenty-seven people wrote to *The Advocate* to say they agreed with Crystal a hundred percent."

Milo kicked at the snow with his heavy boots. "You're getting all worked up over nothing, Emma."

I hesitated. Maybe Milo was right, in some weird, male way. My disposition still wasn't on an even keel, though I'd been able to kick the sleeping pills Doc Dewey had given me back in August when I was averaging as little as three hours of sleep per night.

"At least," I allowed, "Crystal doesn't put out her little rag very often."

"That's right," Milo said, tugging at his earlobe. "Like I told you, I wondered if maybe I should be pissed. But I'm not. Forget it. You won't hear anything from her again for a month."

Given Crystal's past publishing history, I knew Milo was right.

But it turned out that he was wrong.

The snow had stopped when Leo and I drove the two-plus miles from his apartment on Cedar Street to Café Flore just off Highway 2. We had a pleasant, leisurely dinner in the restaurant's French-countryside surroundings. For a couple of hours, Leo could pretend he was in Beverly Hills and I could imagine being in Seattle. The concept bemused us, and we discussed our fantasies at length. While I have been known to confide in my ad manager, and vice versa, I found it best to keep some distance between us. Every so often, I feel that Leo could be a dangerous man. For me. I have a knack for choosing the wrong partners.

It was snowing hard on the way back into town, and I was glad that it was a short trip. Although I've become used to winter driving in Alpine, I still respect the potential treachery of snow and ice.

I also appreciate winter's beauty. As I pulled my aging Jaguar into the carport, I smiled at the sight of my little log house nestled among the snow-covered evergreens. I'd left a couple of lights on, and they glowed warmly in the dark.

The living room still smelled of turkey from the previous day when I'd hosted my staff to Thanksgiving dinner. Vida, who usually spent the holiday with one of her three daughters and their families, had joined us this year. Meg and her husband had gone to Hawaii, Beth had come down with severe stomach flu, and it was Amy's turn to spend the day with her husband Ted's family in Monroe.

After hanging up my duffel coat in the small closet by the front door, I checked the answering machine. One call was registered. I pressed the message button and heard the voice of my son calling from the seminary in St. Paul.

"Mom," said Adam, with that new maturity he'd acquired since discovering he had a religious vocation, "Uncle Ben and I'll both be flying into Seattle on the twenty-third of December. He's meeting me in San Francisco so I can introduce him to my dad. See you soon."

Adam's voice was so assured, so casual, yet so damned *serene*. The news sent me into a paroxysm, and I collapsed on the sofa. I sat there for at least five minutes before picking up the phone and calling Vida.

"Now, now," she began after I'd delivered Adam's bombshell, "why shouldn't your brother finally meet Tommy?"

My former lover and the father of my son was Tom or Mr. Cavanaugh to the rest of the world. But after Vida met him only once, he was Tommy. Naturally, he hadn't seemed to mind.

"Everybody except me seems to be in contact with Tom these days," I replied, anger and frustration causing my voice to tremble along with the rest of me. "It's been almost a year since his wife died, and I still haven't heard a word from him."

Sandra Cavanaugh, the neurotic woman that Tom hadn't quite been able to give up for me, had been found dead in the master bathroom of their San Francisco mansion right after the holidays. Leo, who had once worked for Tom, had finally learned that she had suffered coronary arrest, possibly induced by an overdose of her many medications.

"That's no reason for Ben not to meet Tommy," Vida pointed out. "See here, Emma, you kept Tommy and Adam apart for twenty years. Given the circumstances, I'm not blaming you for that. But when you finally let Tommy meet your son, they began to develop a relationship. It's always sounded mutually beneficial. Why deny the two of them the pleasure of each other's company? Or become upset because your brother wants to meet his nephew's father? You're not using sense."

Sense, as in common sense, was Vida's byword. I sighed into the receiver. "I suppose it's because I'm still mad at Tom. I would have thought he owed me at least a phone call after Sandra died. Or have you forgotten that at one point not too long ago he asked me to marry him?"

"Certainly not," Vida huffed. "I don't forget things. But he had to withdraw the proposal because he was too guilt-ridden to leave Sandra in her precarious state of mental health. I admire Tommy for that. So should you. Now he's probably still feeling guilty because Sandra may have taken those pills deliberately. A full year is the proper period to mourn. As usual, you're being too hard on him, Emma."

Vida was being too easy on Tom. As usual. Still, her words calmed me. "I'll be interested in Ben's reaction to Tom," I said. "He's only heard my side of the story."

"And Adam's," Vida remarked. "As a priest, I'm sure Ben will be very understanding."

Vida, who is Presbyterian, sometimes imbued the clergy with more virtue than I would give them. Ben might be a priest, but he was also my brother. Somehow, I secretly hoped that he would kick Tom's butt. It seemed the least he could do for his poor abandoned sister.

Of course I would never admit it, not even to Vida, but what I wanted most was to hear from Tom.

Chapter Two

ON OUR PUBLICATION date the following Wednesday, we were scooped by a special edition of *Crystal Clear*. There was little comfort in the fact that *The Advocate* was not alone. Crystal Bird had also beaten the met dailies, the other weeklies, and the broadcast media to the punch on a story about a logging ban near Snoqualmie Pass.

"How in hell did she manage to get this leaked to her?" I demanded of my staff as I waved the latest copy around the newsroom. "Who does she know in Seattle or Olympia where this story must have been broken?"

"It might have come out of Wenatchee," Scott Chamoud pointed out. "The timber involved is basically in the Wenatchee Forest. In fact, if you look at the map, the tract is close to Stampede Pass. I don't see it as much of a local story."

As I scanned the big map on the wall behind Scott's desk, I saw that he had a point. Nearby Stevens Pass had been mentioned in Crystal's story only as a point of reference. Or to give the article some local impact, since some of our truck drivers freelanced in other parts of the state. I was still galled, however. "It's the principle of the thing," I groused. "Wenatchee today, the Alpine Lakes Wilderness tomorrow."

Leo rested his chin on one fist. "You're seeing demons where they don't exist, babe. When they start talking about Stevens Pass, and Crystal scoops us, you can pull your hair out by the handfuls."

Scott and Leo were probably right. I acknowledged their words of wisdom with a faint nod, then returned to my office to finish reading the unexpected edition of *Crystal Clear*.

The standard format for the publication was three to four separate articles. She used computer clip art, usually of a generic nature, and displayed a certain visual flair. The logging piece featured a half-column illustration of a cedar tree. The only color in the publication was the logo, the headlines, and the subheads, all of which were deep blue in the current edition. Grudgingly, I admired the graphics, if not the contents.

The second article was an interview with an unidentified woman in Sultan whom Crystal referred to as Zippy. Pointing out that Zippy was not her real name—a damned good thing, in my opinion—Crystal related that the interviewee had escaped from an abusive boyfriend and sought sanctuary in a battered-women's shelter in Everett. Her sanity had been restored, her wounds had been healed, and her life had been handed back to her on a silver platter. Naturally, Crystal went on to point out that if only the local dunces, including me, would take action on a similar shelter, half the female population of Skykomish County would be rescued, and move on to fame and fortune. Or some damned thing. Feeling more perverse than usual, I skipped the last couple of paragraphs. Since I had encouraged at least one battered Alpine wife to leave her violent husband, I felt it was unfair to point a finger at me.

Unfortunately, Crystal didn't stop there. The third and last article was brief, but galling:

Once again, Crystal Bird wrote, and I could see the venom dripping from her word processor, *we suffer from a paucity of leadership as far as the local press is concerned. Emma Lord professes to be a member of St. Mildred's Parish, as well as editor-publisher of* The Alpine Advocate. *If Ms. Lord is so close to Father Dennis Kelly, why can't she use her personal influence to force him into action on social issues? Not only has Ms. Lord been ineffective in the creation of a women's shelter (see above), she hasn't spoken out strongly on a proposed day-care center at Skykomish Community College.*

President Ignacio (Nat) Cardenas utters glib responses to questions about the proposed center. "A committee has been formed to study the issue." "At least three campus sites are being considered." "We are, as always, sympathetic to the needs of our student-parents."

A male-dominated community pays a high price when half its population is neglected. Which, of course, is all the more reason for Emma Lord to step up and speak out on women's issues.

Nor has her staff been active. Carla Steinmetz Talliaferro was replaced by a man whose only qualification for the job seems to be his good looks. We wonder if Ms. Lord was thinking with her brain—or some other, lower part of her anatomy.

That did it. I reached for my Rolodex and looked up the number of Marisa Foxx, a local attorney who also happens to be a member of St. Mildred's.

Unfortunately, Marisa was in conference. Despite assurances that Ms. Foxx would get back to me as soon as possible, I put on my coat and headed outside. Marisa and her partner, Jonathan Sibley, had joined Pratt & Pratt several years earlier after brief stints with the Doukas firm. Winfield Pratt had been dead for thirty years, and his son, Gregory Pratt, was now a superior-court judge.

Marisa and Jonathan made up the firm, though their names had not yet been added to the frosted glass on their old-fashioned door in the Alpine Building.

Pratt & Pratt's offices were directly across the street from *The Advocate*. Thus, I decided to jaywalk in the middle of the block. The snow had stopped, Front Street had been replowed, and midmorning traffic was typically slow.

If I hadn't been so angry, I might have noticed the dirty white van that had pulled around the corner from Fifth Street. Maybe it blended in with the snow-covered sidewalks; maybe I was oblivious. It was the grinding of tire chains that caught my attention. Startled, I looked up and saw the van not more than three feet away. The driver was honking and had rolled down his window.

"Hey, you dumb broad, look the hell where you're going!" he shouted.

"*You* look," I snapped, though my voice was uneven.

"You're jaywalking," he yelled. "You want to get killed?"

"Do you?" I'd recovered from the shock and was still angry.

The driver, who was in his late thirties, had long fair hair and a scruffy beard. I didn't recognize him, and saw that he had a California license plate. No wonder he couldn't drive in the snow, I thought. I was in no mood to be reasonable.

Neither was the driver of the van. He gunned the engine, skidded as he tried to get traction, and came so close that I felt the vehicle brush my sleeve. For one ghastly moment, I thought he was going into a spin that would not only run right over me, but plow through the front of *The Advocate* building.

Luckily, he regained control and roared off. By this

time, three other cars were backed up on Front, so I dutifully waited for them to pass. When I reached the second floor of the Alpine Building, I was even more upset than when I'd left my office.

Marisa's secretary, one of Vida's numerous nieces, informed me that my wait should be brief. The young woman's nameplate on the mahogany desk read JUDI HINSHAW. Vaguely, I remembered that the connection was through Vida's own family of Blatts, rather than her late husband Ernest's Runkel clan.

Marisa greeted me with a surprise that seemed pleasurable, though perhaps her manner was practiced. We had never become friends, though we occasionally chatted after Mass. With women of my own age and interests in short supply in Alpine, I'd often chided myself for not making more of an effort to befriend Marisa.

As it turned out, she had a few minutes to spare before heading for the courthouse. I had gathered all the copies of *Crystal Clear* that I could find, and now presented them to her.

"I know you don't specialize in libel," I said, "but maybe you can tell me if I have a case. I have to admit, I'm not up on the current changes in libel law."

Marisa's smile didn't exactly convey warmth, but somehow it made me feel more at ease. She was actually a few years younger than I, a tall, slim woman with short blonde hair, and a no-nonsense attitude that had been interpreted by some of the locals as a symptom of lesbianism. "I've seen all of these," Marisa said, "except this one." She scanned the first page. "Today's date. I thought *Crystal Clear* came out last week."

"It did. This is an extra edition," I explained, resting my hands on the polished oval table that served as Marisa's desk. "She had something of a scoop. See, that logging-ban story about the Wenatchee Forest."

Marisa's cool gray eyes studied me. "Is that the one that bothers you?"

I shook my head. "Not really. Though I'd like to know how she got hold of it before anybody else did. Go to page four. I assume you've read her other attacks on me."

"Oh, yes," Marisa replied, turning the publication over. "And those on several other people as well. I must admit, she seems to have it in for you."

"That's right." I bit off the words, then waited for Marisa to read the short, if virulent, article. "Well? What do you think?"

Marisa paused before answering. "First, I'd have to study all the issues where she's written about you. Then I'd have to research the current laws. Frankly, they've changed in recent years, specifically with regard to public figures. Which, you realize, is what you are in Alpine."

I let out a hissing sound. "I may be a public figure, but am I a lumplike one? That's how Crystal described me last week."

Marisa waved a slim hand. "Define lumplike under the law. You're aware that I'm no libel expert. If I find that you have a case, I may refer you to someone who specializes in the field."

I nodded. "I understand. Maybe I'm being impulsive or overreacting. But this sort of personal attack drives me nuts. Last week, after Crystal charged that I'd been sleeping with the enemy, I got some of the nastiest letters and phone calls in my tenure at *The Advocate*. And that's saying something! Luckily, most of the letters, as well as the phone messages, were anonymous."

Marisa gave me a knowing look. "But you recognized most of them, I imagine."

"Oh, yes." I sighed. "The worst of it was that there were voices belonging to people who until now had never gotten nasty with me."

"And Sheriff Dodge?" Marisa asked. "Was he also the butt of the article?"

"I don't know," I answered. "Milo's been out of town until last night. He had to attend a sheriffs' conference in Bellingham."

"All right." Marisa sat back in her handsome black leather chair. "I'll get the rest of the issues of *Crystal Clear*. When I've come to a decision, I'll call you. Meanwhile," she added, "this consultation is free."

I hadn't thought of the financial aspect. Contrary to Crystal's allegations, my bank account was far from fat. *Puny* was the word I'd have chosen.

"Thanks, Marisa," I said in surprise. "But you really don't—"

Marisa waved her hand again. "Occasionally, I don't charge for a consultation if it involves a fellow parishioner. I don't have time to volunteer at St. Mildred's, so this is my contribution."

"That's very generous," I said, getting to my feet. "By the way, have you ever met Crystal Bird?"

"Yes," Marisa replied, but didn't elaborate.

I should have known better than to press an attorney for information. But my job involves persistence. "The other people she's attacked in print—have any of them consulted you?"

"I've had inquiries," Marisa admitted, her gaze level but her face expressionless.

"Elected officials?" I waited, but Marisa said nothing. "Academic types?"

Marisa still didn't respond, though the faintest of smiles touched her mouth.

"I wondered," I said, and made my exit. The county commissioners might remain on their dead butts, as was their habit, but Nat Cardenas wasn't likely to take criticism lying down. If nothing else, the college president had a shrewd sense of his political presence in the community.

Shortly after lunch, Paula Rubens called me. "I just read Crystal's latest," she said in a sympathetic voice. "I assume you're furious."

"Assumption correct," I replied. "I've been in a funk ever since I saw it. At this rate, I'm not only going to have to go back on Doc Dewey's sleeping pills, but get him to prescribe some tranquilizers, too."

Paula uttered a truncated laugh. "Just tie one on. In the long run, it's probably easier on your constitution."

I started to tell Paula that I'd seen Marisa Foxx, but thought better of it. So far, I hadn't even confided in Vida. "If I showed up at the liquor store too often, Crystal would start calling me a drunk," I said bitterly.

"Possibly. But I didn't call merely to commiserate." Paula's tone was quite serious. "It occurred to me that maybe you two should get together. Frankly, I can see why Crystal is picking on you. She's frustrated."

"*She's* frustrated?" I shot back. "How do you think *I* feel?"

"I know, I know," Paula said hastily. "That's my point. It's ridiculous for the two of you, who are both involved in publishing—and never mind how silly you may consider *Crystal Clear*—to be at odds. She's obviously angry with you because you're the only other woman around with a real voice in the community. Maybe if you explained your side of it, how you have to deal with advertisers and sources, she'd ease off. Remember, Crystal's never been in the commercial newspaper business. You're articulate, Emma. You might be able to get through to her."

Paula was making sense. "Well . . . Maybe it's worth a try." I doodled on a piece of scrap paper and tried to think through Paula's suggestion. "What's the worst that could happen?"

"More virulent attacks?" Paula said, and laughed. "No, really, it can't hurt. Do you want me to speak to her?"

"You mean to set up a meeting?" I hesitated. Crystal Bird struck me as an unreasonable, perhaps unbalanced, person. "Do you think she'd bend?"

"I'm not sure," Paula answered slowly. "I honestly don't know her that well. I met her years ago when I did a piece of glass for the bank lobby in Portland. Crystal wrote an article about it in their newsletter. Since she moved up here, I've seen her maybe a half-dozen times. Crystal contacted me after she bought that cabin down the highway at Baring. She thought a stained-glass window would add class. Calla lilies, that's what she had in mind. But she didn't want to pay more than three hundred dollars, which was absurd. That type of window would be at least a grand."

"So where does she get her money?" I asked, still undecided about meeting my nemesis.

"I gather the bank gave her a decent package when they let her go," Paula replied. "Plus, her parents passed away within a year of each other. She and her sister sold the family home by the middle school on Tyee Street. I doubt that it went for more than seventy grand, but the old folks might have had some savings. Lester Bird used to own the Venison Inn before he sold it to one of the Iversons."

I hadn't known that Crystal had a sister. "Does she live around here?" I asked after admitting my ignorance.

"Yes," Paula replied. "She's April Eriks. Her husband, Mel, works for Blue Sky Dairy."

I was vaguely acquainted with Del and Luana Eriks, and their daughter, Tiffany. They seemed like decent people. Del and Mel were brothers, according to Vida. "Okay." I sighed. "See if Crystal would deign to meet with me. I suppose it's worth a try."

Vida was alone in the newsroom when I told her about Paula's suggestion. Since it came from another friend of mine, she pooh-poohed it.

"You'll get into a shouting match, mark my words." Vida tapped a pencil on her desk. "I remember Crystal as a little girl. Even then she was ill-tempered, and she gave poor April a terrible time of it."

"You never told me about April and the Eriks connection," I chided.

"Yes, I did," Vida declared. "Back in the spring, when Crystal moved here. You probably weren't paying attention."

That might have been the case. Vida dispenses so much information about so many people that I can't keep track unless I take notes. "I ought to meet her," I said doggedly. "It can't possibly make things worse."

Vida harrumphed. "You think not? Go ahead, confront her. I think it's not only a waste of time, but a bad idea."

I usually heed Vida's words. But I didn't on this occasion, and later I would bitterly regret it.

Paula called late Thursday afternoon to say that Crystal had agreed to see me Friday evening around seven-thirty. I didn't mention the meeting to Vida, and drove home in a bit of a funk. It wasn't my habit to keep too many secrets from Vida, but now I was holding two things back from her: the meeting itself, and my consultation with Marisa Foxx.

Snow had been falling for most of the afternoon. It was slow going as the Jag climbed the hill that led to my log house on Fir Street. Only Front and Alpine Way had been plowed again. By the first week of December, it's taxing work to keep the streets clear and sanded. The snow-removal crew is made up of the Peabody brothers, who are strong of body, but slow of mind.

My spirits lifted a little, however, as I saw several houses with Christmas lights strung over the eaves, and decorated trees, both inside and outside. It was two weeks too soon for me to put up my usual lush Douglas fir, though I'd started to display my Nativity figures. Beginning with the first Sunday of Advent, they emerged one by one from their tissue paper until Baby Jesus would be placed in his crib on Christmas Eve.

The log house was dark when I pulled into the drive, stopping first to get my mail at the box by the street. Mostly bills, I noted, along with a few Christmas cards. Mine weren't quite finished, though I planned to send them out by the tenth.

I gathered a couple of pieces of wood and some kindling from the stash in the carport, then trudged the fifteen feet to my front door.

It was open. Juggling the wood and my handbag, I called in panic: "Who's there?"

No sound could be heard, except for the wind in the evergreens behind the house. Had I forgotten to lock the door when I went to work? I'd been careless once or twice in the past, but not in recent years. Peering at the front yard, I tried to see footprints. There were none, only my own, leaving a trail from the carport.

I called out again. Nothing. Milo had once warned me that it was risky to enter a house that might have been broken into. I reached around the door frame to turn on the lights. I couldn't see that anything had been disturbed. Still, the ominous silence frightened me. Maybe I should get a cell phone. Milo had also urged me to do just that, but I'd put it off, not wanting to spend the money. Common sense required that I get back in the car and drive to the sheriff's office.

The idea angered me. This was my house, my property, my privacy, and it was likely that it had been invaded. Feeling a surge of adrenaline, I stepped inside. I unloaded everything but the larger piece of wood and began exploring the rest of the house. The kitchen, like the living room and dining area, seemed undisturbed. Off the little hall that led out of the living room, I went first into what I still called Adam's room, though he hadn't lived with me on a regular basis for almost ten years. Indeed, he had never occupied the bedroom for more than a few months at a time because he'd started college the same year that I'd purchased *The Advocate*.

He had, however, used the room for storage. Among his treasures was a mason jar filled with pennies, some of which he insisted were rare. The jar was gone from the windowsill. So were his autographed Mariners baseball and several of his heavy-metal tapes.

Cursing, I rushed into my bedroom. My mother's pearls were missing, along with some of my other less expensive jewelry. Pulling out dresser drawers, I saw that an old fox boa that had belonged to my paternal grandmother was also gone.

The closet had been searched, but I couldn't see that anything had been taken. I told myself that it was probably just as well that I'm unable to afford a lavish lifestyle.

I glanced in the bathroom, but saw nothing to alarm me. The shower curtain was pulled aside so I could see that no one was lurking in the tub. Finally putting the piece of wood down on the hearth, I dialed 911.

Beth Rafferty was on duty and expressed sympathy when I told her what had happened. "I can send Jack

Mullins or Bill Blatt." she informed me. "It shouldn't be long unless we get a wreck out on the highway."

I thanked Beth and hung up. Then I poured a stiff bourbon and water before checking the front door. The lock was simple, and apparently had been jimmied. Again, Milo had told me to get a dead bolt. Stupidly, I'd put it off. Without the sheriff to nag me, I'd gotten careless when it came to safety precautions.

I was almost finished with my drink when Milo himself showed up fifteen minutes later. "I just got home and was getting out of my car when I heard your call come in," he said, shrugging out of his regulation jacket. "I told the deputies I'd handle this."

"Thanks, Milo," I said, feeling relief sweep over me. "You're going to be mad. I never got the dead bolt."

He scowled at me from under his heavy sandy brows. "That's really dumb. You know damned well we've had more break-ins around here since the college opened."

"Yes," I said meekly. "Can I fix you a drink?"

"Not until I've checked the place out," Milo replied, returning to the front door. "Jeez, this was like opening a Crackerjack box. Easy as pie." He shook his head, apparently at my stupidity. "They picked the lock. It's the original, isn't it?"

I said that it was. A couple from Everett named Jorgenson had built the log house as a winter ski retreat back in the Fifties when there weren't any other homes on Fir Street. In fact, it had been a dirt road.

"I don't know why the hell you didn't replace the damned locks," Milo declared. For good measure, he kicked the door shut.

"Maybe that's why I got it cheap," I muttered. "By the time I bought it, the Jorgensons were half-dead and could hardly stand up, let alone ski."

"So what's missing?" Milo asked, gazing around the living room.

"Nothing in the living room that I can tell." I had written down the items and handed the list to Milo. "There may be some other stuff, but I'll probably only find out if I need whatever it is later."

Milo looked up from the list. "Liquor? Drugs?"

I pictured the cupboard that served as my liquor cabinet. "I didn't notice anything when I fixed my drink. Bourbon, Scotch, gin, rum, vodka—I think it was all there." I paused and made a face at Milo. "You know I don't do drugs, not even weed."

"I mean prescription drugs. Painkillers and tranquilizers. You got any of those?"

"You know better," I said testily. "Excedrin is my drug of choice. I keep it in the kitchen and it's still there. I took one just before you came."

"I'll check for prints." Milo said. "You build me a Scotch, okay?"

"Okay." Strangely, I hadn't thought about fingerprints. If there were any, no doubt I'd smudged some of them in my frantic search of the house. Surely the burglar had worn gloves. They always did in mystery novels. Besides, it was twenty degrees outside.

I'd built a fire in the grate by the time Milo finished. "I'll have to take your prints," he said, placing his kit on the coffee table. "Too bad I don't have Adam's."

"What do you think?" I asked after he'd finished and I'd cleaned my hands.

The sheriff was lounging in one of my matching easy chairs. In bygone days, we would have sat together on the sofa with my head against his shoulder.

"Kids," Milo replied, sipping his Scotch. "You know the problem. We've had drugs here for years. But now a small percentage of the college students come from bigger towns. They're dealing to the younger kids. To get the money, our local teens are stealing stuff and selling it over in Everett or even in Seattle. We've caught a few who've gotten really careless, but it's tough."

"It must have happened a couple of hours ago," I said. "The snow had covered any footprints or tire tracks."

"Right. I checked. This time of year, it starts getting dark around four, earlier when it's snowing. Did you ask your neighbors if they saw anything?"

I shook my head. "The Marsdens are in Arizona for a couple of weeks. And you know I'm not very friendly with those people on that side," I said, gesturing to my right. "They're the ones with the awful kids."

"Who are old enough to do drugs," Milo remarked. "I'll call on them when I leave."

The people who lived in the houses across Fir probably couldn't see anything through the snow. I had no neighbors in back, only the forest and the steep incline of Tonga Ridge. Which, I realized, set my house up as an ideal target for would-be burglars.

We drank for a few moments without speaking, not the old, intimate silence that had seemed to suit us both so well, but with a melancholy that filled the room like bitter incense. Briefly, I longed for the happier days when I could have found comfort in Milo's arms. Maybe the urge was prompted by the cozy fire, the snow coming down outside, the fright I'd had, or the booze. But we couldn't go back. That road was closed, and I had put up the DO NOT ENTER sign all by myself.

Before Milo left, he asked if I was afraid to stay alone. In which case, he added hastily, maybe I should call Vida. I assured him I was fine. Burglars, as he well knew, rarely returned in such a short time span.

I watched him lope through the snow to the next-door neighbors' house. He is tall, six-foot-five, and despite his fifty years, hasn't gone to fat. That amazes me, because, like me, he never works out and, unlike me, lives on TV dinners.

There was something forlorn about his lanky form as he disappeared among the snowflakes. The evergreens that towered over my yard seemed to dwarf him. Up close, Milo seemed so big; walking away from me, he appeared much smaller. I sensed that he was lonely.

That was definitely like me.

Chapter Three

IN ALL THE excitement over the break-in, I'd forgotten that our bridge club met on the first Thursday of the month. The thought came to me around ten-thirty Friday morning when I was opening the mail, more of which decried my morals and questioned my IQ.

What also occurred to me was that no one had phoned with the usual confirmation. Whoever was hosting the get-together always called the day before we met. This time, I hadn't gotten a reminder.

Heading for lunch through the latest flurry of snow, I decided to take a detour via Sky Travel, which was located across Front Street in the Clemans Building. As I'd hoped, Janet Driggers was on the job. She is a fellow bridge player and the wife of Al Driggers, the local undertaker.

Janet is also very outspoken. She looked up from her own stack of mail as I came in and gave me a big grin. "Well, well," she said, "if it isn't journalism's answer to Jezebel."

"Thanks, Janet. I needed that," I replied, sinking into one of the client chairs. "Did I miss something last night?"

Janet's green eyes gleamed as she leaned forward. "Did you? Who was he?"

I wasn't in the mood to play Janet's ribald games. "I'm talking about bridge club. Nobody called me."

Janet's pretty face sobered. "Oh." The phone rang. Giving me an apologetic look, she picked up the receiver. I tuned out as she tried to handle a client who apparently had been stranded at O'Hare in Chicago. "Look," she said in a sharp tone, "it's not my fault you've been sitting on your ass for three hours. If they say you'll be leaving by one o'clock, believe them. We don't give ticket refunds because Mother Nature is having a tantrum. If you're so steamed, complain to the airline." She paused and gave me a wink. "Have a nice trip, Victor."

Janet hung up. "Russian descent. They're terrible cranks. You'd think they'd be more placid since their ancestors were brought up under a commie regime. If you bitched, you got sent to Siberia. Now, where were we?"

"Bridge club," I said. "Nobody called me, and I forgot."

"Umm." Janet picked up her Starbucks mug and took a sip. "You want it straight or with sugar?"

I shook my head. "I've had enough coffee for one day."

"I'm not talking about coffee, though I should have asked." Janet heaved a big sigh. "First off, forgive me for the Jezebel crack. I was only kidding."

"I know," I said. Janet rarely thought before she spoke. "So what's the bad news?"

Janet made a face. "Some of our fellow card fiends have been upset by the comments in that goofy *Crystal Clear*. The bottom line is that enough of them got their panties in a bunch and felt you shouldn't be included."

I was stunned. I'd known all the members for almost as long as I'd lived in Alpine. We'd played bridge together for most of those years, and usually got along quite well: Edna Mae Dalrymple, the head librarian; Charlene Vickers, wife of Cal who owned the Texaco station; Darlene Adcock, of Harvey and his hardware store; Linda

Grant, high school PE teacher; Francine Wells of Francine's Fine Apparel. There were more, both regulars and substitutes, but none of these women struck me as mean of spirit.

"Dare I ask who?" I said in a hushed voice.

"Honest, Emma, I'm not sure," Janet said with a sad smile. "I could guess. But that wouldn't be fair. It was Linda's turn to give the party, and she called me Wednesday night to say that she'd been on the phone ever since she got home from the high school. At least four of our set had balked at including you. She was in a bind, and asked for my advice. I told her they could go screw themselves, but Linda didn't want to create a situation that would break up the club after all these years."

"So I got screwed instead," I murmured, then shook my head. "Sometimes I forget how small-minded small-towners can be. Just when I think I've become one of them, I realize I haven't."

"You never will," Janet said. "God, Emma, I'm so sorry. But they'll get over it."

I stood up and gave Janet a bleak look. "Maybe. But will I?"

Getting to Crystal Bird's cabin wasn't easy, especially in snow. There was never much more to Baring than a whistle-stop, though at one time I'm told that a couple of saloons, a boardinghouse, a grocery store, and a barbershop existed to serve the men who worked in one of the two local mills. All are gone now, and Crystal's cabin sits on the site of a former railroad logging spur.

I had to admit that Crystal had fixed the place up rather nicely. I presumed the snow-covered roof was made of cedar shakes, though it could have been tin. The shingled exterior was punctuated with small windows accented with bright red paint. A half-dozen steps led to the front porch, and the steel door sported a handsomely decorated glass oval. Maybe that was Crystal's compensation for not getting a calla-lily window.

Crystal was wearing a white terrycloth robe when she opened the door. "Emma Lord?" she said with as much enthusiasm as she would have had for a termite inspector.

"Yes," I replied, then added with a touch of perversity, "Crystal Bird?"

She nodded. Her sideswept bangs were a shock of white; the rest of her hair was golden. The short curls looked damp, and her skin glowed a healthy pink. Without makeup, her small features were bland, except for the gold flecks in her brown eyes. "Come in," she said in a flat, emotionless voice. "I've been in the hot tub. Would you care to join me?"

"No, thanks," I said, following her through the small living room which was filled with old furniture that could charitably be described as antique. "I didn't bring a bathing suit."

"You don't need one," she said, her back still to me. "It's only four steps from the kitchen to the hot tub on the deck."

Crystal didn't need a suit, either. Without embarrassment, she slipped out of the robe and stepped into the steaming tub. Her slim body was in good shape; I suspected she worked out. I eased myself onto a bench and huddled inside my duffel coat. The meeting wasn't off to a good start.

I glanced at my surroundings. The snow had almost stopped except for a few fitful flakes. The deck on which the hot tub sat was small, with the two open sides encircled by evergreens. Candles were placed at intervals on the redwood flooring, and in an alcove where the exterior walls met, I saw a figurine of Merlin, complete with

wand and pointy hat. Tiny crystals flickered in a cave behind him. It took me a few seconds to make the connection with my hostess.

"Care for something to drink?" Crystal asked as she
immersed herself up to her neck and rested her head
against a blue rubber pillow.

"No, thanks," I said, feeling that it would sound silly to
ask for hot chocolate. I assumed Crystal only served
magic potions, à la Merlin. There was already enough
poison flowing between us. I stared at the back of her
head and realized I hated her. I couldn't remember when
I'd harbored such a strong emotion for another human
being.

"I insist you have something," said Crystal in a languid
tone. "There's rum fruit punch heating on the stove.
Here," she went on, nudging at a yellow mug sitting on
the deck behind her. "You can refill mine while you get
some for yourself."

Obediently, I went back into the kitchen, where I noticed other crystal motifs as well as allusions to various
goddesses. I also took in the anti-men slogans plastered
on the refrigerator. MEN SUCK—IN MORE WAYS THAN ONE.
GOD IS A WOMAN—AND IS SHE PISSED. And that old standby:
A WOMAN WITHOUT A MAN IS LIKE A FISH WITHOUT A BI-
CYCLE. I'd never quite figured that one out. Fish have
no feet.

The kettle in which the punch had been heating was
empty when I finished filling the mugs, so I turned off the
stove before going back outside. Crystal thanked me
without looking in my direction.

"Paula Rubens thought we should get together," I finally said, holding the mug in both hands to help warm
my chilly person. "She thinks there may be some misunderstanding between us that we could iron out."

"There's no misunderstanding," Crystal replied calmly. "In fact, I think I understand you very well."

"Oh? Then I guess I don't understand you." I tried to keep my tone light.

"You should." Crystal still didn't look my way. "You've read *Crystal Clear*. The publication is aptly titled. How do you think I haven't made myself clear?"

The condescending amusement in her voice rankled. "Your views are clear," I replied, wishing that Crystal would at least have the courtesy to look me in the eye. "It's the reason behind them that stumps me. Your attacks have grown personal, rather than professional. Why?"

"Isn't it obvious?" Crystal splashed at the water with one bare leg. "You're the only woman in this area who has any influence. You don't use it to benefit other women. Why shouldn't I get personal? You've earned the wrath of women all over Skykomish County. I'm merely their spokesperson."

It was true that I'd gotten more angry letters from the female population since *Crystal Clear* had started coming out. But most of them had been from women I wasn't closely acquainted with, if at all. The bridge club was another matter.

"That's still no excuse for personal attacks in print," I asserted. "Good journalism never lowers itself as you've done. I resent it, and if I have to, I'll take legal action."

Crystal laughed and finally turned her head. "Oh, I'm so scared! Emma Lord is going to sue me. Shall I pack up and run away?"

Silently, I counted to ten as I took a sip of punch. It tasted bitter, but maybe my mood had infected my senses. "Okay. I'm willing to compromise. Contrary to what you may think, I feel very strongly about the women's shelter. You may not have done your homework, but we had one for a short while. The old Doukas house on First Hill was used for that purpose, but there wasn't enough room for more than a dozen women and children at one time. Then the plumbing went out, and it wasn't deemed worthwhile to renovate. As you may know, the house is now closed up, awaiting demolition."

"For six new homes," Crystal said with disgust. "Which, I might add, you wrote a laudatory editorial about because the builder happened to be from your church. I believe that's known in the business as self-serving journalism."

Crystal was partially right about my endorsement. Dick Bourgette, a semiretired contractor from Everett, had bought up the property and planned to erect a half-dozen modest homes on the site. The Doukas house had been vacant for almost five years before the shelter had opened, and was already in disrepair. The churches had banded together to plug the leaks and replace broken windows, but there had never been enough money for serious improvements. It was a losing battle to try to keep the place going.

None of those facts had impressed Crystal. "*The Advocate* is never as self-serving as your handout," I retorted. "*Crystal Clear* is nothing more than you riding all your hobbyhorses."

Crystal ducked under the water, then bobbed up and began blowing bubbles. "Blah-blah-blah, yakkity-yak. Etc. I'm getting bored."

"Then may I finish my proposal?" I snapped, no longer patient.

Crystal gave a toss of her head, drumming her short fingernails on the side of the hot tub.

"I'll write an editorial insisting that the local clergy make a decision by January fifteenth," I said as the snow began to fall harder. "Every week until then, I'll keep after them, in shorter pieces. We'll also run some case histories, like you did with . . . Zippy."

Crystal splashed water over her head, then leaned back against the rubber pillow. "Why January fifteenth? Why not sooner?"

"Because of Christmas," I replied, regaining my reasonable tone. "The pastors will all be busy."

"Christmas." Crystal's voice held a sneer. "I celebrate the winter solstice. It's not nearly as commercial. Go ahead, do as you please. But that's not the only issue at stake."

"I take things one at a time," I replied. "I zero in on issues. The blunderbuss approach doesn't work, especially in a small town. You have to keep everybody focused."

"If you say so." Crystal reached around for her drink. The hand that covered the yellow mug reminded me of a big pink spider. "Your next edition comes out on the tenth of December," she said in a crisp, businesslike tone. "You'd better hit those pious pricks hard, Emma Lord. I'm not a patient woman."

"No kidding," I murmured as I stood up. "However, I'd appreciate a respite. You've been very mean, petty, too. It doesn't become people who have goals."

"Oh, bullshit!" Crystal laughed again. "You're kind of a wuss, aren't you, Emma Lord?"

I didn't respond. As I headed for the kitchen, the phone rang.

"Can you grab that?" Crystal called after me. "I forgot to bring it outside."

The portable phone was on the counter. I set my mug down and picked up the receiver. "Hello?" I said, starting back for the deck.

"Crystal?" The voice sounded puzzled. It also sounded familiar.

"Milo?" I said, equally astonished.

"Who is this?" Milo asked. There was a nervous note in the question.

"It's me, Emma," I replied. "Do you want to talk to Crystal?" I swallowed hard. "She's right here." Without waiting for him to answer, I handed the phone to Crystal.

Then I left. Fast.

It's a miracle I didn't wreck the Jag on my reckless return from Baring to Alpine. The trip was short and I knew the road by heart. What I didn't know was why Milo had called Crystal. Had she also been burglarized? Did she have a complaint about a Peeping Tom watching her nude immersions in the hot tub? Or was I missing the point?

I remembered to enter my house with caution. I also remembered that my father's Colt .45 was hidden in my closet. Unless, I thought with sudden panic, it had been stolen. Making sure that everything in the rest of the house looked undisturbed, I went into the bedroom and hauled out the old jewelry box in which I'd hidden the gun. It was still there. With shaking fingers, I loaded it before I went back into the living room. It was a silly gesture. If the burglar hadn't returned last night, he wouldn't come now.

Sitting on the sofa with the .45 in my lap, I glanced up at the mantel, where the first few pieces of my Nativity set stood by the small wooden stable. In my concern over the meeting with Crystal, I'd forgotten to put out a figure for this sixth day of Advent. Anger, resentment, and growing hatred gnawed at the soul. Advent's gift of grace is ignored when the mind is focused on kicking butt. Setting the gun on the end table, I went to the coat closet where I kept the Holy Family. An angel was due next. Carefully, I removed the tissue and gazed at her graceful wings, white robe, and blonde hair.

She reminded me of Crystal.

I hung her from the roof of the stable and sat back down on the sofa with the Colt .45 by my side. My stomach felt queasy and my nerves were on edge. Even my soul seemed to hurt.

The spirit of Advent still eluded me.

Despite my lack of enthusiasm, I planned to Christmas-shop on Saturday. Another five inches of snow had fallen during the night, but a westerly wind from the Puget Sound basin was dispersing the heavy gray clouds, and the sun was trying to peek through.

The gold tinsel wrapped around the lampposts in the mall parking lot and the jolly Santa cutout at the entrance didn't do much to put me in a holiday mood. Inside the mall, which contains only about twenty stores, I perceived that the other customers looked glum, if determined. Cranky children tried to escape their parents' protective grasp. Tight-lipped couples kept their eyes straight ahead, as if they'd never seen each other before in their lives. Even the elves in the window at Barton's Bootery looked as if they were about to threaten a walkout and join the Teamsters.

Nor did I find much to cheer me inside the stores. The sweater I chose for Ben at Alpine Menswear was sold out in his size; the tennis shoes at Tonga Sport that Adam would have liked cost almost twice as much as I wanted to spend; the blouse I thought would suit Vida at Sky Separates bore a lipstick smudge from a careless customer. Frustrated, I decided to move on to the Front Street shops.

Approaching the sheriff's office, I saw Father Dennis Kelly's Honda parked out front in one of the official-county-business slots. Milo's new red Grand Cherokee was also there, which was unusual for a Saturday. Wondering if the church or the rectory had been broken into, I pulled in across the street.

Neither Father Den nor the sheriff was anywhere in sight. Ron Bjornson, who had been hired the previous July as a sort of jack-of-all-trades, was at the phones behind the curving counter. Deputy Dustin Fong looked up from his computer and gave me a strained smile.

"You heard?" he said in his soft, pleasant voice.

I frowned. "Heard what?"

Warily, Dustin glanced over his shoulder at the door that led to Milo's office. "Maybe I'd better let Sheriff Dodge tell you about it. He's still with Father Kelly."

"Has something happened to Father Den?" I asked in alarm.

Dustin shook his head. He is a young, earnest Asian-American whose city background hadn't prepared him for small-town prejudices. In the two years since he'd been hired, Dustin had slowly managed to adjust. So had most of the local residents, though occasionally some ignorant old duffer would refer to him as "that Chinaman."

"No," Dustin replied in his cautious manner, "Father Kelly's fine. That is . . . well, can you wait a few minutes?"

"Of course." I nodded to Ron Bjornson, who had just gotten off the telephone, then turned back to Dustin. "Can you at least tell me if the church was broken into or vandalized?"

Dustin shook his head. "No, it doesn't have anything to do with the church." He shifted his weight from one foot to the other. "Honest, it shouldn't be long. Sheriff Dodge and Father Kelly have been in there at least twenty minutes."

I glanced at the clock on the opposite wall. It was almost noon. With a smile for Dustin, I sat down in one of the half-dozen chairs that were lined up against the wall across from the counter. Having nothing better to do, I wondered about Milo's call to Crystal Bird.

Ever since hearing his voice on Crystal's phone, I'd purposely put the idea of a social call out of my mind. Certainly Milo wasn't friendly with Crystal. If he had been, I would've gotten some sort of hint in his attitude toward her. It was more likely that in his slow, deliberate manner, he'd finally gotten angry about her allusion to our affair. That made sense, and it was easy to believe.

From my side of the counter, it sounded as if Ron was taking information about a fender bender on Highway 187 near the Icicle Creek Bridge. Two men, one of whom I recognized as Ellsworth Overholt, presented Dustin with a noisy dispute about a cow that couldn't read a NO TRESPASSING sign. I scribbled some notes on both incidents. Scott Chamoud would get the details when he checked the log Monday morning.

At last, Milo and Father Den appeared. They both looked so grave that my heart skipped a beat.

"Emma!" Milo said in surprise. "You got my message?"

I stood up. "No. What's happened?"

"Come on in." The sheriff gestured toward his open door, then shook hands with Dennis Kelly. "Thanks, Father. We'll be in touch."

My pastor and I exchanged anxious smiles as we passed through the swinging door of the counter, going our separate ways. Then I was in Milo's office, which smelled of cigarettes and bad coffee.

"I left three messages this morning," Milo said, easing his lanky form into a swivel armchair. "You must've taken off early."

"Before ten," I said in a taut voice. "Spare me the conversation. What's going on?"

He picked up a pack of Marlboro Lights and shook one out onto the desk. "Where were you last night?"

I didn't like the sharp edge in his usually laconic voice. "I was . . . You know where I was. I answered the phone when you called Crystal Bird."

"That was a few minutes before eight," he said, still in that same official tone. "What did you do after you handed the phone to Crystal?"

"I left. Immediately. I was back home by eight-twenty." Little warning bells were going off in my head. "Has something happened to Crystal?" Given the questions and Milo's attitude, it seemed a logical assumption.

"What happened while you were there?" The sheriff's hazel eyes were very steady as he exhaled a cloud of blue smoke.

"We talked," I replied, feeling the tension build inside me. "Paula Rubens had arranged a meeting between us. It was set for seven-thirty. I might have been five minutes late. The road into Crystal's cabin is tricky, especially in snow."

"What did you talk about?" Milo appeared to have forgotten how to blink.

"Her attitude toward me," I replied. "Why she was so vicious. What we could do to make things better."

"Did you quarrel?"

"No. We argued, but only briefly."

"Then what?"

"We compromised."

"What kind of a mood was she in?"

"Acerbic, which I assume is standard." I leaned forward in my chair. "Look, Milo, you tell me what this is all about or I won't answer another damned question." For emphasis, I slammed my hand down on the desk.

Leaning back in his chair, Milo kept his eyes on my face. "Dennis Kelly called on Crystal this morning. He felt that one of the religious leaders should explain the local churches' position on the shelter and what was being done. Father Den knocked, but no one came to the door, though her sport utility vehicle was parked outside. He went around to what he assumed was the back door. As you know, it leads off the deck." Milo, who is not given to lengthy speeches, paused for breath. "He found Crystal in the hot tub. Her wrists had been slashed and she was dead."

Chapter Four

UNTIL AN AUTOPSY had been performed, Doc Dewey, who also serves as the country coroner, was ruling Crystal's death a suicide. "You're sure Crystal didn't seem upset?" Milo persisted after I'd recovered from the shock of his news.

I summoned up the nerve to glare at him. "You should know. You talked to her after I left. How come, Milo?"

Milo gave a sharp shake of his head. "That doesn't matter."

"The hell it doesn't," I shouted, then lowered my voice. "You had a conversation. How did she sound to you?"

Grimacing, Milo finally looked off toward the opposite wall and his array of NRA posters. "Like she usually does. We didn't talk long."

My eyes narrowed. "It was a business call?"

The grimace turned into a snarl. "*You* don't ask *me* questions, goddamn it. In fact, if you don't have any more information about Crystal, take a hike."

I practically jumped out of the chair. "The only thing I know is that you're a jerk and Crystal was a mean-minded bitch."

"Nice thing to say about the dead," Milo growled.

"Being dead doesn't improve her," I retorted, then managed to trip over my handbag and fall sideways back into the chair. Several four-letter words spurted from my lips.

"Serves you right," muttered the sheriff. Then, perhaps thinking of lawsuits against the county, he asked if I was okay.

"Yeah, fine, swell," I said, standing up and wresting the handbag's strap from where it had gotten caught under one of the chair legs. "Let me know what happens next."

"Aren't you being kind of half-assed?" Milo called out as I reached his door.

"You told me to take a hike. That's what I'm doing." Without turning around, I yanked the door open and tromped through the outer office.

I *was* being half-assed, of course. But our deadline wasn't until Tuesday afternoon, and I refused to give Milo satisfaction. Besides, I had another source. Getting into the Jag, I headed up Fourth Street, turned on Cedar, and pulled into St. Mildred's empty parking lot.

By coincidence, the woman I had helped seek shelter was now working for Father Den. Della Lucci was reeducating herself at Skykomish Community College and living in the rectory with her four children. In a bygone era, two maybe even three priests would have served the county's Catholic parishioners. But the shortage of vocations meant that we were lucky to have a single priest in residence. There was sufficient room left over for the Luccis.

"I don't know where Father is," Della informed me in her wispy voice. She was a plump, docile woman in her forties who had finally left her abusive husband a couple of years earlier. Nunzio Lucci, or Luce, as he was known, had taken up with a woman he'd met at Mugs Ahoy and moved to Arlington. The Luccis had never divorced, and despite Luce's abusive nature and rotten disposition, he and Della had agreed to sell their small frame house by Burl Creek and split the profits.

I smiled reassuringly at Della. She was one of those poor creatures who always seemed to need reassurance. Whatever self-confidence she had as a young woman must have been peeled away by Luce's constant bullying.

"I know Father Den went out earlier," I said. "Would you mind if I wait?"

"Oh, no, Ms. Lord," Della said, wide-eyed, and deferring to me as she always did to those she considered her social betters. Which, I realized, was just about anyone who didn't walk on all fours. "Come into the parlor. Would you like some coffee?"

I declined, but followed Della inside. The parlor had been refurbished since Father Fitzgerald's tenure as pastor. In those days, it had been a dark little corner, full of mohair furniture and sentimental holy pictures. Now the drapes were open and the furnishings more modern, if utilitarian. All but one painting of the Scared Heart of Jesus had been replaced by brightly colored African wall hangings.

For Dennis Kelly was a black man in a white community, and like Dustin Fong and other minorities who had managed to wedge their way into Alpine, he had found resistance, suspicion, and even hostility. But Den had courage as well as charity, and had won over his parishioners, as well as many of the town's more broad-minded Protestants.

I reflected on his fortitude while I waited. Della had gone off to supervise her two younger children, who had put on snowsuits and were going outside to build a fort.

Father Den arrived about ten minutes later, looking strained, but not surprised to see me. "Dodge must have told you about Crystal," he said, sitting down across from me. "That was pretty ghastly."

"For you," I remarked.

"For her." His brown eyes conveyed the merest hint of reproach. "I didn't know her, but she must have been a troubled soul."

"Tell me about what you found," I said. "I didn't beg Milo for the details. He was in a foul mood."

Father Den sighed and crossed his legs. "Dodge told me not to talk about any of this. But I suppose he meant idle gossip."

I saw the glint in Den's eyes. "This isn't idle gossip," I said with a straight face. "This is my job."

Den nodded once. "Then it's okay. Besides," he added, "you're a member of my flock. Dodge isn't." He smiled a bit slyly before starting his recital. "Crystal was floating in the hot tub facedown. At first, I thought she might have passed out. I grabbed her by the ankle and some-how managed to get her up onto the deck. That's when I saw the cuts on her wrists. Of course I knew right away she was dead. I gave her the Sacrament of the Sick, though I've no idea how long she'd been gone."

I refrained from commenting that Crystal would have scoffed at Father Den's administration of what used to be called the Last Rites. While the sacrament was some-times given to individuals who weren't terminally ill, the new name struck me as ironic, especially in a case like Crystal's. I suppose the mutation was intended to give hope; it seemed to me that it was meant to avoid the sug-gestion of death. Crystal, of course, wouldn't have cared if Den had poured a bucket of tar over her head.

"Milo told me you went there to talk to her about the clergy's position on the shelter," I said.

Father Den nodded. He's about my age, a pleasant-looking man whose dark hair is beginning to show signs of male-pattern baldness. "After I saw the special edition of *Crystal Clear* the other day where she berated you over not berating me, I thought about it and prayed on it. Then I decided to extend a hand. I'd have preferred a left hook," he added in his wry manner, "but the Holy Spirit told me it was a bad idea."

"What were you going to tell her?" I asked, relaxing a little for the first time since I'd gotten out of bed. Father Den has that kind of effect on me. He is always the calm place in the eye of the storm.

"Oh—you know, that we're trying to sign a lease for the old Alpine Hotel, but the Californians who bought it a while back are involved in some kind of litigation." He paused and smiled. "Californians usually are, aren't they? Anyway, all I could tell her was the truth, which I assume she already knew but ignored in her crusade for the shelter."

The Californians were actually very nice people who had planned to renovate the old hotel on Front Street. They had run out of money early in the project, but hadn't yet decided whether to sell or lease the property. Like the former Doukas home, the hotel required extensive repairs, but it had been rewired and replumbed, which were big-ticket items. It was also much larger than the house on First Hill.

"What did you do after you hauled Crystal out of the hot tub?" I asked.

Father Den grimaced. "I went inside—the back door wasn't locked—to find the phone. I looked all over the place, but it turned out the portable was right there on the deck. I hadn't seen it."

"No wonder. It must have been an awful shock," I commiserated.

"Exactly." Father Den cleared his throat. "I called for help, and then I stayed out there on the deck with the body and prayed. Milo showed up about fifteen minutes later, along with some of the other emergency people."

"Any sign of a struggle?"

Den grinned. "This sounds like an interview."

"It is." I grinned back. "Remember, it's my job."

"You're not taking notes."

"I don't need to so far. These kinds of facts stick." At some point, I would get out my notebook and a pen. Unlike Vida, who absorbs and retains information like a sponge, I had trouble remembering details. "As I was saying, signs of a struggle?"

"Nothing. The snow around the deck had pretty much filled up whatever tracks had been made earlier," Den said, his high forehead creasing. "Dodge found a straight-edged razor at the bottom of the hot tub. Or so he told me after we got back to his office. I assume he passed that on to you, too."

"He did not," I retorted. "He acted as if I were the one who slashed Crystal's wrists."

Den was silent for a few moments. "I wish I'd known Crystal," he finally said.

"You mean so you could figure her for a suicide?"

He shook his head. "No. So I could have found out why she was so troubled." Den put up a hand. "Don't think I feel I might have helped her. I've no illusions about that. But sometimes in learning what makes people tick, down the road you *can* help someone like them."

"She didn't strike me as the suicidal type," I put in. "Too arrogant, too sure of herself."

"Emma." My pastor gave a sad little shake of his head. "You know better. You're letting your personal resentment get in the way. The arrogant, the overconfident are often masking all sorts of fears and disappointments. I should have thought that Crystal was a perfect candidate for self-destruction. It's not for me to judge, but she may have been killing her soul for a very long time. Killing the body is the final step in denying God."

I considered Den's words. No doubt he was right, but I had trouble accepting his assessment—not on a spiritual or even a rational level, but as a practical approach to people like Crystal Bird.

Thus, when confronted with the ethereal, I chose to deal with the mundane. "The razor was in the pool? That may mean no fingerprints."

Den's smile conveyed what I took as pity. "You don't believe it was self-inflicted?"

I made a face. "I suppose I have to, unless the autopsy reveals otherwise. I suppose that'll have to be done over in Snohomish County. We still don't have the proper lab facilities here."

"Crystal looked like a strong, healthy woman," Den said in his usual reasonable tone. "How do you think someone might have slashed her wrists for her?"

"I don't." I sighed. "But I do wonder why a woman keeps a straight-edged razor around the house."

"Maybe someone left it there," Den replied. "I heard that one of her ex-husbands had been around lately."

My ears felt like they were jutting out from my head. "Where'd you hear that?"

Den frowned. "I'm not sure. One of the parishioners, I suppose."

I searched my memory for the names Vida had mentioned. "Ramsey, that was one of them. I forget the other."

"It wasn't Ramsey," Den said. "It began with a *C*. I believe he's a musician."

"What did you hear about him?" I asked.

"Just that he'd visited Crystal." Den snapped his fingers. "Betsy O'Toole talked about him last Sunday after Mass at coffee and doughnuts. She'd seen him at the Grocery Basket with Crystal."

"Interesting," I remarked as Della Lucci came into the parlor with Vida looming behind her.

"Mrs. Runkel is here to . . ." Della began, but Vida sailed right past her.

"Well!" My House & Home editor planted herself between Father Den and me. "Why did I have to find out about Crystal Bird's death from Harvey Adcock at the hardware store? I thought I was on the staff of a newspaper, which would indicate that I should be kept informed of breaking stories." Her gray eyes raked over me, then took in Den for good measure.

"I was going to come by your house as soon as I got through talking to Father Den," I said, meek as milk. As often is the case, Vida was having trouble remembering who was the boss. So, apparently, was I.

"But I wasn't home," Vida cried. "Nor, I might add, did my nephew Billy call from the sheriff's office to keep me informed."

"I don't think Billy's on duty," I said, referring to Deputy Bill Blatt, who was the usual pipeline between law enforcement and his aunt.

Holding on to her red, white, and blue knit cap, Vida plopped down next to me on the leather sofa. "You found the body, I hear," she said to Den in an accusing tone.

Della lingered in the doorway. She hadn't heard of the tragedy and her eyes were huge. Father Den repeated what had happened for both women. This time I took notes.

"It sounds fishy to me," Vida declared when Den had finished. "Though if I were as hateful as Crystal seemed, I might do myself in out of sheer self-loathing."

Den smiled in his wry manner. "That was my reaction," he said, "if expressed somewhat differently."

"I must call on her sister, April, to offer condolences," Vida said, getting to her feet. She looked down at me. "I should have called on Crystal when she came back to the area instead of letting Carla do a phone interview. It's a shame you never got to meet Crystal, Emma."

I swallowed hard. "Actually, I did. Last night." I felt like hiding behind the leather sofa cushions.

"What?" Vida exploded. "Oh, for heaven's sakes! Come along, it's well past noon. We'll eat something and you can tell me about this aberration of yours." She stalked out of the parlor with a nod at Father Den and Della.

"I guess I'll be going," I murmured. "Thanks, Den." I made a point of patting Della's plump arm. "Thank you, too. How's college?"

"Finals are next week," Della replied, looking nervous. "I hope I pass."

I wished her luck and followed Vida out into the parking lot. She was already behind the wheel of her big white Buick.

"Venison Inn," she informed me, and turned the ignition key.

Vida reached the restaurant first and was bombarded with questions from the other diners. Scooter Hutchins of Hutchins Interiors wanted to know if Crystal had killed herself with a hatchet. Ione Erdahl of kIds' cOrNEr thought it must be the work of a serial killer. Roseanna and Buddy Bayard of Picture Perfect Photography Studio were certain that Crystal's death was tied in to drugs.

When we finally managed to get some privacy in a booth toward the rear of the restaurant, Vida gave me a reproachful look. "I can't believe you didn't tell me you'd met Crystal," she said, as if I'd neglected to mention that her hat was on fire. "Whatever were you thinking of?"

"I wasn't sure until the last minute that I'd go," I said, lying only a little. "Really, Vida, I intended to tell you everything as soon as I ran you down this morning."

Vida uttered a small snort. "Perhaps. Two can play this game, you know."

The ominous tone disturbed me. "What do you mean?"

"Oh . . ." Vida's eyes roamed the grease-stained knotty-pine walls. "A major event. Someone you know extremely well. Huge news, really."

"Vida . . ."

"All right." She all but pounced on the table. "Carla had her baby at six-fifteen this morning. It's a boy, and they're both fine. His name is Omar."

"Omar?" I gave myself a little shake. *"Omar?"*

"Omar Jethro Talliaferro," Vida said with a solemn nod. "I've no idea what the significance of Omar is, but Jethro is Hebrew for outstanding or some such. I think it's rather nice."

I thought it was really awful. But it was typical of Vida, who was usually so critical, to express the opposite opinion.

"Carla is Jewish," I finally conceded, "which accounts for Jethro. But Omar is kind of a tough one to give a poor little kid."

"Children grow into their names," Vida said blithely. "Better yet, they often live up to them. I was on my way from Harvey's Hardware to see Carla and the little one at the hospital when I heard about Crystal Bird. That's when I started driving around town, trying to find you."

"It's a good thing you didn't have to go very far," I remarked.

"How true." Vida turned as the latest in the Venison Inn's series of young, pretty, and not-too-bright wait-resses approached us. This one's name tag read MANDY, and I recognized her as a Gustavson, which meant she was somehow related to Vida on the Runkel side.

After we gave Mandy our orders, Vida bore down on the

questions about Crystal Bird. I told her everything I possibly could, including all the nuances of our conversation.

"You don't think I drove her to suicide, do you?" The terrible thought had just dawned on me, perhaps a late reaction to Father Den's insight.

"Certainly not," Vida asserted. "Maybe it was that ex-husband of hers. Mooching, no doubt."

"You knew he was around town?" I asked, though it was typical of Vida to not always share the information she gathered. There was so much that she filed away in her mighty brain; yet woe to anyone else who withheld the smallest of tidbits from her.

"Oh, yes," she replied as Mandy brought coffee for me and hot tea for Vida. "Jake O'Toole told me about him the other day. Aaron Conley. He's some sort of musician who came up here from California in a ratty old van to borrow money. Jake was sure about that, because he tried to get one of the checkers to run a tab for him on Crystal's account. Naturally, the checker called Jake up front since they couldn't allow such a thing without the customer's approval."

"I didn't know Jake and Betsy allowed people to run tabs at the Grocery Basket," I said.

"They don't, as a rule. But when Crystal first arrived, she was waiting for money from the bank buyout, so she'd made some special arrangement," Vida explained.

"What did Jake do?" I asked as a loud trio of teenagers passed by our booth.

"He called Crystal, who said it was all right," Vida answered, blowing on her tea. "Later, she came back to the store with this Aaron person. Jake said he was much younger than Crystal, maybe in his thirties."

Something clicked in my brain. "Thirties? A van from California? I think he tried to run me down the other day on Front Street."

"Really? I don't doubt it. Musicians are so irresponsible." She quickly amended the statement. "Not all, of course. Roger wants a set of drums for Christmas. I've put in a special order through Music Express at the mall."

Giving Roger drums was tantamount to giving AK-47s to terrorists. Vida's gruesome grandson would use them as weaponry. I pitied his parents, Amy and Ted Hibbert. Maybe they had done their best with the little wretch, but his grandmother not only spoiled him beyond belief, but was blind to his many egregious faults. He was now fifteen, perhaps the worst age for an adolescent boy. I cringed at the very thought of Roger with drums. Indeed, I cringed at the very thought of Roger.

"I didn't see any sign of Aaron Conley at Crystal's house last night," I noted. Unless I could count the straight-edged razor. I mentioned the odd fact to Vida.

"People keep very strange things on hand," Vida said, in apparent dismissal of my theory. "Darla Puckett has never gotten rid of her late father's union suits. He never wore any other kind of underwear, even in summer. And then he'd complain about the heat. You wouldn't remember him, of course. He died at least ten years before your time. Do you want to join me in calling on April and Mel Eriks?" Vida inquired without skipping a beat.

I barely knew the couple. "Maybe you should go alone," I demurred.

Our food arrived, a shrimp salad for Vida, and pancakes, ham, and eggs for me. I'd skipped breakfast this morning; my stomach had still felt queasy.

"Nonsense," Vida said in response to my remark. "You've seen April and Mel a million times around town. They'll appreciate your sympathy."

I wondered if they'd appreciate either of us barging in on what I assumed was their grief. But Vida never passes up a chance at offering condolences. The opportunity is too great for ferreting out all sorts of information the mourners would probably just as soon keep to themselves.

We took both of our cars to the Eriks home, which was located just west of town in what is known as Ptarmigan Tract. The development, which was built in the Sixties, is made up of modest two- and three-bedroom homes that have generally been well kept.

Mel and April's split level was in a cul-de-sac which already was crowded with cars, SUVs, and pickup trucks. Vida and I both parked around the corner and made our way along the unshoveled sidewalk.

The door was answered by Mel, a burly, crew-cut man of fifty. I had indeed seen him many times, usually driving a Blue Sky Dairy truck. He greeted us with surprise, even confusion.

"Is this going to be in the paper?" he asked, ushering us down three steps into the living room, where his wife was on the phone.

"We'll have to run an obituary," Vida said at her most solemn. "It would be wonderful to have a photo."

April Eriks had hung up the phone. She jumped to her feet and hurried to greet Vida, who wrapped her in a warm embrace. "April, dear," Vida murmured. "I'm so very sorry. I was so close to your late parents. Lester and Erla were like an uncle and aunt to me."

I'd never heard Vida mention Lester and Erla Bird, but I suppose it could have been true. The soft soap that Vida applied seemed to make people come clean. April clung to her like moss, and I exchanged awkward glances with Mel, who was picking his teeth with a pipe cleaner.

At last, Vida released April, who began to dab at her eyes with a crumpled Kleenex. "I'm so glad you came by. You, too, Ms. Lord," she added as an afterthought. "We only found out about poor Crystal an hour ago, when

Sheriff Dodge came to see us. I've just been on the phone, trying to reach our kids and some of the other relatives. Whatever shall we do, Mrs. Runkel?"

"Do?" Vida's eyes grew owlish behind the big glasses. "Precisely what do you mean, April?"

April, who was a small, slim, prematurely gray woman with big brown eyes, indicated that we must sit. "About the services. Crystal wasn't a believer. Or so she pretended. I was just talking to Pastor Poole at the Baptist church where we go—well, we go most of the time—and he said we should give Crystal the benefit of the doubt because that's what God would do. What do you think, Mrs. Runkel?"

"I think that's very sound advice," Vida said, easing herself into an orange-and-brown-striped armchair. "We never really know what people believe or don't believe, do we?"

"Crystal had so many opinions," April said, wringing her thin hands. "Still, sometimes I felt she took the opposite view just to upset me. Isn't that right, Mel?"

Mel, who was still stabbing at his gums with the pipe cleaner, grunted. Then he glanced at Vida and me. "You writing all this down?"

"Goodness no," Vida said in a tone that suggested such a notion was impossible. "We're here only to offer a small piece of comfort."

Mel grunted again, then turned his back and stared out the window. April watched him for a moment then clapped her hands to her head. "I'm such a goose! I should have offered you something. Coffee? Tea? Hot cider?"

"No, no," Vida asserted. "We just ate lunch. Tell me, April dear, when was the last time you saw your sister?"

April pressed her fingers against her lips, apparently

trying to remember. "Mel, when did we see Crystal? Was it just after Halloween?"

Mel didn't turn around. "Could be."

"I think it was the first week of November," April said. "She stopped by to see if we had any chains that would fit her car. That was when we had our first big snowfall."

"Yes," Vida agreed. "November fourth. Six inches. How did Crystal seem?"

Again, April had to think about the question. "She was in a hurry. She was afraid she might not be able to get back to her cabin unless she had the chains."

"Cal," Mel grunted.

"I know, Mel," April said. "But she didn't want to spend the money buying chains from Cal Vickers if we had a spare set. As it turned out, we didn't, so she had to go to the Texaco station anyway."

"Tightwad bitch," Mel muttered, still staring out the window and picking his teeth.

"Now, Mel," April admonished, "don't be so hard on Crystal. Especially now that she's dead."

Mel grunted again.

"Her spirits?" Vida coaxed, the smile tightening on her face.

"Oh—yes." April nodded. "She was worried, of course. About the snow."

"But she didn't seem otherwise upset?" Vida asked.

April shook her head. "No, not that I could tell. Of course April was always up in arms about something. She was mad at Mr. Cardenas. You know, the college president."

"Was that about the day-care center?" I inquired, trying to emerge from Vida's shadow.

"I think so," April said slowly. "Although she mentioned something else. Women's studies? Does that make sense?"

"Not to me," Vida retorted. "But I understand what she meant."

"'Had you spoken with her since then?" I asked.

"Oh, yes." April nodded several times. "Thanksgiving was the last time. We wanted her to come for dinner."

"*You* wanted her to come, you mean," Mel put in.

"Of course I did," April responded on a defensive note. "She was my sister. Holidays are for family."

"But she turned you down?" I asked.

"She had company of her own coming," April said, giving her husband's back a defiant look.

"That Russian, I bet," Mel said. "Good thing she didn't try to bring him here. If you ask me, that's why she killed herself." He finally turned around. "Don't quote me."

Mel bent the pipe cleaner a half-dozen times and threw it at the open fireplace.

He missed.

Chapter Five

I SENSED THAT Vida was imploding with curiosity after Mel's remark about the Russian. I was more than a little interested myself, remembering Janet Driggers's conversation with a stranded traveler named Victor.

It wasn't a coincidence. Victor Dimitroff was a naturalized American, born in Paris, according to April Bird Eriks. He was a former symphony player and a composer who had taken up with Crystal in Portland. According to April, he had visited Crystal at least twice since she'd moved back to Skykomish County.

"Really," Vida huffed as we walked back to our cars, "April insisted she didn't know if they were romantically involved. Obviously, Mel thought otherwise."

"If you can decipher the grunts," I noted. "Darn, we've missed a good feature by not knowing about Victor."

"How could we?" Vida retorted, taking umbrage at the merest suggestion that she'd missed a juicy news item. "He'd go straight to her place in Baring without ever coming all the way into Alpine."

"Not necessarily," I said, reaching the Jag. "He booked his trips through Sky Travel."

"What?" Vida almost slipped in the snow. "How do you know?"

I told her about the call Janet Driggers had received Friday from Victor, who apparently had been stranded in

Chicago. "Follow me home," I suggested. "We have quite a bit to discuss."

Among other things, I hadn't confided in Vida about my ouster from the bridge club. Nor had we really talked about the break-in. The item had been culled from the sheriff's log by Scott Chamoud on Friday morning, but we had been busy, with little opportunity for chitchat. And now that Crystal was dead, I could confess my visit to Marisa Foxx.

It was after three when we finally got caught up. Vida wasn't much interested in the legal consultation, but she was wrought up over the snub by my fellow cardplayers.

"Mary Lou Hinshaw Blatt," she said, referring to her sister-in-law with whom she was not on speaking terms. "A veritable worm. You can figure her for one of them. The Dithers sisters. So abnormal, speaking only to their horses. And Edna Mae Dalrymple. Repressed, of course, hiding from the world behind all those books at the library. The others, I expect, would be somewhat more broad-minded."

I didn't quibble with Vida's assessment. "I can't help it, even with Crystal dead, I can't stop hating her for what she's done to me. She was a vile human being."

"Arrogant, yes," Vida conceded. "Opinionated and mean-minded. While I'm the first to not excuse people for troubles they bring on themselves, I must admit that Crystal's life wasn't smooth. One wonders where she went wrong."

"That's what she said about me," I sneered. "Remember her editorial week before last?"

" 'Where did Emma Lord go wrong?' Or some such idiocy." Vida sat back in the chair at my kitchen table. "Yes, yes, I remember it. So silly. What did you think of April?"

"Poles apart from her sister," I said, reaching for the

teapot. "A decent woman. Her grief seemed rather superficial, though."

"Exactly." Vida's eyes brightened. "Shocked, yes. But not devastated. Perhaps not even surprised. Don't you find that curious?"

I considered the question. "Not really. Crystal hadn't lived here for twenty-odd years. I'm assuming the sisters had grown apart. And didn't you say that Crystal gave April a bad time when they were kids? Siblings don't have to like each other."

"Very true," Vida agreed. "Still, I would have expected April to say something about how she wished she might have prevented her sister's suicide. You know—'If only I'd listened,' or some other such useless babble."

"Maybe she'd already said that to Mel before we arrived," I suggested, stirring sugar into my tea.

"Perhaps," Vida allowed. "No doubt Mel grunted, an indecipherable sound that would bring no comfort to April."

"She's used to it, I imagine."

Vida took a last sip from her mug and stood up. "You've had enough tea. We must go see Carla and Omar."

I'd almost forgotten about the Talliaferros. On this trip, we drove to the hospital in Vida's Buick. As usual, she rubbernecked for the entire five blocks to Pine Street.

"Richie Magruder shouldn't take his grandchildren sledding down Fourth. Very dangerous. It's Seventh that's been closed just for that purpose." "Why on earth is Veda Kay MacAvoy pushing that grocery cart uphill in the snow? So silly, considering her varicose veins." "Oh, good heavens! Here comes Durwood!"

Vida slammed on the brakes as Durwood Parker, the worst driver in Alpine, plowed through the intersection on a red tractor. As was customary, he didn't look to right or left, but stared straight ahead through glasses so thick they could have stopped bullets.

"Where did that old fool get that tractor?" Vida demanded, wrestling with the steering wheel. "The Parkers don't own a farm. They have a perfectly nice house in town, though I can't say much about their garden. Durwood's useless, and Dot has no sense of color. One year, all her annuals were white."

"Since Durwood had his license yanked, maybe he got the tractor so he could still get around town," I suggested as Vida finally managed to move the car forward.

"Perhaps." Vida's expression was prunelike in its disapproval. "It shouldn't be legal."

"It's an item for 'Scene,' though," I said, referring to Vida's gossipy front-page column that chronicled Alpine's minutiae.

"Yes," she agreed. "It's that until he runs over someone, and then it becomes news."

We parked on the street by the hospital, though it wasn't easy to find the curb. The sun was still out, but the temperature remained below freezing. The only melting I'd detected was on some of the utility poles and the eaves of buildings with east-west exposures.

Omar Talliaferro was the only newborn in the nursery. He was still red and wrinkled. His black hair stood up like a whisk broom. Although he wasn't crying, he refused to open his eyes while Vida and I inspected him through the window.

"Homely," Vida murmured. "Most babies are. Roger was one of the exceptions. So handsome, right from the start."

Since Roger had evolved into something like the shape of a bowling ball and had squinty, piglike eyes, I made no comment. I had thought that Adam was quite good-looking from the moment the midwife in Mississippi held him up for my inspection. Ben had thought so, too. I had gone to stay with my brother during the last stages of my pregnancy. He had been serving in a delta mission church near Fort Adams at the time.

Our office manager, Ginny Erlandson, was just leaving when we arrived at the door to Carla's room. "Poor Carla," Ginny whispered as she waylaid us in the corridor. "She had a terrible time. Did you know it was a breech birth?"

I felt like saying that it figured: Carla did most things backward, including her news stories. Vida, however, expressed great sympathy as she greeted the new mother.

"So difficult." She sighed, squeezing Carla's hands. "But such a beautiful baby. He has your hair and Ryan's eyes."

Carla, who definitely looked wan, frowned at Vida. "Omar's eyes are blue."

"Yes, yes," Vida said hastily. "All babies have blue eyes. I mean ... the way they're set. In his head. Near each other."

I suppose it was better than saying his eyes were close together. I leaned over the bed and patted Carla's shoulder. "Have you slept much since Omar was born?"

"A little," Carla answered in a tired voice. "They're going to let me stay an extra day. Otherwise, I'd go home tomorrow."

My gorge rises whenever I hear how quickly new mothers are dispatched. The equivalent of major surgery, one of the greatest major life changes—and the medical profession can't induce the insurance carriers to allow a poor woman some time to collect her mental and physical faculties. I made up my mind to write an editorial about it. It would do no good, but I'd vent some spleen. It was one woman-related subject on which I would have needed no goading from Crystal Bird.

"Maybe tomorrow I can find some time to write the rest of the wedding-gift thank-yous," Carla said. "I was hoping I'd get them done before Omar came along."

Carla and Ryan, who taught at the community college, had been married in early November at the Petroleum Museum in Seattle. Vida was still yapping about the unusual site, but I'd found it rather whimsical. The nostalgia of old gas pumps and oilcans had somehow put me in an appropriately sentimental mood. I'd envisioned bride and groom in an old jalopy, roaring away from a church with tin cans and streamers tied to the bumper. Reality had been Carla, eight months pregnant, and Ryan, looking as if he were about to faint.

"Your mother's coming from Bellevue, I understand," said Vida, who had sat down in the only visitor's chair. I'd considered parking myself on a portable commode, but decided I'd rather stand.

"Yes," Carla replied, pausing to sip water from a plastic glass. "That's for the first week. Then Ryan's mother is coming over from Spokane. By the time she's ready to go home, it'll be Christmas."

"Carla," I said, "surely you aren't going to start work right after New Year's."

"Why not?" Carla responded. "Winter quarter doesn't begin until January fifth. That gives me exactly a month."

Carla had signed on as the adviser to the student paper at the college. The thought of her instructing impressionable young minds in the art of journalism made me cringe.

"It won't be full-time," she went on to say. "President Cardenas doesn't expect to put out the first issue until spring quarter. The monies allocated from the student funds won't be available until then."

Vida was shaking her head. "It's not wise to push your-self. The wedding, the baby, the holidays—you must allow time to recuperate."

"I'll be fine," Carla asserted. "Hey—what's this I hear about Crystal Bird killing herself?"

"Unfortunately," Vida replied, "it's true. She slashed her wrists."

"Bummer," Carla remarked. "I interviewed her once on the phone. She was loaded with attitude."

"Yes, she was," Vida agreed, rising from the chair. "We must go. Too many visitors are tiring."

"That's right," I said. "Get some sleep."

Carla grimaced. "If I can, with that moron next door yelling every ten minutes for painkillers. Men are such babies. All he's got is a broken leg. Big deal."

"Oh?" Vida's head swiveled. "Who is it?"

"Some foreign dweeb," Carla replied. "He ran his car into a ditch last night down by Eagle Falls. Ever since they put me in here, I've had to listen to him moan and groan. He's quiet now. Maybe they finally knocked him out. I hope they used a hammer."

Vida bolted from the room. Blowing a kiss at Carla, I ran after Vida. She had stopped next door and was boldly removing the medical chart that rested in a metal holder.

"Ah!" she exclaimed in her usual stage whisper. "Vic-tor Dimitroff. I wondered." Vida peered around the door frame. "Carla's right. He's asleep. Here, have a look."

A chunky nurse was coming down the hall. I recog-nized her from Vida's stay in the hospital a few months earlier. "Mrs. Runkel," she said in a surprised voice. "How nice to see you. Are you visiting Mr. Dimitroff? I'm afraid he's resting."

Vida wasn't pleased at the interruption, but she made the best of it. "Emma and I have been calling on Carla

Talliaferro, However, we learned that poor Victor had been in a wreck. Since it's the weekend, we haven't checked the police log for accidents. How did it happen?"

I had gotten only the briefest glimpse of Victor Dimitroff. Black hair, black beard, and muscular arms were all that I could discern. I stood back, waiting to see how much Vida could wheedle out of Constance Peterson, LPN. Or so her name tag read.

Constance backpedaled, presumably out of Victor's hearing range. If he was listening, of course, which didn't appear likely.

"It happened last night," the nurse responded, looking grave. "He was going along Highway 2, right around Eagle Falls. He either turned off the road or skidded and landed in a ditch. Barclay Creek comes in there, so we assume he went into the area where it joins the Sky. It's hard to tell, with all this snow."

"Yes," Vida said. "And he broke his leg, correct?"

"In two places," Constance replied. "Nasty breaks. He'll be on crutches for a good six weeks."

"Tsk, tsk," Vida clucked. "Was he alone?"

Constance looked vaguely surprised. "I think so. No one else was brought in with him. Why do you ask?"

"For *The Advocate*," Vida answered. "Of course we'll get the details Monday from the sheriff's office."

"Oh. Of course," Constance said, in apparent understanding. "Shall I tell Mr. Dimitroff you came by?"

"That's not necessary," Vida said, starting off down the hall. "Thank you, Constance. It's nice to see you."

"Eagle Falls, huh?" I said when we were out of earshot. "Barclay Creek. Are you thinking what I'm thinking?"

Vida gave a single nod. "Certainly. They're right there at Baring, where the road leads into Crystal's cabin."

* * *

When I got home shortly before five, there was a frantic message on my machine from Paula Rubens. I called her back immediately.

"Do you mind if I come up to see you?" she asked in an unsteady voice. "I heard about Crystal this afternoon when I was talking to Shawna Breseford-Hall at the college."

I told Paula to come ahead. As usual, I had no exciting plans for Saturday night.

Paula must have left right away, since she arrived twenty minutes later from her house on the Wallace Falls road at Gold Bar. Her long red hair was more disheveled than usual and the flowing caftan that covered her ample figure looked as if she'd put it on backward. Of course with caftans, it's hard to tell.

"I can't believe it," she declared by way of greeting. "Who would have figured Crystal would do such a thing?"

I didn't quote Father Den. "People are hard to figure," I said, ushering her into the living room, where I'd just finished building a fire. "Can I fix you a drink?"

"Please." Paula collapsed into one of my matching green armchairs. "Not too stiff. I'll have to drive home."

I remembered that Paula was a gin drinker, and mixed my best version of a martini along with the standard bourbon and water for me. She gave me a grateful smile when I returned from the kitchen.

"I feel terrible," she said, raising the glass to her lips. "I meant to call you first thing to find out how the meeting went." She paused, then lifted the glass in a toast. "To Crystal. Poor crazy Crystal."

I leaned forward and we clicked glasses. "Do you mean that? Was she crazy?"

"Oooh . . ." Paula flung her free hand in the air. "Aren't we all? Let's say that Crystal was kind of obsessed. She'd had two lousy marriages, which is enough to make any woman spin out."

"What happened?" I inquired.

"Crystal got married almost straight out of high school, to some guy from around here. Sultan, I think. His name was Dean Ramsey, and he had a scholarship to Oregon State University." Paula paused to remove the olive from her drink. "They moved to Corvallis, and she worked to help put him through school. I don't think the scholarship was for a full ride, maybe only the first year. Anyway, she had a couple of miscarriages before they had a daughter. After Dean graduated, he got a job with the county. I forget what he did—something agricultural, like an extension agent. They lived in Salem, where Crystal worked as a bank teller. After about ten years, she left him."

"She left him?" I wanted to be clear on the background.

"That's how she put it when she told me," Paula replied, chewing the olive slowly. "Crystal felt the relationship had come apart. They couldn't communicate, and she was stifled. After they separated, she moved to Portland."

"What about the daughter?" I asked. "Her sister, April, never mentioned her."

Paula made a sad little face. "She ran away when she was seventeen. It happened while Crystal was married to Aaron Conley. I think the girl's name was Amber."

I was trying to calculate ages and dates. I figured Crystal to be about my age, which meant she had probably graduated from Alpine High School in the late Sixties. Ten years later, at the time of the divorce from Dean, she would have still been under thirty.

"Crystal got very caught up in the women's movement," Paul continued. "She went to work for another bank, but also enrolled at Clackamas Community College. It took her three years, but she got her associate-of-arts degree, and finished up at Portland State circa the mid-Eighties. That was when she got on with US Bank. The rest you know."

I shook my head. "I don't, actually. I mean I know she got some kind of buyout from the bank and moved here, but what about Husband Number Two?"

"Oh." Paula made a face. "An easy omission. She never told me how she got mixed up with Aaron. He was about ten years younger and yearning to be the next Kurt Cobain. That marriage didn't last long."

"Did you know he's in town?"

Paula's eyes widened. "No kidding! Did Crystal tell you that?"

"Crystal didn't tell me much of anything," I said, and was surprised that the memory of our brief encounter could make me sound so irritable. "I heard about it from my usual source. Vida."

A hint of amusement played at Paula's lips. "Of course." She paused and let out a big sigh. "We're the smart ones, Emma. We never married. How many women do you know who are happily wed?"

I was surprised by her comment. "Several. Shall I count the Merry Wives of Washington?"

"Don't bother." Paula made a slashing motion with her hand. "My parents were miserable all the years that they were both alive. But they never divorced. I often wondered why not."

I didn't want to get sidetracked in a debate over marriage. My own feelings were strong about the merit of struggle and endurance, of commitment and love. Except, of course, that I'd never had to do any of it.

"Tell me," I said, "if Crystal had a current man in her life."

Paula shrugged. "There was some guy, a tuba player, I think. Or maybe he's a composer. Russian name—I forget."

"He's in the hospital. His name is Victor Dimitroff, and he was in a car wreck Friday night."

Paula choked on her drink. "Really! Goodness." She dabbed at her chin with the back of her dimpled hand. "Then he must have been on the scene more than I realized. Did you talk to him?"

I shook my head. "I heard about him by chance. Vida and I went to see Carla Steinmetz. Carla Talliaferro, I mean. I can't get used to her married name. She had her baby early this morning."

"Well." Paula gazed into her glass, which was just about empty. "That's interesting."

"It's a boy," I said. "They named him Omar."

"What?" Paula's eyes took a moment to focus on me. "Oh. Omar? That's . . . different."

"I think so," I agreed, standing up. "Can I fix you another?"

"Half," Paula replied, giving me her glass. "On second thought, why not a whole one?" she called as I started for the kitchen.

"Do you want to stay for dinner?" I asked, pausing at the kitchen door. "I've got some chicken breasts thawed."

"Okay," she said. "That way, I'll be sober by the time I go home."

I put the chicken breasts in the oven, set a pot of water on to boil for rice, and got out a can of French-style green beans. After replenishing our drinks, I returned to the living room.

"Tell me," I said, after using a poker to turn one of the logs in the grate, "why do you think Crystal killed herself?"

"That's a tough one." Paula stared into the fire, which

was again crackling brightly. "If, as you mentioned, Aaron Conley is in town along with Victor, maybe they sent her into some kind of emotional tailspin. Honestly, I can't say, except that Crystal had mood swings."

"Depression?" I asked.

"Could be." Paula settled back in the armchair, balancing her drink on her lap. "She didn't talk about—what do I want to say? Her innermost thoughts, I guess. She was always so involved with issues. If I had to guess, I'd go for manic-depressive, or whatever they call it these days."

"When did you see her last?" I was beginning to feel somewhat mellow. The second bourbon, the sweet scent of wood burning, the shadows dancing around the room all contributed to an improvement in my own mood.

"Let me think," Paula said. "I spoke with her on the phone Thursday about meeting with you. In fact, I called her late Friday night to see how things had gone, but she didn't answer." She gave me a sad little smile. "I guess I know why now. But the last time I actually saw her was Tuesday. She came by the college to look at the exhibit."

"How'd she seem?"

"Okay." Paula paused, apparently thinking through her perception of Crystal. "If anything, she was kind of revved. I thought she was being enthusiastic about my glass pieces, but in retrospect, it may have been more than that."

"Like Victor?"

Paula shrugged. "Could be. I'm not sure how serious that relationship was. I'm guessing it wouldn't be because of Aaron. That guy was nothing but trouble."

Trouble was what Crystal seemed to have found, enough of it to force her to take her own life.

I wondered if Milo knew where those sources of

trouble might have come from. Aaron Conley or Victor Dimitroff, perhaps.

Or even Milo.

But I didn't want to think about that possibility.

Chapter Six

THERE WAS SOMETHING of a buzz about Crystal after Mass Sunday morning. Francine Wells, who seemed friendly if a bit uncomfortable in my presence, said she'd never met Crystal but figured her for an oddball.

"Most women come into my shop to at least *look*," she told the little circle that had gathered around Father Den on the wood-framed porch of St. Mildred's. "Not Crystal. Somebody told me she wore nothing but ethnic outfits."

"She wasn't wearing anything at all when I saw her," I put in. "She was in the hot tub." I glanced at Father Den, who acknowledged my statement with a slight incline of his head.

However, Ed and Shirley Bronsky's heads turned as if they were on springs. "You met Crystal?" Shirley gasped, huddled in her black mink coat. "I thought you two hated each other."

"And a meaningful Advent to you all," said Brendan Shaw, wearing his insurance agent's grin. "Hey, Father Den—maybe we should go back and start over with Mass. I don't think it took the first time."

Everyone laughed except Shirley, who was still regarding me with a curious expression. It was pointless to keep my meeting with Crystal a secret. In Alpine there are no secrets. The grapevine is long and active, even without Vida's considerable help.

"Gosh," Ed said in wonderment when I'd finished my brief recital, "you must have been about the last person to see her alive."

"It's possible," I allowed, darting a furtive glance at Den.

"I don't get it," Ed declared. "People shouldn't kill themselves. Life's full of surprises. Look at me, for instance."

I did. Ed Bronsky had worked—well, sort of—as *The Advocate*'s ad manager until a few years ago. He was full of gloom and complaints, lacking in ambition and energy, and it was only my soft heart and softer brain that prevented me from canning him. Then an aunt in Iowa had died and left him several million dollars. Ed had quickly retired to a squire's life and built a so-called villa above the railroad tracks. He and Shirley were the quintessential nouveaux riches, hosting the occasional lavish party "to show off," as Vida put it, and often asking the guests to bring along "a little surprise." Like the booze or the steaks or the hot dog buns. Ed was that kind of guy.

"We're looking at you, Ed," Francine said in a dry tone. "Your point would be . . . ?"

"That if you live right, everything will turn out fine," Ed asserted, sweeping a pudgy hand over the luxuriant length and considerable width of his fur-trimmed camel-hair overcoat.

Father Den flinched. "I don't think that was the same kind of camel-hair outfit that John the Baptist wore in the desert," he said, alluding to this morning's gospel from St. Mark.

"Huh?" Ed gave our pastor a curious look. "No, I guess not. It was hot over there in the Holy Land. You wouldn't need a coat."

Marisa Foxx had slipped between Shirley and me. "On the other hand," she said in an undertone, "you saved yourself the price of a lawsuit."

"Did I have one?" I asked, turning to look at Marisa.

She smiled and shrugged. "I don't know. I was going to check into it this afternoon at home. I don't mean to be callous, but Crystal saved several people some trouble."

"Did she?" I wanted Marisa to elucidate, but Brendan Shaw had caught her attention. My gaze wandered out to the parking lot, where vehicles were making their way through the unplowed snow. It occurred to me that Ed could have used his idle time to help out Father Den by clearing the lot. In fact, I recalled that Ed had originally been in charge of the shelter project, as St. Mildred's liaison with the other churches. As usual, he had kept a low profile, burrowing down in Casa de Bronska.

"Hey, Ed," I said, grabbing him none too gently by the camel-hair sleeve, "what kind of progress have you made with the women's shelter?"

Ed stared at me. "Progress? How do you mean? The Alpine Hotel site is all mired down in legal stuff. You know those Californians."

"That was months ago," I said. "How recently have you checked in with them?"

Ed turned to Father Den. "You talked to somebody in Santa Barbara a while ago, didn't you, Father?"

Den shook his head. "I thought you were going to do that."

"Gosh." Ed removed his expensive fedora and scratched at his bald spot. "I guess I got mixed up. I'll give them a buzz tomorrow."

Shirley tugged at Ed's arm. "You can't, Ed. You're going into Bellevue tomorrow to meet with your publishers."

Ed smacked himself alongside the head. "Right! Gosh, I can't keep up with everything these days." He offered Father Den and the rest of us an ingratiating smile. "The meeting tomorrow is huge. Skip and Irving didn't like the offer from Spielberg. To tell the truth, I didn't either, though *Mr. Ed* is a natural after that big war movie he's got coming out. In fact, we played around with changing the book title for the movie and calling it *Saving Mr. Ed.*"

Having read the original manuscript, I felt there was no possible way of saving *Mr. Ed.* The only thing I could save was myself, and I quietly ducked out of the little group as Ed raved on about other film deals, tossing around names like Coppola and Lucas and Cameron as if they were on his Christmas-card list. Maybe they were. I wouldn't put anything past Ed.

That afternoon, I drove over to the college to see the glass exhibit. I'd promised Paula that I'd take it in, though I had assigned Scott to cover the story. He'd gotten the photos back from Buddy Bayard on Friday. They looked okay, though it was a shame we couldn't run them in color.

All the works had been done as windows or door insets. Most were mediocre, though there were a handful—including three by Paula—that were quite beautiful. I was surprised to see that one of the names on a luminous sunset was Melody Eriks.

I was admiring the delicate pinks and lavenders and blues when a young woman came up beside me. "Do you like it?" she asked in a shy voice.

I turned. Even without the name tag identifying her and stating her credentials as an exhibitor/guide, I would have recognized Melody Eriks. She was a younger, prettier version of her mother, April. The daughter was taller, but small-boned, with the same big brown eyes. The fair hair hadn't gone gray, but the mouth and the nose were almost identical to her mother's.

"Yes," I responded, looking again at the sunset, "it's beautiful. You must have a gift for glasswork."

"I love art," Melody enthused. "I've always drawn and

painted. But this is much more interesting. I'm working on a sunrise to match."

Holding out my hand, I introduced myself, then waited for Melody's reaction. There was none.

"Do you like stained glass?" she inquired.

"Very much," I said, nodding to the Episcopal rector, Regis Bartleby, and his wife, Edith. "I'm a friend of Paula Rubens. One of these days I'm going to splurge and buy a piece from her."

Melody's face brightened at the mention of Paula's name. "Ms. Rubens is the most wonderful teacher. If you signed up for her class next quarter, you could make your own. There were several older students taking it fall quarter."

My smile was strained. There were some days when I didn't mind being middle-aged. There were very few when I enjoyed being reminded that most of my forties were in the rearview mirror.

"I met your parents yesterday," I said, changing the subject. "Mrs. Runkel and I stopped in to offer our condolences."

"Because of Aunt Crystal?" Melody sounded open to other ideas. Certainly she didn't seem aggrieved by the reference.

"Yes. How is your mother doing today?"

"Okay." Melody gave a little shrug, then strolled over to the next exhibit. "Mom and Aunt Crystal weren't close. What do you think of this one? It's my cousin Tiffany's. We took the class together."

Tiffany Eriks, whose family I knew better than Melody's, had done something with a seagull. It was perched on a piling with the ocean in the background. As clichés go, it was adequate. At least I could tell it was a seagull.

"The colors are a bit muted," I said. It was a kinder description than *dull*.

"I don't think Tiffany's really into it," Melody said without malice. "She has trouble focusing. That's why she's never finished college."

I figured Melody for nineteen, maybe twenty. Tiffany was a few years older, and currently working for Platters in the Sky at the mall. She had bounced around between jobs over the years, which meant she didn't focus on a career, either.

"My brother's *too* focused," Melody said as we moved on to the last piece, which was another of Paula's. "He's starting his master's next quarter at the University of Washington. Thad wants to be a Wall Street wizard."

My eyes widened in surprise. Seldom had I heard Wall Street mentioned in Alpine, and upon those rare occasions when it came up, the context was always derogatory, as in "Those bloodsucking bastards on Wall Street."

"Your brother must be an ambitious guy," I remarked.

Melody giggled, a rather unmusical sound, considering her name. "He wants to get rich. He's been reading *Forbes* and all those other magazines since he was fifteen." She pointed to Paula's final piece. "Isn't that great? Look at those colors."

The stained glass was also large, intended, perhaps, for a tall window on a staircase landing. The central figure was a breast-plated goddess, with her sword raised on high, and the ruins of a city in the background.

"Minerva?" I guessed.

"No, Hera," Melody replied. "This shows her after she helped the Greeks destroy the Trojans. Isn't she magnificent?"

She was. Her armor, sword, and shield were a burnished gold, which was reflected in the flames of Troy. The flowing skirts seemed to move, and the handsome face was exultant.

"How long did it take Paula to do this?" I asked.

"I don't know," Melody said. "A long time, I'd guess. The detail is so rich." She looked beyond me and made a face. "Here come the old folks. Reverend Nielsen brought a vanload in from the Lutheran retirement home. Excuse me, I've got to show them through."

I studied Hera for a few more minutes, then headed out of the RUB. On the way to the parking lot, I spotted Nat Cardenas, looking as if he'd just come off the ski slopes.

"Emma," he said in that charming tone he reserves for civic leaders, the press, politicians, and whoever else he figures can do him some good. "How are you?" He whipped off a heavy glove and put out his hand.

"You've been skiing?" I asked.

Nat shook his head. He was a rugged, handsome man in his fifties with thick iron-gray hair and deep-set dark eyes. "Snowmobiling," he answered, then gave me his engaging smile. "It's not a good day for it, though. I decided to come back to the campus and get some work done before I went home."

"I was taking in the glass exhibit," I said in a conversational tone. "Paula and her students have turned out some nice things."

Nat gave a single nod. "Paula's an excellent instructor. She has rapport with the students and she knows how to teach. We were lucky to get her."

"You've been able to hire some first-rate people," I said, hoping the praise wasn't too transparent. "After three years, does Alpine feel like home?"

Nat tipped his head to one side, gazing up at the snow-covered evergreens that had been left standing as a backdrop for the campus. "Yes, it does. Of course, it's quite a change from L.A." He laughed in his self-deprecating manner.

Skykomish Community College had recruited Nat from

a JC in Los Angeles. His previous years had been spent in various parts of the Southwest, and his Hispanic roots were from somewhere in Texas, where he had grown up poor but ambitious.

"Alpine is a huge change," I remarked. "I'm glad you've adjusted. Many people who come to the Pacific Northwest from sunnier climates often find this part of the world depressing."

Nat gave an emphatic shake of his head. "Not at all. I like the weather changes."

"Good for you." I smiled. "You've been here long enough to know you can take it. The rain and snow drive some people over the edge. Which reminds me," I continued, not needing any such reminder and finally weaving my way to the subject of my quest, "you have to wonder how much effect all our snow had on Crystal Bird. I lived in Portland for years, and some winters we didn't have any snow at all. She must have felt isolated down there at Baring when the roads got impassable."

Nat's charming facade disappeared. The expression that emerged was distant, even austere. I actually liked it better. "I figured she enjoyed being alone in her little aerie," Nat said.

"All the better to sharpen her claws on the rest of us?" I forced a small laugh.

Nat made a noise that sounded like "Hmm-mm-m." Then he cleared his throat and put the glove back on his right hand. "Public figures are always fair game. Or so the expression goes. I've never seen anything fair about it." The glove was back on; so was the mask. "Now, if you'll excuse me, Emma," he said with his big smile, "I'd better head for the office so I can get home in time for dinner. Justine is making something special."

Justine was Mrs. Cardenas, a rather handsome, if somewhat asocial, woman. I sensed that she came from money, and wondered if her bank account had helped put Nat through graduate school. As Crystal had done with Dean Ramsey—but with less fortunate results.

As soon as I got home, I called Ben in Tuba City. For once, he was at the rectory.

"What's up?" he asked in his crackling voice. "Did you get Adam's message?"

"I did. I've tried to call you four times this week, but you were always out. How come you never called back?"

"Because my answering machine is broken," Ben replied. "It *seems* to take messages, but it's only a tease. I never get them at this end. Bob Spotted Dog is coming to fix it tomorrow."

Bob Spotted Dog was the Navajo handyman who could fix just about anything. He had been invaluable to my brother, who could fix nothing, and had long ago given up trying.

"I'm not really happy about you and Adam visiting Tom Cavanaugh," I said, disdaining small talk. "How come?"

"How come?" Ben sounded puzzled.

"Don't be dense," I retorted. "You aren't in San Francisco. Neither is Adam."

"But that's where I'm going for a two-day meeting," Ben replied. "Thus, Adam will fly in from St. Paul and meet me there instead of going straight through to Seattle. It gives me a chance to finally meet my nephew's father. Why are you pissed?"

I'd been asking myself the same question for a week. "Because I seem to be the one factor left out of this entire equation," I said. "Tom and I are Adam's parents. Tom has, upon occasion, declared his undying love for me. Tom is now a free man. And, while everyone else seems to be yukking it up with Tom, including my ad manager, I have not heard word one from the SOB." The last few words fell from my tongue like hot lead.

My brother is a compassionate man, a priest who has devoted his life to God and to the service of others. He lacks neither charity nor patience. Ben's virtues are admirable, enviable. But he is human.

"You know," he said, his voice deeper but still crackling, "I'm damned pissed with all your melodrama. What's wrong—you don't have a phone? How the hell did you call me? You can't do the same with Cavanaugh?"

"It's not up to me to call," I snapped. "I'm not the grieving spouse."

"Bullshit. How many times do I have to tell you that you enjoy all this thwarted-passion crap?" He stopped to take a quick breath. "How's this? I tell Tom you want to marry him. I insist he gives me an answer. If he says, 'Yes, yes, yes, I cannot go on without the help and support of the woman I love,' what do you say?"

"You wouldn't dare."

"I would."

I didn't doubt Ben. But I doubted myself. "I'd say yes."

"Liar."

"Try me."

"I will." Ben paused again. "Do you want me to bring him gift-wrapped and stuff him under your Christmas tree?"

"Let's not get ahead of ourselves," I said, sounding unintentionally sarcastic. "I want to hear his answer to your question first."

"Do you."

There was no question in Ben's voice. But there was sarcasm to match my own.

On Monday morning, I sent Scott Chamoud to interview Victor Dimitroff at the hospital. According to the sheriff's log, Victor's accident had occurred Friday night at ten-forty. He had been traveling eastbound at the time.

When Vida heard about Scott's assignment, she flew into my office. "How could you? Talk about sending a boy to the mill! Why wasn't I given this Russian?"

Looking up from the Wenatchee Forest news release that had showed up at *The Advocate* Friday, I offered Vida my most innocent expression. "Because it's an accident story. Because it's hard news. Because it's Scott's beat."

"How often do you interview people who've been in auto accidents?" Vida demanded, leaning on my desk. "If you did, Durwood Parker would be an entire series."

"Okay," I allowed, sitting back in my swivel chair, "so this *is* a little different. But if Victor Dimitroff really is a composer, it's a feature. He's going to be released today, and for all I know, he's leaving the area. You don't do this kind of feature, Vida."

"I do culture." She resumed standing straight up. "Just last week, I had the Merry Methodists' Musicale. This issue, I'm writing up the Burl Creek Barbershop Quartet's trip to Monroe."

There was indeed a fine line between such assignments. Basically, they depended on who received which news release. The established groups, such as the churches and private organizations, sent most of their releases to Vida. In the past, anything else was parceled out between Carla and me. As the new mother's successor, Scott had taken over the stories I wouldn't or couldn't do.

I didn't mind offering Vida an apology, however. "Maybe I should have let you interview Victor. But I need to load Scott with work so that he gets a sense of urgency and makes his deadlines. As you may recall, he hadn't finished two of his features for last week's issue, and we had to fill the holes with holiday recipes."

Vida inclined her head, which was covered with a faux-fur hat sitting so low on her forehead that it almost obscured her eyebrows. "You have a point. However, you should have considered that an interview with Victor—at least as conducted by me—would not have been limited to musical composition."

"I know," I admitted. "But what's the point of digging around in the guy's private life? Crystal's dead, he's probably out of here, and anything you find out would be inappropriate in an article about his musical background."

The eyebrows merged with the fur. "There's always curiosity."

"I know," I said, grinning at Vida. "To be frank, I want to forget about Crystal and move on. She was a sour chapter in my life. For once, I'm not curious about the rest of her miserable life. Just hearing about it would get me mad all over again. The poor woman killed herself, and that's that. Which reminds me, you do the obit, and I'll do a brief page-one story."

"You have confirmation from Milo as to cause of death?" Vida inquired as the hat slipped still farther and her eyebrows disappeared, gobbled up by the animal on her head.

"Not yet," I said, "but Jack Mullins told Scott that they expected to hear from the ME in Everett by this afternoon. Surprisingly, it was a slow weekend for dying in Snohomish County."

"Not surprising," Vida responded, turning toward the door. "This time of year, so many sick and elderly people are determined to hang on until Christmas. You know what the obituary page in *The Seattle Times* and *P-I* look like the last ten days of December. A half, maybe even a third of a page from the nineteenth until the twenty-ninth. Then—whoosh!" Vida's arm flew up. "They have to jump the death notices to a second page."

I knew Vida was right. To make up for not having given her the Dimitroff assignment, I told her about Crystal and Dean Ramsey's runaway daughter.

"Now where did you hear that?" she demanded, leaning back into my office.

"Paula Rubens," I said without apology.

Vida sniffed. "I trust she knows what she's talking about. How long ago did the girl run away?"

Paula hadn't said. "Several years," I estimated. "Amber was seventeen, and Crystal was married to Aaron. I suppose the daughter would be in her early to mid-twenties by now."

Vida's expression was enigmatic. Then without further comment, she walked away in her splayfooted manner while I went back to the timber ban story. Leo, meanwhile, was on the phone, getting a jump start on his calls for the annual double-truck Christmas church advertising. The two center pages of the December 17 issue would feature each house of worship's special holiday services.

The mail was late that morning, no doubt due to the Christmas rush. Ginny arrived in my office around eleven with her arms full of envelopes and a couple of parcels.

"Carla's on her way home," she said, dumping everything into my in-basket except for the parcels. "I'm taking a casserole over tonight for their dinner. Do you want to make something for tomorrow night?"

"I thought Carla's mother was coming up from Bellevue," I said.

"She is. I mean, she did. But Mrs. Steinmetz doesn't cook." Ginny pulled her red hair into a ponytail and slipped on a green scrunchy to hold it in place. "Did you know that they're rich?"

"I always wondered," I said. "Despite the lowly salaries

I can afford to offer, Carla never seemed to have any money problems."

"I'm sure that both the Steinmetzes and the Tallia-ferros helped them buy that house in Ptarmigan Tract," Ginny said. "Carla's hinted as much, but I hate to ask."

Vida and I had driven by the Talliaferros' home when we called on April and Mel Eriks. Carla and Ryan had bought one of the larger houses, with four bedrooms and a triple garage.

"You're probably right," I said. "College professors don't make that much and Carla certainly didn't earn enough to save money. Which reminds me—how much of a Christmas bonus can I afford to give all of you?"

Ginny not only worked as our office manager, but as our bookkeeper. It was an ideal situation, since her husband, Rick, handled our account at the Bank of Alpine.

"Mmm." Ginny pressed her lips together. "About the same as last year. Maybe fifty dollars more each if Leo pulls in a lot of advertising the last three weeks. Oh, and there's the Christmas-card printing. That should do it. Everybody's due to pay up by the end of the year."

Revitalizing the back shop under Kip MacDuff had added much-needed revenue the past three years. "Good. We'll issue the checks a week from Friday, on the nineteenth."

Ginny nodded and headed back to the front office. It was a relief not to see her dragging little Brad around with her. The Erlandson offspring was going on two, and his mother had brought him to work with her on a daily basis until September, when she finally put him in the day-care center run by her sister-in-law, Donna. Even though it had been my idea for Ginny to bring Brad, he had gotten to be a nuisance after he became ambulatory. The last straw had occurred when he'd somehow man-aged to open a printer cartridge and poured it into Vida's ever-present water glass. She hadn't noticed, and her teeth had turned black. The Reverend Bartleby had come by with a story about the newly appointed choir director, taken one look at Vida, and become hysterical. She had been on the verge of calling for help, when he finally simmered down enough to explain. It was hard to tell which of them was the most embarrassed.

It was almost noon when Milo came into my cubby-hole and closed the door. I was surprised at the gesture, and steeled myself for a personal confrontation.

I was wrong. Without asking my permission to smoke, the sheriff took out a cigarette, lighted it, and looked around for an ashtray.

"Here," I said, reaching into the bottom drawer of my desk. "You know I quit."

"Often," he remarked. "Thanks." He inhaled, exhaled, and leaned his elbows on the desk. "We got the autopsy report back from SnoCo. Crystal Bird died from an over-dose of sleeping pills. Her wrists were slashed after she was dead. We're not sure we're looking at a suicide. Foul play may have been involved. It could turn out that she was murdered." Milo held the cigarette a few inches from his mouth and gazed at me with shrewd hazel eyes. "What do you think of that, Emma?"

On the surface, I was shocked; deep down, I wasn't surprised. Then I made the mistake of saying so.

"Crystal certainly didn't act like somebody who was contemplating suicide," I said, flipping to a clean sheet on my notepad. "You'd better give me the particulars."

"That can wait," Milo replied. "It's only Monday. Now I want you to tell me exactly what happened while you were at Crystal's cabin Friday night."

I know Milo well enough to realize when he's immersed in his role of sheriff. In a town like Alpine, there are times when he can be on duty, but still one of the boys. I've seen him talk fishing and hunting to the locals, then turn around and arrest one of them for felonious assault. Milo doesn't work in a big office building, isolated from the citizenry; he has to live with these people, from gassing up the Grand Cherokee at Cal's Texaco to standing in line at the Grocery Basket. He can josh and laugh and joke as he makes his inquiries, but Milo gets the job done.

I forced a laugh of my own. "If Crystal was murdered, am I a suspect?"

Milo just looked at me. He wasn't laughing. Neither was I.

Chapter Seven

DETAILS.

Though only two full days had passed since I'd been with Crystal Bird, it seemed like much longer. Maybe that was because I was determined to erase her memory from my life. She had created an anger and a hostility that had soured my soul.

But I had to think back to Friday night. Piece by piece, I recounted what had happened from the time I arrived at seven-thirty until I left around eight.

"You poured the rum punch for yourself and Crystal?" Milo asked when I got to the part about my hostess's request.

"Yes. She was in the hot tub."

"Was Crystal eating or drinking anything else?"

"No." I tried to picture the kitchen. There had been a partial brick of cheese on the counter and some fruit in a glass bowl. I'd seen no signs of actual food preparation.

"Were you wearing gloves?"

"Not when I got the punch. I took them off. Otherwise, I couldn't have gotten my fingers through the handles on the mugs." *Damn.* My prints were all over the place.

"How much punch did you drink?"

"Do you think I killed Crystal in a drunken rage?" I snarled. Then, seeing that Milo was unmoved by my wrath,

I answered the question. "About two swallows. I didn't like it. It tasted bitter." *Just like Crystal. Just like me.*

"What did you do with your mug?"

"I . . ." My mind was blank. I'd been angry when I left the deck. I'd gone into the kitchen to make my exit and the phone had rung. "I don't remember. I was on the way out when you called."

"Right." At last, Milo's gaze shifted away from my face. "You left after that?"

"I went back out onto the deck and set the phone down. I told Crystal who was calling. Then I left." It was my turn to offer a hard stare. "How come, Milo? Why did you call Crystal?"

"That's irrelevant." He stubbed out his cigarette and the hazel eyes resumed their hold on me.

"Did you go there that night?"

Silence. Then, just as I was about to explode, he asked if Crystal had mentioned anyone else who might have been coming to see her.

"We didn't chitchat," I responded frostily. "It was all business."

"Did you see any sign of anyone having been there?"

I'd noticed only the Merlin motif and the crystals and the goddesses. There'd also been the older, if sturdy, living-room furnishings. The rest was a blur.

"You mean like a straight-edged razor?" I asked in a dry voice.

Milo had left his sense of humor in the Grand Cherokee. "Like anything that obviously didn't belong to Crystal."

"No. I really didn't." I gave the sheriff a helpless look. "Have you checked up on Aaron Conley and Victor Dimitroff?"

The muscles tightened in Milo's face. "What do you know about them?"

I couldn't tell if he meant there hadn't been time to

question the men or if he'd never heard of them before. I
recounted what little I knew about Aaron, then added
the even sketchier information on Victor. "He's being released from the hospital today," I said in conclusion. "He
may already be gone."

This time, Milo couldn't hide his surprise. "This is the
same guy who was in that wreck the other night?"

"So you didn't know he was a friend of Crystal's?"

"No," Milo admitted. "I knew about Conley, though."

"Is he still around?"

"We're checking on that." Milo stood up. His head almost touched the low ceiling. "Don't leave town."

I grimaced at the cliché. "I wasn't planning on it."

I'd lost my appetite. The news office was empty by the
time Milo left. Ordinarily, I would have expected Vida to
stay through the noon hour until she found out why he'd
come, but she was taking her sister-in-law Nell Blatt to
lunch at the ski lodge for her birthday.

My hands were opening the mail, but my mind was de-
ciphering the sheriff's words. Why would anyone slash
the wrists of a woman who was already dead? To indicate
suicide, perhaps. On the other hand, it was still possible
that Crystal could have taken the sleeping pills herself.
None of it made sense.

What bothered me most, of course, was Milo's suspicions. Even more disturbing was that if I thought he'd
called Crystal on a nonprofessional basis, he himself
could be a suspect. He wouldn't tell me anything about
their relationship. But someone must know. I'd talk to
Toni Andreas or Jack Mullins or one of the other county
employees. Discreetly, of course.

My brain was still going 'round and 'round when I
opened the last of the morning mail's news releases. It
was from the state department of agriculture, announcing

the retirement of Hector Tuck as extension agent for Skykomish County, effective December 31. Tuck, according to the story, had served SkyCo since 1967.

Replacing Mr. Tuck is Dean Ramsey, former extension agent for Marion County in Salem, Oregon. Mr. Ramsey has been training with Mr. Tuck since December 1.

I read the news release twice. By chance, maybe by design, Crystal Bird's first husband was moving—probably had moved—to Alpine. It seemed like too much of a coincidence, even in a town where former residents often came home to their roots. I dialed the courthouse, but Hector Tuck was out to lunch. So was Dean Ramsey.

I tried Milo next. If I was going to be a suspect, I might as well spread the misery around. The sheriff, however, wasn't in his office.

"He should be back by three," Toni Andreas informed me.

Maybe it was just as well that I didn't speak directly to Milo. I gave Dean Ramsey's name to Toni.

"He was married to Crystal many years ago," I said, always careful to be specific with the sheriff's receptionist. "It may be just a coincidence that he came here about the same time that Crystal died."

"Dean told me he didn't even realize Crystal was living here," Toni said. "In fact, he just stopped by. He feels awful about her death."

"You know Dean Ramsey?" I said, surprised.

"Sure," Toni responded. "He introduced himself the first day he started training with Hector. His family's not here yet. I guess they wanted to have Christmas at their old house in Oregon."

I was chagrined at not having run into the newcomer on my regular treks to the courthouse. Even more curious was the fact that Vida apparently hadn't known about Dean Ramsey's appointment.

"Where's he staying?" I asked.

"At the Lumberjack Motel," Toni said. "He's a real nice guy."

"So Sheriff Dodge knows he's here?"

"Sure. They had dinner together last week."

I grimaced into the phone. "I must be the only idiot who didn't know about Ramsey," I said. "Hey, Toni—tell me something. I know this sounds indiscreet, but were Milo and Crystal friendly?"

Toni seemed to hesitate. "I don't really know. She called in a couple of times about some vandalism at her place. He went up to see her at least once. Gosh, do you think they were dating?"

That's what *I* wanted to know. "I've no idea," I admitted. "Probably not," I added. There was no point in starting idle rumors.

But of course I already had. "Wow!" Toni exclaimed. "Dodge and Crystal Bird! That's wild!"

"Now, Toni, as far as I know there's absolutely no—"

"He's been pretty miserable since you guys broke up," Toni interrupted. "Maybe he was desperate. Wasn't Crystal sort of weird?"

"We're all a little weird," I said, more tersely than I'd intended. "Thanks, Toni. I've got to run."

Just as I set the phone down, Scott Chamoud rapped on the door frame. It was a habit of his, despite the open-door policy I had with my staff. Unless the door was closed.

"Dodge stopped in to see you, I hear," he said, easing his six-foot-something physique into one of the visitor's chairs. He saw me nod, and continued. "I've talked to Mullins and Fong. They've given me all the details, including the kind of sleeping pills that killed the Bird woman." He gave me an off-center smile. "Sorry. Don't mean to disrespect a dead woman. Anyway, here's all the data."

Scott laid a couple of sheets of notebook paper in front of me. "Dilantin," I said, noting the name of the sleeping drug. "That sounds familiar. Hunh—'time of death, nine P.M. to two A.M.' That's plenty of latitude."

Scott nodded. "That's because she was in the hot tub. The water kept the body warm."

I frowned at Scott. "Don't those things turn off automatically as a safety feature?"

Scott's limpid brown eyes grew musing. And more limpid. "They do in public places. I'm not sure about the ones people have in their homes."

"They should," I said. "People are far more careless at home. Of course, the tub could have shut down and been turned on again."

Scott grinned, revealing wonderfully white teeth. "You trying to solve this on your own?"

I almost told Scott that I felt compelled to find the killer—assuming there *was* a killer—to exonerate myself. But he didn't need to know that—yet. "It's an occupational hazard," I explained. "When you cover crime, especially major crimes, in a small town, you get caught up. The old investigative-reporter skills come to the fore. Journalism is seeking Truth. But of course you know that."

"Totally," Scott replied. "Truth is tight. But you can lose sight of all that on a daily basis."

I nodded. "I'll have you do the sidebar pieces on the coverage. In a situation like this, I usually cover the straight news."

"Sidebars?" Scott blinked. "Like what?"

"We'll see what develops," I replied, though I already had a few ideas in mind. As if changing the subject, I asked Scott about his interview with Victor Dimitroff.

Scott made a face. "He was pretty much of a butt. To be fair, though, he was getting ready to check out, and Doc Dewey was putting him through the rehab paces. All I got was some background and a couple of quotes. Six inches, maybe. He wouldn't let me take his picture."

"Interesting," I remarked. "Is he afraid somebody will recognize him? Like the cops?"

"Would you want your picture taken in one of those hospital gowns?" Scott asked with a snicker. "Dimitroff hadn't gotten dressed yet while I was there."

The explanation was logical, but I hung on to my suspicions. "Okay, let's have that story ready by three o'clock. Then I'll give you a couple of other assignments for tomorrow's deadline."

Scott winced. "Wow, it takes a lot of copy to fill an issue, doesn't it?"

I smiled. "Yes, it does. And you and I are the ones who have to do it. Vida's got plenty of work to do covering her House & Home section."

"Amazing," Scott murmured as he got out of the chair. "It's sure different from what I imagined *The Washington Post* to be."

"This is Alpine, Washington, not Washington, D.C.," I said, as if Scott needed the reminder. The tin roof in my cubbyhole had begun to leak again under the accumulated snow. "By the way, tell Kip to see if he can do anything about this." I pointed to the slow drip that was emanating from somewhere in the low ceiling behind my chair.

Scott gave me his terrific grin and went out through the newsroom, presumably in search of Kip. It was almost one-thirty, and Vida wasn't back yet, so I decided to go over to the courthouse to see if I could find Dean Ramsey.

The clouds were moving in again, gray on gray, with a

touch of blue. The lull between snowfalls left Front Street covered with dirty slush. I was crossing Fourth when Vida honked at me. *Toot-toot*—pause—*toot-toot-toot*—pause—long *toot*. It was like a duck call; she never varied.

"Where are you off to?" she shouted after rolling down the window.

I teetered on the curb. "The courthouse. See you later."

"What's going on at the courthouse?"

"Later," I repeated. Three cars were stuck behind Vida at the four-way stop.

"Wait." Vida drove through the intersection and pulled into her spot by *The Advocate*. In less than a minute, she was at my side. "Don't tell me those county commissioner old fools have actually done something?"

"Of course not," I said. "Did you know about Dean Ramsey?"

"Dean Ramsey?" Vida looked momentarily puzzled as we crossed Front Street. "Crystal's first husband? What about him?"

I backed up before answering directly, telling Vida about the autopsy report and Milo's interrogation. Somewhat to my surprise, she seemed unruffled.

"It all makes sense," she said, nodding at an elderly couple I knew by sight but not by name. "Crystal angered a great many people besides you, which might have made her a victim. As for Milo, he's doing his job. You know how he goes by the book. Now what's this about Dean Ramsey?"

We were passing the Bank of Alpine. Rick Erlandson waved at us from his assistant manager's desk. "He's taking over for Hector Tuck. Ramsey's been in town since the first of the month."

"Well." Vida probably wiggled her eyebrows, but I

couldn't tell. The fur hat had slipped again. "That's very puzzling. How could I not have known?"

We trudged by the Burger Barn, whose aroma of grease made me realize I hadn't eaten since breakfast. "The news release arrived only this morning."

"That's no excuse. Dean Ramsey has actually been in Alpine for over a week. How could that happen without my noticing him? Why didn't someone tell me?" Vida's annoyance was escalating.

"It's a busy time of year," I offered. "People get caught up in the holiday rush. Your informants have probably been Christmas shopping."

"That's no excuse." Vida didn't wait for the light at the corner of Third but stomped right through the intersection. A goateed man in an SUV honked in protest. I didn't recognize him; presumably, he didn't recognize Vida. "Dean Ramsey's staying at the Lumberjack?" she asked as we reached the corner by Alpine Ski.

"Yes. Toni said his family is coming later, after the holidays. I suppose he's looking for a house."

"Absurd," Vida muttered, in apparent reference to not knowing about Dean Ramsey. "I saw Hector and Opal at church Sunday, and he mentioned retiring. But the way he put it, the date was off in the future. Typical. Hector has always been obscure."

As we approached the Clemans Building, Janet Driggers came through the door of Sky Travel. She greeted us with a windmill wave.

"Late lunch," she announced. "Hey, remember that guy who got stuck in Chicago, Emma? The Russian? He finally got in and then ran his car off the road and broke a leg. Serves him right for bitching. Now I've booked him on a flight to San Francisco. He'll probably run into fog. Ha-ha."

"He's leaving town?" I asked.

"Not until Friday," Janet replied. "I gather he has some things to take care of around here."

Vida leaned over my shoulder. "Where has he been staying?"

Janet shrugged inside her powder-blue parka. "I don't know. He didn't make any arrangements through us."

"Interesting," Vida murmured as we headed across Second Street. "Do you suppose that Crystal Bird offered Victor Dimitroff hospitality?"

"Could be," I said, wishing I'd paid more attention to my surroundings when I'd been at Crystal's cabin Friday night. The kitchen counter might have revealed a notation of Victor's flight arrival, or a Chicago-area phone number jotted down somewhere that would have suggested his imminent arrival. Of course Milo would have checked for such signs. But would he have known what they meant?

The homely, durable courthouse was built during the Depression. Its two stories of brown brick, with tan trim around the two-paned windows, give it the air of a Depression-era survivor: simple, austere, hardy. There is a rotunda of sorts, or at least an open area with a functional skylight in the roof. Sixty-odd years ago, when county government was new to Alpine, the double staircase and the tile floor must have lent a sense of spaciousness. In the waning years of the twentieth century, several desks and a couple of cubicles all but filled the building's core.

Vida marched right up to Madge Gustavson, who was the longtime receptionist and some shirttail relation. The dressing-down of Madge was brief. Vida rebuked her for not passing on the news about Hector Tuck's imminent retirement and his replacement by Dean Ramsey. Then she asked if the newcomer was in. Luckily—perhaps more so for Madge than for us—the new county extension agent was in his office on the second floor.

There was an elevator, but we took one of the two sweeping staircases. I don't know what I expected Dean to look like, but I hadn't envisioned the small, seemingly meek man who got up from behind a table in what was still Hector Tuck's office.

"Mr. Tuck's at the Overholt farm," Dean began, his thin, prematurely lined face regarding us with what appeared to be foreboding. "He should be back around four."

"We're not here to see Hector," Vida said curtly. "We're here to meet you." She held out a gloved hand. "I'm Vida Runkel, and this is Emma Lord, editor and publisher of *The Alpine Advocate*."

"How nice," Dean Ramsey said in a voice that didn't sound convincing. "I'm flattered that both of you would want to interview me."

Vida's head swerved around, surveying the crowded room. There were three chairs—the one in which Dean had been sitting, a faux-leather chair behind the desk that still belonged to Hector Tuck, and a spare wooden armchair that was apparently for visitors.

"Here," Vida said, going behind Hector's desk and shoving his chair closer to Dean's table. "I'll take this." She nodded at me. "The armchair looks quite comfortable, Emma."

Like an obedient child, I pulled the chair up to the table and sat down. Dean rather warily reseated himself at the table. "I'm just getting my feet wet," he said, "but I can tell you about what I did in Marion County. I was there for over twenty years."

"We're more interested in the personal angle," Vida said, finally pushing the fur hat up higher on her forehead. "As I recall, you grew up down the highway in Sultan. Have you yearned to come back to your roots?"

"Yes." Dean nodded several times. His brown hair was thinning and streaked with gray. He wore glasses with heavy black frames that drew attention away from his short chin. I guessed him to be in his late forties, though he looked older. "In fact, I'd applied earlier this year for positions in Snohomish and Chelan counties. You see, my parents moved to a retirement home in Monroe a couple of years ago, and neither of them is very well. They can't make the trip to Salem anymore, so Jeanine and I decided we should move closer. Jeanine's my wife," he added with a small smile.

"Yes," Vida said, smiling back. "Your second wife, I believe. Do let us offer our condolences on the loss of your first wife. Her death has been quite a shock to the community."

Dean turned toward the window, where icicles had formed like clear plastic swizzle sticks. "Oh, yes," he said in a virtual whisper. "To me, too. The worst part is that I hadn't had time to call her. I only arrived in Alpine a week ago Sunday."

Once again, I had to assert myself in Vida's presence. "How did you find out about her death?" I asked.

"Hector told me," Dean replied, fiddling with a key chain on the table. "This morning. I couldn't believe it."

"That she was a suicide?" Vida put in.

Dean nodded. "That's not the Crystal I remember. Of course I hadn't seen her in several years."

It appeared that Crystal's ex hadn't yet heard about Milo's suspicions. The word would spread quickly enough. Dean was probably still undergoing the isolation that newcomers experience when they arrive in a new town.

"But you remained friendly?" Vida's smile looked like

the Cheshire cat's. In fact, with that goofy fur hat, all she needed was a set of whiskers.

"Well . . ." Dean grimaced and set the key chain aside. "She moved to Portland after we split up. I didn't have much contact with her, really. But I'd run into her a couple of times when I was in Portland. We didn't hold any grudges. It was just one of those things. Too young, maybe." He was looking away from us, out the window toward the snow-covered slopes of Mount Baldy. Perhaps he was recalling a pair of teenagers in love, and how it had all gone sour.

"I understand you and Crystal have a daughter. Have you any idea where she might be?" I asked.

Sadly, Dean shook his head. "I heard from her twice after she ran away. She was in Reno, then Vegas. She told me not to worry, she was fine. That's all, both times. It was years ago." Tears had welled up in Dean's eyes.

"Do you know why she left?" I asked.

Dean shook his head. "Only Crystal's side of it. Amber was resentful of authority." His face hardened. "Why wouldn't she be? Crystal had one of those blasted 'Question Authority' bumper stickers on her car. Amber had been raised to resist being told what to do. Crystal never realized it could backfire on her."

"Foolish," Vida remarked. "Shortsighted."

Dean didn't respond, but kept staring at the icicles. Maybe he thought they were small daggers, piercing his heart.

"Will you be looking for a house?" I asked, feeling a need to back off from Dean Ramsey's regrets.

"What?" He turned, staring at me through the heavy-framed glasses. "Oh, yes. We have two children, one in high school, the other in middle school. I've looked at a couple of places around Sultan. It's closer to Monroe and my folks, but not that far from Alpine."

Vida's smile had faded. "If you're working for the county, wouldn't it be more suitable for you to live here?" There was disapproval in her tone. Vida didn't favor the idea of people living anywhere but Alpine.

Dean looked surprised. "Does it matter whether my residence is in Snohomish or Skykomish County?"

"Legally?" Vida sniffed. "I don't know. But it's much more pleasant here. Sultan is becoming very spread out."

This didn't seem like the moment for a debate on the amenities of Sultan versus Alpine. "Will you be attending Crystal's services?" I asked.

Dean grimaced again. "Yes . . . yes, of course. Do you know when they're scheduled?"

"No," Vida admitted, "but we'll find out by tomorrow. We have a deadline."

"I'm having dinner tonight with April and Mel," Dean said. "I hadn't called them, either, until I heard about Crystal. They very kindly asked me over."

"How thoughtful," Vida said, getting out of Hector's chair. "By the way, did you know—and this is certainly a coincidence—that Crystal's other ex has also been in town?"

"Aaron?" Dean clutched at the edge of the table. "No. I thought he'd fallen off the face of the earth. What's *he* doing here?" There was anger in his voice, as if his successor had no right to be anywhere, least of all in Alpine.

"Apparently," Vida said in her most casual voice, "he came to see Crystal."

"Came to mooch is more like it," Dean growled. "He probably wanted money for his drugs."

"That's possible," Vida allowed, never turning a hair, though the fur hat had begun to slip again. "I'll be by later to take your picture. Will you be here?"

Dean said he would. He didn't bother to show us to the door, but remained seated, again staring out the window.

"Drugs." Vida sighed as we trudged back down the stairs. "I should have guessed. A musician. Wouldn't you know it? And that Victor also has something to do with music. I don't recall Crystal ever being interested in any of the arts."

"She was interested in men. Or was in the past," I said, recalling the anti-male slogans on the refrigerator. "Maybe their backgrounds weren't the attraction."

We had reached the lobby, where Vida nodded briskly at Madge Gustavson, but didn't speak. I suspected that Madge was probably going to be in the deep freeze for at least a couple of days.

"Billy has also been remiss," Vida murmured as we exited through the revolving door. "He didn't call me this morning about the autopsy report. What do you know about Dilantin?"

Before I could answer, Bill Blatt pulled up to the curb in his deputy's car and called to his aunt. "Could I treat you to some ice cream this evening?" he asked in a humble voice.

"Why, Billy," Vida replied, "how nice. In fact, let me treat you to dinner. The ski-lodge coffee shop at six? I lunched there with your dear mother today, and the food seemed especially good."

Bill Blatt slapped a hand to his head. "Ohmigosh! It's her birthday, isn't it? I forgot." His florid complexion deepened. "We'll have to get together tomorrow night. But you're coming to the house after work, right?"

"Oh." It was clear that Vida had also forgotten, at least the part about the family birthday celebration. "Of course. How silly of me. We'll talk then, all right?"

Bill assured his aunt that it was. I had the feeling that he'd lost out on a free meal. Vida would wheedle everything she could out of the poor guy before the candles were extinguished on Nell Blatt's cake. The dinner date would be superfluous.

Al Driggers had called while we were gone to say that the funeral services for Crystal Bird would be held Thursday at eleven A.M. at First Baptist Church. There would be cremation, because that was what April Eriks thought her sister would have wanted. It may have been, but second-guessing the dead has always seemed self-indulgent to me.

Shortly after four, Scott turned in his brief story on Victor Dimitroff. There wasn't much more in it than we'd already learned from April: Victor's parents were political dissidents who had fled to France shortly before World War II. Their son had been born during the German occupation, and after the war, the Dimitroffs had moved to Vienna for a time, and then back to Paris. Young Victor had studied the tuba in both cities, and had eventually been hired by the Paris Opera. In the mid-Seventies, he had joined the New York Philharmonic, remaining with the orchestra for almost twenty years. During that period, he had begun to compose, and finally chucked his career as a performer to create his own music. He had not bragged about successes, so I assumed he was still struggling.

"Scott," I said, standing in the doorway to my cubby-hole, "this is fine, except that you didn't include why Victor was in the Alpine area."

Laboriously, Scott looked up from his next assignment, covering ski enthusiasts' reaction to the new back-side runs and lifts at the pass. He had a habit of making every story look like an onerous task, and maybe it was or else it wouldn't have taken him so long to produce his copy.

"Dimitroff didn't say," Scott replied.

"Nothing? Not a skier, not a tourist? Was he headed

for eastern Washington?" Nobody simply passes through Alpine, though they pass it by when heading across the pass. "Why would he have Janet Driggers making his travel arrangements if he didn't have a reason to be in the area?"

"I don't know. He didn't say," Scott repeated with a shrug.

"Didn't? Or wouldn't?"

Scott gave me that terrific grin. "The latter, I guess. I did ask. But he was kind of in a rush to get out of the hospital."

"Okay." I went back into my office, cursing myself for not having sent Vida in the first place. At the time, I had believed there was no real importance in Victor Dimitroff's visit. But I was wrong. Now that murder was a possibility, his relationship with the dead woman loomed large.

The phone rang, and I picked it up in a distracted manner.

"Can you come over right away?" the terse voice asked.

"Milo?" He sounded very strange, alarmingly harsh. "Yes. Why?"

"Just be here, ASAP." He hung up.

Not only had I barely recognized Milo, I suddenly felt afraid of him. But I obeyed. After all, I was a suspect.

It was icing up underfoot, and I almost fell twice in my rush to reach the sheriff's office two blocks away. Milo was sitting in a haze of blue smoke, drinking yet another mug of his vile coffee. He had two space heaters going, one aimed at his chair, the other in the middle of the room.

"What's with these?" I asked, pointing to the heater nearest my visitor's chair.

"We blew all the fuses this morning and killed the

heating system," he replied in a detached voice. "Ron Bjornson's working on it. Coffee?"

"No, thanks." There was a two-inch story in the blown fuses, but I'd get to that later. "Why am I here?"

Milo set his mug down and riffled some papers on his desk. "Jack and Dwight Gould drained the hot tub at Crystal's this afternoon. They found a pill bottle stuck in the drain. The printing on the prescription label was pretty washed out, but we were able to bring it up under the microscope in the lab." The sheriff lifted his long chin and stared at me with chilling hazel eyes. "The empty bottle had contained Dilantin, and it was made out to you."

Chapter Eight

I asked Milo for a cigarette. He held the pack out while I fumbled around. Then he leaned forward again and lighted the damned thing for me. All the while, his gaze never left my face.

"This is crazy," I finally said in a strange parody of my own voice. "How can that be? Can I see it?"

"The bottle?" Milo shrugged. "Why not?"

He opened a drawer and fished out a plastic bag. In it was the small amber plastic bottle that I'd bought at Parker's Pharmacy, where Doc Dewey had phoned in my sleeping-pill prescription.

"Jesus," I whispered.

"How many were in there?" Milo asked, putting the evidence away.

"Ohhh . . ." I held my head in my hands, elbows resting on the desk. "A dozen, maybe. I'd had it refilled once, then I finally went off the blasted things. You remember—I must have told everybody in town how glad I was to be able to sleep on my own again."

"Alone." The word slipped from Milo's lips and he reddened. I don't think I'd ever seen him blush before. "Scratch that." Briefly, he turned away, and I sensed that he was swearing at himself.

"The break-in," I said suddenly. "Whoever broke into my house stole that bottle."

114

"What?" Milo had recovered, and was looking at me again. "Oh." He tugged at one ear, then picked up his coffee mug. "You think so?" There was no inflection in his voice.

"Isn't it obvious?" The idea had put steel in my spine; finally, there was something I could hold on to besides the cigarette. "Did you ever recover the other things that were stolen?"

"No."

"Did you try?"

Milo stared at me, but didn't respond.

"I know, I know," I said hastily. "It's almost impossible to find stolen goods because they go to Everett or Seattle or Damascus. But I don't think petty theft was the reason for the break-in. Come on, Milo. Crystal's murder was premeditated, and somebody's trying to set me up."

"Who?" There was still no emotion in his voice, and it was beginning to gall me.

"Paula Rubens arranged the meeting," I said, "though I can't imagine why she'd want to kill Crystal. In fact, I can't imagine Paula killing anybody. But everybody in town knew Crystal and I were at odds, and probably half the population knew I was going to meet her that night. Paula's a nice woman, but she talks. And you know how word gets out around here."

Milo drained the mug's dregs into a sickly-looking cactus. If it survived only on the sheriff's coffee, the plant's condition was probably terminal. "How well do you know Paula?"

"Fairly well," I replied, beginning to relax a bit. "I like her. We share quite a few interests. You've known her as long as I have. She lives near Honoria's old place."

Milo grunted. He rarely liked being reminded of his former girlfriend, who had put him through a fair share of misery. "I know Paula," he allowed. "She's kind of deep."

To Milo, that meant Paula read the news before the sports page. "Do you agree with me about the break-in?" I asked, taking the last puff off my cigarette.

"It's possible." He didn't seem enthused with the idea.

"Don't be a jackass," I shouted, pounding a fist on the desk. "You know damned well I didn't kill Crystal Bird. Why are you wasting your time grilling me?"

Milo tucked his chin into his chest. "Admit it, it doesn't look good."

"Screw you."

He kept looking at me, but a muscle twitched along his jaw. "What?"

Angrily, I waved a hand. "Poor choice of words. I'm sorry. And make up your mind—are you interrogating me or taunting me? I thought we were past all that stuff."

Milo heaved a deep sigh. "So did I. Okay. When did you last see that pill bottle?"

I couldn't remember. My medicine cabinet, which was above the sink, contained the usual assortment of over-the-counter remedies. The only prescription drugs I had were an ointment for a rash, tetracycline to keep my skin from erupting into adolescent zits, the hormone replacements—and the sleeping pills. I didn't take a daily inventory.

"I wish I could remember," I said, "but I can't. I open the medicine cabinet twice a day. In the morning, when I'm still fogged in with sleep, and at night, when I'm dead tired. My powers of observation are at a low ebb both times."

Milo grunted. "If you're right about how many pills were left, it was definitely enough to kill Crystal. Especially since she'd been drinking rum. Was she drunk when you were there?"

"I don't think so. But then it's hard to tell with some people, especially when you don't know them." I paused, thinking back to her demeanor. She had scarcely looked at me the whole time. I had little memory of her face, and almost none of her eyes.

"What do you know about this Dimitroff guy?" Milo asked.

"Funny you should ask," I murmured, then tried to recite all the facts from Scott's story.

Milo gave a faint nod. "I checked with Janet Driggers. She said Dimitroff made his flight arrangements a couple of weeks ago. But she didn't know where he was staying. Do you?"

I shook my head. "Did she tell you he wasn't leaving until Friday? Surely you can run him down."

"We've got an APB on the guy. Let's hope he wasn't headed for Seattle."

"Could he drive with that broken leg?"

Milo shrugged. "Doc Dewey said maybe, if he took it easy."

"What about Aaron Conley?" I remembered the incident on Front Street where I'd almost been hit by his van. "I could describe his vehicle."

"Conley's in custody," Milo replied.

"What?"

"We picked him up a couple of hours ago. He was trying to pass a forged check on Crystal's account."

"Wow." I couldn't help it, I reached for another cigarette. Unfortunately, Milo obliged. "What's his story on Friday night?"

"He was in Monroe, jamming or whatever they call it these days, at a tavern." Milo's expression was dour. "He's got witnesses, but since when are a bunch of drunks reliable?"

I didn't know, either. Impulsively, I grabbed one of

Milo's hands. "You don't really think I'm a killer, do you, Milo?"

He gave my fingers a quick squeeze. "No. But damn it, Emma, I have to go by the book."

I knew that. Milo always does.

Despite a little coaxing and a lot of badgering, I couldn't get Milo to open up about Aaron Conley. On the way back to the office, it occurred to me that Scott might have better luck. The sheriff's office was part of his beat, and he was already developing some rapport with Dustin Fong.

"Here's your first sidebar to go with the homicide story," I announced.

Scott jumped. "So soon? It's officially a homicide?"

"That's the way Sheriff Dodge is treating it." *And the way he's treating me,* I wanted to add, but didn't. "This is a first, I assume?"

Scott nodded. "You don't cover crime when you work for a suburban shopper," he said in reference to his previous job on an Eastside weekly.

I was giving him the details when Vida sidled over to Scott's desk. "So Milo's convinced Crystal was murdered?"

I nodded. "We can discuss the details later."

"When?" Vida folded her arms across her bust. "It's almost five. I have a birthday dinner to attend."

"Tomorrow, then," I said with a cheer I didn't feel. "Don't worry. You've got Billy to pump at the party."

Before Vida could respond, April Eriks entered the news office. "I have a photo of Crystal," she said. "Mr. Driggers told me I should bring it by for the obituary."

"That's right," Vida said, holding out her hand. "I do death notices. Thank you, April. How are you managing?"

April lowered her eyes. "Okay. Fine. Reverend Poole

asked if someone from the family wanted to give a eulogy. Our son Thad has volunteered."

"That's very kind," Vida declared. "I didn't realize he was close to his aunt."

"Neither did I," April responded. Without looking at any of us, she turned on her heel and left.

"Well!" Vida licked her lips. "Now what does *that* mean?"

I shrugged. "My guess is that April's resentful because her son wants to put in a good word for his aunt. Let's see the photo."

It was a five-by-seven black-and-white glossy, probably taken in a studio at least ten years ago. "A corporate photograph," Vida said, "no doubt for the bank's files."

"Yes." I studied the face closely. Frankly, I hardly recognized it as belonging to the Crystal Bird I'd seen in the hot tub at Baring. This version was not only younger, but considerably softer. The shoulder-length fair hair was styled in thick curls, a very Eighties look. Crystal wore makeup—lipstick, eye shadow, liner, mascara, and, if the photo had been in color, blush would have shown on her cheeks. Despite the severity of the no-nonsense suit and severe blouse, she looked almost beautiful.

"What changed her?" I mused aloud.

"Life," Vida replied. "It does that to people."

"Yes," I agreed, "but it's both style and substance. She was thinner when I saw her, harder, plainer."

"Older, of course," Vida noted.

Scott was looking over my shoulder. "She's pretty, but she doesn't look very friendly. That smile is bogus."

Scott was right. The smile didn't go past her nose.

Vida took the photo over to her desk while Scott shifted his weight from one foot to the other. "There's no point in getting started on this Aaron Conley story, is there?" he asked. "It's five to five."

Technically, there wasn't. But at his age, I had always been willing to work past the hour if I felt even the slightest sense of urgency about deadlines for *The Oregonian*.

"That's okay," I said, submitting to a different time, place, and generation. "But get on it first thing tomorrow."

I, too, decided to call it a day. On the way home, I stopped by the Grocery Basket to replenish the larder. The owner, Jake O'Toole, was up at the front end of the store when I checked out. Juggling two bags of groceries, I approached him with a smile.

"Confide in me," I said in my most winsome manner. "Did Aaron Conley try to pass a forged check here?"

Jake wrinkled his aquiline nose. "Aaron Conley? Oh— you mean that ex-husband of Crystal Bird's? No, why?"

I explained about Aaron's arrest. Grimly, Jake shook his head.

"He's a piece of work, all right," Jake said. "If it's true that Crystal was murdered, I figure he did it. That guy's got trouble written all over him."

"Tell me," I said, wishing I hadn't bought five pounds of potatoes and ten pounds of sugar on this expedition, "were you here when Crystal came in with Aaron?"

"You mean after we went through that rigmarole about him charging on her account?" Seeing my nod, Jake continued. "Yeah, I was here. When am I not here?" His eyes raked the store, though his expression conveyed affection as well as resentment. For Jake, the Grocery Basket was like a much-loved but demanding mistress.

"How did they interact?" I inquired.

Jake shrugged. "Nothing special. If I hadn't known better, I would've figured them for a big sister–little brother act."

"No show of affection? No harsh words? No tension?"

Jake passed a hand over his face. "Well . . . Maybe there was kind of a strain between them. You know, the way people act after they've just had a fight, but they've patched it up."

I appreciated Jake's insight. He ought to know: Betsy and Jake O'Toole were famous for bickering in public, despite the fact that they were a devoted couple.

"Did you get the impression that Aaron was staying with Crystal?" I asked as Jake's brother, Buzzy, approached with a clipboard in hand.

"Yeah, I did," Jake answered, giving Buzzy a high sign. "They were buying stuff for dinner. Hey, Emma, got to go. Buzzy needs some help with tomorrow's produce order."

My arms were about ready to fall off by the time I got home. After dumping the grocery bags on the kitchen table, I went into the bathroom and opened the medicine chest. As far as I could tell, the only missing item was the bottle of sleeping pills. It had sat between the estrogen and the cortisone ointment, but whoever had taken it had moved the remaining bottles closer together so that I wouldn't notice a gap.

Milo had checked for prints and found none that didn't belong. It figured. The thief had worn gloves. I was angry all over again, not only at being set up—or so it appeared—but because the staged robbery had included Adam's possessions. What, I wondered, had the intruder done with the jar of coins and autographed Mariners baseball?

There was one call on the answering machine, and it was from Paula Rubens. "I just heard that Crystal was poisoned. Good God, Emma," she continued in an agitated voice, "I can't believe it. Is there any chance we can get together tonight after I'm done with my final? Call me, *please*."

Since it was going on six, I assumed she'd be on

campus. I dialed her number there and she answered on the first ring.

"Class doesn't start until six," she said, sounding somewhat calmer. "All I have to do is collect the term project from each student, ask a few questions, and get the hell out of there. Could you meet me at the bar in the ski lodge at seven?"

I could. Dinner consisted of macaroni and cheese, a hamburger patty, and an ear of corn that tasted as if Jake had grown it in his basement. No wonder Buzzy needed help with his produce order.

The bar at the ski lodge has a handsome Viking motif, featuring various figures from Norse mythology. Rough stone and stained wood provided a perfect setting for the big glass panel that evoked the northern lights. The first time Paula and I had met at the lodge for drinks, she had commented on the glass, informing me that the Seattle artisan who had designed it was one of the most outstanding and underrated craftsmen in the country.

Now, however, Paula didn't even glance toward the bar itself, where the glass glowed and a small waterfall trickled off to one side.

"Tell me everything you know," she demanded before she'd even sat down. "I had to hear about this from Nat Cardenas himself. Do you know he seemed pleased to deliver the bad news? The man's a skunk."

The college president no doubt had reason to feel a certain amount of satisfaction. Or relief. Certainly he had taken his lumps in *Crystal Clear*. I reminded Paula of the attacks on Cardenas.

"So what?" Paula retorted. "That doesn't excuse his attitude. The least he could do is put up a good front. Nat does that very well. He strikes me as a first-class phony."

We hadn't met to argue about Nat Cardenas. "I imagine there are quite a few people around here who aren't weeping and wailing over Crystal's demise," I said in a mild tone. "Me, for instance."

"But you're not gloating," Paula countered. "Okay, give me the lowdown."

Before I began to relate what I knew, we gave our drink orders. Then I lighted a cigarette from the pack I'd purchased in a weak moment at the lodge's gift shop. Paula made a face.

"Must you?" she asked, though there was amusement in her tone.

"Yes, I must. It's been a rough day."

"Okay, so I'll indulge you." She laughed. "Now talk."

I told her almost everything I knew, though I reserved the part about the pill bottle. Milo wouldn't make that public, and neither would I. Newspaper publishers don't need to incite the readership any more than is necessary.

When I had finished, we were halfway through our drinks. Paula sat back on the banquette and frowned. "So Conley's in the slammer," she remarked. "Is it just the forged check or is Milo holding him as a person of interest?"

"I don't know. Both, maybe." I lighted my second cigarette, careful to blow the smoke as far away from Paula as possible. "What do you know about the guy?"

Paula fingered the stem on her martini glass. "Crystal didn't talk about him much, unless she'd been drinking." Pausing, she met me with her level gaze. "Don't get me wrong. Crystal was no boozer. But, as some of us do once in a while, she'd get a little tight and feel sorry for herself."

"I can do that sober," I remarked.

Paula gave a faint nod. "Can't we all. Anyway, that's when she'd go off on her exes, husbands and lovers."

"Lovers, such as Victor Dimitroff?"

Turning quickly to catch our server's attention for another round, Paula wagged a finger. "I don't know much

about that one," she said, "because he must have been a
newcomer. But there were a couple of guys in Portland
who'd given her a hard time. One of them was a married
coworker from the bank. The other taught at Reed College. Frankly, I don't remember their names."

"And Aaron?" I prompted.

"Aaron." Paula inclined her head. "She met him in
Portland when he and his band were performing at some
tavern on Burnside. I think they were called The Hoods—
for the mountain, not the criminals. They hit it off, and
were married just a few months later. In fact, the ceremony was held on a barge under the Burnside Bridge.
Let's call them an ill-starred couple. It didn't last long."

I put out my cigarette and promised myself I wouldn't
smoke any more for the duration of the evening. "The
age difference was a factor, I suppose."

"That, and Aaron's problems with the band, which
broke up just before the marriage did." Paula paused
while our fresh drinks were delivered. "There were also
drugs, which Crystal didn't use. Oh, she smoked weed
now and then, but had nothing to do with the hard stuff.
Aaron didn't have a real job, though he sometimes
worked as a waiter. Crystal supported him, which was
pretty old with her. She'd already put one husband
through college."

"Aaron sounds like an all-around loser," I commented.

"He was. Is, I guess. The last I heard of him, he took off
for California to make it big in L.A. He didn't." Paula
gave me a wry look.

"Do you know when he showed up here?" I asked.

Paula's high, smooth forehead wrinkled. "A couple of
weeks ago, maybe? When I talked to her on the phone,
she mentioned that he was staying with her. She thought
it would be just for a day or two, because he had plans to
go across the pass to Spokane. His former drummer had

gotten a gig over there, and Aaron intended to bunk with him for a while. I guess he got comfortable, though, because he was still hanging out with her as of last Wednesday." Paula lowered her head. "That was when I arranged the meeting with the two of you. It was the last time I spoke with her."

Crystal Bird must have had some good qualities. Otherwise, Paula wouldn't have befriended her. Maybe the second drink was giving me the courage to ask.

"What did you like about Crystal? What did I miss?"

Again, Paula's gaze was level and unwavering. "She was brave. She had the courage of her convictions. I don't think I ever met anyone who was so honest and open about her feelings. I suppose," she went on, growing thoughtful, "I admired her as much as I liked her."

"I see." I supposed those were good enough reasons.

Paula, however, knew what I was thinking. "I realize you and she had very little common ground. I'm not unsympathetic with the way she attacked you and some of the other people in Alpine. But you must admit, her causes were just."

"They were." I couldn't argue against the women's shelter, day-care centers, or the environment. "But you don't have to support a cause by tearing down other people. As I told her the night I met her, personal attacks aren't good journalism. She was asking for trouble."

Paula laughed. "She always did. That was part of being Crystal."

I wasn't laughing. "She found it."

Immediately, Paula grew serious. "Yes," she said in a hushed tone. "She did."

As I dealt with the exigencies of deadline the next morning, I tried to sort through what Paula had told me.

There really wasn't much new. Certainly there had been nothing to point the way to Crystal's killer.

Scott returned around nine-thirty from his morning run to the city and county offices. He looked harried as he spread out a pile of notes on my desk.

"Dustin wasn't in, so I had to deal with Jack Mullins," Scott complained. "Jack's full of it."

Jack Mullins sometimes lets his sense of humor get the better of him. "You'll get used to it," I said. "What about Conley?"

"Mullins insists they're only holding him on the forgery deal," Scott replied, tinkering with the tape recorder he always used as a backup. "He can post bail, but so far he hasn't."

"He's broke," I put in. "Did you talk to Conley?"

"I tried." Scott made a face. "He wouldn't even look at me. He's one surly dude."

"So what are we talking about? A dead end as far as Aaron Conley's concerned?"

"You got it." Scott looked at me with those limpid brown eyes. "Sorry. But I did find out something kind of strange."

I leaned forward in my chair. "About the murder?"

"No." Scott tapped one of the notes on the desk. "Yesterday when I checked the log, I noticed that there was no name by one of the weekend DWIs. That struck me as odd, but we don't run those anyway, so I didn't pay any attention."

During Marius Vandeventer's reign, he had always run the DWIs and the DIPs, which stood for Drunk in Public. According to Vida, Marius felt that putting their names in the paper might deter them from repeating the performance. Naturally, Vida agreed with him, but I felt differently. Public humiliation wouldn't cure alcoholism, and was just one step above the stocks as a form of punishment.

"But today you got curious about the anonymous sot," I said with a smile of approval. It was one thing to not publish names; not knowing them was another matter. "Who was it?"

Scott grinned. "Nat Cardenas, college president. He got picked up last Friday night for crossing the center line on Highway 2 just this side of Baring."

Chapter Nine

VIDA HAD COME into my office right after Scott made his startling announcement. Naturally, she was agog.

"Astounding," she murmured, rubbing her gloved hands together. "How many people do we now have in the vicinity of Baring Friday night?"

I gave Vida a droll look. "Including me?"

She shook her head, which was covered on this snowy Tuesday morning with a most inappropriate feathered toque. "You don't count. I mean Victor Dimitroff, Nat Cardenas, and—who?"

"The killer?" I responded. "Or do you think one of them did it?"

"It's certainly possible," Vida said, assuming a defensive stance with her bust jutting like the prow of a Boston whaler.

"I don't get it," Scott put in. "Do people like Cardenas get special treatment from the sheriff?"

"What?" Vida barked.

Scott waved the sheet of notes in front of her. "Cardenas's name didn't appear in the log. But the other dozen or so who were picked up over the weekend got IDed."

Vida grimaced. "Yes, I see what you mean."

"I'm not sure that they ever list first offenders by name," I said, feeling a need to come to Milo's defense.

128

"Or maybe it was a courtesy. What's the point, really? We're the only ones who check the log, and we don't ever run the names."

"We should," Vida muttered. "Marius Vandeventer did."

I ignored the remark, and addressed Scott. "Did you ask Jack about this?"

Scott nodded. "He said it was a gentlemen's handshake."

"Oh." That explained it. Milo had in fact gone easy on Nat Cardenas. He'd probably done the same over the years for Mayor Fuzzy Baugh, the county commissioners, and maybe a couple of clergymen. Since Carla had covered the log on her beat, she might never have noticed the omission of names.

"Tricky," Vida was saying as she tapped a foot. "How do we find out what Nat was doing near Baring without letting on that we know he was drunk?"

"Isn't that up to the sheriff?" Scott asked.

Vida didn't exactly scoff, but there was pity in her expression. "Our job is to investigate as well as report. Besides, Milo needs all the help he can get. Short-staffed, you see."

As Scott started for the news office, he looked skeptical. He's learning, I thought. At least about Vida.

My House & Home editor sat down in the chair that Scott had just vacated. "I've heard no gossip about Nat Cardenas's drinking. Have you?"

I shook my head. "Those things can be kept a deep, dark secret, though."

"My, yes," Vida agreed. "Even in a town like Alpine. Take Arthur Trews, for example. So straitlaced, so proper. No one ever suspected him of drinking. But after he died and his children tore down the old chicken coop, they found dozens and dozens of empty whiskey bottles. His wife was shocked, poor thing. She knew he spent a great deal of time with the chickens, but she merely thought he was fond of them. It never occurred to her that the names he called each one were suggestive. MacNaughton. Seagram. The Old Crow. I forget the others, and naturally he didn't speak of them outside of the house. The odd thing was, those hens rarely laid any eggs."

I couldn't resist smiling. "In Nat's defense, it's not unusual for someone to drink too much once in a great while. Especially this time of year. As you know from your section, the party season is upon us, and has been since Halloween."

"Perhaps." Vida was still looking troubled. "Do you think that person you know at the college could find out what Cardenas was up to Friday night?"

"What person?" I knew very well that Vida was referring to Paula Rubens.

"Your . . . friend. Paula." Vida's lips puckered like a prune.

I shook my head. "Dubious. Paula's a part-timer, and in any event, I don't think she and Nat are particularly close. He socializes some with the administrators, but not the faculty. Frankly, Justine Cardenas isn't much of a hostess. She's either shy or she doesn't want to bother herself."

"Not a very helpful sort of wife," Vida murmured, then brightened. "We've only done one feature on Justine. Wouldn't it be nice to interview her about Christmas customs in other parts of the country where she and Nat have lived?"

I started to dismiss the idea out of hand, then hesitated. "I suppose that's not the dumbest thing I've heard this week. You're assigning this to yourself, I gather?"

Vida glared. "Dumb? Certainly not. It's a House & Home piece, isn't it?"

"Yes, it is. But I don't know what you expect to find out from her about her husband's whereabouts Friday night and why he was trashed."

"We'll see," Vida said, standing up.

I didn't give voice to further doubts. If anybody could get anything out of Justine Cardenas, it would be Vida.

I half expected to be summoned back to the sheriff's, but by noon, there was no word from Milo. I should have been relieved and left well enough alone, but on impulse, I dialed his number and asked if he wanted to meet me for lunch at the Heartbreak Hotel. Somewhat to my surprise, he did.

The Heartbreak Hotel is a new Fifties-style diner that opened just in time for Halloween. Two brothers, John and Dan Bourgette, built the restaurant on the site of an old warehouse that had burned down the previous year. They suffered through a number of rather gruesome obstacles before they could lay the foundation, but had missed their completion date by only a month. So far, business seemed brisk, especially from college students and skiers.

The restaurant is on Railroad Avenue, between the train tracks and the river. Appropriately enough, the gleaming steel building looks like a dining car. I maneuvered the Jag into a diagonal parking place between a battered pickup and a brand-new Taurus.

Milo hadn't arrived yet, so I asked for a booth in the smoking section. I didn't intend to indulge my vice, but I knew the sheriff would. I also knew he'd order coffee. The heavy white mugs arrived just as Milo came through the door. The Heartbreak Hotel hadn't been open during our affair. It held no memories. But the name itself was a reminder of what had been between us.

"Another wreck out on Highway 2," Milo said, clumsily getting into the booth with its bright red vinyl upholstery. "Damned fools. Half the people in this state don't know how to drive in snow."

I agreed. "Anybody hurt?"

Removing his hat, Milo nodded. "Three of them had to be taken to the hospital." He paused, looking alert. "There they go now."

Above the jukebox's rendition of "Rock Around the Clock," I heard the siren wail as the ambulance raced along Alpine Way, half a block from the diner. "Locals?"

"No." Milo picked up the menu. "Locals know how to handle these roads. I think they're from Everett or Mukilteo. You'll see it in the log."

I gave Milo a strained smile. "It's Tuesday. Scott'll have to check it this afternoon to make deadline."

The sheriff gave a lazy wave of one big hand. "Oh. I forgot."

He always did. To be fair, most people paid no attention to our deadline. Over the years, an untold number of readers had needed reminding that delivery of a news item on Wednesday morning couldn't possibly make it into *The Advocate* that same afternoon.

"Tell me about Nat Cardenas," I said, stirring an extra measure of sugar into my coffee.

Milo grimaced. "That's a bitch. I don't like the guy, but I feel for him."

"You're a nice guy," I remarked, and meant it. "You didn't have to leave his name off the log."

Milo scratched his head. "No. But local VIPs have some perks. They shouldn't, but they do. Marius Vandeventer wouldn't bend the rules for anybody, and gave holy hell to my predecessors if they tried to cover up. When Eeeny Moroni was sheriff, the two of them had a couple of real fistfights about it. Then Eeeny threatened to arrest Marius for assaulting an officer of the law, and Marius said he'd charge police brutality and go to the big-city papers and TV stations. It got pretty ugly, but Marius won. He had the Constitution behind him. Eeeny only had his badge."

"I understand Marius's position," I said, "but I don't agree with it. The law punishes people, not the press. At least not when it comes to DWIs."

"The press does its own kind of damage," Milo noted. "Anyway, even if you don't put Cardenas's name in the paper, the story'll leak out."

"Maybe not," I replied. "Everybody's occupied with Crystal's murder."

Milo didn't respond directly; the waitress, whose name I'd forgotten but recognized from her tenure at the Burger Barn, had arrived to take our orders.

"Who picked Cardenas up?" I inquired when we were alone again.

"Dustin," Milo replied absently as he lighted a cigarette. "Funny thing—Cardenas waived the test and admitted he'd been drinking. I suppose he didn't want anybody to know how much he'd had."

I, too, thought it a bit unusual, but people are unpredictable, and I didn't know Nat Cardenas well enough to speculate. "How long do you plan to hold Aaron Conley?" I asked, deciding I might as well change the subject while the sheriff was in a cooperative mood.

Milo shrugged. "We charged him yesterday. But you already know that," he said, waving away the cloud of smoke that lingered between us. "Unless he raises bail, he's stuck until the trial. That could be another couple of weeks."

"Which doesn't upset you in the least," I noted.

My remark didn't seem to cheer Milo. Instead, he ran

an agitated hand through his graying sandy hair and shifted his weight in the booth's narrow confines.

"This is some damned mess," he muttered, accidentally hitting his coffee mug and splashing a couple of drops on the vinyl table. "Homicides are supposed to be easy," Milo went on, swiping at the spilled coffee with his bare hand. "Two guys in a bar, one knifes the other, two dozen witnesses, even if most of them are hammered. Wife catches the old man in the sack with another woman, whips out a shotgun, and blows them both away, then cries all over herself, saying how she didn't mean to do it, and she still loves the SOB. That's the way it usually is. That's the way it should be."

The sheriff stopped his diatribe while the waitress delivered his cheeseburger and my hamburger dip. "But not this case, not some of the other ones I've gotten stuck with in the past few years." Milo went on. "Life used to be simpler, especially in small towns."

"That's true," I allowed. "Everything is more complicated. Even murder."

"It ought to be easier," Milo asserted after he'd taken a big chunk out of his cheeseburger. "We've got all this technology going for us. DNA, for instance. But then some clever bastard uses poison. Wouldn't you know it'd take an old-fashioned murder to screw up new methods?"

I offered Milo a genuine, if somewhat uncertain, smile. "Then you don't think I'm the clever bastard?"

"Shit." Milo permitted himself a half grin. "I can't see you going to all that trouble. You'd be more likely to pick up a fireplace poker and split somebody's head in two."

"And then cry all over myself?"

The sheriff nodded. "Probably."

We grew silent for a few moments, each of us chewing away on our respective burgers. My gaze traveled to the counter and beyond to the murals of crew-cut and ponytailed teens doing the Bop. Small replicas of Fifties cars hung on wires from the ceiling: a turquoise Chevy convertible, a maroon Mercury with huge tail fins, a classic red T-bird. The jukebox was playing Elvis, "Love Me Tender." I winced. It hadn't been the Fifties, but Tom had crooned the song to me over drinks at the Thirteen Coins across the street from *The Seattle Times*. It didn't matter that he couldn't carry a tune in a ten-gallon bucket.

"The problem is," Milo was saying without any apparent notice of my emotional state, "you'd better watch yourself."

"Huh?" I stared at him. "Watch what?"

Milo's grin widened. "You're a target. Dueling editors. Women at war. One whacks the other. It's juicy stuff."

"That's funny?" I frowned at the sheriff. "What are you hearing that I'm not?"

"Nothing." The grin faded and the hazel eyes were unusually wide.

"Liar."

"No, really, Emma." He finished the last french fry and lighted another cigarette.

"I don't believe you," I said, bracing my hands against the table. "You're hearing rumors or innuendos or some damned thing. 'Fess up, Dodge."

Milo sighed and flicked ash onto his empty plate. "Maybe a weird look or some half-assed comment. No big thing. I swear it."

"Great." I put both elbows on the table and held my head. "Now I'll have to write an editorial proclaiming my innocence."

"That's not a good idea," Milo cautioned.

"Of course it isn't. I was kidding."

At least I hoped I was.

* * *

Scott had gotten the information about the latest vehicular accident, though he hadn't managed to finish the story until ten to five. Vida, meanwhile, had set up an appointment for Friday morning with Justine Cardenas.

"She was unwilling at first," Vida said as she wound a very long and very ugly orange-and-green scarf around her neck. "But I coaxed. So good for the college. So homey. So positive."

Kip MacDuff entered the news office before I could reply. "Ready?" he asked with the usual cheerful grin on his freckled face.

I grinned back. "I think so." Kip deserved the biggest bonus of all. He was my most underrated staff member, yet he had evolved from a carrier to a delivery-truck driver to running the entire back shop. Still in his early twenties, he had learned every aspect of the business, except for writing and selling ads. It had occurred to me that if he ever acquired a knack for either talent, he'd be a natural to take over *The Advocate* someday.

But that was far off in the future, and for all I knew, Kip didn't intend to spend the rest of his life in Alpine. I never asked about his long-term plans for fear they didn't include the newspaper. I honestly didn't know what I'd do without him.

Vida and Scott left at the same time, but Leo was still on the phone. "All these special Christmas promotions," he said with a sigh as he finally rang off. "I'm not knocking them, but some of our advertisers can't make up their frigging minds about what they want. Just now Clancy Barton changed his mind for the fifth time. He's decided that elves peeking out of Florsheims would be a terrific idea."

I'd gathered up my belongings and was halfway to the door. "You dissuaded him, I trust?"

Leo shook his head. "Not yet. I'm going to let him

sleep on it. Maybe he'll get the idea that just because he owns a shoe store, he doesn't always have to show the damned shoes."

Leo's phone rang again. I glanced at the clock, which said that it was two minutes after five. Maybe Clancy had already changed his mind. Again.

But as Leo listened to the caller, his face froze for just an instant. "Yeah, right, good to hear from you," he said, then put his hand over the mouthpiece. "Nothing important. Go home."

I paused on the threshold. Leo was chuckling into the phone, his face turned away from me. That seemed odd. Maybe Leo had a new lady in his life. With a little shrug, I made my exit. Leo deserved his share of happiness. We all did.

I wondered what had happened to mine.

At home that night, I made some notes about Crystal's murder. Victor Dimitroff and Nat Cardenas had been in the vicinity about the time that the killing had occurred. Of course time of death couldn't be pinpointed, because the warm water in the hot tub had complicated matters. Victor had wrecked his car around ten-forty. According to the sheriff's log, Nat had been cited for drunken driving at ten seventeen. Until then, I hadn't noticed how closely the two incidents had followed one another. Notepad in hand, I picked up the phone and called Vida.

"Goodness," she said after I finished reciting the times, "they must have barely gotten Victor's car towed before they arrested Nat. It was Dustin who was on patrol, correct?"

"That's what Milo told me," I said. "Don't you find this kind of odd?"

"Certainly." Vida paused, apparently reflecting upon the coincidence. "Did the two men meet somewhere?

Did they know each other? Were they both calling on Crystal?"

"Nat might have gone to see Crystal for the same reason that Father Den and I did," I suggested. "To reason with her."

"Not that you could," Vida broke in.

"I know, but that's not the point," I said. "We had our hopes. But it's possible, especially if Nat had a few drinks to buoy himself up."

"He may have had drinks with Crystal," Vida pointed out.

"Dubious," I said. "You'd have to drink about a gallon of that rum punch to get really drunk, and you'd probably get sick first. It tasted awful. I also doubt that Crystal was a serious drinker." I didn't want to rile Vida by quoting Paula Rubens, who had said that her late friend was no boozer.

"Vodka," Vida put in. "If Victor was staying there, he'd have vodka on hand. You know those Russians."

"Not all Russians drink," I said, but allowed for the possibility. "I wonder how solid Aaron Conley's alibi is. I should have asked Milo when we had lunch today."

"It's no alibi," Vida scoffed. "Taverns close at two A.M. Crystal might have been still alive by then."

Again, Vida could be right, though I recalled that two was the outside limit given by the ME. "We don't know when Aaron left the tavern in Monroe. Milo must be having trouble pinning that down. The bartender might be the only one who'd have any idea."

Vida sniffed. "I don't frequent taverns, though I'm aware of what goes on. Accuracy, like neatness, doesn't count."

"The real question is motive," I pointed out. "Was it a crime of passion or of gain?"

"Not passion," Vida replied without hesitation. "It was planned, don't you think?"

I uttered a mirthless laugh. "Planned to frame me. Or was I just a scapegoat?"

"Probably the latter," Vida said. "Which of these possible suspects knew about your sleeping pills?"

I sighed. "Any of them could have known, because I blabbed about them so much. The only doubtful one is Victor. It appears he hasn't been around much. Besides, he's a stranger, and who'd feel compelled to tell him that the local newspaper publisher was taking sleeping pills?"

"Crystal," Vida answered promptly. "Can't you just hear her? 'That ridiculous *Advocate* editor is so upset over my lambasting of her that she's had to resort to sleeping pills.'"

Unfortunately, the remark suited Crystal. "Why me?" I asked in a peevish tone. Of course I already knew the answer.

"Because you had a motive," Vida said reasonably. "As did Father Den, Nat Cardenas, and heaven knows who else. But—to my knowledge—they hadn't gone around town making announcements about their sleeping pills. The pity is that Milo wasn't able to find any evidence concerning who stole your pills in the first place. Indeed, has it occurred to you that they weren't stolen in the robbery?"

It hadn't. But Nat Cardenas had stopped by my house shortly before Thanksgiving to drop off a news release that his overworked PR person had forgotten to give me. I'd offered him a drink at the time. To my surprise, he'd accepted, though he barely touched it until the ice had melted. A public-relations gesture on his part, I'd assumed, though he asked only for a soda because he didn't drink.

He didn't drink. Excitedly, I recounted his statement to Vida.

"In public," she said.

"Well . . . maybe so," I admitted.

"Who else?"

"Father Den," I said. "You know he was here for Thanksgiving because you were here, too. Not to mention Carla and Ryan Talliaferro and Leo." I thought back to when I'd quit taking the pills, which would have been when I'd quit paying attention to their presence in my medicine cabinet. "I went off the blamed things right after Halloween. I don't exactly hold open house around here, but quite a few people have been in and out. In fact I had bridge club the first week of November. Just about everybody used the bathroom that night, except the Dithers sisters. They never go to the bathroom."

Vida harrumphed, apparently in disapproval of the toilet reference—or of the Dithers sisters in general. "What about your friend Paula?"

"Yes," I agreed, "she dropped in, too. So did Edna Mae Dalrymple, even when she wasn't playing bridge. Carla came twice without Ryan, and Mary Jane Bourgette, who wanted some help with the parish bulletin."

"And Milo?"

"The only time Milo's been here recently is when I called about the break-in." I was growing impatient with Vida's grilling.

"He could have taken the sleeping pills then," Vida said in a too calm tone.

"What?" I practically dropped the phone.

"There've been rumors," Vida said, still overly calm.

I hadn't told her about the sheriff's phone call to Crystal on the night of the murder. I wasn't about to do that now. "You're being crazy," I declared. "What have you heard?"

"They dined," Vida replied.

"They . . . When? Where?"

"At the ski lodge, a week before Thanksgiving. November twentieth, I believe."

"Like a date?" I was incredulous.

"I'm not sure. Marje Blatt saw them. She has a new beau, from Index. Quite a nice young man, but suffering through an unfortunate divorce."

"Why didn't you tell me this earlier?" I demanded.

"It didn't seem important." Vida cleared her throat. "Perhaps it is now."

"I hope not. Vida, can you honestly think Milo . . . ?" I couldn't finish the question.

"Really, Emma, you never know what people will do. Just because Milo is a law-enforcement officer doesn't mean he's not human. But then," she added, with an edge to her voice, "you already know that."

Chapter Ten

THE REVEREND OTIS Poole dominated the pulpit at First Baptist Church. He was a big man, well over six feet, with white hair and a barrel chest, who would have looked equally at home as the foreman of a construction crew or in the cab of a logging rig.

But he'd heard the call forty years earlier while harvesting corn on his father's farm in Nebraska. After serving in churches throughout the upper Midwest for the first ten years after his ordination, Pastor Poole had started his western migration, first to North Dakota, then Idaho, and finally Washington. He'd arrived in Spokane fifteen years ago. It was his first big-city calling, and his wife had hated it. According to Mrs. Poole, after much prayer—and probably even more bitching—they'd ended up in Alpine.

On this snowy morning in December, Pastor Poole's baritone rolled out over the small gathering that had come to pay its respects to Crystal Bird. There were perhaps forty people in attendance at First Baptist, including the Wailers, a group of women who attended all local funerals, and let out a chorus of high-pitched moans and groans at intervals, both appropriate and inappropriate.

Vida, who didn't miss many funerals herself, ignored the quartet, who looked like four crows on their favorite perch in the last pew. All of them were dressed in black, including their hats and stockings. In a town where weight is great, they were tall and spare, and, according to Vida, three of them were sisters and one was a sister-in-law. When the sister-in-law's husband had died some ten years earlier, they had put on quite a show of vocal mourning. Apparently, it had given them the impetus to expand their talents, and they had begun attending virtually every funeral in the vicinity. None of their fellow mourners ever said out loud that they minded, but of course they did. You could tell by the grimaces and winces and curious stares from the uninitiated when the performance began with the customary slow, rolling moan that suddenly turned into an outright shriek.

But there were others on hand besides the Wailers, those who had actually known and perhaps even loved Crystal Bird: her sister, April, and brother-in-law, Mel, along with their two children, Melody and Thad; Aaron Conley, let out of jail for the occasion, and accompanied by Milo Dodge; Paula Rubens, with Dean Ramsey on her left, and Victor Dimitroff on her right; Del and Luana Eriks, offering comfort to their relatives; and Father Den.

Vida gave me one of her bruising elbow nudges. "Why is your priest here?" she asked in that stage whisper she seems to reserve for solemn occasions.

"To pay his respects, I suppose," I whispered back. "After all, he found the body."

Vida clucked her tongue. "Poor taste. People will talk."

"Vida!" Sometimes her devious mind could still dismay me.

"A promiscuous woman. The contemporary clergy." Sadly, she shook her head. "Conclusions will be drawn." Just for good measure, she nudged me again. "People are also staring at *you*."

They were. Some of the Eriks clan, two of the Wailers, and a couple of people I didn't recognize were looking my way and talking behind their hands. I set my jaw and stared straight ahead.

Pastor Poole concluded his eulogy, which had consisted mostly of praising Crystal for her enterprising spirit and alluding to her good sense in moving back to the Alpine area. A hymn followed, accompanied by much practiced wailing. Then Thad Eriks rose from the congregation and went up to the pulpit.

Thad was a pleasant-looking young man in his early twenties, a slimmer, trimmer version of his father. He seemed much more self-possessed and articulate than Mel Eriks.

"My aunt was a pioneer," he began, his eyes making contact with his listeners, one by one. "Crystal Anne Bird set a course for herself and never veered from it. There were some who challenged her or disagreed with her, but they couldn't ignore her. She had a powerful voice, and it was heard."

"Piffle," murmured Vida.

"Social conventions were obstacles to be trampled, not observed," Thad went on, his voice steady and secure. "Aunt Crystal had spent a lifetime discovering not just the world around her, but herself. The real tragedy is that just as she had begun to understand who and what she was, her life was brutally ended. Aunt Crystal had finally found her mantra."

"Fiddlesticks," Vida muttered.

I saw Victor Dimitroff frown and Dean Ramsey give a slow shake of his head. Maybe they were hurt because they hadn't been part of Crystal's so-called mantra. Meanwhile, Aaron Conley stared into space, as if in a daze. If he hadn't been in custody, I would have guessed that he was strung out on his drug of choice.

"Aunt Crystal had goals," Thad continued, "which she was determined to reach. She had her own approach, particularly through her newsletter, *Crystal Clear*. Critics and naysayers couldn't deter her. She marched to her own drummer, but the route she took always followed her social conscience."

"Conscience indeed." Vida sniffed. "Twaddle."

As Thad Eriks further lauded his aunt, I tried to turn a deaf ear. Neither his words nor the Reverend Poole's homage had moved me in the slightest. Vida was right. Thad was spouting meaningless drivel. As for the minister, I couldn't fault him. He didn't know Crystal Bird from Larry Bird. His intentions were good, his faith apparently genuine. But I felt no compassion for Crystal. I still hated her. It would have been much better if I'd felt nothing at all. I was beginning to hate myself.

My gaze wandered about the church, which was unadorned, except for a plain cross on the altar, a stained-glass window depicting the Good Shepherd, and an American flag. The Wailers had remained mercifully silent during Thad's eulogy, which was beginning to wind down. Two rows in front of me, I saw the Eriks clan. Only Melody seemed moved by her brother's words. The rest sat as stone-faced as Al Driggers, who stood discreetly off to one side, waiting to tend to his duties as funeral director.

Thad finished and joined the rest of the family. A final prayer was offered by Pastor Poole. Then the organ played another hymn and the service was concluded except for a few last bleats and shrieks from the Wailers.

Crystal had been cremated, and a solemn Al Driggers now moved to the urn and held it up in front of him, like a priest offering the wine at Mass. No one looked at him. With Mel Eriks in the lead, the family all but bolted out of their pews. The rest of us weren't far behind.

We didn't get far. Aaron Conley had stopped by the pew where Dean Ramsey was patiently waiting for Paula to help Victor with his crutches. Aaron lunged toward Victor; the sheriff grabbed him from behind.

But Milo couldn't stop his prisoner from shouting: "You and your precious, pretentious talent! There's no truth, no life, no guts in what you do, you big phony! You ruined Crystal! By God, I'll bet you killed her!"

The last words were uttered as Milo dragged Aaron down the aisle. The remaining mourners froze momentarily in shocked silence. Then, as if pushed by a giant hand, everyone moved forward practically at a gallop.

At the door, I turned to look over my shoulder. Al Driggers had also disappeared. The church was deserted; the urn again sat on the altar.

It was a sad reminder that everyone had left except Crystal. She wasn't going anywhere. She was already gone.

"Amazing," Vida declared after we were outside. "I wouldn't have thought that a musician like Aaron would be so articulate."

"Or so angry," I said as the rest of us began to file out of the church. "Aaron must deeply resent Victor. I wonder if it's because they're both in the music business, or if it's more personal."

"The latter," Vida responded as we paused at the edge of the parking lot. "I can't imagine a rock musician or whatever they call themselves these days would care about a symphony-orchestra player. But it would appear that they both cared about Crystal."

"Or about her money," I put in. "Victor may have advised Crystal to cut Aaron off."

"If so," Vida noted, tucking her plaid scarf inside the collar of her tweed coat, "he failed. As far as we know, Crystal was still helping Aaron financially."

"True," I admitted. "But not anymore."

"Yes," Vida said, looking up at the gray clouds that

hung so low they obscured the trees on the face of Mount Baldy. "Aaron is on his own." Her gaze shifted to Dean Ramsey, who was getting into a county vehicle which no doubt belonged to the extension agent's office. "They're all cut off. It makes you wonder, doesn't it?"

It did, of course. "Don't you find it odd that no one took the urn from Al Driggers?"

Vida touched her upper lip with her gloved hand. "Perhaps there was some confusion about the arrangements. Still," she went on in a musing tone, "it is rather strange."

"I thought so," I remarked, but didn't elaborate. It had grown colder, and my black raincoat might have been appropriate for a funeral, but not for subfreezing weather.

Vida and I had come in our separate cars. Reluctantly, I steered the Jag in the direction of the Erikses' house. I would have preferred going back to work to get a jump start on next week's edition of *The Advocate*, but felt duty-bound to attend the family reception.

Since the Wailers never show up for postfuneral events, and Milo had escorted his charge back to the county jail, the reception attendees were small in number.

Paula had brought Victor with her. "Despite what Doc Dewey said initially, he really can't drive," she explained as we selected cookies provided by the Upper Crust Bakery and accepted coffee from Luana Eriks.

"Where's he staying?" I asked.

Paula made a face. "With me. He couldn't be on his own at Crystal's, and he despises hotels and motels. It seems he's spent too much time in them while traveling with various orchestras. Anyway, what could I do? It seemed like a last favor for Crystal."

We had moved away from the dining-room table to a spot by the fireplace. Vida was across the way, in a head-to-head conversation with Melody Eriks. Pastor Poole and Father Den were in the far corner, perhaps engaging in an ecumenical discussion. I'd always been struck by the contrast between the two men in both style and appearance. The white offspring of a Nebraska farmer and the black son of a career army man had bonded long before Crystal's attacks on the clergy. Yet they found common ground, even when poles apart. Each understood compromise, and out of willingness to give and take, a friendship had been formed. I thought of Crystal's apparent inability to bend an inch and how much grief her intransigence had caused, perhaps even her untimely death.

I must have frowned. Certainly I'd lost the thread of conversation, and Paula had to prod me. "Are you there, Emma? Knock, knock." She made a pounding gesture with her fist.

"What? Oh!" I laughed in embarrassment. "Sorry. I was mulling over the differences in temperament between people. I'd meant to say that Victor leaves tomorrow," I noted, recalling Janet Driggers's words at the travel agency.

Paula shook her head. The masses of red hair had been tamed in deference to the solemn occasion and tucked under a silver turban that Vida no doubt envied. "Doc Dewey insisted Victor shouldn't travel—especially by plane—for another week. Unfortunately, I'm stuck with him."

"Is he a problem patient?"

"You bet. Very demanding, very unappreciative." Paula eyed Victor, who was sitting in an easy chair with his fiberglass-encased leg propped up on a footstool. "He was quick to inform me that my pathetic little house in Startup is not the Ansonia in New York City. Which, I gather, is where he's headed eventually. Like so many artists, he calls it his spiritual home. About now, I wish it was a ten-story walk-up."

I glanced at Victor, who was being waited on by Thad Eriks. "Maybe I should pay Victor a condolence call."

"For what?" Paula retorted. "His broken leg? His rotten disposition? His supposed sense of loss?"

Paula's tone was caustic, but I couldn't blame her. She had become an unwilling nursemaid to a stranger. House-guests of any kind could be bad enough. But maybe I had lived alone too long. Maybe Paula had, too.

Thad had just delivered a plate of cookies and a cup of tea to Victor when I sidled up next to the easy chair. "I'm Emma Lord," I said in my brightest voice. "I was visiting a friend in the hospital when you were there."

Victor's granite-gray eyes narrowed. "Whose friend?" His accent was barely noticeable, his voice a basso profundo.

I explained about Carla and my connection with her through the newspaper. Victor was clearly bored.

"Babies," he said. "There are too many babies. The world cannot hold them all. We are already overcrowded, like pilchards in a tin."

"Have you ever seen Saskatchewan?" I shot back, and immediately felt silly.

Victor, however, ignored my implication. "Only Van-couver, Toronto, Winnipeg, and Montreal have adequate musical talent," he replied. "In all of North America, there are no more than six outstanding orchestras."

I was an opera, not a symphony, devotee. "Which is the best?" I asked, deciding to appear humble.

Victor frowned. Seated, he appeared to be a big man, with broad shoulders and a large head. What was left of his dark hair continued into a neat beard and mustache, all sprinkled with white. His eyebrows were thick, his nose almost delicate. Had the gray eyes not been so cold and penetrating, Victor Dimitroff would have looked almost benign.

"Best?" he echoed, clearly thinking my question idiotic. "Best conductor? Best strings? Best woodwinds? Define your terms."

I tried not to look as stupid as I felt. "In general."

Victor spewed peanut-butter cookie crumbs all over his lap. "You should refer to interpretation, performance. Which composer? Beethoven? Bruckner? Sibelius? Rimsky-Korsakov?"

"Such fine points," I murmured, trying to save face. "As a mere listener, I don't understand. Though," I added, "I suppose I can see why a rock musician such as Aaron Conley would resent other musical forms."

Victor's frown deepened. "He doesn't begin to understand music. He is part of a fad, and personally unsuccessful. What will endure of his sort of music? Fifty, even ten years from now, who will recall what so-called song sold the most copies?"

The statement was certainly grounds for an argument, but I declined to take part. "Did you know Aaron before you visited Crystal?"

"We had met." Victor bit off the words. "In Portland, some time ago. Crystal used poor judgment when it came to love, though it's understandable. As the product of a small town, she married too young the first time."

Victor finally had a point. I was growing tired of standing next to the easy chair, however. Gingerly, I placed one knee on the footstool. "I'm sorry about your accident. How did it happen?"

Now it was Victor's turn to look discomfited. "Why do you ask? Is this an interview for your little newspaper?"

I reined in my temper, which was always ignited by any slights to *The Advocate*. "It's my job. I'm covering the story. In this week's issue we wrote about the main facts, along with a background piece on Crystal's life and the official obituary. Next week we'll follow up with some of the details."

"The details of my life are private," Victor declared, scowling at me from under those thick eyebrows. "Why does my misfortune make news except in your traffic-accident reports?"

The truth was, I had no good reason to interrogate Victor. But he had given me an idea. "That's the point," I said. "We're not just interested in your accident and any connection with Crystal, but we plan on doing a winter driving article. With so many newcomers in the area, not to mention the skiers, we thought it would be helpful to tell drivers how to avoid mishaps. Naturally, we need a few examples." Naturally, I'd had no such story in my head. Now that it was there, I'd pawn it off on Scott.

Victor was still scowling. "To show me off as a bad example?"

"No, of course not. I wouldn't even use your name." I resurrected the bright smile with which I'd begun the conversation. "We'll talk about when to put on chains, front-wheel drive, studded tires, black ice, compact snow, fresh snow—"

As I'd hoped, the litany obviously bored Victor. "Yes, yes," he interrupted. "But this is of no importance. If you must persist in interviewing me, then speak of my work, my compositions. Your callow young reporter didn't bother to probe. Now I shall explain what I'm trying to do with my music."

My knee accidentally slid forward, knocking against Victor's cast. He let out a yip and I hastily withdrew from the footstool. "Sorry," I gulped. "Are you all right?"

Judging from Victor's fierce expression, I might as well have set off a dozen sticks of TNT under his leg. "Of course not! I am in pain. I suffer. Mightily." He leaned forward, grasping the cast.

"To get back to the accident itself," I began, keeping my distance from the footstool. "Did you—"

"Enough!" he bellowed, causing some of the Erikses to turn and stare. "What of my oratorio?"

The fish was fighting on my line, and I was about to lose him. "Please, Mr. Dimitroff, could we get this minor matter out of the way so we can concentrate on your wonderful music?"

Incredibly, the ploy worked. Victor uttered a huge sigh and leaned back in the chair. "Very well. It won't take long. My accident was of a simple nature. The car I'd rented had studded tires, but no chains. I am not used to driving in snow. Indeed, until recent years, I have not been used to driving at all. No one of intelligence has a car in New York or other large cities."

"That's so." I nodded with what I hoped was encouragement.

"The car was a standard-model medium-sized sedan, a Ford, I think." He paused, perhaps trying to recall the model. "In any event, I lost control and it skidded off the highway." Victor struck his right fist into his left palm. "Kablow! The car hits a rock, a log, who knows? It is impossible to tell with so much snow. And I am in terrible pain, in delirium. I know immediately that my leg is badly injured. Fortunately, someone with a cell phone stops and calls for help. I think I pass out at least once. The next thing I know, I am being removed from the car and put in an ambulance. Is that what you want to know?"

"Exactly," I replied, though it wasn't the truth. "Were you wearing a seat belt?"

Victor looked embarrassed. "No. That was a mistake on my part. You may use my carelessness as your bad example."

"A reminder," I said, now smiling in sympathy. "Seat belts are mandatory in this state, but it's amazing how many people forget to put them on."

"Yes." He nodded. "I forgot. That was very stupid."

"We all forget things sometimes," I remarked. "I'm sorry to have bothered you with all this when you must be in pain. Physical, as well as emotional. You must feel Crystal's loss deeply."

Victor lowered his large head onto his big chest. "Yes. We had been good friends. Though she had no true appreciation for music. Happily, she had other qualities. She was a humanitarian and politically aware. While she didn't understand my current composition, she encouraged me."

"What is it that you're composing?" I asked, trying to pretend that I hadn't heard the word *humanitarian* in connection with Crystal Bird. "You mentioned an oratorio."

"Yes, about the fall of France. It will be brilliant in its contrasts. The cowardice, the bravery, the entire gamut of raw human emotions." Victor smiled, more to himself than to me. "I call it *Vichy*."

My gaze was wandering around the living room. Father Den was taking his leave, shaking hands with April and Mel. Vida now stood at the picture window, talking to Thad. Pastor Poole was with the rest of the Eriks clan, though he, too, seemed to be edging toward the front door. Dean Ramsey stood alone by the TV set, looking lost. Paula, who had been refilling her coffee cup at the dining-room table, joined him.

"Your oratorio sounds very ambitious," I said, for lack of a better word.

"Of course." Victor shrugged his wide shoulders. "What else would be the point?" Apparently, he'd also spotted Paula. "I'm very tired now and need my medication. Would you please inform my escort?" He slumped in the chair, his body as limp as laundry after the rinse cycle.

Paula noticed, but took her time breaking away from Dean. Victor's cave-in signaled my move in Vida's direction. She had just concluded her conversation with Thad, and was looking sour.

"I'm going now," she murmured as I caught up with her by the coat closet. "We'll discuss this fiasco at the office."

Not wanting the Eriks family to think that Vida and I were leaving on some sort of cue, I lingered until she made her farewells. Dean Ramsey, however, beat me to the coat closet.

"I have to get to work," he explained. "It was really kind of Hector Tuck to let me take this much time off when he's breaking me into the job."

I didn't know the present extension agent that well, but he'd always seemed like an easygoing man. "I'm sure he understands," I said as Dean put his navy-blue parka on over his dark suit. "Was this awfully hard for you?"

"Well ..." Dean tugged at one ear. "It sure brought back a lot of memories. The funny thing is, they were mostly good ones. Until today, I didn't think there were that many of them."

I gave Dean a wry smile. "As time passes, we tend to repress much of the unpleasantness. I've often felt that was a shame. It would be easier to miss people if you only remembered the bad stuff."

Dean turned up the collar of his parka. "Oh, I still remember plenty of bad stuff. Crystal had a real mean streak, right up until the end."

"Divorce is always sad," I said. "Maybe you were lucky to end the pain she caused you."

Briefly, Dean seemed puzzled. "Yes, of course. I was lucky." He offered his hand, then moved to the door.

When he left, he still looked lost.

* * *

"Worthless," Vida declared half an hour later as she munched carrot and celery sticks in my office. "The Erikses are not a communicative family. What's worse is that they are so obvious in their personality traits. April, feeling inferior to Crystal and intimidated by her, even in death. Mel acting subdued, yet clearly callous about his sister-in-law's death. Melody trying to be a grown-up in a world she doesn't yet understand. And Thad, so arrogant and extremely defensive about his aunt. One wonders why."

"The heir?" I offered, taking a bite out of the chicken-salad sandwich I'd picked up at the deli in the mall. It was going on two o'clock, and a couple of cookies hadn't been sufficient to stave off my hunger pangs.

"The heir to what?" Vida said scornfully. "I can't imagine that Crystal had accumulated any fortune. Yes, she had the bank buyout, and perhaps she'd made some investments along the way. But," she added, averting her eyes, "I doubt Crystal had any substantial savings."

My gaze was reproachful. "Vida—you didn't."

Her head snapped up. "Certainly not. Just because I work with Ginny doesn't mean that her husband, Rick, would violate customer confidentiality. But one can't help noting when a statement is left in plain sight on some-one's desk."

I could imagine the wheedling and cajoling and per-haps even threats that Vida had used to get Rick Er-landson to print out a copy of Crystal's account at the Bank of Alpine. "How much?" I sighed.

"A bit over fifty thousand dollars. Crystal was living off of it, of course," Vida went on, once again making eye contact. "She didn't solicit advertising for her silly newsletter, and I doubt she had any other income."

"Still," I said, "fifty grand would make a nice nest egg for graduate school."

"Thad's not the only one who could use that amount, I suppose." Vida paused to sip from her mug of hot water. "Aaron certainly needed money, not merely for his drugs, but to live on. I can't guess at Victor's financial status, since I've no idea what kind of salary tuba players earn." She made a face. "Such a silly instrument. All that oompah."

"Do you think Crystal had a will?" If anyone would know, it'd be Vida.

But for once, she pleaded ignorance. "It's doubtful, isn't it? She was still a young woman. Have you made a will?"

I had, in fact, but only because of a fluke. The fiancé of my youth, a Boeing engineer, had made me the beneficiary of his company life-insurance policy. Though we had parted and Don had married someone else, he'd neglected to change the policy. When he died of a sudden heart attack at forty-five, I had come into five hundred thousand dollars. After months of litigation from his deserved heirs, I ended up with the entire sum. Somewhat guiltily, I used the money to pay off my legal counsel, purchase *The Advocate*, and buy my secondhand Jag. Thus, in one of my wiser moments, I'd asked the attorney I'd been forced to hire to draw up a simple will. I'd designated Adam and Ben as my sole heirs.

"Milo should know about the will," I said.

"Yes." Vida carefully peeled a hard-boiled egg, another basic item in her ongoing attempt to diet. "There was one conversation of interest at the reception, now that I think about it."

"Which was?"

Vida sprinkled the egg with the tiny packets of salt and pepper she guiltlessly lifted from the Burger Barn. "Mel was grumbling about the expenses for the funeral and reception. Thad spoke rather sharply to his father, saying that if he—Mel—and Mom—April—ever saved any money, then he—Thad—wouldn't be . . . something-or-other. I couldn't quite catch the last of it."

"Indicating that the family wasn't going to inherit?" I suggested.

"Perhaps." Vida carefully cut her egg into quarters. "It might also indicate they don't yet know who gets the money. One assumes, if Crystal hadn't made a will, everything would go to April as next of kin."

"As I said, Milo might know whether there's a will." I paused, tossing the sandwich's plastic container into the wastebasket. "I'm betting Crystal had one."

Vida didn't comment as she finished her low-calorie lunch. I called Scott in and gave him the winter driving assignment. He didn't look pleased, but spared me any protest.

Having requested and received a photo of Dean Ramsey, I typed up the slightly skewed interview Vida and I had conducted Monday. We could have run it in this week's edition, but I'd deemed it in poor taste to carry the story of his new appointment in the same issue that contained coverage of his ex-wife's untimely demise. Besides, now we had time to do a feature on the departing Hector Tuck. That assignment would go to Vida. She knew the Tucks better than I did, and it would fit as neatly on her House & Home page as in the straight news section of the paper.

Around four o'clock, I was about to call Milo and ask if there had been any new developments, or if he knew about the existence of a will. But the phone rang before I picked up the receiver. I heard the vaguely familiar fragment of a masculine voice at the other end just before the lights flickered and the line went dead.

"Power failure," I called to the news office, though I wasn't sure if anyone was there.

Leo strolled into the office as the lights gave one more blink and then went completely out. "I'm still not used to living with a mountain PUD." He sighed, opening a fresh pack of cigarettes. "Damned good thing I'd just hit the save key on my computer."

I nodded, shoving the candle I kept at the ready toward Leo. "It happens even in good weather," I said. "This is the first one since Scott came aboard. I must warn him. Is he out there?" I gestured toward the news office.

Leo shook his head as he lighted the candle first, then his cigarette. "He went over to the courthouse to check something-or-other. Hey, babe"—he grinned—"want to play some games in the almost dark?"

I grinned back. "Like what? Guess whether my automatic save actually worked and I haven't lost the feature I was doing on the candlelighting ceremony at Old Mill Park?"

"You were there?" Leo slipped into one of my visitor's chairs.

"No. But Scott took pictures for this week's edition. Don't tell me you missed them."

Leo grinned again. "No, of course I saw them. There were only captions accompanying them. What's with the feature?"

"I should have written it the week before the ceremony," I said in a rueful voice, "but I didn't get around to it. I'm writing about the history, how it was started in 1918 by Carl Clemans at the old mill site on December sixth, St. Nicholas's Day, then stopped for a few years after he shut down operations, and was finally resurrected the day before Pearl Harbor."

"I didn't know that," Leo said, the candlelight casting all sorts of weird shadows across his craggy face. "Say, would you mind if I took off for L.A. over Christmas? I've still got two days' vacation coming, and since the holiday falls on a Thursday, I thought maybe I'd take the twenty-fourth and twenty-sixth."

The lights gave a flicker, but went off again. "Sure," I said, blinking at Leo. "You'll be able to have everything put together for the next issue?" I tried to peer at my calendar, but failed to make out the dates. "It'd be the thirty-first, New Year's Eve day."

"No problem," Leo said. "I can do most of the layouts in advance since it's another special edition for the year end."

"Do you plan on seeing your kids?" I asked, hoping not to sound like a snoop.

"They actually invited me," Leo replied, looking vaguely sheepish. "I guess they really have forgiven dear old Dad for drinking his way to divorce."

It had taken Leo's three grown children a long time to work their way through their father's borderline alcoholism and subsequent destruction of the Walsh family as a single unit. His ex-wife, Liza, was remarried, and she and Leo had resumed speaking, though I wasn't sure how amiably.

I tilted my head to one side and smiled at my ad manager. "Was that who called yesterday afternoon just as I was leaving?" Leo had seemed a little surprised, if pleased, when he answered the phone.

"What?" Leo drew back in his chair, then inhaled deeply on his cigarette. "Oh—that call right at five. No, that was somebody else, an old pal from my advertising days in Southern California. Hey," he went on, once again leaning forward, "it's after four, it's dark in here, what's the point of diligence? Want to grab a drink at the Venison Inn?"

I started to mull, and then the lights came back on. We

both held our breath and waited. Nothing happened. The power seemed to have been restored.

"That's your answer," I said. "We stay. We work. We are diligent."

Leo nodded and got to his feet, then blew out the candle. "The offer still stands at five," he said over his shoulder.

"I'll consider it," I said, wondering why I didn't give Leo a straightforward answer.

But I knew. In that brief moment as the lights had come on, I had seen his face unguarded by shadows. Leo was lying to me about the phone call. I suddenly felt uneasy.

Chapter Eleven

I DIDN'T GO out for drinks with Leo that evening. Instead, I went directly home, still feeling unsettled. My ad manager wasn't inclined to hide his love life from me. Was it possible that he was covering up something to do with Crystal? Like Milo, he might have known Crystal, though if memory served, he'd said they'd never met. But my memory was sketchy. As I grew older, there didn't seem to be as much room on the computer disk in my brain.

Or maybe my mind was disintegrating along with my body. Just to make sure I still had all my appendages, I paused as I changed clothes in front of the full-length mirror that hung on my closet door. Perhaps it was the insufficient lighting in the bedroom, but I didn't look as bad as I felt. There was no gray in my brown hair yet, nor had I any noticeable wrinkles. The figure was reasonably trim, though I'd never had much of a waist, even before Adam was born. A bit of sagging along the jawline and the possible presence of emerging turkey neck were really the only signs that betrayed my forty-seven years.

So maybe it was only my mind that was going. Taking small comfort in that fact, I stepped into a worn-out pair of wool pants and pulled a Mariners sweatshirt over my head. Leo's suggestion of a drink sounded like a good idea, even if I wasn't going to have it with him.

I was heading for the kitchen when my doorbell

sounded. As usual, I left the porch light on at night as a security precaution. Not that it had done me any good, since my break-in had occurred during the day.

A man in a heavy dark jacket stood outside my door. I hesitated, not recognizing him at first. Then he looked up and I saw that it was Nat Cardenas.

"Good evening," I said, putting out my hand. "Come in out of the snow."

Nat's usual genial mask had been stripped away, replaced by a sheepish, almost fatuous, expression. "Sorry to disturb you, Emma," he said, stamping his booted feet on the mat. "Are you busy?"

I assured him I wasn't. Taking his jacket, I gestured at one of the matching armchairs. "Can I get you a drink? I was about to make one for myself."

"A diet soda would be fine," Nat said, easing himself into the nearest chair.

"No diet stuff around here," I replied. "Will a real 7UP or Pepsi do?"

"That's fine," Nat said quickly.

I went into the kitchen to pour a Pepsi for the college president and a weak bourbon and water for me. When I returned, Nat was rubbing his hands together, apparently trying to warm himself.

"I haven't built a fire yet tonight," I said, sitting down on the sofa. "Shall I?"

"Please, don't go to any trouble." Nat sounded as if he meant it.

"No trouble," I said, stuffing old newspaper under the half-burned logs and adding some kindling. "I like a fire. I couldn't live in a house that didn't have a fireplace, especially with all the snow we have in Alpine."

"This is a cozy place," Nat remarked. He had been to my log house at least twice, the last time before Thanksgiving. Had he used that opportunity to take the sleeping pills from my medicine cabinet? I shivered in spite of being next to the fledgling fire.

"Thanks," I said, and wondered if I should be afraid. The phone was in reach; Nat wasn't behaving like a man with murder on his mind.

On the other hand, Nat wasn't behaving much like his usual confident self. As I reseated myself on the sofa, he spread his hands. "Emma, I feel like such a fool. Still, I want to thank you for keeping my name out of the paper. I pulled a stupid stunt last Friday night. If that story had gotten out, I could lose my job."

"Oh." My shoulders slumped in relief. Maybe he didn't intend to kill me after all. "That was Milo's doing. It's kind of a tradition, dating back, I suppose, to when sheriffs were elected, rather than appointed."

"I should thank him, too," Nat said, taking a sip of soda. "I acted recklessly. I usually don't drink. I suppose that was the problem."

I pointed to his glass. "I understand." Maybe that explained why he had nursed the drink I'd offered him on his last visit until it was mostly melted ice and water. "But this is the party season."

"Yes," Nat replied with a rueful expression. "You know how that goes—you stop in to see a friend, they insist you join them in a cup of cheer—and the next thing you know, you've had two."

I doubted that two drinks would make even a neophyte boozer drunk. But that depended on several factors, including metabolism. I wanted to believe Nat, if only because he was big and strong, and I was alone with him in my living room.

"Crystal's funeral was this morning," I said, changing the subject. "It went off well." Unless, of course, I counted Aaron Conley's verbal attack on Victor Dimitroff. "Vida and I attended."

"Why?" Nat asked, scowling.

"You couldn't keep Vida away," I said with a twisted smile. "And I"—my eyes roamed to the pieces of my Advent set on the mantel—"I suppose I felt some kind of obligation. Guilt, for disliking Crystal so much."

"She had an unpleasant way about her," Nat said with a touch of the condescension that often shaded his attitude. "By the way, I gather that your . . . Vida, I believe . . . is going to interview my wife tomorrow. She'll go easy on Justine, won't she?"

I gave Nat a curious look. "Of course. The story's about Christmas customs in the various parts of the country where you've both lived." At least that was Vida's cover, but Nat didn't need to know.

"Justine," Nat began, not looking at me, but gazing into the fire, "is extremely shy. She strikes some people as standoffish, but that's not the case. She's the youngest of three daughters, a latecomer in her parents' lives. Her sisters were six and eight years older." He turned, and offered me his engaging grin. For once, it looked like the real thing.

"Justine grew up with an inferiority complex," he went on, "even though she was just as pretty and as smart as her sisters. It's been very hard for her to put on a public face and play faculty wife. She'd much rather stay home and work on her crafts."

Picturing Justine in my mind, I could well imagine that some would think her a snob. I'd wondered myself. She was not merely distant, but seemed cold. "We all have our armor," I said, more in response to my own thoughts than to Nat's words.

"Armor?" The grin dwindled into a faint, ironic smile. "Yes, I suppose you could describe her detachment that way. It *is* armor, or at least a shield. I'm afraid Justine feels she lacks social skills. Over the years, I've done my best to convince her otherwise, but she doesn't believe me. It's very painful for Justine to host even a faculty tea. And speaking in public is impossible." The small smile now turned pleading. "That's why I asked how Vida would handle the interview. Your House & Home editor seems like a very dominating personality."

"She is that," I admitted. "I'll mention it to her before she sees Justine. Tactfully, of course."

"Thank you." His laugh was strained. "I seem to be spending my time being grateful. I feel like an idiot."

Again, Nat sounded sincere. Apparently, I was seeing another side of President Cardenas. It was vulnerable, and I shouldn't have been surprised. He had come from humble roots, no doubt fighting prejudice and humiliation along the way. But this evening, a glass of Pepsi, a dancing fire, and his self-confessed peccadillo had allowed me to penetrate a bit of Nat Cardenas's own armor.

"It's nice to have someone say thanks," I said. "That doesn't happen very often in the newspaper business. Usually, readers tell me *I'm* the idiot."

A light flickered in Nat's eyes. "Have you taken the brunt of this thing with Crystal?"

"You mean letters and such?" I nodded. "Oh, yes. Everything, including accusing me of murder." The missives were still arriving, another half dozen, all unsigned, having come in the morning mail. "I didn't realize Crystal was so popular."

Nat put down his glass and stood up. "She's undoubtedly more popular dead than alive." He gave me a remorseful look. "Sorry. I didn't mean that the way it sounded."

I also got to my feet. "I know what you mean. And you're right. It happens. Martyrdom is the best way to restore a flawed reputation."

Nat picked up his jacket from the back of the sofa. "How

true. But now we don't have to cringe while waiting for the next edition of *Crystal Clear*. It's over."

I walked with him to the door. "Not quite. There's still a killer out there."

He hesitated with his hand on the knob. "Of course. I meant that—" He stopped and shook himself. "I meant that what Crystal did to the rest of us is over."

I supposed that was what he'd meant. Thoughtfully, I watched him trudge through the unplowed walk to his car, which was parked behind mine in the driveway. I felt that I'd seen more deeply into Nat Cardenas in the last half hour than I ever had before.

"Really," Vida snapped after I cautioned her to use a kid-gloves treatment on Justine Cardenas, "what do you think I intend to do? Grill her like a lamb chop?"

"No," I responded, "you know I didn't mean that. I'm just saying that she's very shy. And don't mistake it for snobbishness."

"Propaganda," Vida muttered. "How do you know that Nat Cardenas isn't pulling the wool over your eyes? His wife seems very sure of herself. Too sure, if you ask me."

Vida's judgment was usually on target, but she tended to be overly critical. "I don't think Nat was trying to dupe me," I responded. "Why should he?"

Vida harrumphed, but offered no rejoinder. Pulling her orange wool hat over her ears and snatching up her camera, she stomped out of the office.

Before I could carry my third cup of coffee to my desk, Ginny entered the news office. "More letters." She sighed. "Not to mention Christmas cards. I'll dump them in your basket after I get rid of Leo's and Scott's. Vida has so many cards that I have to make a separate delivery."

Leo and Scott were out on their morning rounds. I went into my cubbyhole and sorted the wheat from the chaff. I'd open the cards later, since they were mostly from local merchants and a couple of politicians. Except for the half-dozen letters that were signed and vented spleen on such issues as moving the bridge over the Sky (two for, two against), a rumored bypass of Monroe (both for), and Averill Fairbanks stating that he'd seen a flying banana land in his backyard, the other ten were from readers all wrought up about Crystal. Three, who actually signed their names, expressed regret over Crystal's death, but not over the demise of her newsletter. Somewhat to my surprise, Molly Freeman, the high-school principal's wife, praised me for my restraint in not taking Crystal to task in my editorials.

Ms. Lord must be commended for not responding to Ms. Bird's biased and often unfair attacks. I decided to call Molly and thank her personally. I hoped her attitude was shared by Linda Grant, the high school PE teacher and my fellow bridge player.

The unsigned letters were another matter, calling me everything from a slut to just plain evil. I recognized at least two sets of handwriting. They were the same cranks who had never forgiven me for taking Marius Vandeventer's place. They never would, and I usually managed to ignore them. The odd thing was that they could pass me on the street or in the grocery aisles, and nod and smile. I often wondered if they thought I was too stupid to recognize them as the vindictive letter writers. But I'd fingered them early on, and refused to give them the satisfaction of acknowledging their hostility.

Finishing the rest of the mail, most of which were the usual handouts, I headed for the sheriff's office. It was well after ten, and Scott should have already covered his beat. I didn't want him to think I was checking up on him.

Milo was in, drinking his wretched coffee and eating a cinnamon twist. He regarded me with neutral hazel eyes, and, as usual, asked if I wanted some coffee. As usual, I declined.

"I've been thinking about something," I said, sitting down across the desk from him. "Who uses a straight-edged razor these days?"

"Old-timers, mostly," Milo replied without hesitation. Obviously, the same thought had crossed his mind.

"Certainly not Aaron Conley or Victor Dimitroff, both of whom have beards," I noted.

Milo rested his chin on his chest. "So you deduce that . . . ?"

I made a face. "Don't get cute, Dodge. There's not much to deduce, just guess at. Yes, there's a 'third man' theme here, but have you heard anything about another guy? Especially," I added with a touch of sarcasm, "an old-timer?"

"There's always Crazy Eights Neffel," Milo said, refer-ring to our local head case who had last been seen on Thanksgiving, wearing red spandex and leading two turkeys on a leash into the midst of the morning service at First Presbyterian. Vida, naturally, had been irate, re-fusing to put the tidbit into her "Scene Around Town" column.

"Right," I drawled, "except that Crazy Eights has a beard, too."

Milo's eyes twinkled. "Not anymore. Ask Vida."

I was astonished. "You mean he shaved after all these years? I thought he had birds living in that mess."

"Nope. He shaved off the beard right after Halloween. He told Jack Mullins it scared some kids who came trick-or-treating. Jack figured it wasn't the beard, but the shot-gun Crazy Eights was holding. You ought to keep up with the news around here, Emma."

"Hunh." I leaned back in the chair. "Okay, but let's

leave Crazy Eights out of this. Have you been able to identify the razor in any way?"

"No." Milo deflated a bit. "It's old, it was somewhat rusty, it hadn't been sharpened recently, and it was made in England. It could have belonged to anybody. My guess is that it came with the cabin when Crystal bought it."

That seemed reasonable. According to Vida, the cabin had belonged to a family from Seattle for use as a vacation retreat. But their children grew up and moved away, then the dad died, and his widow sold the property to Crystal. Perhaps Milo was right. The previous owner could have had a straight-edged razor.

"No help there," I murmured. "It sounds as if it hadn't been used recently. What about the house itself? Did you find anything of interest?"

"We finished up this morning," Milo answered. "We still have to sort through a few things. Crystal got her share of hate mail, but how many letter writers carry out their threats? You ought to know."

I nodded. "If they did, I'd have been dead years ago. Were the letters signed?"

"A couple of the more reasonable ones were," Milo said, dumping the dregs of his coffee in a sickly jade plant. It wasn't hard to figure out why it was sick. I'd be, too, if I drank the sheriff's coffee regularly. It was no wonder that Toni Andreas kept having to buy new ones from Alpine Gardens. "There weren't that many," Milo continued, "and they were all postmarked within the last few days before Crystal died. In fact, three of them came in after that. We opened them, of course. I guess she'd thrown the rest out."

"I would," I admitted. "What about Aaron? Has he posted bail yet?"

Milo looked pained. "Somebody did that for him. He got sprung this morning. Don't worry, Scott took the info."

"Who?" I asked.

"Dean Ramsey," Milo replied.

I was astonished. Again.

I owed Dean a follow-up interview, so I went back to the office to get my camera, and retraced my steps past Milo's office and hurried across Front Street to the courthouse. It wasn't snowing, but it felt colder than it had been so far this December. My guess was that it had dropped into the teens. The sidewalks had been shoveled and swept, but the footing was still precarious.

Luckily, Dean was in his office, studying county maps. He evinced mild surprise when he saw me knocking on his open door. "Ms. Lord, right? I can't get over how things have changed since I lived around here, especially in Snohomish County. It's amazing, isn't it?"

"Call me Emma," I said, and sat down next to his worktable. "You're keeping warm this morning."

Indeed, the old-fashioned radiators were producing wheezing, hissing noises. Dean smiled rather diffidently and nodded. "Now that Hector's so close to retirement, he feels he should visit every client in the county. A farewell tour, I guess."

"He's been on the job a long time," I remarked. "Speaking of farewells, I gather you said goodbye to Aaron Conley this morning."

Dean's thin face turned bright pink. "Posting his bail was the least I could do. I felt I owed it to Crystal."

"Why?" I asked bluntly.

Dean lowered his gaze, his long fingers pawing nervously at one of the maps. "I don't know. Why are you asking me?"

I'm not as glib or as devious as Vida. "Because," I said, feeling a faint sense of remorse, "I'm nosy. That's part of being a journalist. Most of all, I need to clear my name."

My answer wasn't much of an excuse, but it seemed to soothe Dean Ramsey. "I suppose I still felt bad because our marriage failed. If we hadn't divorced, Crystal would never have gotten mixed up with a young guy like Aaron. He's not really a bad person, just one of those would-be musicians who never grow up. Crystal saw him through rehab twice, but it didn't work. Even she shouldn't have had to put up with that. It can get real ugly."

I tried to give Dean a sympathetic look. "Yes, it can. So you bailed Aaron out as a posthumous peace offering?"

Dean pressed his back against the chair as if to shore up his spine. "It couldn't have been one-sided. With Crystal and Aaron, I mean. I know what she was like to live with. We had something in common, and somehow, with both of us showing up in Alpine shortly before her death, I figured I owed Aaron, too. I guess I *was* making a peace offering. But mostly for myself."

It made a certain kind of sense, I supposed. "So where does Aaron go now?"

"He's going to stay at Crystal's place for a while," Dean responded, his color returning to normal and his hands at rest. "He has a right to, after all."

"Yes," I allowed. "I can't see any harm in it. The house is vacant until the estate disposes of it. Do you know if Crystal had a will?" In my astonishment over Dean's posting bail for Aaron, I'd forgotten to ask Milo.

"I couldn't say," Dean said, and he sounded as if he was telling the truth. "There's no need for complications. Aaron can stay at Crystal's as long as he wants. The house belongs to him now anyway."

I leaned forward in the chair. "What do you mean?"

Dean's expression was quizzical. "Don't you know?" He saw the blank look on my face and uttered a hoarse little sound that might have passed for a laugh. "Crystal and Aaron separated a long time ago, but they never divorced. He inherits whatever she had, including the house."

It was turning out to be a day of surprises. After asking Dean a few cursory questions about how he planned to handle his new job and then taking what would probably turn out to be a rather bad picture of him, I slunk back to *The Advocate* in a befuddled state of mind.

Fortunately, Vida had returned from her interview with Justine Cardenas. "She's a cold kettle of fish, I don't care what her husband says. I never trust a woman who wears a French roll."

"Francine Wells wears one," I pointed out.

"I don't trust Francine," Vida shot back. "Have you ever known me to buy a piece of apparel from her store? Goodness, such prices! I marvel that she stays in business in a town like Alpine. Think of the markup!"

I *had* thought about it, especially on my rare forays into Francine's Fine Apparel. But Vida was right about one thing: she wouldn't be caught dead buying anything that bore even the hint of a designer label.

"Did you find out much except for Christmas customs in Texas and California and wherever else the Cardenases have been?" I asked, trying to keep from exploding with my own latest information.

"Not really," Vida admitted. "Three of their four children and their families are coming here for the holidays. Actually, the younger two aren't married yet." She sat down at her desk, whipped off her glasses, and began rubbing her eyes in that familiar, agitated gesture I knew so well. "Ooooh! I tried everything to get her to talk about Nat and last Friday night. The woman is a clam. It was so frustrating!"

I could imagine. Anyone who could resist Vida's cajoling, blandishments, and just plain nerve had to become The Enemy. I suspected that Justine Cardenas had gone down in Vida's books as not only standoffish, but hostile.

Thus, I changed the subject and told Vida about Dean Ramsey and Aaron Conley. Naturally, she was agog.

"Not divorced! Oh, my!" Vida put her glasses back on. "Which, this being a community-property state, means Aaron inherits everything."

"Unless she did have a will," I pointed out, and then confessed that I'd forgotten to put the question to Milo.

For once, Vida didn't scold. Instead, she grew thoughtful. "I'll call Billy right now. If Milo knows, he'll know." She picked up the receiver and began to punch in the sheriff's number.

I wandered back into my office. The wall calendar, courtesy of Sky Dairy and featuring snow-covered Tonga Ridge, told me it was December 12. Twelve days until Christmas Eve. Less than two weeks before Adam and Ben arrived. I questioned my lack of excitement. Usually, a combination of Christmas and my favorite relatives' imminent arrival would make me giddy with anticipation. So far, I felt nothing. I wondered if my soul was dead. Hating someone, as I had hated Crystal, can kill in more ways than one.

"There is a will." Vida stood in my doorway, startling me out of my reverie.

"Then there's a way," I retorted without thinking.

"A way for what?" Vida looked mystified.

"Sorry." I gave her a sheepish grin. "I was being silly. Did Bill have any details?"

Vida tapped her fingernails against the doorjamb. "He was very reticent. All those ridiculous scruples. I've no idea where he got them. Certainly not from his mother."

"Did he say anything at all that was helpful?" I asked, trying not to look too amused.

"Only that shortly after she arrived in Baring, Crystal asked Marisa Foxx to draw up a will. Which means," she added, squaring her wide shoulders, "I'm off to the courthouse. It should have been filed by now."

Briefly, I thought about going with Vida. But somebody needed to hold down the fort. While I waited for her to come back, I mulled over the case—again. Milo had to be making some progress, if only eliminating certain suspects. Aaron's alibi must have held up, or the sheriff wouldn't have let him go. But it appeared that Aaron had the best motive. Perhaps Milo had no legal grounds to keep him, but had warned him not to leave the area. Picking up the phone, I decided that I needed to get the sheriff in a mellow mood.

"I can't," Milo replied when I asked if he'd like to have a drink after work. "My kids are coming up for an early Christmas."

"So soon?" I asked. "How come?"

"Old Mulehide," he said, referring to his ex, "is taking them on a ski vacation to Vail." The sneer in his voice crept over the wire.

"Wow. Where did she get the money?"

"Probably that phony she married the second time around shelled out," Milo said in a disgruntled tone. "He claims to ski, too."

I commiserated briefly with Milo, then surrendered. My next call was to the PUD to find out about the power failure. As is often the case, a tree limb had blown down over a wire, in this case, one near the Overholt farm. I'd just finished typing up the two-paragraph story when Ed Bronsky came into the office.

"Ed!" I exclaimed, forcing an optimism I didn't feel.

"How's the shelter project? Are you bringing good news?"

Ed stumbled a bit over his glossy designer boots, but finally managed to wedge himself into one of my visitor's chairs. "I've got good news, but it isn't about the shelter." He gave me a half-assed smile. "This isn't the time of year for that kind of thing, Emma. Everybody's too caught up with Christmas."

"Yeah, gee, you're right, Ed," I replied. "Those poor women out there are having such fun getting their heads pushed into the wassail bowl and being decorated with the kind of punch you never drink. Why should we worry?"

Ed made a face. "I'm not worrying. I mean, it's really a shame, and I'll get onto it right after the holidays, but for now, I've got an announcement. Page-one stuff. You ready?"

I was never ready for Ed, but I took a deep breath and pretended. "Okay. What is it?"

Ed beamed. "A TV miniseries, based on *Mr. Ed.*" He beamed some more. "How do you like them apples?"

Ed had the power to render me speechless. I stared. Finally, I managed to croak out a coherent response: "The project has been green-lighted?"

Ed nodded, still beaming. His chins bounced off the fur collar of his cashmere overcoat. He looked like a circus bear. All he needed was a funny little hat with bells.

"Irv and Stu wrapped up the deal this morning," Ed explained, finally subduing his grin. "It'll be on cable, the HOPE channel, probably in the fall, maybe even Sweeps Week."

I wasn't familiar with the HOPE channel. Maybe we didn't get it in Alpine. Maybe nobody got it. Maybe I was dreaming.

"That's great, Ed," I said, and forced enthusiasm into my voice. "You're positive? I wouldn't want to run this without confirmation."

Ed nodded some more. "My agents faxed me a copy of the contract this morning. We'll seal the deal over the weekend. In fact, Shirl and I are driving into Bellevue this afternoon. We'll stay at the Hyatt Regency to celebrate."

I took notes. I had no choice. "What's the name of the production company?"

"Family Something-or-Other," Ed replied, and scratched his head. "Gee, I forget exactly. Shall I call you?"

"You can tell me when you get back," I said. "We'll have plenty of time before deadline."

"Sure." Ed stood up and preened a bit. "I doubt that I'll have much to say about casting. Still, I'd like to see Leonardo DiCaprio as the Young Ed. Maybe De Niro when I hit middle age. Wouldn't he be perfect?"

Since the only resemblance I could see between Ed Bronsky and Robert De Niro was that they were both male and had probably had two parents, I didn't reply directly. "I think you're right," I hedged. "Usually, the author doesn't get involved in the filming process."

"It's too bad, really," Ed said, literally filling the door. "I've got some terrific ideas, especially for the opening about how my mother went into labor."

Dare I ask?

I didn't need to. "It was right after World War II," he began, "and my folks had a little Victory Garden. You know, carrots and radishes and beets and stuff like that, to help beat the Nazis and the Japs."

"You can't say Japs, Ed," I interrupted.

"Huh?" Ed looked surprised. "You could then. Anyway, Mom was digging up the old vegetables when she got her foot stuck in a hole and fell down. Her water broke, and the next thing you know, whoosh! I was practically born in the cabbage bed."

"No kidding," I said, trying to envision such an opening for a TV miniseries. I suppose it had its comic possibilities.

Ed nattered on about the rush to the hospital, the delivery in the hall, the great excitement among family and staff because he was such a *big* baby. I pictured a smaller version of the present Ed, in diaper and bonnet, gnawing on a chicken.

Naturally, Ed mistook my amusement for approval of his proposed opening scene. "See, Emma," he said, "I've got a genius for TV drama. Maybe I could talk Irv and Stu into letting me have . . ."

I tuned Ed out. Eventually, he ran down. "Got to pick up Shirl and head for the Hyatt." At the door, he called back to me. "You want some pictures? I've got a great shot of Shirl and me by the pool from last summer. It has that Southern California look."

As in Sea World? I wanted to say, but didn't. In bathing suits, Ed and Shirley resembled a couple of beached whales. "I doubt I could use it for this issue, Ed," I said with what I hoped sounded like regret. "We've got so much Christmas stuff. Not to mention the follow-up on Crystal's murder."

"Oh, that." Ed dismissed Crystal with a wave of one hand. "I thought Dodge arrested her ex."

"Not for murder," I said. "Anyway, he's out on bail."

"Hunh," Ed responded, looking momentarily bemused. Then he puffed himself up and departed.

I marveled that Ed could be so self-centered. Crystal could have died in his own hot tub, and he'd still be picturing Robert De Niro as the Lord of Casa de Bronska. I might have hated Crystal, but I was affected by her death. At least I hoped I was.

Vida returned five minutes later. "Heavens!" she exclaimed, flopping down across the desk from me. "I almost ran into Ed. Fortunately, I saw him coming out of *The Advocate*, so I ducked into Sky Travel. By the way, Janet Driggers told me that no one has come to claim Crystal's ashes."

"Really?" I said. "That's odd."

"More than odd," Vida agreed, stripping off her gloves. "That hasn't happened at Driggers's Funeral Home since Frosty Phipps died in 'sixty-nine. Frosty was so ornery that nobody wanted him, not even in his cremated form. Al's father, Owen, finally mailed the remains to Charles, the eldest Phipps child, who passed them on down the line—there were four children in all—until they got to Neva, the youngest. Her little ones got hold of the package before she did, and since it was close to one of their birthdays, they thought it was a present and opened it and dumped it in their sandbox. Neva and her husband, Doyle, always said it was the only time that their kiddies had ever played with Grandpa. He was *that* mean."

I smiled as Vida paused for breath. "Terrible. What about the will?"

Vida's eyes sparked. "Ah, yes. The will. Most interesting. The cabin and its contents go to Aaron. The money is divided forty-sixty between Thad and Melody. Thad gets the sixty share. What do you make of that?"

"If I were Thad, I'd make a nest egg of it for graduate school," I said. "Whatever Melody gets will be nice for her, too. Do you think they knew about the inheritance?"

"We'll have to find out," Vida declared.

" 'We'll'?" I echoed.

"Well . . ." Vida pursed her lips. "It might be more discreet if I called on the Eriks children alone. I *have* known them since they were born. More or less."

Inasmuch as Vida knew everyone in Alpine, I acknowledged her superior qualifications. "Go for it. What's your plan?"

She was vague, but I didn't doubt her sense of purpose. I wouldn't have put it past her to get the urn from Al Driggers and cart it over to the Eriks home. Meanwhile, I felt as if the case had hit a wall, at least as far as I was concerned. If Milo had any leads, he wasn't sharing them.

Feeling vaguely depressed, I threw myself into next week's editorial. For all of Ed's indifference, somebody needed to get moving on the battered-women's shelter. I'd issue another call to action, and sit back to see if anything happened. It probably wouldn't. As much as I hated to admit it, Ed was right about the Christmas season. It was hectic, and the irony was that most people were too busy to help others.

By mid-afternoon, Vida came back to the office bursting with news. "I was most fortunate," she exuded. "The Eriksons had just been to see Marisa Foxx. Thad and Melody pretended to be surprised about their windfall, but I think they were acting. At least Thad was. On the other hand, I didn't feel that April and Mel knew anything about the will. Mel was very grumpy at being left out, and April was sulking."

"Interesting," I remarked, less amazed at Vida's news than at her ability to wheedle information out of her fellow human beings. "You're sure Thad and Melody knew about the will before Crystal was killed?"

"They made a slip," Vida said, looking a trifle smug, "indicating that they had foreknowledge. Melody mentioned that Aaron didn't deserve the cabin at Baring. She said that he was a loser, that they should have been divorced a long time ago. Then Thad said, and I quote, 'You wouldn't live in that place. You never counted on having your down payment so soon anyway. What do you need a house for? You're still a kid.' Unquote."

"Implying that Melody knew she would someday get money from her aunt," I mused. "What did Melody say to that?"

"She made a nasty face at her brother and mumbled something about 'You wouldn't use it for a house anyway. You'll want a mansion by the time you're ready to settle down.' "Vida adjusted her glasses and gave me her owlish look. "Thus, I gather that both Thad and Melody had visited their aunt at the cabin. They seemed to know all about it. But April and Mel appeared to be in the dark. Mel complained that it wasn't fair, April was Crystal's sister. She should have gotten everything."

"And April sulked?" I said.

"Definitely. She seemed quite off her feed. Of course," Vida went on, "she may be mourning Crystal. I don't want to be mean-minded about the relationship. They *were* sisters, after all."

After Vida returned to her desk to type up her story on the Cardenas-family Christmas customs, I mulled over what she had told me. Thad had certainly spoken glowingly about his aunt at the funeral. That was fitting, since she'd left him approximately thirty grand. But was it a motive? I didn't know Thad well enough to tell. Vida had overheard him taking his parents to task for not saving money. Maybe his only prayer of graduate school—and resulting riches—was his aunt's inheritance. Melody, on the other hand, had seemed unaffected by Crystal's passing. Maybe it was just a difference in personalities.

By five o'clock, it had started to snow again. Shivering in my raincoat, I trudged out to the Jag and used a scraper to clear the windshield. Then I headed home, up the series of small hills that led to my log house. It was much nicer than Crystal's place, at least in my opinion. She hadn't had a fireplace, only a Franklin stove. *Ha-ha*, I thought, and immediately hated myself. I was losing the

Advent season as swiftly as the relentless snowflakes were filling up the tire treads on the side streets.

By the time I turned onto Fir, I was in a real funk. There were no plans for the weekend, no names on my dance card. That wasn't news, but it sure was depressing.

It was snowing so hard by the time I reached my driveway that I didn't notice the car pulled up by my mailbox until I started back to get the daily delivery. It was a medium-sized compact, a newer Ford Taurus. The more recent model always reminded me of a teapot. Maybe the car didn't belong to anyone connected to me. Sometimes the neighbors had visitors who parked in front of my place, especially if they were hosting a party.

Carrying the mail, I headed for the front door.

That was when I saw the tall figure of a man standing off to one side. He raised a hand. Startled, I stopped. Through the snow, I couldn't make out who it was. It was too tall for Leo. Nat Cardenas again? Milo, with a change of plans?

I got within five feet of the porch and recognized Tom Cavanaugh.

Chapter Twelve

THERE ARE NO stars on a snowy night, but I swear I saw them. There are no bells and whistles after the mill has shut down, yet I definitely heard them. The winter storm swirls around, driven by the wind from off the mountains, but the earth doesn't quake, though I felt it rock beneath my feet. I should have fainted, but I stopped short of being a complete cliché.

Instead, I just stood there with my mouth open. Tom moved to the first of the three steps and held out his hand. "Did I scare you?"

I stumbled and fell forward. Tom caught me and laughed, that rich, merry sound I hadn't heard in years. He held me close to his chest, and like a damned idiot, I started to cry.

Tom Cavanaugh is a patient man, a virtue that has cost me dearly. He waited for at least a full minute, and then spoke over the top of my silly head. "Do you have a key?" he asked in an amused tone.

Still unable to speak, I nodded. He let me go, and I rummaged in my purse. I couldn't find my keys.

"You never could find anything in those satchels you call a purse," he said, still amused. "Did you drop them?"

Stupidly, I turned and stared through the snow. "Yeah . . . maybe." Testing my legs for weakness, I started back the way I'd come. Tom followed me.

"Here," he said, and scooped them up. Then he put his arm around me and led me back onto the porch. "Oh, Emma, I'm so damned glad to see you. I told Leo I wasn't sure I should come."

"Leo?" I echoed, trying to insert the key in the lock.

"I called him the other day to ask his opinion. I was up in Vancouver at a meeting and—" Tom stopped and firmly removed the key chain from my uncertain grasp. "Here, let me."

No wonder Leo had acted strangely when I'd quizzed him about the five o'clock phone call. And he hadn't really lied. Tom *was* an old pal from Leo's advertising days in Southern California, having been my ad manager's boss on one of the Cavanaugh weeklies.

"Are you really here?" I asked, wiping away the tears as he let us in and flipped on the lights.

Tom closed the door. "Yes. I'm here."

I stared up at him. He'd changed, of course. His dark hair had more gray and the lines in his face were deeper. Otherwise, he looked much as I remembered him. Handsome. Attractive. Wonderful. I started to cry again.

"I'm a boob," I blubbered, struggling with the raincoat.

Gently, he extricated me, then took off his heavy jacket that had probably come from Brooks Brothers or some other expensive San Francisco emporium. "I hope you didn't have plans for the evening," he said, hanging up both coats in the closet by the door.

Strangely, the comment wasn't made lightly. Tom sounded genuinely worried that he might have intruded. "Actually," I replied, staying on my feet to make sure they were still there, "I'm not busy. But why didn't you call first?"

"I just got here," he said, hands in the pockets of his well-tailored slacks. "I thought about it, but just outside of town, the snow really started to come down. I figured

I'd be lucky to get up these hills with the rental car. It doesn't have chains."

I finally found my smile, and it must have been unsteady. How many times had I imagined this reunion with Tom? Despite his solid presence, his voice, his touch, I felt as if I were in a dream. They say imagination can take you only so far. But sometimes it overlaps with reality.

"Well," I said, "you made it. But it sure took you long enough."

Tom's face darkened and he lowered his head. "It did, didn't it? Frankly, I wasn't sure of the reception I'd get."

"Shall we start with a drink?" I tried to keep my voice light.

Tom gave a nod. "Sure. Bourbon's good."

It always was, being Tom's beverage of choice. "Water and rocks?" I asked from the kitchen.

"Fine," Tom answered from the living room.

Making drinks settled my nerves. I didn't drop anything, which was a plus. Bearing our cocktails, I came back into the living room and asked Tom if he'd like to sit down.

"Sure," he said again, and seated himself in one of the armchairs. I didn't know whether to take that as a bad or a good sign.

"Have you talked to Adam lately?" I inquired, touching off the logs in the fireplace while getting a firmer grip on my composure.

Tom shook his head. "I'm supposed to see him as well as your brother when they come through San Francisco on their way up here."

"You approve of Adam's decision to become a priest?" I asked as I sat down on the sofa.

Tom shot me a wry look. "Adam doesn't need my approval. Or anyone else's. If he has a vocation, then I pray that he becomes a good priest. I assume you feel the same way." There was a formal note in his voice and it jarred me.

"Of course," I replied. "I'll be honest, though. At first, I was upset. It was selfish on my part, but I guess it was because I realized I'd never have grandchildren."

"That matters?" Tom seemed surprised.

"Yes," I responded. "Maternal instincts die hard."

Tom smiled. "I suppose they do. I haven't had much experience with them."

"Meaning?" I leaned forward, encouraging Tom to elaborate.

"Meaning," he said slowly, "that Sandra's maternal instincts must have been repressed. I don't want to speak ill of the dead, but facts are facts. She concentrated too much on herself and her problems to be a real mother."

"But she had problems," I noted. "Or so you always told me."

Tom's expression was hard to read, especially in the firelight. "Yes, she had problems. Horrendous problems. Early on, my theory was that when Sandra did become a mother, she'd stop dwelling on them and maybe they'd lessen. But after having had our two kids, she didn't change. In fact, she only got worse. Sometimes I felt she was jealous of them."

So I'd been sacrificed for an unsuccessful cure. Or so I calculated, since Tom had been forced to choose between Sandra and me when we became pregnant at the same time.

"Gee," I said, and didn't try to hide the asperity that surfaced, "it's a good thing *I* wasn't crazy. You might have had to marry me after all."

Tom gave a little start. "What do you mean by that crack?"

"I thought it was obvious." Along with my composure,

anger had welled up. "Forget it. We can't undo twenty-six years."

Tom's face had darkened under what always seemed like a perpetual tan. "We can't?"

"What do you mean?" I asked with a frown.

Tom's deep blue eyes avoided me. "Never mind. For now. I'd assumed you wanted to hear how it was between Sandra and me."

"You always kept me apprised," I said stiffly. "It was one crisis after the other."

For a long moment, Tom didn't reply. He sat gazing into his drink, the firelight glancing off of his glass. "That's what it was," he said simply. "Continual crises." His eyes locked with mine. "You weren't there, Emma. You couldn't possibly understand."

I had to admit that much. "Still, knowing that, why did you string me along, especially when you promised to leave her and asked me to marry you?" I could hear the bitterness in my voice.

"Because," he said, and sounded angry, "it was my only hope. I had to have something to hold on to all those years. You were my strength."

"But it wasn't fair!" I burst out. "You used me. That was an awful thing to do."

"Was it?" His face was solemn.

"Yes, of course it was." I spoke in a rush, all the resentment, the anger, and my own dashed hopes filling my words. "You should have let me go. Why should I waste my life waiting for you? Good God, I was barely twenty-two, I could have married and had more children."

"Emma." A faint smile touched his lips, even though he spoke my name with reproach. "We didn't communicate for almost twenty years after you ran off to Mississippi to have Adam. How can you accuse me of ruining your life? That's not fair, either."

It wasn't. Tom was right. It was only after he reentered my life seven years earlier that I'd considered a future with him. The years in between had gone for nothing, lost in a sea of rekindled passion and noble promises. I was kidding myself. It's one of my worst habits.

But I wasn't completely giving in. "You got my hopes up after that weekend at Lake Chelan," I said, sounding dangerously close to a sulk. "That should never have happened. I was doing just fine until then."

"So was I." The words sounded hollow, and Tom immediately took them back. "No, it wasn't. I was hanging on by a thread. I needed you. I needed to feel alive again. If that's selfish, then there it is. And now I'm here."

"For what?" The sulky note lingered.

Tom set his glass down on the side table and put his hands behind his head. "I don't know. That's what I came to find out."

For some unknown, perverse reason which is so much a part of my emotional makeup, I wanted to stall. "Tell me about Sandra. What happened? How did she die?"

"I thought Leo told you," Tom replied, looking pained.

"He did. That is," I clarified, "he told me she took an overdose of something-or-other."

"That's right," Tom retorted. "Did you think I'd killed her?"

I didn't detect any humor in his tone. He was wearing his belligerent expression. I'd forgotten how daunting that was. But under that sophisticated, gentlemanly exterior lurked a man who did battle in the newspaper wars. Tom hadn't gotten where he was without being tough.

"Of course not," I declared. "But was it deliberate or accidental?"

"On her part?" The faintest hint of a smile touched his mouth as he saw me nod. "I honestly don't know. Sandra had threatened suicide so often. It was one of her favorite ploys to keep me in line. She'd actually attempted it four or five times, but she was so well acquainted with her medications that she always managed to pull through. I'm guessing—if only because it makes me feel better—that she wanted to kill herself. The kids had moved away, so had some of her closest friends, and her older relatives were dying off. Her coterie of sympathizers was shrinking."

My initial reaction was contempt, but it was quickly replaced by pity. How pathetic to live life only to gain the compassion of others. It was a waste, and I said so.

"Yes," Tom agreed, "it was. Sandra was smart, she was beautiful, she'd been given everything. I suppose that was the problem. Her wealthy parents had spoiled her. She never stopped wanting to be spoiled. And, to be fair, she was unstable, even when I met her. Like a fool, I thought marriage—and motherhood—would change her."

"We don't change," I said sadly. "We simply become more of what we already were."

"So it seems." Tom had removed his hands from behind his head and was finishing his drink.

"Do you need a refill?" I asked.

"I don't know." He gave me another wry look. "Do I?"

"Probably. You've had a long drive," I added hastily.

"Yes." As I took his glass, he grabbed my wrist. "I've come a long way. Have you?"

I was trembling. "I don't know," I said. "I'm still in shock."

"Should I go?" Tom looked very earnest.

I shook my head. "No. Please. Let me collect myself. I'll get us another drink."

He released my hand and I staggered out into the kitchen. I was getting more ice when I heard the crash. Spilling several cubes on the floor, I dashed out into the living room.

"What was that?" I cried.

Tom was at the picture window that looks out onto my front yard. "Christ," he murmured with a startled laugh as he bent down to pick something up. "This is crazy. It's a brick. With a note."

"What?" I was incredulous as I joined him.

He held the note in his hands. "It was tied to the brick," he explained, and with a look of disgust, handed me the folded tablet-sized piece of paper. "What's all this about?"

With shaking hands, I unfolded the note. It had gotten wet and the ink had started to run, but it wasn't too difficult to make out the big block printing. *Killer whore*, it said.

"Damn!" I gasped, then stared at the jagged hole in my front window. "Damn, damn, damn!"

Tom put an arm around my shoulder. "Call a glazier right away. You can't get along without a new window in this weather."

I looked up at Tom. "Are you kidding? There's one glazier in town, and if you think he'll dash out on a Friday night, you're nuts. This is Alpine."

Tom looked vaguely nonplussed, then examined the window's two-foot gash. "Have you got any heavy cardboard?"

"Somewhere." I was already shivering, and snowflakes were swirling on my hardwood floor. "I'll check."

Five minutes later, I was back with part of a box and a roll of duct tape. Tom had collected the broken glass and put the shards in a bowl.

"Did you see anything?" I asked.

"You mean who threw the damned brick? No. I was sitting there, admiring your Monet print, and suddenly there was a crash. I turned around." He paused, getting to his feet. "And by the time I realized what had happened, the SOB must have taken off."

"In a car?" I asked as Tom bent down to apply the cardboard.

"I don't think so," he replied. "My guess is whoever did it was on foot. They may have parked in that cul-de-sac down at the corner."

"Rats." Then I brightened. "There must be footprints. Maybe I should call Milo."

"Go ahead," Tom said, carefully applying tape to cardboard and glass, "but I doubt he'll get anything by the time he arrives. It's probably too late right now. Look out there, it's practically a blizzard."

Tom was right. The flakes were small but thick, blowing down from the north and piling up against the house. "Bummer," I muttered. "I'd love to catch that jerk."

Finishing his task, Tom stood up. "What set whoever it is off?" He glanced at the note, and his face darkened with anger.

I let out a big sigh. "Let me get our drinks first. Then I'll tell you all about it."

Having spent his career in newspapers, Tom wasn't surprised by the brick-throwing business. But he was shocked when I told him that an attempt had been made to set me up as Crystal Bird's killer.

"Who hates you both?" he asked when I finally wound down.

I stared at Tom. "I never looked at it quite that way. I don't know that Milo has, either."

"I remember Milo," Tom said with a thin smile. "He's not the sharpest scalpel in the surgery tray."

"He's not dumb," I said in a defensive tone. "Milo goes by the book. He has to."

"You're very protective of Milo," Tom remarked.

I tried to be casual. "We have to work together, especially on big investigations like this. Believe me," I added, hoping I didn't sound bitter, "when we've had ... disagreements, the cooperation level all but disappears." I didn't go further; I had no idea what, if anything, Tom had heard about Milo and me from Leo Walsh.

Tom's expression was noncommittal. "Milo didn't fall for the setup?"

"The setup?" I wasn't sure what he meant. "You mean by the killer? No, he didn't." I didn't add that Milo knew me too well to fall for it. There was no need for Tom to find out how well the sheriff and I really knew each other. Not now, at any rate. "Besides, I think Milo may have known Crystal on a personal basis."

I told Tom about the phone call from Milo the night of the murder, and also added some of the other details, including Victor's accident, Nat's drunken driving, and Aaron's arrest.

"It sounds pretty complicated," Tom said with a smile. "But you enjoy these homicidal puzzles. By the way, are you going to call Milo to report this?" He gestured at the picture window.

"I'd better, if only for the record." Dutifully, I picked up the phone. Sam Heppner answered. He sounded surprised in his own quiet way, then asked if I wanted an officer to patrol the house.

"No, Sam, but thanks," I said. "You've got what—two men?—on duty and there's bound to be some more nasty accidents. I'm fine."

"But this isn't the first incident," Sam pointed out. "Your house was broken into a while back, right?"

"Right." I hesitated, wondering if in fact the two occurrences might not be linked. "Still, it's okay. People who throw bricks usually don't burgle as a sideline."

"Maybe." Sam sounded grudging. "It's up to you."

I reiterated my statement about the deputies being needed elsewhere. Sam didn't argue further.

When I'd hung up, Tom asked me more about the break-in. "It was over a week ago," I told him. "But I'm not sure that's when the sleeping pills were taken. Any number of people had been in the house since I last took them. In fact, I think the burglary was kids. They took the kind of things that kids take."

"It could have been a cover," Tom pointed out.

I admitted that was possible. Despite the cardboard, the living room still felt chilly. Going over to the fireplace, I threw in another log.

"Are you staying for dinner?" I asked, standing between Tom's chair and the sofa.

"I was going to take you out," Tom said, then added wryly, "if you didn't throw me out first."

"It's snowing too hard to go anywhere," I said. "I've got plenty of stuff in the freezer. Steak? Chicken? Pork chops?"

"Pork chops," Tom replied with a wistful smile. "Do you know how long it's been since I had home-cooked pork chops?"

"I thought you and Sandra had live-in help," I said, perching on the sofa's arm.

"We do. We did," he corrected himself. "Sandra had a full-time nurse, a housekeeper, and a cook. Only the nurse lived in. We had gardeners, too." He lifted his head, giving me a glimpse of that profile that looked as if it had come off an ancient coin. "I sold the house this summer and bought a condo on Nob Hill. I don't need servants. I don't want them. It was never my style."

It probably wasn't. Tom had come from a very middle-class family. His father had worked for the Burke Mill in Seattle. Entering the newspaper business had never been a way to get rich. But marrying money was, and Tom was sufficiently human to be impressed by wealth. Still, I'd always believed that wasn't Sandra's main attraction. Sandra had been beautiful and smart as well, the whole package. She had also been crazy as a bedbug.

"I didn't realize you'd sold the house," I said.

"The kids were gone. Why would I want to rattle around by myself in that big place in Pacific Heights? Besides," he added, "I travel a lot. It didn't make sense not to sell it. At least at the time."

I eyed Tom quizzically, but he didn't say anything more. For a long moment, we were both silent. He was gazing into his almost empty glass; I was staring at the fire. The reality of his presence in my living room had only begun to sink in. Why had he come? Why didn't I ask?

"Pork chops it is," I said, getting up and heading for the kitchen. "You want a refill?"

"Half," he replied, getting up to join me. "I'll fix it."

While I made dinner, we spoke of other, neutral things. He was intrigued by Crystal's murder. I was interested in his newspaper empire, which was still thriving despite competition from other media.

"It won't stay that way," Tom said as we finally sat down in my little dining alcove. "If I were smart, I'd start selling off and buying up TV or radio stations."

"Why don't you?" I asked, glancing out the window to see that the snow hadn't yet let up.

He gave me a cockeyed grin. "You know why. It's not the same. I've still got printer's ink in my veins. So do you." Abruptly, he grew serious. "How's *The Advocate* doing financially? Have you ever considered selling?"

I uttered a strange little laugh. "No," I gasped. "Never. At least not seriously. I mean, as long as we're showing a profit, why would I?"

"That's when you sell," Tom said in the tone of voice that he must use in high-powered business meetings. "You don't wait until you start losing money, or even flattening out."

I shook my head. "With any luck, we can hang on until I'm ready to retire. Alpine's growing, Tom. The college has meant a lot to this area in terms of the economy."

"That's good," he said between bites of pork chop. "But you're talking about initial impact. Over time, that growth may level off. Let's face it, college students aren't big spenders. Once the plant has been built, money injected into the community comes mainly from faculty and staff. What's the projected growth pattern for the next five years?"

I passed Tom the mashed potatoes for a second helping. "I don't know exactly. But they expect quite a bit of growth. In the next couple of years, they'll be adding at least three new programs."

Tom gave a single nod. "That's fine, too. But what does that mean? Four, five new faculty members? Another forty or fifty students? And where will they go after they get their two-year degrees?"

I put my fork down next to my plate. "What's your point?"

Tom waved a hand. "Nothing. I was trying to offer some friendly counsel."

"It doesn't sound as if you're taking it yourself," I pointed out as I resumed eating.

"True." His smile was ironic. "Maybe I should. I've been thinking that it's time to pare down. That idea came along after I sold the house."

Tom was fifty-four. Perhaps he was looking down the road at retirement. I suggested as much, but he shook his head.

"I can't imagine retiring," he declared. "That's one thing about owning newspapers—if you hire the right people, you can assume a hands-off role. That's why I was trying to steal Leo a while back." Tom's expression was faintly sheepish.

I recalled the incident, which had resulted in Leo delivering the fateful news about Sandra, and me losing it in the middle of the bar at the Venison Inn. The whole story of my relationship with Tom had come out then, and Leo had been a comfort. But he couldn't explain why Tom had never contacted me in the ensuing months.

"Leo likes it here," I said lightly. "Why didn't you call me? Why did I have to find out about Sandra from him?"

Tom hesitated before spearing a second pork chop from the oval platter. "I suppose that made you mad," he said.

"You bet." I'd finished eating and folded my arms across my breast. "Not an unreasonable reaction, you must admit."

"Probably not." Tom didn't seem disturbed, however. "I intended to, of course."

"And?" I prodded.

He gave a shake of his head. "I didn't do it."

"Why not?"

He chewed for a moment, then lifted one shoulder. "There was a lot to do after Sandra died. Not just the estate, but because of the way she died. It took me months to get through all the details and red tape. Six months later, when I finally put the house on the market at the end of June, I felt I was out of the woods. As it turned out, I wasn't."

"How come?" I had a feeling I wasn't going to like the answer.

"Kelsey got herself into some trouble," he replied, the blue eyes solemn. "She had a boyfriend in New York, where she'd gone to work after she dropped out of college. He fancied himself a writer, but was making ends meet by working for a messenger service. It turned out that he was delivering more than messages."

"Drugs?" I put in.

Tom nodded. "Anyway, Kelsey got pregnant. To my

horror, she wanted to marry this moron. It killed me to interfere, but I had to. Oh, I went back to meet him—his name was Thor, for God's sake—and he was everything I'd dreamed of—in my worst nightmares. I'll be damned if I know how she could have picked such a loser."

I could hazard a guess, but I didn't. Kelsey had grown up mothering her mother. Sandra's death had left a hole in her life. I suspected she'd been looking for someone else to take care of. But I wouldn't rub that in.

"Anyway, I talked her out of it," Tom continued, putting his plate aside. Maybe just talking about Thor had caused him to lose his appetite. "I tried to be reasonable, and to my amazement, it worked. God, she's only twenty-four—why should she screw up the rest of her life?"

I'd been twenty-one when I'd gotten pregnant with Adam. Had that event screwed up my life? Maybe. Through the misty vista of twenty-six years, I wasn't sure. If it'd been screwed up, I'd done it myself.

"So what happened?" I asked.

Tom uttered a heavy sigh. "That was the hardest part. If she wasn't getting married, Kelsey decided she'd have an abortion. I hit the roof."

I winced. "Oh, Tom," I said, "that must have been rough."

"It was. We spent two days arguing about that." He gave me a wry smile. "It only took six hours to talk her out of Thor."

"And?" I felt like I was watching a soap opera and had come to the end of the Friday episode that leaves viewers on the edge of their seats.

"She finally gave in," he said, "but not on spiritual or moral grounds. Kelsey began to see the baby as a replacement for her mother."

"So how's she handling it now?" I asked with a sense of relief.

Tom made one last foray into his second pork chop. "The baby's not due until mid-February. She quit her job the first of December, and is moving back to San Francisco next week. Graham will be home around then for Christmas, too."

Graham was Tom's elder child, the boy with whom Sandra had become pregnant while I carried Adam. In her case, fertility and stability hadn't gone hand in hand.

"Well," I said, with an uncertain smile, "you're going to be a grandfather."

Tom ran a hand through his hair, which, I realized, didn't come quite as far down on his forehead as it used to. "Yes. Strange, huh? You wish you could be a grandparent, and I'm not quite as enthusiastic over the prospect."

"So what will Kelsey do?" I asked, never having met the girl and only having seen a high-school graduation photo that had depicted a pretty blonde with an air of innocence. I wondered what she looked like six years later with innocence lost.

"She'll stay with me," Tom replied. "The condo has two bedrooms. Three, really, if you count the den. We'll work out the rest of it after she gets there."

"I see." Unfortunately, I thought I did, and my heart sank. Like Kelsey, Tom couldn't seem to free himself from caring for someone else.

Maybe he read my mind. Tom reached out and grabbed my hand. "You understand the position I'm in, don't you?"

"Do I?" The words sounded shaky.

"It doesn't change my feelings for you," he said quickly, squeezing my fingers. "I swear it, Emma. I still love you."

"Great."

"Shall I go?"

"Where?" I started to laugh. "Poor Tom, wandering in

the blizzard. We'll find him curled up against a western hemlock, frozen stiff as a two-by-four."

"Please. Don't be a smart-ass." Tom stood up, pulling me with him. In the process, I knocked my knife on the floor and upset the salt-and-pepper shakers.

"Don't," he commanded, and his voice was gruff. Then he was kissing me and I wasn't laughing anymore. The hysteria was gone; so were the tears that had threatened to spill.

We were in my bedroom, where all the anger and bitterness and resentment floated away as softly as the snowflakes that fell outside my window. December surrounded us, but inside, it felt like May, and we were young again.

Chapter Thirteen

I'M STILL NOT sure exactly how or why Tom decided he'd call on Marisa Foxx the next morning, but I think it had something to do with his status as a newspaper baron. Over breakfast, he had conjectured that libel was a viable motive for murder. Somehow, he'd gotten it into his head that if he talked to Marisa, he might find out more about the possible suits that had been filed against Crystal.

"I don't get your reasoning," I admitted as he prepared to walk through the two feet of new snow that had blanketed Alpine during the night. "Isn't it the other way around? Wouldn't the defendant, Crystal, have more of a motive than the plaintiff? I know how much of an estate she had. It wouldn't make for a very big settlement after legal fees and court costs."

"Were you going to sue for money or satisfaction?" Tom asked, putting on a heavy pair of boots he'd gotten out of his luggage.

I admitted that money hadn't been foremost in my mind when I'd gone to see Marisa. "Do you think she had some serious dirt on somebody in Alpine?"

Tom allowed that might be possible. "I was thinking that an aggrieved party could get more satisfaction out of murdering Crystal than being awarded a paltry monetary settlement. Not to mention that it would end her harassment and provide swift revenge." Then he kissed me and headed off into the quiet morning.

He got about two feet before he sank up to his knees in the snow. "I tried to warn you." I laughed. "It's far too deep. We have to dig our way out."

Judging from Tom's expression, I surmised that he hadn't shoveled snow since moving out of his parents' home thirty-odd years ago in Seattle's Fremont neighborhood.

"I don't have hired help," I reminded Tom as he got back onto the porch, "but I do have two shovels."

Hands on hips, Tom surveyed the front yard and the street beyond. The snow had dwindled to a few drifting flakes, but it was very cold, fourteen degrees on the thermometer outside my kitchen window. At least three feet of snow had accumulated over the past week with drifts against the house reaching almost to the eaves. The hole in the front window was no longer a problem, since it was packed with driven snow.

"What do you people do in weather like this?" Tom asked.

"We shovel," I replied as I led the way into the house. "It takes me about half an hour. Usually, the plows are out by now, but it's Saturday. The Peabody brothers like to sleep in on the weekends."

"I take it the Peabody brothers are the snow-removal crew?" Tom asked dryly.

I nodded. "That's it. Come on, have another cup of coffee. Why don't you just telephone Marisa back and talk to her over the phone?"

Apparently, that idea appealed more to Tom than shoveling did. But coffee appealed to him even more. "Okay, so who do you think might have sued Crystal?"

"Might *want* to, as opposed to actually doing it?" I queried, and saw Tom nod. "Not Nat Cardenas. He'd try everything else before going public. The man's a real politician." I paused, thinking about the people Crystal had excoriated in her newsletter. "None of the clergy. They're all pretty decent, and would try to avoid scandal."

"Scandal?" Tom looked curious.

"Not in that sense," I amended. "The attacks weren't personal. I meant that some of the issues could cause rifts in the congregation, especially among the women who favor the shelter. As for the county commissioners, they probably never read *Crystal Clear*. I'm not sure if they *can* read."

"What about Milo?" Tom asked.

"Good question." I turned slightly as a Steller's jay perched on the windowsill, eyeing me hopefully. "I should feed the birds. Milo won't tell me if he knew Crystal in any way except in an official capacity," I went on, going to the bread box and getting out several crusts. "If there was no personal involvement, the sheriff may have been giving Crystal advice on burglar-proofing her cabin. It's isolated, and a perfect target for troublemakers."

Tom was looking thoughtful. "I take it you haven't heard any rumors linking Milo and Crystal romantically?"

The phone rang before I could respond. It was Paula Rubens, sounding not quite like herself. "What's the weather up there like?" she asked in a worried voice.

Startup was just a few miles down the highway, but far enough west and considerably lower in altitude. We didn't always share the same kind of weather. "There was a blizzard last night," I replied. "Have you checked the radio? They ought to be giving pass reports."

"Stevens Pass reopens at eleven," she said. "How is it in Alpine?"

"Bad," I said. "My street's a mess, but they may have plowed Front and Alpine Way by now. What's wrong, Paula?"

I heard her take a deep breath. "It's probably nothing.

One of my students called a few minutes ago to say that he was cross-country skiing through town and saw the sheriff go into Nat Cardenas's house. Benjy—the student—said he was sure it was Dodge because he's the only one in town with a new red Grand Cherokee. I called Nat, and Justine answered. She sounded very upset, and said she couldn't talk. Do you have any idea what might be happening?"

"None," I replied, glancing at Tom's curious face. "If I hear anything, I'll let you know."

"Please do," Paula urged. "I figure that if the weather up your way is really bad, it must be something important to send Dodge over to Nat's."

Paula was right. Milo's Grand Cherokee had four-wheel drive, but even that had its limitations in a hilly town like Alpine. However, Nat and Justine lived in the upscale development known as The Pines, where they could probably pay or bribe someone to plow the streets.

"It must be urgent to get Milo out on a morning like this," Tom remarked.

I agreed. "I'll try to call him in a little while. Do you want to talk to Marisa first? I'll get you her home phone number."

Not surprisingly, Marisa was in. While Tom wandered into the living room with the gypsy phone nestled between his ear and his shoulder, I tidied up the kitchen. I felt as if I were in a dream. The fresh snow piled outside, the birds in the feeder by one of the big Douglas firs that grew in my backyard, the two of us doing everyday things, like a real couple. But the snow would melt, and so would my dream. Reality was Kelsey having a baby and a two-foot hole in my front window.

Tom's conversation with Marisa was relatively short. Just as I was turning on the dishwasher, he returned with the phone and placed it on the counter.

"Marisa takes client confidentiality seriously," he said. "I gather you haven't found any cases on file at the courthouse?"

"That's Scott's beat," I said, then, seeing Tom's puzzled expression, I quickly explained how Scott Chamoud had been hired to replace Carla. "He definitely would have mentioned anything about Crystal that was a matter of public record."

"Scott didn't miss anything," Tom said, pouring yet more coffee. "Marisa Foxx was able to tell me that no one had gone as far as to file a suit, and that, in her expert opinion, no one would now that Crystal is dead. However," he went on, the blue eyes twinkling, "she did say that there had been at least three inquiries. One was somebody in the timber industry, and another was a member of the clergy. Which pastor has the most clout in this town?"

"Nielsen," I answered promptly. "He's the Lutheran pastor, and they're definitely a majority. The timber-industry person could be Jack Blackwell, who owns a logging company and has never met trouble that he didn't want to make worse."

"The third party?" Tom asked as he leaned against the counter, mug in hand.

"Me." I gave him a feeble smile. "I went to see Marisa right before Crystal was killed. How the heck did you get this much out of her?"

Tom's smile was sly. "I told her I was a West Coast publishing magnate canvassing some of the independent weeklies. I wanted to know how often the present owners encountered legal problems. You, apparently, don't get involved in litigation."

"Luck," I responded. "And caution."

"Which then led me to ask about any other publications in the county," Tom said. "That brought up *Crystal*

Clear. I professed amazement at how such a one-horse newsletter could rile so many people. That was bull, of course. It's always the self-published rags that stir up trouble because that's their owners' intent. If they didn't have an ax to grind, they wouldn't go into the business."

"That's true," I remarked. "Congratulations. Frankly, I thought you'd hit a stone wall."

"I was very magnatelike. I think I impressed her." Tom grinned over the rim of his coffee mug.

"You're very impressive," I gushed as the phone rang. Reaching behind Tom, I heard Milo's voice at the other end.

"Good," Milo said. "You're home."

"Where else would I be on a day like this?" I countered.

"The Peabodys are plowing," Milo said, and judging from the interference, he was on his cell phone. "They're up to Cedar, so you'll be clear in another four blocks. Mind if I stop by? I've something to tell you."

"Ahh . . ." I locked gazes with Tom. "Can't you do it now? It'll be at least half an hour before the Peabodys get here."

"No," Milo replied. "This thing's breaking up. Hell, I can park on Alpine Way and walk to your place. Besides, I owe you one. I've been kind of a butt lately."

The admission must have cost Milo. But I'd have preferred him not finding Tom at my house. I didn't need the awkwardness; I'd rather not embarrass any of us. "It's five long blocks from Alpine Way to here," I said. "Believe me, it's all but impossible to get through. You know how the snow gets deeper higher up. I'm marooned."

"Then I'll shovel you out," Milo said, though the squawks and tweets on the line made him barely audible. "See you in a bit."

"Great." I stood there holding the receiver and looking bleak. "Milo's coming."

"So?" Tom's gaze was level.

I started to throw up my hands, then opted for discretion. "You don't mind him seeing you here?"

Tom shook his head. "Where else could I have gone last night?" The twinkle was back in his eyes.

So Tom didn't mind. But I did. Not for my own sake—somebody in town already thought I was a whore and a killer—but for Milo's. I might never have been in love with him, but I cared.

"To hell with it," I said, picking up a dishrag and slinging it at the sink.

Tom stepped in front of me. "Don't get upset. I didn't expect you to live a celibate life. I've always wondered about you and Dodge."

"Oh." I let out a big sigh. So that's what accounted for his attitude toward the sheriff. Tom already knew, and didn't condemn me. Not that he had any right to criticize. "Milo and I were friends, then lovers. Now we're friends again, but he doesn't like that very much. Still, I'm very fond of him."

"A good choice," Tom remarked, brushing my hair with his lips. "Solid. Dependable. Reliable."

I jerked away. "That was always the problem. Describe Milo, and you're describing a Kenworth truck."

Tom's expression was droll. "You prefer a sportier, less trustworthy type?"

"You're not that," I said in a tired voice. "I trust you. But I couldn't rely on you. You weren't here."

"And Milo was." Tom spoke lightly as he moved away and picked up his coffee mug. "What do you think he wants to tell you?"

"Something about Nat Cardenas, I suppose." A sudden chill came over me. "Good God, do you think Nat killed Crystal?"

The phone rang before Tom could reply. This time it was Vida, and as I should have predicted, she was agog.

"Billy called me from the sheriff's office," she announced. "He was ever so reticent, though he knows better than to hide things from his aunt. They found some incriminating evidence about Nat Cardenas at Crystal's cabin."

"Such as what?" I scribbled Vida's name on a notepad I kept on the counter. Tom, looking amused, nodded.

"That's what Billy, the little wretch, wouldn't tell me," she groused. "The only reason he called was because he was supposed to have the weekend off, and he promised last night that he'd shovel my walk. Then he called this morning to say he couldn't come. He had to work, as there had been some sort of emergency. The most I could get out of him was that it had something to do with Nat Cardenas."

I was reluctant to admit that Milo was on his way. What was worse, I didn't know if I should tell Vida that Tom was with me. In her contrary way, she would be ecstatic.

Tom made the decision for me by gently but firmly removing the phone from my grasp. "Hello, Vida. It's Tom Cavanaugh. How are you?"

I could hear Vida's gasp from six inches away. Then she sputtered and glowed, though I couldn't make out much of what she said to Tom.

"Yes"—he laughed—"It's been quite a while. I hope I'll see you while I'm here."

More sputters, more glowing. I heard the words *dinner* and *lovely casserole*. Vida's casseroles weren't lovely. They usually tasted like library paste. Finally, Tom handed the phone back to me.

"So wonderful," Vida enthused. "Didn't I tell you? Aren't you thrilled? Patience is such an outstanding virtue." Then, her tone much altered, she asked again about Milo. "What should we do? Shall I call?"

"He's coming here," I confessed. "I'll let you know what he has to say as soon as he leaves."

"Coming to your house?" Vida shrieked. "Oh, my! Oh, dear."

"Don't fuss, Vida. I'll manage."

"Call me at once," she commanded. "Or should I try to come, too?"

"You can't," I said. Vida lived on Tyee Street, two blocks from where the Peabody brothers had last been reported working.

"Nonsense," Vida retorted. "Billy said the Peabodys were on their way. I can always walk. It's not that far."

It was a good five blocks, two of them uphill. The side streets were always the last to be cleared. "Don't," I insisted. "It's too dangerous. Maybe later in the day we'll all be able to get out."

"Rubbish," Vida replied, though not as forcefully. "We'll see." She hung up.

Tom was laughing. "She's a marvelous old girl. I wish I had one like her on every paper."

"You'd think twice," I muttered, "if you had to cope with her on a daily basis. Sometimes she can be pretty overbearing."

"You'd be lost without her," Tom remarked, and of course he was right.

A pounding at the side door startled us both. I hurried to peer out the kitchen window and saw what must have been Milo, looking like a very large snowman.

"Come in," I urged. "You must be half-frozen."

Snow fell from the sheriff, creating its own little drift at the entrance to the kitchen. Milo wasn't wearing his regulation clothes, but a heavy parka over snow pants and a hat with flaps that tied under his long chin. All I could make out was his mouth and nose.

He took one look at Tom and swore. "Son of a bitch," he muttered, "it's Cavanaugh."

"Sheriff Dodge," Tom said, extending a hand. "Your bravery does you credit."

Milo reached out a wet, stiff glove. "Bravery? This is nothing. I'm used to it." He glanced at me. I didn't know if he was referring to the snow or to our breakup.

"Coffee?" Tom inquired, nodding at the carafe on the counter.

Milo shook his head. He was shedding snow all over the floor, but didn't seem to notice. With a struggle, he pulled off his gloves and removed the heavy flannel hat.

"When did you get in?" he asked Tom.

"Last night," Tom replied evenly. "Just before the blizzard hit. Did you hear about Emma's brick?"

"Sam told me." Milo's hazel eyes regarded me with something I couldn't quite fathom. Disappointment? Anger? Irony? "It's not the first time."

"It's the first time at the house," I put in, realizing that I hadn't spoken until now. "The other rocks and such have arrived at the office."

"It's the weekend," Milo said, apparently dismissing my brick. "Yeah, I will have some of that coffee." He moved in front of Tom and went to the cupboard. "Don't bother. I can fend for myself."

I winced. I seemed to be in the middle of a turf war. Milo was establishing his familiarity with my kitchen—and thus, with me.

"I had to question Nat Cardenas this morning," Milo said as he got out a mug and poured his coffee. "Sam and Dustin finally got around to going through all the stuff we'd taken from Crystal's place last night. They called me first thing to tell me what they'd found." The sheriff sat down in the chair Tom had vacated. "It was pretty damned interesting."

"In what way?" I asked, also sitting down.

Milo had unfastened his parka and was taking out a pack of cigarettes. "We'd taken all of Crystal's business papers, along with her financial statements and computer disks. We saved the disks for last, which was probably dumb, since we didn't turn up much in the other stuff." He paused to light a cigarette, then offered the pack to me. I declined; Tom looked surprised. "She had her newsletter files on three of the disks," Milo continued. "Some of it was obviously being saved for future editions. One of the files was on Nat Cardenas. It seems he's a bit of a playboy."

My jaw dropped. "Nat cheats on Justine? Did Crystal name names?"

"Only one," Milo replied. "Some woman in Olympia. We'll question her, too. But there were others. Crystal referred to them—three different women—only by vicinity. Sultan, Monroe, and Everett. I went to his house today to ask him about this mess."

I was still staring. "In front of Justine?"

Milo chuckled. "Hell, no. Even I'm not that insensitive." He shot a quick look at Tom, who had remained standing. I wondered if the sheriff thought I preferred Tom because of his sensitivity. If so, he was wrong.

"Cardenas denied anything serious," Milo continued, "and did the usual, 'Why can't a man have a woman for a friend?' bit. We all know it doesn't work that way." This time the sheriff's pause was barely noticeable. "At least not with four different women. Not that I blame Cardenas in a way—Mrs. C. is so frosty that you could freeze a chicken on her butt."

If Tom was comfortable with this monologue, I certainly wasn't. Shifting in my chair, I managed to hit my knee on the table leg. "So what happened this morning?" I asked, grimacing with pain.

Milo's smile was thin. "Cardenas would rather hang himself from the roof of the college ad building than be embarrassed in public. Just because he's a big shot, he figures he can get away with things. Maybe even murder."

"Did you arrest him?" Tom broke in.

Milo shook his head. "No, not yet. I'm not jumping the gun this time."

The allusion was to a different homicide, where the sheriff had uncharacteristically moved too soon to make an arrest and almost ended up with a lawsuit in his lap.

"But I kept pressing him," Milo went on, finally taking off his parka. "It seemed kind of funny to me that Dustin had stopped Cardenas so close to Crystal's place the night she was murdered. After about twenty minutes of badgering, he admitted he'd been in contact with her and had gone to Baring to try to reason with her."

"You mean about the information she had on him?" I asked.

"Right," Milo answered. "She'd called him a week or so earlier to tell him she planned to run a piece on his affairs. Unless he could think of a good reason why she shouldn't."

"Blackmail?" Tom suggested.

Milo tugged at his ear. "I don't know about that. None of the other stuff we've found out about Crystal leads me to think she was a blackmailer. Her withdrawals way outnumbered her deposits at the Bank of Alpine. Of course she could have had another account somewhere that we haven't found yet."

"So she was—in her perverse way—doing Nat a favor?" I said, getting my nerves under control now that we seemed to be on less dangerous ground.

"Maybe," Milo allowed, "she was covering her own

ass. I'm hearing only his side of it. Crystal knew about these women. Somebody actually told her the name of that one, Astrid Something-or-Other, who's a lobbyist for higher education in Olympia. The one in Sultan is an ex-student—not a kid, an older woman, older than Cardenas. I'm not sure about the ones in Everett and Monroe. Anyway, Cardenas said there was nothing romantic with any of them. Crystal thought otherwise. So Cardenas went to Baring to explain, and when he got there, Crystal was already dead. He was going to call our office from her place, but he heard a noise outside and said he panicked and bolted. He was so upset—according to him—that he drove erratically, which is why he got picked up. Cardenas didn't want to admit he'd left the murder scene, so he made up the story about having a few drinks. That's why he didn't take the Breathalyzer test. He wasn't drunk, just scared. Or so he says."

"Do you believe him?" I asked, trying to make sense out of everything Milo had told us.

The sheriff sighed and put out his cigarette in an ashtray I'd taken from one of the kitchen drawers. "I don't know. If he isn't lying, then I'd sure as hell like to know who made the noise that scared him off."

"The killer?" I shuddered at the thought. For all I knew, the killer could have been in the house while I was there.

"Could be," Milo admitted. "But now we've got to look closer at this Dimitroff accident. What made *him* drive like a madman?"

"Fill me in on the time frame," Tom requested, finally having fetched one of my dining-room chairs into the kitchen.

Milo took a notepad from an inside pocket of his parka. "Ten-seventeen when Cardenas was cited. Make that closer to ten-twenty, ten twenty-two. Dustin likes to

keep his watch a few minutes fast, though I wish he'd syn-
chronize like the rest of us. He'd just sent Cardenas on his
way and gotten back in the squad car when somebody
called him on a cell phone to report Victor Dimitroff's
accident. He was at the scene half a mile down the road at
ten-forty. Dimitroff, by the way, was heading west."

"Dimitroff's the composer and possible boyfriend,
right?" Tom saw Milo nod. "Except that Crystal was still
married to Husband Number Two, Aaron . . . I forget."

"Conley," I put in as another loud knock sounded at
the back door. "Now what?" I got up to peek outside.

Only Vida could have done herself up to look like a
clumsily wrapped Christmas package. She was wearing
wavy red, white, and green stripes. Under the patches of
snow, the fuzzy garment seemed to be mohair and might
have been a coat. Something that might have been a belt
was wound around her torso at least three times. The
collar was pulled up to her nose and she wore a red-and-
white striped knit hat. She'd collected so much snow on
her person that she looked as if she had rolled all the
way from her house at Sixth and Tyee to mine at Fourth
and Fir.

"Well!" she exclaimed, tromping into the kitchen. "It
looks like you have company. Good morning, Milo." She
gave the sheriff a nod. "Tommy!" Vida engulfed him in
an embrace. "How nice!" she cried, her voice muffled.
"And such a surprise."

"Vida." Tom grinned, pretending not to notice that he
was now covered with crusted snow. "You look . . .
amazing."

Vida beamed and finally stood back. "Yes. Well, now."
She paused, and Tom took the cue.

"Let me get a chair from the dining room," he offered.

"Thank you, Tommy." Her gaze traveled to me. "I hate

to ask, Emma dear, but could I have a cup of hot tea? It's rather brisk outside."

Dutifully, I put the teakettle on the stove. "You're lucky you didn't break something," I remarked, and almost wished she had. What had started out as a romantic snowbound idyll was now utterly shattered. In novels, Tom and I would have whiled away the hours in bed. In real life, I had a jealous sheriff and a snoopy House & Home editor crowding my small kitchen.

"You could use more coffee," Milo said, trying in vain for a refill.

"I'll make some more," I muttered. "Sit down."

"Are you having fun?" Milo whispered as he passed me on his way back to the table.

"Shut up," I snapped, observing that Vida apparently couldn't hear us. She was in the kitchen doorway, talking to Tom and unlayering herself from the mohair shroud.

It took ten minutes for Milo to bring Vida up to speed. It took half that time to make her tea and put on another pot of coffee. Since it was going on noon, I asked if anyone wanted a sandwich. Tom and Vida declined. Milo asked what I had to offer.

"Tuna, chicken, or ham," I replied, giving the sheriff an evil look.

"Ham," Milo replied. "Got any cheese?"

While I made Milo a sandwich and piled some chips on a plate, Vida commented on the sheriff's interview with Nat Cardenas.

"After he found Crystal, do you think he searched for her files or notes or whatever you call those computer things?"

Apparently, Milo had wondered about that, too. "He might have. Which could explain why he didn't call us. He was too busy."

"Where were the disks?" I inquired, handing Milo his plate.

"She had boxes of the stuff," Milo answered, "which is why it took us so long to get through all of it. It would have taken Cardenas hours and hours to make a search. Crystal's labeling system was kind of weird. She used sort of a code, with just key words or letters. The Cardenas disk had 'ICU' on it. When Dustin first saw it, he figured it had something to do with the hospital and the need for another doctor. You know, Intensive Care Unit."

I shook my head. "I think it's a pun. Nat's first name is actually Ignacio. Crystal probably needed three letters for her computer files. Hence, ICU stood for 'I See You.' "

Milo grunted. "Some pun." He turned to Tom, who was at the window, watching the birds in the feeder. "How come you're not having lunch?"

"It's a bit early for me," Tom said pleasantly. "I'll fix something later on."

"You must feel at home, too," Milo remarked.

"Emma is very hospitable," Vida put in, apparently to save an awkward situation. "Too hospitable. It seems that someone knew what to look for in her medicine cabinet."

"Cardenas, maybe," said Milo. "The way I see those files, they're a motive for murder."

Vida frowned. "I thought you were still suspicious of Victor."

"I am," Milo replied. "That's the problem. Too many suspects. I don't have a motive for that Russian guy, but what was he doing at Baring right after Crystal was killed? What if he made the noise that scared Cardenas off? And now it turns out that Conley's alibi isn't worth shit."

Vida gasped, and shot Milo a disapproving look. He ignored her. "Dwight Gould went back to that tavern in Monroe," Milo said. "It turns out that Conley was gone for at least an hour, between nine and ten. He went off with some girl but she decided she didn't want any after all. She took off, but was bragging the next day about how she'd made it with this big-city-type rock musician. Her girlfriends knew she was lying, so we checked her out, and she'd gone straight home. Which means Conley can't account for that missing hour. He did show up again at the tavern to play another set around eleven. I guess he got there about ten-thirty. Unfortunately, my deputies weren't as savvy as her pals. They believed her the first time."

"So what are you going to do now?" I asked.

Despite talking so much, Milo had wolfed down half the sandwich. It occurred to me that he was probably hungry. I pictured him getting up early and struggling through the snow to get to Nat Cardenas's house. The sheriff had probably skipped breakfast. After all, he had no one to look out for him. The thought made me feel sad and just a little guilty.

Milo ate two chips and lightly touched my arm. "What kind of stuff are you really made of?" he asked.

I wrinkled my nose. "How do you mean?"

"Technically, you're still a suspect," he said in an even voice. "I'd like to lull these other bastards until we collect some solid evidence. I can't afford a mistake like I did last time and make a wrongful arrest, especially with somebody like Nat Cardenas involved. How would you feel if I used you as a smoke screen? I want to let everybody know that you're the prime suspect. Can you take it?"

I sagged in the chair. "Why should I?"

Milo's eyes darted in Tom's direction. "Let's say you owe me."

I bit my lip and reluctantly agreed.

* * *

Naturally, Tom thought I was crazy. Vida, however, felt that Milo's suggestion made sense.

"Don't discourage him," she said under her breath as she stood at the back door, winding herself back into the mohair outfit. "For once, he's showing some imagination. You must admit, he's not getting anywhere as it is."

"The thing is," I said, an ear cocked to the apparently innocuous conversation between Tom and Milo at the kitchen table, "I wish I hadn't agreed. You know how people jump on negative things and ignore reactions. My reputation will take a beating."

"Nonsense," Vida declared, yanking the ski hat over her gray curls. "You either killed Crystal or you didn't. When Milo arrests the real killer, your name will be cleared."

"What if he never does?" I asked in a bleak voice.

"Well . . ." Vida's eyes, which were almost hidden by the ski hat, veered toward the kitchen table. "That could be a problem," she said in a tone that was far too chipper for my taste.

I felt more than bleak. Frankly, I was scared.

Chapter Fourteen

By TWO O'CLOCK, Tom had a path shoveled from the house to the street. He'd also cleared off his rental car, which had all but disappeared under the previous night's snowfall. Tom seemed exhilarated by the task. Although he kept himself in good shape, he wasn't used to manual labor.

"I haven't shoveled snow since 1964," he said, grinning at me and leaning on the shovel. "My dad had hurt his back, so I came home from my apartment on Eastlake to clear the walks for him and Mom. It was just about this time of year."

Meanwhile, the Peabody brothers and their plow had reached Fir. If necessary, we could get out in Tom's car, though mine was still blocked by the snow in the driveway.

"I was going to get my Christmas tree today," I said, standing in front of the broken picture window. "Maybe I can do that tomorrow. It's still not snowing much."

"Isn't it early to get a tree?" Tom asked. "Sandra never ordered ours until the eighteenth."

"Ordered?" I gave him a curious look.

He nodded. "She always had Neiman Marcus deliver and decorate our tree. Last year—the last one she picked out—was all burgundy and gold."

I started to say that it sounded very beautiful, but candor got in the way. "I think that's horrid. What about

217

tradition? What about using ornaments that have been handed down through three generations? What about letting the kids decorate the damned tree?"

Tom gave a faint shake of his head. "That wasn't Sandra's way."

I didn't comment further. My gaze wandered to the mantel, where eleven pieces of my Nativity set reposed. I'd neglected to get out the twelfth piece the previous night, having been too caught up in the throes of passion. Instead of a sheep, I should have put up a figure of Salome.

"I'm an Advent disaster," I said out loud. "I don't know why I'm criticizing Sandra. I'll bet I'm worse than she ever was."

"What are you talking about?" Tom was standing in front of the TV set, having turned on a college basketball game.

I didn't feel like elaborating, so I went to the closet and took out two more sheep. "Have you ever hated anybody?" I asked, arranging the sheep between the shepherds.

Tom hit the mute button on the remote control. "I don't think so. Hatred is actually rare, and requires some very strong feelings. I've never gone beyond despising a few people."

"That's not the same," I asserted, turning my back on the Nativity scene. "I mean hating someone so that you'd like to wring their neck?"

"Their? Or her?" Tom looked amused.

"It's not funny." I glared at Tom. "It's a terrible thing, like a cancer. It eats away at you. That's how I feel about Crystal, even now that she's dead. She didn't know me, and yet she must have hated me. Here," I said, going to my desk and pulling out the back issues of *Crystal Clear*.

"Read this to see how Crystal took a hatchet to poor old Emma."

Since I'd highlighted the stories that attacked me, it didn't take Tom long. To my chagrin, he still seemed amused when he finished.

"Except for the part about you and Milo, it doesn't sound all that bad. Mostly, it's Crystal's opinion. I don't think you would have gotten far with a libel suit." He put the newsletters back on the desk. "Isn't it your pride that's hurt?"

I'd never thought of it that way, and Tom's suggestion angered me. "It's a hell of a lot more than my pride. It's my professional competence, my virtue, my ethics, my integrity," I said, my voice rising. "Not to mention my lack of Christian charity."

"For Crystal?"

The irony wasn't lost on me. "That's my point," I retorted. "I haven't got any charity for Crystal Bird. That's why I feel so crummy."

"You'll get over it," Tom said, glancing out the window. "It's stopped snowing. Want to go for a walk?"

"No." Arms folded across my breast, I plopped down on the sofa. "People will probably throw rocks at me. Or snowballs, at any rate."

"That's possible," Tom replied, a bit too breezily for my taste. "But I require some fresh air."

He went to the closet and put on his jacket. "G'bye," I muttered.

With a wave, he was gone. I pouted for another couple of minutes, then turned off the TV and dialed Vida's number. She should be home by now, unless she'd stopped too often with her usual gawking into open windows. By foot or by car, Vida couldn't resist peering into people's houses. I honestly believed she not only knew who lived at every address in Alpine, but what they did in their daily routine.

"You'll never guess who I ran into on the way home," Vida said. Then, before I could say anything, she went on: "Dean Ramsey. He was walking around town, looking at some of the houses that are for sale. He was particularly taken with the Burleson place by the football field on Spruce. They've moved into the retirement village, you know. It was in 'Scene' two weeks ago. They wanted to get settled by Christmas."

I didn't know the Burlesons, but I evinced interest. Vida, however, had zigzagged back to Dean Ramsey. "Dean seems like a very nice man, if a bit timid. Naturally, we talked about Crystal. He's been lying to us, Emma."

"About what?" I asked in surprise.

"Crystal. He saw her at Baring." Vida, I imagined, was looking like a cat in cream.

"Did he say so?" I inquired.

"No, not directly. But you recall the timber-parcel story that she got before we did? He told her about it. Dean apparently had some advance notice from Olympia."

"How did you wheedle that out of him?" I asked, even though I could imagine the answer.

"Oh, we got to chatting," Vida said airily, "and somehow it came up and I told him how mystified we were that Crystal had the news first and he became very apologetic and said it was his fault, he'd mentioned it. What do you think of that?"

"I'm thinking, why? Why, I mean, did he see—or at least talk to—Crystal?"

"I can think of several reasons," Vida said, her voice now jerky. "First, they *were* married. A courtesy call wouldn't be amiss. Didn't he—" She stopped for a moment and I heard a rustling sound in the background. "Didn't he tell us that he'd *intended* to see Crystal? But because she was . . . Oops!"

More rustling and a few cheeps ensued. I sighed, realizing that Vida was doing something with her canary, Cupcake. A bath, perhaps, or a claw clipping. Maybe she was putting his feathers up in rollers.

"So let's say," Vida went on, apparently subduing Cupcake, "that he had indeed seen her or spoken to her, but he didn't want to admit it after she was murdered. It would be quite natural. After all, they had a . . . Oof!"

"Vida, what are you doing?" I asked in a beleaguered tone.

"I'm changing Cupcake," she replied grimly.

"Changing him? He now wears pants?"

"Of course not," Vida huffed. "I mean, I'm changing the papers in his cage. In fact, I'm using old copies of *Crystal Clear*."

"That's fitting," I remarked. "What were you saying about Crystal and Dean?"

"They had a daughter. Maybe there'd been some news of her. Ah. Cupcake is secured."

"Good." I paused, just in case the blasted bird tried to shoot his way out of the cage. "I asked Dean about the daughter when I reinterviewed him. He said he still had no idea where she was."

"But perhaps Crystal did," Vida suggested.

"Could be. Are you trying to find a motive in all this?"

"It comes to mind," Vida said.

"Milo's already got too many motives," I pointed out.

"No," Vida countered. "Milo has too many suspects. He only has two motives. Nat Cardenas's and Aaron Conley's. There's nothing I've heard that suggests Victor Dimitroff has a motive."

"Jealousy," I said, "of Aaron. He and Crystal were still married. Remember how Aaron lashed out at Victor after the funeral?"

"Victor strikes me as someone who cares only about his tuba."

"Not his tuba so much as his musical compositions," I said, going to the front window to see if Tom was coming back yet. "Honestly, I can't tell with him. I can see Victor easily enraged, though, and possibly violent."

Vida didn't agree, and then proceeded to read my mind. "Where's Tommy?"

"He went for a walk."

"Oh." Another pause. "Weren't you thrilled to see him?"

There was no sign of Tom outside, just two kids pulling a sled along the quiet street. "Of course. I almost passed out."

"Do you have plans?" Vida sounded eager.

"No."

"No? Why not?"

"It's complicated." I sighed. "I'll explain later."

"No, you won't. Explain now."

I collapsed onto the sofa. "Tom's daughter Kelsey has moved in with him. She's having a baby and the father is a drug addict or a drug dealer or both. Tom can't make plans. He has to take care of Kelsey. When the baby's ready for college, check back with me."

"It's not as bad as all that," Vida asserted. "The daughter—Kelsey?—won't want to live with her father forever."

"Oh, no?" I shot back. "After this experience, she's probably off men for the rest of her life. She'll never marry, and Tom won't want her to take a job because he'll feel that she should be a full-time mom. It would have been nice if he'd felt that way about me twenty-six years ago."

"You're working yourself into a lather," Vida scolded. "You don't know anything of the sort. Do be patient. Sandra hasn't been dead for a year."

"Vida, I've been patient for a quarter of a century. If it's not Sandra, it's Kelsey. If it's not Kelsey, then it'll be his son, Graham. Or a crisis with the newspaper business or another San Francisco earthquake or some damned thing. I'm resigned. Forget it."

"Would you say yes?"

The unexpected question caught me up short. "That's beside the point."

"Hardly. Would you?" There was a dogged edge to Vida's voice.

"Don't ask," I replied in a sulky tone. "I can't possibly answer that question unless I know what I'm getting into."

"You know," Vida said accusingly, but she backed off. "It's a good thing Tommy is here. You're going to need him. The word is out."

"What word?"

"About Milo suspecting that you killed Crystal."

I made a face into the receiver. "How could it be? Milo was still here an hour ago. He couldn't possibly have spread the word so fast."

"True," Vida allowed. "But I could."

First Presbyterian Church had what was called a Telephone Tree to inform the faithful of deaths, births, and convalescences. As a lifelong member of the congregation, Vida perched on top of the tree, ready to spread the news.

I held my head. "Vida. You didn't." Then I started to

laugh. "But of course you did. It makes perfect, infuriating sense."

"You couldn't expect Milo to do it on his own," she said, bridling. "Especially on a weekend with the weather so bad. Crystal has been dead for over a week. People are starting to question Milo's competence. Not to mention that so many elderly and infirm are housebound in this snow and are afraid that the killer might be out to get *them*."

"Not a chance," I retorted, though small-town paranoia was annoyingly familiar to me. "Did you volunteer or did Milo ask you?"

"I volunteered," Vida responded indignantly. "I called the sheriff as soon as I got home. Then I got busy. It only takes a few calls when you're at the top of the Tree."

I wished I'd been a very big bear and Vida had been up a very small tree. "Vida—" I began, then stopped. "Never mind. I guess somebody had to do it. I still wish I'd refused to go along with this stupid stunt. I'm not even sure it'll work."

Naturally, Vida felt differently. We argued a bit, but I knew that trying to change her mind was useless. I didn't even bother pointing out that I thought Milo had gotten his bright idea as some sort of weird retaliation for Tom's presence under my roof and in my bed.

I'd just hung up when I saw two figures approach my house. Neither of them was Tom. They had almost reached the porch when I recognized Melody and Thad Eriks.

Amid much stamping of feet, they apologized for intruding. Curious, I showed them inside and offered coffee.

"No, thanks, Ms. Lord," Melody said, still looking apologetic. "We've come with a request." She turned to her brother. "Thad?"

Thad cleared his throat. "We heard some really bad news this afternoon. Somebody called my mother and said that Sheriff Dodge was going to arrest you for Aunt Crystal's murder."

Even in the aftermath of a blizzard, news travels fast in Alpine and reaches out beyond the Presbyterians. I flopped down on the sofa and indicated that Melody and Thad should also sit. They declined and remained standing stiff as a pair of snowmen.

"We shouldn't be here," Thad declared, with a nervous glance at the broken window. "We know it could be dangerous, but we let Sheriff Dodge know where we were headed."

Watching Melody's scared wide eyes and noting that Thad's usual self-confidence was in abeyance, I realized there might be an amusing side to being an alleged murderess.

"You're very brave," I said with just a touch of sarcasm. "What prompted such audacity?"

The siblings exchanged quick looks, perhaps seeking mutual encouragement. "You used to live in Portland, right?" It was Thad who spoke up.

"Yes," I replied. "For a long time. I moved to Alpine about nine years ago."

"You knew Aunt Crystal there, right?" It was Thad again, apparently the official family interrogator.

"Did I?" Until Thad mentioned it, I'd never made such a connection. While living in Portland, I wouldn't have known Crystal from the queen of the annual Rose Festival.

"That's how we figure it," Thad said. "You were still there when she married Aaron. How come she didn't divorce him?"

"Maybe she still loved him," I suggested.

"No," Melody put in. "She never did. It was an infatuation. She should have just had an affair and let it go at that."

"So," I queried, "why do *you* think she stayed married to him?"

Again, brother and sister exchanged glances. "It looked better, staying married," Thad finally said.

I frowned at the pair. "How do you mean?"

"*You* know," Thad said, his jaw thrust out.

I didn't, of course, but I decided to pretend. "Your aunt wasn't a conventional woman."

"Exactly." Thad brightened, as if I'd said something brilliant. "You knew her a lot better than we did. The problem is, everything would have been okay if she'd divorced Aaron like we thought she had."

"And why did you think that?" I asked.

"Somewhere along the line," Thad began, "like maybe five years ago, she wrote to my mother to say she'd separated from Aaron and was moving, so she had a new address. I didn't pay much attention at the time, I'd just started college up at Western in Bellingham, and I guess Mom and Dad figured Aunt Crystal got a divorce. We didn't know she hadn't until after she got killed."

"It was really upsetting," Melody said, her gaze straying to the window. Maybe she was hoping the sheriff would cruise by. "It doesn't seem fair that Aaron gets anything. He meant nothing to Aunt Crystal."

"He meant enough that she let him come here and live off of her," I pointed out.

"That's because she was so softhearted," Thad said.

It wasn't the way I'd have ever described Crystal, but I didn't say so. "It's a matter of law," I explained. "This is a community-property state. As long as they were still married at the time Crystal died, Aaron is entitled to everything she had except for the bequests she made to the two of you in her will."

"That's our point," Thad said earnestly. "That's why we're here. We're sure Aunt Crystal never intended for

Aaron to get any of it. We think she made a second will just before she died."

Candor was my only option. "I don't know. Have you asked Marisa Foxx? I understand she made out the first one for your aunt."

"I called her right after the funeral," Thad said. "Ms. Foxx insisted there wasn't a second will, or if there was, she hadn't made it for Aunt Crystal. Anyway, she said that if she had, it'd probably not be a new one, but a codicil."

"We thought that since you knew Aunt Crystal from way back," Melody said, sounding pettish, "you might know what she'd done about the will. After all, you were the last person to see her alive."

I bit back a denial. "I don't know anything about it. I really don't understand why you think there is a second will or a codicil. Your aunt didn't expect to die, you know."

"She didn't expect Aaron to show up, either," Thad declared. "That's why we think she would have changed everything."

"I think you're wrong," I said.

Brother and sister started for the door, though they didn't turn their backs on me. "You ought to know," Melody said in a sullen tone.

"No," I asserted, standing up, "I don't know. And if I were you, I'd think twice about changes in your aunt's will. What if she left everything to her daughter, Amber? What if she cut you both out of your inheritance?"

"Never," Thad shouted. "We were the children she wished she'd had instead of that weirdo, Amber."

Melody was looking pugnacious. "Amber ran away a long time ago, about the time I started high school. Nobody knows what happened to her and nobody cares.

Anyway, Aunt Crystal wouldn't have left her a dime. Amber was a narrow-minded little bitch."

"How do you know that?" I demanded, trying to look menacing.

"Because Aunt Crystal told us all about her rotten daughter," Melody replied, backpedaling in step with her brother. "It wouldn't surprise me if she was the one who killed her mother."

Apparently, my killer act had bombed, at least with the Eriks offspring. Or maybe they preferred to believe that their cousin had done the deed. That would certainly sew up the inheritance for them if Amber ever resurfaced and took the matter to court.

As Melody and Thad skittered away, they almost collided with Tom on the plowed path to the street.

"Who's that?" he asked, puffing a little as he came through the door.

While Tom eased himself out of his boots, I explained, including how it felt to have someone look at you as if you might have killed another human being.

"Did you scare them away?" He grinned as he sat down next to me on the sofa and held my hands. His fingers were like ice.

"Well," I began, "that's the funny thing. Melody and Thad acted nervous, but there wasn't much else there. Either they're too shallow to comprehend what it's like to talk to a killer, or they know I really didn't do it."

"You think one of them did?" Tom asked, wiggling his toes in his thermal socks.

I grimaced. "I don't know. I don't think so. But I have to wonder why they're so insistent about another will or a codicil. If such a thing exists, Marisa Foxx didn't draw it up. If she didn't do it, who did? And wouldn't Crystal have kept a copy? Milo never mentioned finding anything of the sort."

Tom looked puzzled. "You say these kids insisted Crystal wouldn't leave anything to Aaron? Why not, if she was helping him financially?"

"I don't know, because I didn't know Crystal. Melody and Thad did, if briefly. Another thing," I added as three people passed by on foot and swiveled in the direction of my picture window, "those kids don't think much of their runaway cousin."

"The missing daughter?" Tom leaned back against the sofa. "How come?"

"I don't know that, either. I suppose Aunt Crystal told them tales. Melody and Thad are a couple of gullible, small-town products," I explained. "Kinship is very important— unless you're in a family feud. I figured that poor Amber was driven away by her ornery mother. But the Eriks kids aren't going to see it that way, not when they get the bulk of her estate."

For a few moments, Tom was silent. "Melody and Thad don't know who killed Crystal. I'll bet they really don't believe you did it. They may have come by to see how you'd react."

A couple of cars crept along Fir. I had the feeling they, too, were rubbernecking, out to see what a real live murderess looked like. As if they didn't know, having seen me around town for years.

"None of it makes sense," I said. "As for drawing conclusions that I must have known Crystal in Portland, I suppose that makes more sense. If I'd actually killed the wench, we might have had a history."

Tom lifted my chin. "You're bitter."

"I'm pissed. At Milo and Vida, for getting me into this mess."

Tom gave a shake of his head. "I don't know, Emma. It sounds to me as if it's working. You've already had a couple of callers. Maybe you can just sit here and have the whole mystery unfold in your living room."

"Don't be a smart-ass, Tom." I looked outside as a pickup stopped by my mailbox. A gangly man with a scruffy beard got out and planted a sign at the edge of the street. "Oh, shit!" I started for the door.

Tom was right behind me. In fact, he pushed me aside and headed into the yard, shouting for the man to stop. Unfortunately, Tom hadn't put on dry shoes. He took ten steps before his thermal socks began to freeze on the path. Tom swore while the man in the pickup truck drove off, honking his horn.

"Hand me my boots," Tom called. "I'm going to get that sign."

I obeyed. Moments later, Tom stomped back to the porch, sign in hand. It read, YOUL FRY.

"Charming," I remarked. "I wish I'd be harassed by people who can spell. You should see some of the letters I get. Especially the ones addressed to Emmy Lard."

"I've seen a few like that in my time," Tom said grimly. He took the sign directly to the fireplace and stuffed it in the grate.

I threw my arms around his waist. "God, but I'm glad you're here. I'm scared."

"You? Scared?" Tom hugged me tight. "I didn't think that was your style."

"It isn't. Not as a rule. But this caper is creepy. Look, it isn't quite four, and it's already getting dark."

"I'm not going anywhere." Releasing me, Tom knelt by the hearth and began to build a fire. "Have you ever thought of this scam as Milo's cry for help?"

"What?" I was incredulous.

"He's stumped. Or baffled, as they say in the head-lines." Tom paused while he stuffed kindling on top of the wretched sign and a handful of old newspapers. "He can't ask you for help, because you and he are on the outs. Dodge has pride, you can see that. By putting you in this rather awkward position, he knows you'll knock yourself out to help solve the case."

"That's Machiavellian," I responded. "Too much so for Milo."

"Maybe not consciously," Tom said as he lit a match. "But I'll bet that's part of it. He's feeling desperate. Didn't you say he made a wrongful arrest a while ago?"

"He did," I admitted. "It could have gotten really ugly, but he bailed himself out."

"So he's feeling unsure of himself." Tom sat back down next to me. "What do you want to do first?"

I stared at him. "About what? Solving the stupid case?"

Tom nodded. "Where do we start?"

"I already did. I've talked to Dean Ramsey and Victor Dimitroff and the Eriks family—you're right," I interrupted myself. "I haven't even officially met Aaron Conley."

"When should we drive down to Baring?"

I glanced outside. Despite the encroaching darkness, there was no sign of a new snowfall. "Now. The pass is open, and the main thoroughfares in town are plowed. But if we take my car, we'll have to dig it out first."

"The rental will do," Tom said, getting up to make sure the fireplace screen was secure. "It has studded tires."

Ten minutes later, we were waiting at the railroad crossing for the Christmas train from Leavenworth to pass. Every December, the Bavarian-style town on the other side of the summit put on a tree-lighting ceremony. It was an event that Alpine could have borrowed if not stolen, but no one in town could agree on exactly what kind of festivities we should host. Maybe Crystal should have gotten up in arms about that issue. I would have ridden the hobbyhorse right along with her.

I glimpsed happy tourists through the windows. Every year, I promised myself I'd drive to Leavenworth and enjoy the ceremony. And every year, I got too busy to do anything but run in place. Feeling frantic didn't make my spiritual journey any smoother.

The safety barriers went up and we crossed the bridge over the Sky, heading for Highway 2.

"It's beautiful up here," Tom remarked as we wound our way downhill past small waterfalls that were frozen in place and trees heavy with new snow.

"It's a long winter, though," I pointed out. "Actually, the snow came late this year. I don't think they've had any yet over in Leavenworth. The altitude there is much lower than in Alpine."

The cross-state highway was busy on a late Saturday afternoon. The ten-mile stretch between the turnoff to Alpine and the whistle-stop of Baring was familiar to me, but relatively foreign to Tom. He took his time, not risking to get around the slow-moving trucks that blocked our way.

We passed the ranger station, the road that led into Skykomish, and tiny Grotto, with its modest little sign. Then, just as the river edged closer to the highway, I showed Tom where to turn for Crystal's cabin.

"It's peaceful up here," he said, steering cautiously up the twisting road where the bare vine maples arched over us like a portal. "Except for the occasional murder, of course."

"Of course." I smiled a bit thinly. Was Tom trying to talk himself into something? "It's contentious, though. Little things become big things. Cleaning the bird poop off Carl Clemans's statue in Old Mill Park can trigger a small war. The money—all one hundred bucks of it—could be better spent on planting begonias around the flagpole. The next thing you know, the town is up in arms. People who think that little places like Alpine are utopias don't really understand what goes on."

"I know what goes on," Tom said as he parked behind the dirty white van that had almost run me down in the middle of Front Street. "I own several small-town papers, remember?"

"It's not the same as living in those small towns," I said.

Tom didn't respond, but got out of the car and stood gazing up at the cabin. "So this is the House of Death," he said as I joined him. "It looks pretty ordinary."

"That's the secret of all these little Edens tucked away amid nature's glory. They're very deceptive."

Tom knocked three times. We could hear loud music, mostly bass, inside. Finally, the door opened to reveal Aaron Conley, dressed in T-shirt and jeans. He could have been on the beach at Malibu instead of in a snow-covered cabin at Baring.

"I know you," he said, jabbing a thumb in my direction. "You're from the paper."

He started to close the door, but Tom had already put out a hand. "Hold it. We just want a few minutes of your time. Don't you want to have your side aired?"

Boom-thump-whump-boom went the bass. I flinched as we stepped inside.

"My side of what?" Aaron said in a sullen tone. "And who the hell are you?" He jabbed his thumb at Tom.

"Turn that thing down," Tom ordered in an irritable voice.

"What thing?" Belligerence was written large on Aaron's bearded face.

Crystal's CD player—now legally Aaron's—was in a corner, by some bookcases. Tom strode across the room and punched the power button.

"There," he said, putting out a hand to Aaron. "I'm Tom Cavanaugh, a longtime friend of Emma Lord's. How do you do?"

The return to quiet—and civility—apparently had an effect on Aaron. He shook hands docilely enough, then sat down on the leather couch. The coffee table in front of him bore an almost empty bottle of wine and a bong. I recognized the smell of marijuana.

"What's up, man?" Aaron asked, slouching on the couch.

Not having been invited to sit, I leaned against the bookcase. Tom stood in the middle of the room, hands in pockets. "We hear your alibi's shot," Tom said in an amiable tone. "Now what?"

Apparently Aaron wasn't on the Presbyterian grape-vine or its extensions. "Hey, I don't give a shit," he said with a little laugh. "I didn't do Crystal. She was cool."

"Even though she left you?" Tom asked.

Aaron raised both hands. "So? Shit happens. We weren't doing it for each other anymore. What's to save?"

"What about Amber?" I asked.

"Amber?" Briefly, Aaron looked mystified, then he grinned, revealing a space between his front teeth. "Oh, you mean Lolita. She booked. Long time ago." The grin faded, but his pale blue eyes seemed hopeful. "Has she turned up?"

I shook my head. "No. I take it you haven't heard from her?"

"Hell, no." He lighted a cigarette, of the legal, if still lethal, variety. "She wouldn't have shit to do with me. Not anymore. She was a real little priss."

"I thought you called her Lolita," I said.

Aaron laughed. "That was *my* perception, not hers."

"Is that why she ran away?" I asked. "Because you made moves on her?"

"Hell, no." His face fell. "At least, I hope it wasn't. I never thought about that."

"Why did she leave?" Tom queried as he sat down on a ladder-backed chair that had thrift store written all over it.

"Amber and her mom didn't get along," Aaron replied from behind a blue haze of smoke. "You could call it a personality clash." He laughed again. "Hey, you guys don't really think I killed Crystal, do you? Man, I'm clean on that one. I was puking up my guts in an alley behind some tavern down the road."

"Really," I said in distaste. "And now you're nicely settled in. Do you plan to stay in Baring?"

"Why not?" Aaron gave me what might have passed for a friendly grin. Or maybe it was a leer. "I snowboard. This setup's perfect for the winter, a hell of a lot cheaper than Tahoe or even Timberline."

Moving a pile of what appeared to be literary magazines from a leather hassock, I, too, sat down. "Tell me, Aaron, why did you come to see Crystal?"

He shrugged. "Why not? Like I said, we were mates. As in friends. No hard feelings. I was in Seattle, chilling with some guys I'd met in L.A. I thought, what the hey? I'll go see Crys. That's what I always called her. Crys."

"You were broke," I said.

"So? What else is new?" Aaron snickered as he puffed on his cigarette. "That's not a crime."

"Didn't you find it odd that Dean Ramsey posted your bail?" I asked.

"Ramsey?" Aaron frowned, as if he were trying to

place the name. "You mean old Dino. No. He's a straight-up kind of guy. You have to admire anybody who's so to-tally uncool."

"Do you think," Tom put in, "that Dean killed Crystal?"

Aaron looked contemptuous. "Never. That's too weird. Old Dino wouldn't hurt a bug. Besides, why should he care? They split up about a thousand years ago."

"He doesn't always tell the truth, though," I remarked.

"Dino?" Aaron scowled. "I don't think so."

"He told me a lie," I asserted. "He said he hadn't been in contact with Crystal since she moved here. But that's not true. He talked to her, at least."

"Could be." Aaron had turned indifferent as he slugged down the last of the wine.

"Why would Dean lie?" I persisted.

Aaron shrugged again. "Maybe he forgot. Or maybe it was none of your business." He gazed somewhere in my direction through half-closed eyes.

"Did you know he'd seen Crystal?" I wasn't giving up easily. So far, I considered our visit to Aaron Conley a big fat flop. What was worse, he seemed to be heading for a distant planet. I felt a sense of urgency to get at least a smidgen of information out of him before his spaceship went into orbit.

Aaron picked at something in his beard. "I don't think he mentioned it. But then we never had time for a real one-on-one talk, you know?"

I suppressed a sigh. If Aaron's eyes had been a little foggy when we arrived, what little I could see of them now looked utterly glazed.

"One last question," I said, getting to my feet. "At the funeral, why did you burst out at Victor Dimitroff so angrily?"

The eyelids lifted slightly, like window blinds on a

faulty roller. Aaron opened his mouth, then hesitated as if he were concentrating. Finally, he spoke:

"Who's Victor Dimitroff?"

Chapter Fifteen

"A washout," I pronounced as we got back into the Taurus. "I don't think Aaron knows what universe he's in."

"Maybe your next question should be put to Victor," Tom said, turning the key in the ignition, "to see if he knows Aaron."

"I talked to Victor at the funeral reception," I said, "and he certainly knows who Aaron is. He mocked Aaron's kind of music, claiming it has absolutely no value."

Tom looked dubious. "That doesn't mean Victor knows Aaron on a personal basis. He may only have heard of him from Crystal."

"Hunh." I was still annoyed. "We're no better off than before we drove to Baring. The only thing I gathered from that dim-bulb conversation is that Aaron is too flaky to commit murder. Especially a well-planned one like Crystal's."

"So it seems." Tom braked before turning back onto Highway 2. "It could be a ruse."

"I don't think so. You don't, either."

"But he did have a motive," Tom said. "A roof qualifies these days."

"That cabin suits him," I said. "But why pretend not to know Victor?"

"Don't ask me," Tom replied.

"He must have known Victor. They were both staying with Crystal."

"Where? The cabin didn't look as if it had more than one bedroom."

"That's so." I thought back to what I'd heard about Victor's visit earlier. "You're right. I think Victor was staying at the ski lodge, even if he did hate hotels and such. Maybe that's why he checked in there, instead of going to Crystal's. Aaron was already bunking at the cabin."

"Might that not rule out a passionate affair between Victor and Crystal?" Tom suggested.

I drummed my nails on my knees. "I'm trying to get a clearer picture of them both. Not to mention Aaron, who is fuzzy by definition. What's coming through isn't exactly passionate relationships. Victor's not the type, Aaron's too mellow, Crystal herself was . . . cold, detached."

"You never know about people," Tom said with a nudge.

"Never mind me. But you're right," I allowed. "I suppose a man as passionate about his music could also be passionate about a woman. Still, there's something about the Crystal-Victor-Aaron triangle that doesn't ring true."

"You left out Husband Number One," Tom said as we continued our steady climb up the pass.

"Dean." I drummed my fingers some more. "He's another unlikely candidate for a murder. Look, this was carefully planned, premeditated, the works. I can see Victor threatening Crystal in a fit of rage. Maybe Aaron doing ditto in a drunken stupor. Dean's another matter. He just doesn't fit either a cold-blooded killer or a homicidal fury. Besides, as I keep saying, this is premeditated."

Tom nodded. "Have you considered what I mentioned earlier about who'd want both of you out of the way?"

"Because I was set up as the killer?" I shook my head. "I can't think of a soul. There are plenty of people in this town who dislike me, they may even think they hate me, but they resort to things like letters, bricks, and signs in the front yard. In other words, they vent in a relatively harmless way. I don't think anybody really wants to send me to prison with no possible hope of parole. What would be the point?"

"Nobody's offered to buy you out lately?" Tom asked as we approached the turnoff to Alpine.

I laughed. "Hardly. In all the years I've owned *The Advocate*, I've never had more than two offers, and they weren't serious. In fact, *you've* never made an offer."

Tom chuckled. "Do you want me to?"

I turned in the passenger seat. "What kind?"

He let out a big sigh. "I don't know. Yet."

"Hey!" I looked in the side mirror. "You passed the turnoff. I should have reminded you. Now you'll have to wait until we get to a wide spot in—"

"We're not turning off," Tom said quietly.

"We're not?"

"We're going to Leavenworth."

"Tom! What about the murder?"

"It's not going anywhere."

"And we are? How come?"

"When that Christmas train went through Alpine, you looked wistful. Why not go see the Yuletide fun Bavarian-style?"

In all the years that I'd known Milo, as friend and as lover, we had often talked about going over to Leavenworth for the December tree lighting, the Oktoberfest, the January winter carnival, the summer river rafting, or just to sightsee. We'd never done it. Milo wasn't the impulsive type, and I didn't fancy myself a nag.

Now I was with Tom, and we were heading up over

Stevens Pass and down the eastern slope of the Cascades. I was smiling all over myself, which didn't prevent me from protesting.

"I look like a bum," I said. "I'm wearing crummy clothes."

"You look terrific," Tom reassured me.

If Tom said so, it must be true. I had, in fact, dressed a bit more carefully that morning, simply because Tom was there.

"We don't have reservations," I said.

"We won't need them. Didn't you say the tourist train had already left?"

"Yes, but lots of people stay over. The restaurants will be crowded," I pointed out, reverting to my usual perversity.

"We'll wait."

"You don't have chains. It could start to snow again."

"I'll buy some. Besides, we aren't coming back tonight."

"We aren't?" I stared at Tom.

"Do you really want to stay at your place and have a bunch of nuts come by slinging God-knows-what?" Tom shook his head at me. "Not smart. It'd ruin your disposition."

"They might wreck the house," I declared.

"I'm sure Milo has somebody watching it. Call him when we get to Leavenworth."

My arguments, feeble as they were, justifiably faded away. "I will," I said. "I'll call whoever is on duty." There was no point in rubbing it in with the sheriff. "I should call Vida, too. She'll fuss if she calls and I'm not home."

"She'll know you're with me."

"She might think you left."

"Emma . . ." There was a reproachful note in Tom's voice.

"Okay, okay. I'll shut up."

I leaned back against the seat. It was different, it was strange, it was *good* to turn my life over to someone else for a change. My cherished independence could sit on the shelf for a few hours. I wondered if I could get used to it.

Leavenworth in December glitters like a Hapsburg jewel. The old railroad town's Bavarian-style architecture with its rococo storefronts and picturesque painted exteriors looks even more authentic at night. Thousands of fairy lights are strung along the main streets, and visitors bustle from shop to shop. There was no snow on the ground, only on the mountains that rose above the town. That suited me fine. I'd seen enough snow during the last few weeks.

I slipped my arm through Tom's. "This is wonderful. I'm glad we're here."

"So am I." He patted my hand, then looked up at one of the shimmering trees that towered over the town.

I looked up at Tom. Despite the deep lines etched on his face, he still had that Roman-like profile and those keen blue eyes. Last night in bed, he'd told me more about how he earned those lines and the gray hairs. I realized that when I thought of Tom, which I often did, I always pictured him presiding over business meetings, or heading out on the town to whatever gala event San Francisco had to offer. I never dwelled much on what his life was really like. Inside that big brick mansion in Pacific Heights, there had been misery I couldn't possibly gauge. It showed in Tom's face, if not in his manner.

After calling Sam Heppner at the sheriff's office to let him know I wouldn't be home, we explored the shops. I bought a fierce-looking nutcracker for Ben, a denim shirt for Adam, and several varieties of German cheese. Tom and I also picked up some necessities, including toothpaste, toothbrushes, and a change of underwear. Then, in a fit of extravagance, I splurged and bought an Austrian ski sweater and a pair of black slacks which I wore out of the store. My vanity had gotten to me.

Inside one of the shops that featured Christmas decorations, I was entranced by a Madonna and Child carved out of wood. Their star-spun halos were made of something that looked like gold. Maybe it really was gold. The statue cost five hundred dollars.

"You really like that, don't you?" Tom asked.

"It's beautiful," I said, and started to turn away.

Tom signaled to the saleswoman, who seemed to belong in a Bavarian shop. She was tall and buxom, with blonde hair pulled back in a tidy knot. Her name tag read MARTA.

"Is that the only one of its kind?" Tom inquired.

Smiling pleasantly, Marta nodded. "The artist is very well-known in Germany. Everything he does is one of a kind." She tapped the Virgin's mantle. "See here? The folds are so graceful, so realistic. And look at the Infant's face. Isn't he precious?"

"Do you have a box?" Tom asked.

Marta nodded. She had the faintest of accents, and I wondered if somewhere along the line she had married an American serviceman. "Certainly. Are you shipping it or taking it with you?"

"We're taking it with us," Tom said, and got out his Visa card.

"Tom!" I exclaimed. "You can't. It's too expensive."

"I can. I will." He slipped the card to Marta. "I did."

I slumped against the counter. "I don't know what to say."

Tom grinned. " 'Thank you' comes to mind."

I hugged him around the waist. "I've never had such an expensive present. Never."

"Merry Christmas," Tom said, and kissed the top of my head.

With Tom carrying the statue in its sturdy cardboard box, we wandered off to Café Mozart for dinner. From there, he called the Leavenworth Village Inn to see if they had a vacancy. They did—amazingly, one of their two luxury suites. I grew dizzy with happiness, full of Viennese pastry and Rhine wine.

Unlike the previous night, when I felt that Tom and I were making up for lost time, we made love leisurely on the rug in front of the fireplace, in the tiled spa, and under the canopy of the four-poster bed. Sometime around midnight, I fell asleep in Tom's arms and didn't wake up until almost nine.

At first, I was confused, almost panicky. Then I saw Tom coming out of the bathroom, wearing one of the white terrycloth robes the inn provided.

"Mass is at ten," he said. "I checked. The church is called Our Lady of the Snows."

"No snow here," I murmured into the down pillow. "Would people condemn us for going to Mass after we've made love like minks?"

"Of course." Tom smiled, opening a package of new socks. "But that's not the point of going to Mass, is it?"

"No," I replied, prying my eyes wide open, "it's not. It's for sinners. Like us."

"Then get your rear in gear so we can have breakfast first," Tom said, slapping me on the behind. "They serve it continental style in the Garden Room."

Stark naked, I stumbled out of bed and headed for the bathroom. *This can't last,* I told myself as I stuck my head under the shower. *Enjoy it while you can.* I had to shed my usual perversity and seize the moment. *Carpe diem, carpe diem,* I repeated as the warm water beat down on my body.

I panicked. Hurriedly toweling off, I threw on the matching robe and rushed into the bedroom.

"What happens next?" I all but shouted, throwing myself against Tom.

"Hey!" He braced my elbows with his hands and held me away from him so that he could see my face. "What are you talking about?"

"This." I freed one arm and lashed out at the luxury suite. "Us. Tomorrow and next week and next year—"

Tom laid a finger on my lips. "Hush, Emma. Why are you so upset?"

"B-b-because," I sputtered, "th-th-this isn't real. This is a fairy tale, a dream. I'm going to wake up tomorrow in that crappy little cubbyhole I call an office and go over my useless editorial on the women's shelter and make sure Leo's got enough ads for all our special editions and check up on Scott to see if he's making his deadlines and—" I broke off and looked away. "I don't know what's wrong with me. I thought I was having fun."

"I thought you were, too." Tom looked very serious, even worried. Maybe he wondered if I was as crazy as Sandra.

"Damn." I staggered over to the closet where I'd put my new sweater and slacks. "I feel like a fool."

Tom, who was already dressed, sat down on the bed. "I can't tell you what's going to happen tomorrow or after that. I don't know. Some of it's up to you. Some of it's up to me. And most of it's up to forces we can't control. We're not kids anymore, Emma. We have burdens and we have responsibilities. Why can't you accept whatever happiness comes your way and not try to spoil it with worry?"

"I am," I said. "Therefore, I worry."

Tom sighed. "I know you do. You always have, as far as I can tell. And that's another thing," he went on, getting to his feet and pacing the width of the bedroom. "We don't know each other that well. We did twenty-six years ago, but that's a long time. Our lives have changed us. You're not a wide-eyed twenty-one-year-old girl. I'm not a mixed-up twenty-eight-year-old working the slot in the city desk. We've both traveled some bumpy roads, and done it alone, for the most part. When we first met, where did you think you'd be twenty-six years later?"

I had no answer. "Have I changed so much?"

Tom shrugged. "I don't know. I haven't been around you enough to find out."

Of course I had changed, in the sense that we all become more of how we began. But sometimes we are the last to understand how those changes affect us. We can't really see ourselves, except in dreams. And even then, there is illusion.

Illusion. Maybe that was all I was seeing now. This was a dream, and it would pass. The here and now felt very fragile. I hadn't seized the day or the moment. Instead, I was spoiling our precious time together. I wanted to cry.

"Just wait," Tom said, putting a hand on my shoulder.

"Wait?" I practically choked on the word. "That's all I've ever done."

"Then you ought to be good at it," Tom said lightly. He squeezed my shoulder. "How about getting dressed?"

I did, with hands and feet that felt like lead. We stopped in the Garden Room to eat some fruit, muffins, juice, and coffee. Then we walked to the church, which was a rather nondescript white building.

As the priest and the small procession of acolytes and lectors came down the aisle, I glanced at Tom, who was singing his head off. The man had a terrible voice, off-key and almost adenoidal.

I started to smile and put my hand over my mouth. Tom looked at me and frowned, but he didn't stop singing.

Maybe he thought I was on the verge of hysterics. To ease his mind, I patted his arm. The hymn ended and the priest began the Mass by inviting us to recall our sins.

Was gloom a sin? Pessimism was, which is the same, and hope is a virtue. I concentrated on the altar and felt my spirits rise. Not very high, but no longer completely stifled by *gloom*.

After checking out from the inn, we spent a couple of hours seeing the sights around Leavenworth, then had lunch at a restaurant called Lorraine's. The main square was packed again, with visitors admiring Father Christmas in his crushed-green-velvet robes, the life-sized teddy bear sitting outside of the chocolate shop, and the man who carried a huge cross depicting the crucified Christ.

On the way home, we encountered no new snow and arrived at my house a little before four. As I expected, there was a message on the machine from Vida. Actually, there were four messages, each one more anxious than the others.

"I should have known," she exclaimed in an overwrought voice, "whoever killed Crystal has gotten you, too. Couldn't Tommy stop them?"

Tom was laughing. "Vida thinks I'm Superman?"

"Apparently." I smiled, dialing her number.

At the sound of my voice, Vida let out an ear-shattering squawk. "Emma! You're alive! Where on earth have you been?"

"In Leavenworth," I replied. "With your so-called Tommy."

"Oh." Vida immediately deflated. "You should have called. I worried so."

I didn't explain, though I knew I'd eventually tell all to Vida. There was no way to avoid it, unless I had my vocal cords surgically removed. "Did anything happen in my absence?"

"Wellll . . . ," Vida hesitated. "In a way."

"What way?" I asked with an amused glance at Tom, who was rebuilding the fire we'd abandoned the previous day.

"After church, I decided to swing by the Methodists," Vida said, speaking very fast lest it occur to me that the First Presbyterian was in the opposite direction from Vida's house. "The Driggers attend services there, you know. I had to ask if anyone had collected Crystal's ashes."

Figuring this would be a fairly long story, I sat down on the sofa. "And?" I waved at Tom as he went outside to the carport, presumably to get more wood.

"Janet is so forthcoming," Vida declared. "I can almost forgive her rough tongue. In any event, she told me that the urn had been turned over to Melody and Thad. They intended to spread the ashes in the river, which may or may not be legal."

"You can dump them at sea," I pointed out. "Why not a river, especially this time of year, when it's running high and fast?"

"Exactly," Vida agreed. "And who needs to know? It put my mind at rest."

"Why the delay?" I said.

"Precisely my question," Vida responded. "Janet and Al didn't know, so I just happened to run into April and Mel in the Safeway parking lot. They stumbled and stuttered through their explanation—really, such a dim couple, so like Mel's parents, who could barely get out a simple sentence. Must that sort propagate dimness? Of course one wouldn't want them marrying someone too bright. The other spouse would go mad." Vida stopped. "Where was I?"

"Talking to Mel and April, who couldn't get out a

simple sentence," I said dryly. "I think I got lost somewhere at the 'dim couple' detour."

Vida ignored the remark. "Yes. It seems they delayed picking up the urn because they weren't sure what Crystal would have wanted. An excuse, of course, for not carrying out their duty. Then yesterday someone called their house to ask what was being done about Crystal's remains. April answered, and she was embarrassed to tell this person that so far nothing had been done. She hastened to add—because she was shamefaced, I imagine—that they were picking up the ashes that afternoon. Which Thad and Melody did."

"Who called to inquire?" I asked, wondering what was taking Tom so long to fill the wood bucket.

"Ooooh!" Vida sounded agonized, and I assumed she had whipped off her glasses and was punishing her eyes in a fit of frustration. "So vexing. April didn't know who it was. You'd think she'd have the sense to ask. She told me she got rattled. All she knew was that it was a woman."

"A woman?" I echoed as Tom came back inside. "Who could that be? Somebody who knew Crystal in Oregon?"

"Possibly," Vida said. "She must have had friends there. Al Driggers no doubt sent the obituary to the Oregon papers as he always does with people who've lived out of state."

Tom was putting the wood into the bucket on the hearth. I started to smile at him, then noticed the grim expression on his face. "I'd better go, Vida," I said hurriedly. "I'll see you in the morning."

I turned to Tom, who was standing by the sofa. "What's wrong?" I asked as alarm rose up inside me.

Tom grimaced. "You're not going to like this." He paused, then reached down to take my hand. "Somebody took a sledgehammer to your Jag. It's a mess."

* * *

The freezing weather didn't bother me. I was too upset at the sight of my precious car. The roof was dented, the windows and headlights were broken, and the tires were slashed. There was other damage as well, but the rage in my soul prevented me from taking in the details.

I stomped back into the house and picked up the phone. "That does it! I'm calling Milo!"

I dialed the sheriff's home in Icicle Creek. He answered on the third ring. When I told him what had happened, he said he'd be right over.

"Do you think it's totaled?" I asked Tom after hanging up.

Tom shrugged. "I don't know. The hood—or bonnet, as you British car owners would say—is jammed. I can't look inside."

"The body looks bad," I mumbled, then flipped through my Rolodex to find the home phone number for Brendan Shaw, my insurance guru.

Fortunately, he was home. After commiserating with me, he expressed guarded optimism. "You'll have to get an estimate from Bert," he said, referring to Bert Anderson, owner of the local body-and-chop shop. "Get it towed out there now before it starts snowing again. Gosh, Emma, I'm sorry. You've had some lousy luck lately. We missed you this morning at Mass."

"I was in Leavenworth," I said rather vaguely. As I knew it would, as I feared it would, the over-the-pass idyll now seemed as distant as last spring. Or did it? I had the memory, which made a difference. Which maybe, in some small way, reaffirmed me as a woman.

"Leavenworth, huh?" I could hear the smile in Brendan's voice. "Nice town, especially this time of year." He paused, then became more businesslike. "The problem with the Jag, Emma, is that it's not exactly new. Ten, twelve years old?"

"Thirteen," I said.

"Okay. Then we're talking about *Blue Book* value, which might not be enough to get it fixed. But talk to Bert, see what he has to say. And take it easy, will you? You've got your fans out here."

I thanked Brendan with more warmth than I thought I could muster. As soon as I hung up, Milo arrived. He looked upset.

So was I. "Where was your deputy?" I asked, trying not to sound completely outraged. "I thought you were going to watch this place."

"I was. I did." Milo glared at me, then turned to Tom. "Come on, Cavanaugh, let's have a look."

"Wait a minute," I snapped. "It's *my* car. Where was your damned deputy?"

"On the job," Milo snapped back. "Your little cabin isn't the only hot spot in the county." He started for the back door, then turned to look at me again. "Where were you?"

"Leavenworth." I bit off the word.

Milo didn't respond, but led the way outside. Doggedly, I followed the men, feeling like some woman in a third-world country bringing up the rear behind the tribal chieftains.

The wind was blowing from the south, whipping its way through the carport. I wished I'd grabbed a jacket. With my arms folded across my chest and my hands tucked up the sleeves of my sweater, I watched the two self-appointed experts study the Jag.

"It was done by something like a sledgehammer, all right," Milo said after several minutes of silent scrutiny. "Maybe during the night. Some of the snow has blown into the dents. Even if my guys had driven past the house, they wouldn't have seen anything out of kilter unless they'd caught whoever did it in the act. You didn't hear anything?"

"I told you, I wasn't here," I replied.

"It's pretty bad," Milo said in a tone that sounded a trifle too cheerful. "The front doors and the trunk won't open, and we can't look under the hood. Have you thought about a nice American car?"

Trying to keep my teeth from chattering, I turned my back and stomped into the kitchen, with Milo and Tom trailing behind me. "Have you thought about who's doing all this? Have you any suspects? Evidence? *Police work?*"

Tom, who avoided looking at me, closed the door behind Milo. The sheriff pulled off his heavy gloves. "How many names can you give me?" he asked in a reasonable tone. "You know damned well who your critics are in this town."

"You think it's one person or several?" I shot back. "Are they acting separately or is it some sort of conspiracy? Anyway, that's not the point. I want it to stop before I end up dead."

"You're safe." Milo glanced at Tom. "You've got protection. Round-the-clock, right?"

Even though I understood Milo's attitude, it was galling. If his wounds had begun to heal before Tom's arrival, they'd been reopened. That didn't surprise me. It was the depth of Milo's hurt that was disturbing. Had he really cared that much or was his masculine pride greater than I realized?

"Protection's not the point," I said, trying to calm my temper. "I've suffered from cranks before this. It's part of the newspaper business, especially in a small town. But this is different. It seems more dangerous." I turned to Tom. "Don't you agree?"

Tom didn't answer right away. "Maybe," he finally allowed. "But then I've had a newspaper burned right out from under me."

I was startled. "You have?"

He nodded. "It was a few years ago, over in San Bernardino County. A couple of rednecks took exception to my editor's stand on immigrants."

"I didn't know," I said in a low voice. "Were you there?"

He shook his head. "No."

Milo, who had been gazing somewhat longingly, if futilely, at the liquor cupboard, started for the living room. "Come down and fill out a complaint."

"Can I do it tomorrow? I want to get the car towed to Bert's Auto Shop."

"No, you don't," Milo said as Tom and I joined him by the front door. "You want it towed to the parking area behind my office. If you're getting serious about this, we have to go by the book."

Of course. "Do you expect to find anything?" I asked.

Milo shrugged. "Who knows? Too bad they didn't carve their initials into the roof."

The sheriff left. Tom, who hadn't yet lighted the fire, picked up the matchbox and then set it back down on the mantel.

"Let's eat out," he said. "You choose."

My gaze remained on the mantel. Once again, I hadn't put up a Nativity piece. I hadn't been here to do it the previous night. "Okay," I said, "but wait."

I went to the box in the coat closet and got out the last sheep. "There," I said, positioning the small figure next to one of his brethren. "How about the ski lodge?"

Tom was still looking at the stable and its growing number of residents. "Don't you pray when you put up something?"

I felt embarrassed. "Yes, usually. Something short, anyway."

"Then let's." He took my hand and bowed his head.

So did I. But all I could pray for was that the scuzzy bastards who had wrecked my car would run off the road and go over Deception Falls.

That didn't seem to fit the spirit of Advent, either.

Chapter Sixteen

VIDA ARRIVED BEFORE I did the next morning, breathing enthusiasm. "I've been thinking," she said, blowing on her steaming mug of hot water, "we must speak to Victor again. I sense that he holds a key to this whole business with Crystal."

"If we go," I said, "we'll have to take your car. Mine's wrecked."

"What?" she shrieked, almost spilling some of the hot water. "You wrecked your car? Were you *drinking*?"

"Of course not," I replied, sitting down in the extra chair next to her desk. "Somebody did it for me."

I proceeded to tell her what had happened while Tom and I were in Leavenworth. It took a while, since she kept interrupting to ask me several nonpertinent questions, including if we'd spent the night, where we stayed, what I bought, and did I see anyone from Alpine which would make an item for "Scene Around Town."

"Vida," I finally said in exasperation, "let me finish. Please. Or are you going to include my getaway with Tom as grist for your gossip mill?"

"Hardly," she retorted, looking askance. "Since when did I ever include love nests in 'Scene'?"

"Love nest" wasn't quite the way I would put it, but I let the subject drop and Vida allowed me to continue. Leo, Scott, Ginny, and Kip had arrived by the time I got to the climax. When I announced in somber tones that my poor old Jag was probably a car of the past, they all offered their sympathy.

"That was one sweet automobile," Kip said in a mournful voice. "I'll bet there aren't more than half a dozen Jags in Sky County."

"I saw a new one the other day gassing up at Cal's," Scott put in. "It was black, beautiful. Will you get another one, Emma?"

I made a face. "It's not dead yet. I have to wait for Bert Anderson to decide."

"Bert's nice," Ginny said. "Isn't it true he lost an eye up on Tonga Ridge? I went through school with his daughter, Cammy."

"Is Christine Anderson Bert's wife?" Leo asked. "She's the one who puts the Amway ad in the paper."

"That's Carolyn Anderson," Vida said. "Carolyn is married to Bert's brother, Ken. Ken sorts packages for UPS in the warehouse. He suffered a punctured lung working for Blackwell Timber."

Leo looked puzzled. "I thought Ken Anderson worked for Sears."

Vida shook her head. "That's Kent Andersen. With an *e*. He has two missing fingers on his left hand. Another logging accident."

Scott was looking dazed. "I'll never figure out who's who in this town. Not to mention how many of these guys have lost body parts. Wouldn't you think they'd be glad not to have to risk their necks cutting timber?"

"Heavens, no," Vida replied. "It's their calling, like the sea. How many crabbers do you know who have gone down off Alaska?"

"None," Scott answered. "I'm from Portland."

"So you are," Vida murmured. "A shame, really." She

turned to me just as I headed for my office. "When do you want to drive down to Startup?"

I glanced at my watch. "Not for a while. It's only eight-thirty."

"Then we'll leave around eleven," Vida said. "Perhaps you should call first."

I agreed, then began my day behind my desk. Kip had repaired the leak in the roof, which meant one less distraction. The snow had held off, and as I walked downhill to work, I felt that the temperature was rising. Tom had offered to drive me, but wasn't yet dressed. I had let him sleep in because last night he'd confided that he was only beginning to get back into a natural sleep pattern. The past few years with Sandra had practically forced him to keep one eye and one ear open. They'd had separate bedrooms for some time, but there was an intercom, and she frequently called to him for help in the wee small hours.

That was another thing I hadn't known about Tom.

I finished the editorial on the women's shelter shortly after nine. Scott brought in the contact prints from his photo shoot of the St. Lucy's pageant held on Saturday night at the Lutheran church. He had some excellent shots, no mean feat since there are only so many ways you can photograph young blonde girls with candles on their heads.

Ginny arrived a few minutes later with the mail, which brought yet more ugly letters. I skimmed them, but decided they could be evidence and stuffed the most recent ones into an envelope for Milo.

Around ten I called the sheriff to ask if he'd found anything helpful in or on the Jaguar. So far no luck, but Ron Bjornson, who knows his way around almost any kind of vehicle, wasn't finished checking.

At ten-thirty I phoned Paula's house in Startup and got the answering machine. I figured she was at the college, grading finals. Her students' term projects weren't the kind that could be brought home. When the glass pieces had been graded, the students would keep their creations, no doubt using some of them as Christmas presents.

"Nobody answers down there," I called to Vida. "I suspect Victor wouldn't bother himself to pick up the phone."

"Then we'll have to surprise him," Vida said, and looked pleased at the prospect.

"Okay," I said without enthusiasm. Surprising Victor Dimitroff sounded like an early wake-up call for a grizzly bear in hibernation. "We'll leave at eleven."

Vida scowled, but didn't say anything. I knew she was champing at the bit, but I wanted to call Tom to see if he was meeting me for lunch. He'd been in a sleep-induced fog when we'd made a tentative date to eat at the new diner. The drive to Startup and back, along with the interview, would take over an hour. One o'clock would be a more realistic time for lunch.

Tom didn't answer, so I assumed he was in the shower. I left a message, though I suspected he wouldn't check the machine. Milo was right. A cell phone was becoming a necessity, not a luxury. I called Stuart Electronics, formerly Stuart's Stereo, and asked them to make me their best offer. Ten minutes later, my head was reeling and Cliff Stuart had sold me "not the cheapest, but a quality item." It better be. My new necessity was in a luxurious price range.

On a late Monday morning, there wasn't much traffic along Highway 2, except for the blasted trucks. I frankly considered them a menace, especially on a two-lane, undivided road. For the past year or more, I'd considered starting an editorial campaign to get the trucks off the highway and load the freight onto trains. Or planes or ships or dogsleds. But I knew my feeble protests would go nowhere, and that in a community where trucks had been part of a once-thriving livelihood, I'd make even more enemies. Thus, I often seethed, particularly when stuck behind a semi on an uphill grade.

Vida, however, showed remarkable patience. "Victor can't go very far," she remarked as we passed the Money Creek campground. "He may even be glad to see us. I imagine he's getting cabin fever by now."

I was about to express my doubts when a horn honked as a driver passed us on a straight stretch of road.

"Really," Vida huffed, "I despise people who feel they must—goodness," she exclaimed as the red Grand Cherokee pulled back into our lane, "isn't that Milo?"

I strained to see who was at the wheel, but the Cherokee was too far ahead of us now. "I haven't memorized his new license plate yet," I admitted.

"It's the same as the previous one," Vida responded. " 'LAWMAN.' "

"Sorry," I apologized. "I didn't catch it."

"He's turning off," Vida said in surprise. "Isn't that the road into Crystal's cabin?"

"It sure is," I replied, and was far from amazed when Vida hit the turn signal and we, too, left the highway.

"Milo isn't going to like this," I said as we wound along on the gravel road. "Assuming that *is* Milo." Maybe I could appease him by telling him about the cell phone I'd ordered.

Sure enough, the sheriff was at the front door to Crystal's cabin when we pulled in behind the Cherokee. He turned, saw us, and threw up his hands.

"I should have guessed when I saw you on the highway," he shouted, sounding irritated. "How did you find out so soon? Bill Blatt?"

Naturally, the question was addressed to Vida, who gave a little start, then squared her wide shoulders. "Not Billy," she said in a vague voice. "I do have other sources."

I had no idea what she was talking about, and was pretty sure she didn't, either. But I could bluff right along beside her. We were going up the steps to the front porch when Aaron Conley opened the door about two inches.

"It's The Man," Aaron mumbled. "Dudester Dodge. The Lawmeister. How's business?" Then, before Milo could respond, Aaron saw Vida and me, and slammed the door shut.

"Come on, Conley," Milo shouted, trying the knob. "Open up."

This time, Aaron only gave an inch. "Not with those broads around. Hey, forget it. Nobody stole anything. They didn't even get in. I scared 'em off. I only called because . . ." He paused, apparently trying to remember why he had in fact summoned the sheriff. "Because of Crystal. I mean, like, maybe the killer returned to the scene of the crime."

Milo's shoulders slumped. "Jesus, Conley, I don't have time for jokes. Did you or did you not have a break-in?"

"Not exactly." The door moved another inch. "I mean, whoever it was, got scared off. Honest. I yelled when I heard the noise and then all I saw was somebody take off in a car."

"What kind of car?" Milo asked, obviously trying to keep his temper under control.

"A dark one. Older model. Maybe a Chev, or one of its spawns." Aaron seemed to be trying to cooperate, though even from my viewpoint on the porch, I could see his eyes were dilated and not quite focused.

"What about the noises?" Milo persisted.

"I was chilling in the hot tub," Aaron said. "I guess it was the front door. Right here." He rapped on the sturdy wood with its calla-lilly window. "By the time I grabbed a towel, there was nobody here. Then I heard somebody around the side of the house, sort of stumbling around in the snow. I went back inside and put on a pair of pants and some boots. By the time I got out on the deck, I heard the same noise, only more toward the front of the house. I came back out here and that's when I saw the car start down the road. It wasn't parked all the way up behind my van, like you are. It was just down there, by the bend." He pointed to the road a few yards beyond Vida's Buick.

Milo nodded. "That's it? You call that a break-in?"

"I call it damned weird," Aaron shot back, sounding almost like a normal person. "Who comes sneaking around like a freaking burglar and won't say who it is? Hey, Dodge dude, you think it's *fun* to stay in this place after my wife got killed?"

I kept forgetting that Crystal had still been legally married to Aaron at the time of her death. Mr. Weed didn't strike me as a typical widower.

"You can take off after your trial," Milo said, and poked a finger at Aaron. "It's set for January fifth, you know. Meanwhile, Merry Christmas." The sheriff turned on his heel and almost bumped into Vida. "Let's go," he muttered. "I'm done here."

"Aren't you going to look for footprints?" Vida asked.

"Hell, no," Milo shot back. "Do you really think Pothead in there heard anything besides what runs around in his burned-out brain?"

"I'll look," Vida declared, and moved quickly down the steps and around the side of the house.

Milo, however, was getting into the Cherokee. "Come on, Vida, get your damned car out of the way. I've got another call, out by Cass Pond."

But Vida wasn't deterred. I watched her for a moment, then joined Milo by the Cherokee. "What about Nat Cardenas?" I inquired. "Could he have been the person snooping around?"

Milo frowned. "You mean to see if there was more dirt

on him? No. What's the point? We have those computer disks, and we'll hang on to them until he's cleared. Then he can have them and throw them in the Dumpster. For all we know, he may be telling the truth. Those women are only friends. Like us." He shot me a perverse look.

Vida reappeared, waggling a finger at Milo. "There definitely are footprints," she announced. "Medium-sized. Aaron wasn't hallucinating."

"I never said he was," Milo retorted. "Not exactly. I mean he could have heard ten people outside, and by the time he wandered around in his usual daze, they'd given up. Face it, the guy's unreliable."

"Still," Vida began, "I should think you'd—"

Milo silenced her with an emphatic wave of his hand. "Forget it. There was no crime. It's not against the law to knock on somebody's door and then, when they don't answer, to go looking around the rest of the house. Conley's van is parked right there." He gestured at the dirty white vehicle that had almost run me down. "Who-ever it was had a right to assume he was home. End of story. Now let's get the hell out of here."

We did, with Milo turning back toward Alpine and the Buick heading west to Startup. Ten minutes later, we were at Paula's place. Vida had never been there, and, as expected, her reaction was critical.

"This was the Merrill farm, fifty years ago," she said, tromping to the door in her sturdy overshoes. "The Mer-rills were peculiar. They raised goats, but refused to sell them. By the time Marva Merrill died back in 'sixty-two—Curtis had passed on in 'fifty-eight—the goats were living in the house and Marva was sleeping in the barn. Ruby Siegel—she was in Sultan at the time, but had lived in Alpine many years ago—told my mother that the whole place smelled like an abattoir. Ruby never should have moved. She was bored in Sultan, which is why she joined the Ku Klux Klan and the Communist party. She didn't believe in either of them, but the meetings kept her busy. Unfortunately, she once got mixed up on the dates and appeared in her bedsheet at a Communist rally. The party members chased her all the way across the highway and down to the cemetery before she could tell them who was wearing the pointy hat."

I shook my head in an incredulous manner. Small-town ways could still amaze me.

Vida was already at Paula's front door. "All this glass," she said with a sweep of her hand. "Whatever happened to the walls?"

"The goats ate them?" I suggested.

"Hardly," Vida said, pushing the doorbell. "At least two other owners lived here before your friend Paula came along."

Victor didn't seem to be answering the door. "Maybe he misplaced his crutches," I said.

Vida rang the bell again. "Maybe he's antisocial."

Still, no response. I moved down the wide porch and peered through a window that was decorated with wild roses. "He's there, sitting in a recliner."

"Is he alive?" Vida asked in an irked tone.

"He's moving. He just turned a page in his book."

"Oh, for heaven's sake!" Vida rattled the door handle. Surprisingly, it opened. "Yoo-hoo!" she called. "Mr. Dimitroff? You have company."

"I don't want company," Victor called back in his deep, accented voice. "Go away."

"Don't be so ornery," Vida commanded, striding into the living room. Paula had removed all but the necessary walls and beams to open up the house into a continuous large room. Only the bathroom was enclosed. Vida took it all in, and looked disapproving.

"Mr. Dimitroff," she said, planting herself in front of Victor, "you remember us. From *The Advocate*."

Victor remembered, but didn't look pleased at the recollection. "Paula is not here. She is at the college."

"We didn't come to see Paula," Vida said, now exuding charm. "We came to see you. Goodness, are you quite comfortable? That recliner seems to be at an awkward angle."

"It's broken," Victor replied in a petulant tone. "Paula is not always a conscientious housekeeper. She should be more vigilant concerning repairs."

"Let me," Vida said, bending down. "Shift your leg away, if you will."

Despite his skeptical expression, Victor complied. Vida yanked at the footrest, gave it a tremendous pull, stepped on it with her considerable weight—and, amazingly, it reverted to its proper place.

"There! Much better." She smiled ingratiatingly at Victor. "Now, shall we chat?"

Victor looked uncertain. "Chat? Why should we chat?"

"We've just been to Crystal's cabin," Vida said, sitting down in an antique wooden rocker. "Aaron Conley had called the sheriff to report a break-in. There hadn't actually been such a thing, but it got us to thinking."

It had? I marveled to myself. I hadn't been thinking much of anything, except wondering if I could use Paula's phone to call Tom about lunch.

"Anyway," Vida went on, shedding her tweed winter coat, "we wondered about the night Crystal was killed and your auto accident. Is it possible that you actually went to Crystal's cabin and interrupted another break-in? Or was it the murderer?"

The color drained from Victor's face. "You are saying that *I* am the murderer?"

Vida uttered an uncharacteristic fluttery laugh. "Heavens, no! I mean that you may have encountered the person who killed Crystal. Which is why you were so upset and went off the road."

To my surprise—but probably not to Vida's—Victor looked shaken as well as pale. "What do you mean?"

"I've been perfectly clear," Vida asserted. "I believe that you drove up to Crystal's cabin the night she was killed. Either you found her already dead, or you heard her talking to the killer. Which was it, Victor? You can tell us. We aren't the police."

"Then why should I tell you anything?" he asked in a belligerent tone.

Vida started to speak, but I interrupted with a brainstorm. "Because you are a creative genius. Because you shouldn't keep trivial things to yourself. They clutter the mind and fetter the soul." I didn't dare look at Vida; my soft-soap blather was, as my father used to say, enough to gag a goat. A Merrill goat at that. "Because," I continued, on a shameless roll, "you don't need to be bothered with the menial matters that vex the rest of us."

Victor was no fool. The gleam in his eyes told me that. But I'd managed to prick his ego just a little. He closed his eyes and exhaled, as if the letting out of breath was preface to unburdening his troubled heart. Or something like that.

"I saw no one," he began, his voice growing even deeper. "There was no answer to my knock, yet I knew there was someone inside. This person made much noise. Of course I thought it *was* Crystal. There was no car parked there, except for hers. I couldn't understand why she didn't come to the door, so I went around the side of the house. The hot tub was running, I could hear it. I called to Crystal, but she didn't respond." He paused, passing a hand over his high forehead. "There was a tree near the deck, so I started to climb it in order to get up high enough to see into the hot tub. Alas, I kept slipping, then I heard what sounded like the slamming of a door. I started back to the front of the house and saw a figure running down the road. I could not recognize who it was, but I knew it wasn't Crystal. Too large, in every way."

"A man?" Vida interrupted.

"Perhaps. It was very dark. And," Victor added on a note of candor, "I was startled. Even afraid."

"So what did you do then?" I asked.

Victor cleared his throat. "I started back to the front door. But before I could get up the stairs, I heard the motor of a car. Whoever had fled must have been parked off to the side of the road. I hadn't noticed when I arrived. There is, you see, a sort of . . . what do you call a space to turn around or avoid running into a car coming from the other direction?"

"Turnout will do," I offered.

"Yes," Victor agreed solemnly, "a turnout. So I proceeded up the stairs and discovered the door had been left wide open. Perhaps the noise I made outside had frightened off the other person. I went inside, calling for Crystal, looking in the other rooms, going to the deck because I'd heard the hot tub running. Then—" He stopped, closed his eyes once more, and took a deep breath. "Then I saw her. There was no doubt that she was dead. I went quite berserk, I think. Frankly, I do not recall exactly what I did next. I assumed I'd just crossed paths with a killer. Would he return? Was I also to die at the hands of a madman?"

"Or woman?" Vida put in.

Victor frowned. "A woman? Perhaps. But dubious. In any event, I tried to find the phone. Crystal had one of those portable phones, and in my shock and distress, I could not find it. So I weep for a while, and then I am again afraid. I leave, driving back to the highway with tears in my eyes and shaking in my limbs. That is why I crashed the car. I was in terror and sick with grief."

"But," I pointed out, "you didn't mention finding Crystal to the deputy."

"No," Victor said in a sad voice, "I did not. I was afraid, you see. I thought the police would believe that I had killed her. In Europe, the police are not always understanding. Or so was my experience when I lived there many years ago."

"Poor man," Vida said with what sounded like genuine sympathy.

Victor finally met Vida's gaze. "I almost crashed many times before I reached the main highway. The road is crooked, narrow. Indeed, I missed a tree by millimeters. That's when I saw where the car could have been parked."

Paula's two Siamese cats, Rheims and Rouen, came out from behind the counter that divided the kitchen and living room. They slithered across the floor and came to rest at Vida's feet. She is not a cat lover, and gave them an intimidating look. The cats stayed in place. They always seem to know who hates them most.

Cars were parked in strange places outside of Crystal's cabin on the night of the murder, then, according to Aaron, again this morning.

The thought of Aaron brought another question to mind. "How well do you know Crystal's husband?"

"Husband?" Victor frowned. "Which one?"

"The second one, Aaron Conley." I eked out an encouraging smile. "He spoke rather sharply to you after the funeral. We talked about it later, at the reception. You criticized his kind of music."

"Justifiably," Victor responded. "That kind of so-called popular music is grease that escapes from the roasting pig."

"Yes," I said without conviction. The cats were now rubbing against Vida's boots. She gave them each a nudge, but they persisted. "Aaron and Crystal were never divorced. Perhaps you knew that."

Victor shrugged. "It is of no importance now, is it?"

"Not to you," I said carefully, "though I wondered how you knew Aaron."

"I didn't," Victor replied. "It is only his kind of music I know. Trash, excrement, debris on the musical path to what really matters in composition."

"I see." I didn't, but the musical path seemed to have reached a dead end as far as I was concerned. "May I borrow your phone?"

Victor hesitated, then gave a nod. On my way to the counter divider where the phone was kept, I picked up Rheims and Rouen. They wriggled in my grasp and let out that unearthly piercing cry that is typical of the Siamese breed.

As I walked away, I heard Vida mutter, "Wretched pests. Of what use are they?"

As I picked up the receiver, the cats escaped and raced off to their food dishes by the stove. Back in my log house against the mountains, the phone rang four times before again switching over to the answering machine. This time I left a message, saying that I would meet Tom at the diner around one. Maybe he'd figure out that I was trying to call him. On the other hand, it was almost twelve-twenty. He'd probably already left and was sitting in a booth at the diner, twiddling his thumbs.

Vida had put her coat back on and was starting for the door, offering profuse thanks to Victor along the way. I, too, thanked him, and then we were gone.

"Whose car was pulled off the road?" Vida asked as we got into the Buick.

"Your guesswork in approaching Victor was brilliant,"

I remarked. "Mine wasn't so bad, either. The car belonged to Nat Cardenas."

"Of course." Vida put the Buick into reverse and turned around. "So Nat wasn't drunk, and Victor wasn't as bad a driver as he pretended. Now, why didn't Nat call the police when he discovered that Crystal was dead?"

"The same reason that Victor didn't," I replied. "He was upset, in shock, and afraid that he'd be the prime suspect. Incidentally, you're making an assumption."

Vida's head swiveled. "Which is what?"

"That Crystal was dead when Nat got there."

"True." She grew thoughtful as we headed out onto the highway. "You know him better than I do. Would he do anything as insane as killing Crystal? You've said he's very political."

"That's right, but it cuts both ways," I answered. "He was protecting his reputation. Let's say he went to see Crystal to reason with her, beg, plead, whatever. She laughed in his face. She certainly laughed in mine. So Nat goes berserk and—" I stopped and shook my head. "It doesn't wash. The murder was carefully planned. I think you were right the first time. He found Crystal dead when he got there and then conducted his search. He came up empty and left in a panic. Maybe he heard Victor outside. All that tromping around and tree climbing must have made some noise. Victor isn't exactly a puma cat."

"Cats!" Vida exclaimed. "Especially Siamese. How do people put up with that awful cry they make? It's inhuman."

"That's because they're cats," I said. "Paula adores them. She's had them as long as I've known her. She couldn't keep cats in some of the other places she lived, especially apartments."

"Silly," Vida declared. "Can you imagine what they'd do to Cupcake?"

I could, and it was not a pretty sight. Yellow feathers drifted before my eyes. "Paula named them after two of the French cathedrals, Rheims and Rouen. For the stained glass."

"Ridiculous," Vida scoffed. "How can you be friends with anyone who'd name their pets after *windows*?"

I decided to drop the subject. We were passing the turnoff to Crystal's cabin again. All seemed quiet, but of course it was impossible to see beyond the first bend in the road. Who had been hanging around the cabin this morning? One of the Eriks clan? Dean Ramsey? Paula? No, not Paula. She drove a minivan. But I could imagine her stopping by to ask Aaron for a keepsake. As strange as it seemed, Paula had been fond of Crystal.

"We're going at this all wrong," I declared. "Instead of motive, we should be looking for a certain type of person, someone with an organized mind, an eye for detail, and a lot of patience."

"Not to mention," Vida said as we passed the Skykomish Ranger Station, "someone who had no qualms about pinning the murder on you."

"Which reminds me," I said in a waspish tone, "I hold you at fault for getting my poor Jag wrecked. You and Milo both, with your goofy plan to make people think I really did do it."

"Nonsense!" Vida huffed. "You agreed. How could we know someone would behave so viciously?"

"Viciously?" The word brought me up short. "It *was* vicious, wasn't it? I wonder. What if it wasn't just an irate subscriber? What if the killer did that to my car?"

"To what purpose?" Vida asked.

"I'm not sure. Maybe to make it look as if people really think I killed Crystal. Reinforcing the idea." I gave an impatient wave of my hand. "Never mind. I don't want to sound paranoid."

"Personalities," Vida mused as she turned off to Alpine. "You're quite right. Let's consider the Eriks clan. April appears to be a bit insipid, though I suppose that may mask something more sinister. Mel is mentally lazy. I see nothing cunning about him. Melody, I suspect, is easily led, especially by her brother. Yes," she said with emphasis, "I could see the two of them planning such a crime. Or Thad, acting alone."

We were crossing the bridge over the Sky. "Why don't you drop me off at the diner?" I said. "Tom's probably waiting for me there."

"Oh. Certainly." Vida took a left onto Railroad Avenue. "Do you see his car out front?"

I gazed at the parking lot, which was almost full. "No," I said, frowning. "There are at least two Tauruses, but neither of them is Tom's rental. He must have gone over to *The Advocate* to find out what happened to me."

"No doubt," Vida remarked, turning up First Street. "Goodness," she said, her eyes darting up and down Front, "couldn't Fuzzy Baugh find some money in the city treasury to buy new civic decorations? That gold tinsel and those artificial wreaths are beginning to look a bit shopworn."

"The city and the county can't find money for the women's shelter," I pointed out. "Or so they tell us. It's odd, isn't it? Crystal's fifty grand could have gone a long way toward making one of her pet projects a reality."

Vida turned to stare at me. "Are you saying that since she'd made a will, she should have left money to a shelter fund?"

"That's right." I paused as Vida backed into the diagonal parking place in front of the office and I scanned the street for Tom's car. "She didn't put her money where her mouth was."

We got out of the Buick and trudged through what had

become dirty slush in the last twenty-four hours. "I don't see it," I said in a worried voice.

Vida was opening the door to *The Advocate*. "Crystal's attitude, you mean?"

I lingered on the sidewalk. "No. Tom's car. I don't see it anywhere."

"Well," Vida said, tapping a booted foot, "come inside. I'm sure he's been inquiring about you."

Except for Kip MacDuff, who'd gotten takeout from the Burger Barn, the rest of my staff hadn't yet come back from lunch. Kip had seen only a couple of people placing classified ads.

"I've been in the back shop mostly," he said between bites of cheeseburger. "But when we get visitors, they buzz me and I come right out."

"I know you do," I reassured Kip. "You're very conscientious."

We left Kip and returned to the news office, where I immediately hurried into my cubbyhole to check messages. There were several, but none from Tom. Then I noticed the folded sheet of paper on my desk.

I opened it with shaking hands. I was already sensing the worst, and the bold, slightly illegible penmanship justified my feelings.

Dear Emma, the letter read.

I feel like a heel. But I called Kelsey this morning to check on her, and she's having some problems with her pregnancy. In fact, she was on the way to the hospital. It seems she's developed some bleeding, and the doctor fears a miscarriage.

I debated with myself—an agony, I assure you—but realized that my duty lies with my daughter. I'm heading for Sea-Tac and hope to catch a one-forty flight to San Francisco.

Please try to forgive me. Our time together was precious, wonderful, magical. I pray that it won't be long before we can be together again. I'll call you tonight and let you know what's happening.

I love you. I really do. Don't be angry, don't be sad. Yesterday was the third Sunday of Advent, when the pink candle is lighted as a sign of hope. Remember that. Please.

Chapter Seventeen

Scott had returned from lunch, so I summoned Vida into my office and asked her to close the door.

"Read this," I said, handing her Tom's letter.

Vida gave me a quick, sharp glance over the rims of her glasses. "Oh, dear," she said. "I have a feeling . . ." She lowered her gaze and absorbed the one-page message, then set the letter down on my desk. "Poor Tommy."

"Poor Tommy, my butt!" I exclaimed. "Come on, Vida, what about poor Emma? Why do you always take his side?"

Vida pursed her lips. "For one thing, he's a man. They're so much more helpless than we are. For another thing, in this particular instance, he's facing yet another possible tragedy. If Kelsey loses the baby, it would mean that Tommy will have had two great losses in one year. You, on the other hand, are miffed because he had to leave town in a rush. You're feeling sorry for yourself, which is natural, but you'll get over it. And," she added, narrowing her eyes, "please watch your language."

The last comment made me even angrier. "I have a right to feel sorry for myself. I've been in love with this bozo for over twenty-six years. He's virtually ruined my life. Now he shows up, an eligible widower, and he's got yet another millstone around his neck. It's as if Tom can't survive unless he's taking care of somebody else. Maybe that's admirable, but for once in his life, why couldn't that somebody be me?"

Vida gave a little shrug. "Because you don't need him. Not as Sandra did then, not as Kelsey does now."

"Bilge." I turned away, my face set in a grim line. "I've had lousy luck with men. Maybe I should give up on them. All they've ever given me is a lot of grief."

"Perhaps," Vida said quietly. "Twenty years ago, Ernest left me a widow with three teenage girls to finish raising. There was great grief, but we'd had many happy years together. I wouldn't have had our daughters without Ernest. Nor would you have had your son without Tommy."

"I could have had six sons if I'd never met him and married someone else," I countered, once more meeting Vida's gaze head-on.

"Did you *want* six sons?" Vida looked mildly aghast.

"Maybe." I felt my lower lip protrude.

"Bother," Vida breathed as she got to her feet. "You're being perverse."

I said nothing as she stomped out of my cubbyhole. As usual, she had a point. But so did I. If Tom hadn't ever come back into my life, I might have married someone else. Of course, he'd stayed away for twenty years. That should have given me time to find another prospect. But I hadn't. The few lovers I'd taken over the years had all been deeply flawed.

So was Tom. I heaved a big sigh. Maybe I had fixated on him, like an obsession. Somewhere, in my brief surge of adolescent romanticism, I'd read about a woman who had fenced in her man. The gist of it was, did she love him so much that she had to lock the fence—or did she love him enough to let him go?

At the time, I had practically wept over the brave

woman whose noble love had given her man his freedom. But thirty years later, I thought she was a sap. Selflessness has its limits. I wanted something out of life for *me*.

What I didn't want was Ed Bronsky looming in front of my desk. So lost in thought had I become that I hadn't heard him enter the news office.

"What's bigger than big?" Ed asked, beaming like a Kewpie doll.

"You?" I retorted without thinking.

But Ed was unfazed. "You got it." He wedged himself into a visitor's chair. "The TV project's moving ahead. Shirley and I had a bang-up time in Bellevue. Irv and Stu are really on the ball. They've got a script in the works."

"The cable network green-lighted the project?" I asked, unable to hide my surprise.

Ed's smile faded a bit. "Well . . . not quite yet. That's why Irv and Stu are having a script written. They figure that'll clinch the deal."

"Who's writing it?" I asked, cringing at the thought that Ed might have volunteered his own talents. In my experience with him on the job, his writing skills had been limited to phrases like *year-end clearance, deep discount,* and *factory blowout sale.*

"A freelance guy who lives on the Eastside," Ed replied. "Andy Butz. He's done quite a few scripts. Did you see that documentary a while back called *Squirrel Madness*?"

"No. I missed it." Miraculously, I kept a straight face.

"It was terrific," Ed asserted. "It was all about how squirrels commit suicide in the months of March and September. You know, they run right in front of your car and . . . splat! Then you feel real bad, but you shouldn't because that's the way the squirrel wanted to go out. I guess not too many die of natural causes."

"Maybe not." I was now biting my cheeks.

"So here's the news release I put together," Ed continued, taking out a sheaf of papers from his hand-tooled leather briefcase. When he worked for me, he had a vinyl number, and the only thing he usually kept in it was his lunch.

The self-promo was four pages long and included glossy photographs of Ed, Ed and Shirley, Ed and Stu, Ed and Irv, Ed and Stu and Irv. Now I had no problem trying to control my laughter.

"I'll go over all of this a bit later," I said, trying to exhibit at least a smidgen of enthusiasm. "We'll certainly run it in this week's edition." We would, if I could find an extra inch and a half in the paper.

"Great." Ed beamed as he stumbled to his feet and then winked. "You know, Emma, you may end up seeing yourself on TV. I spend quite a bit of time telling about my advertising career. Who do you think should play you? Anne Archer? Sela Ward? Jeanne Tripplehorn?"

"I'll give that decision some real hard thought," I said. "You'd better concentrate on Vida. She may be harder to cast."

Ed shook his head. "She's a cinch. Angela Lansbury."

Not even close, I thought, but in bygone days, I'd have nominated Dame Martita Hunt, with an extra thirty pounds. I waved Ed off and went back to my blank computer screen. The muse wasn't upon me. All I could think of was Tom, probably about to board a plane for San Francisco.

The phone's ring startled me. It was Milo, another of life's major disappointments.

"Vida's up to her old tricks, I see," he said in a weary voice.

"What do you mean?"

"She called Bill Blatt to tell him about your morning's sleuthing. Damn it, Emma, can't you two leave well enough alone?"

"What's well? Or have you made an arrest?" I sounded tart, and didn't care.

Milo sighed. Or was it a groan? "One of these days, you two are going to get yourselves killed. In fact, unless your memory's shot all to hell, you both almost did a while back."

"I recall the incidents," I said dryly. I had faced off with a murderer, and Vida had been shot. There was a serious rationale behind Milo's cautions.

"Admit it," I said, "you didn't know that Victor had been at Crystal's cabin the night of the murder."

"I figured as much," Milo said in a grumpy voice. "Don't you ever give me any credit?"

I was about to contradict the sheriff, but he was right. I didn't give him much credit for imagination or coloring beyond the lines. Yet he did use guesswork and intuition in his investigations. The problem was that he never shared anything he couldn't prove with hard-and-fast evidence. That, I supposed, was also to his credit.

"So what do you conclude?" I inquired, trying not to sound so testy.

"I don't. The fact that Cardenas and Dimitroff were both there doesn't prove a damned thing," Milo said, exasperated. "Don't you want to hear about your car?"

"Oh! Of course." I steeled myself for the bad news.

It came quickly. "The Jag's totaled. Bert and Brendan both did their damnedest, but they couldn't make the numbers come out right. Too bad I traded in my old Cherokee Chief. I could've given you a good deal on it."

"Thanks," I said glumly. "How much will I get from my insurance company?"

"Don't ask me, ask Brendan," Milo replied. "I figure a couple of grand."

A new car, even a new used car, was definitely not in my year-end budget. In anger and frustration, I threw a pen across the room. "Okay. I'll get a nice old American beater from the Nordbys," I said, referring to the local GM dealers, a couple of brothers who were nicknamed Trout and Skunk, though God—and Vida—only knew why.

"Not a bad idea, as long as it runs," Milo said blithely. "Got to go."

"Wait. Don't you have *anything* new on the homicide investigation?" It was my turn to needle Milo.

"Nope. Which makes it easy to spread the word that you're still our prime suspect, right?"

The hint of a chortle in the sheriff's voice infuriated me. "What a surprise. Police baffled. Goodbye, Milo." I hung up first.

Men. Tom, Ed, Milo—they were all driving me nuts. No doubt Scott would be late with his deadlines. Leo still wasn't back from lunch, though in fairness, he was probably wooing an advertiser or two.

Once again, I tried to turn my attention to the blasted women's shelter. What could I say that I hadn't already said fifty times earlier? Crystal was right about one thing—it was the men who were dragging their feet. If the project had involved the golf course or fishing regulations or a contest to see who could manipulate the TV remote control the fastest, all the good ol' boys would have piled on as if they were recovering a goal-line fumble.

Which is exactly what I wrote. I sounded as angry, as vitriolic, as waspish as Crystal. Maybe I hadn't given her credit, either. She'd been nasty about me, but Paula was right: Crystal had the courage of her convictions, and she'd run roughshod over anyone who stood in her way.

If she saw me as a weenie, she might not have been too far off the mark. I often tended to tiptoe around controversial issues for fear of offending not just our subscribers, but our advertisers. It was the way of the newspaper world. But this time I was going to stand up and be counted. We women *should* stick together. I wrote a paragraph to that effect, urging Alpine's female readers to form a united front.

Don't be cowed by the opinions of husbands, lovers, fathers, or sons, I wrote. *Their priorities are often different from ours. If we are without power, it's because we won't fight for it. Let your voice be heard, and use your influence to see that all women, including the battered, abused, and homeless, receive a chance to better themselves. The shelter is only the first step. Is a roof too much to ask to salvage dignity and restore self-esteem?*

I sat back in my chair, smiling. I hated to admit it, but the piece was worthy of Crystal. Although she was right, I still thought she was loathsome. Her way was not entirely my way: I hadn't attacked anyone on a personal basis.

But writing the editorial had given me an idea. It was just the grain of a thought, and it was a little crazy, but there it was. I didn't much like it; maybe I'd become completely perverse. Telling Vida was tempting, but I decided to wait. I didn't want her to think I'd gone 'round the bend.

That night around seven-thirty Tom called me from San Francisco. Kelsey was doing okay, but the doctor had suggested complete bedrest in order to prevent a premature birth.

"I'll have to stay here for a while," he said, sounding abject. "How angry are you?"

"Pretty angry," I replied, and then softened. "But I understand. Maybe I'm more disappointed than anything else. I thought we were having fun."

"We were. Can you hang on to that?"

Sure, sure, any damned fool can grasp a twig after falling over a hundred-foot cliff. But what good will it do?

"I guess so," I said, trying not to pout.

"Pray for Kelsey," said Tom.

"Of course." I was startled, not by the request, but because I hadn't thought of it on my own. What was becoming of me? Was I turning into Crystal?

"Look," Tom said, sounding strained, "I've got to go. Kelsey is staying overnight at the hospital—that's where I'm calling from—and I want to see her before Nurse Ratched calls for lights-out. You take care of yourself. Please?"

"Sure." I paused. "I will. Really. You, too."

But he wouldn't. Tom could only take care of others.

My idea was growing, burgeoning into something that was taking on a life of its own. I tried to resist it, and failed. Once again, I thought of telling Vida, and reached for the phone. Then I pulled away. Vida wouldn't think I was nuts. She'd egg me on, but for all the wrong reasons. It was better to keep my ugly little brainstorm to myself. I could be wrong.

Paula called about ten minutes after I finished talking to Tom. "Victor's gone," she said in an agitated voice. "Should I tell the sheriff?"

"I think so," I told her. "I'm not sure he was supposed to leave the vicinity. When did he leave? *How* did he leave? He can't drive."

"He left this afternoon while I was on campus," Paula said. "He left a note, a brief note, in which he failed to thank me for my hospitality. He'd hired a car from somewhere and was having it take him to the airport. Where would he get a car hire? Seattle?"

"Everett, maybe." I shook my head. Tom and Victor flying on a plane; Tom and Victor causing us a big, fat pain. "Do you know his destination?"

"I can't guess. It might have been San Francisco, but it could be New York. That's where he lives, at the Ansonia. I'll call Dodge right away." She hesitated, then went on quickly. "I could use some company. Care to join me for a festive eggnog?"

I debated. It was only seven forty-five. My social calendar wasn't exactly chock-full. I reflected briefly on my crazy idea.

"Why not? The sky's clear as a bell. I can see stars from my still-broken window. The glazier can't come until tomorrow. I'll be there shortly."

I hung up. And remembered that I had no car. I couldn't ask Vida to go with me; she was jealous of Paula. Nor would I presume on Milo. Leo was attending the annual chamber-of-commerce Christmas dinner. I paced around the living room, then realized I had to place a camel in my Nativity set. If I had a real camel, I thought, I could ride it to Startup. Standing in front of the mantel, I said a prayer for Kelsey, for Tom, for all of us, including Ed, despite the fact that he was a world-class ninny.

But the ninny had two cars, a Mercedes and a Beamer. It might cost me five inches in this week's edition, but I needed transportation. I hurriedly dialed his number at Casa de Bronska.

Ed was only too glad to accommodate me, not because he's generous, but because he likes to show off his wealth and extravagant toys. He picked me up ten minutes later in the black BMW, with Shirley following in the white Mercedes to cart him back home. I was profuse in my thanks, and made a mental note to buy the Bronskys a substantial Christmas present that they could all enjoy. Like a herd of beef cattle.

Since I had wheels under me, I stopped at Stuart's to pick up my new cell phone. Usually, the stores closed at six or seven during the rest of the year, but because of the holiday season virtually all of the merchants stayed open until nine. To my surprise, Cliff Stuart had already charged the battery.

"I thought you'd come by sooner to pick it up," he said, showing me my cell number on the small lighted screen. "Then I heard about your car. That's a real shame, Emma. The Jag was a classic around here."

I tried not to think about my rotten luck and took off in Ed's Beamer, which was also something of a classic in Alpine. But then so was Ed. In a way. And while the car was handsome on the outside, it was something of a mess on the inside. No wonder it had tinted windows. All the better not to have admirers see the empty McDonald cups, the Wendy's hamburger wrappers, the Itsa Bitsa Pizza boxes, the Burger King french-fries containers, or the object that looked like a dead possum but was probably one of Shirley's fur hats.

The weather was still holding, and the road was dry once I got past the ranger station. As I pulled into the driveway that led to Paula's house, I noticed that she had put up strings of icicle lights that cascaded from the eaves of her house. They looked lovely, especially when reflected off of the big stained-glass windows.

As she ushered me inside, I complimented her on the decorations.

"I haven't been able to do much until Victor left," Paula explained. "He made so many demands, and between him and the end of the quarter and finals, spare time has been at the top of my Christmas wish list."

"It is for all of us working girls," I responded, sitting down in the chair that Victor had recently vacated.

Rheims and Rouen sidled up to me, then settled on the braided rug at my feet.

Paula, who was wearing a purple caftan shot with silver threads, floated around behind the counter bar. "One eggnog coming up. I assure you, it'll beat the socks off of Crystal's rum punch."

I stared at Paula as she poured what looked like a jigger and a half of rum into a red mug. "I'll bet it will," I replied. "I have to drive home, remember."

"Then I'll go easy on the refills," Paula said, pouring an equal amount of rum into a green mug for herself. "Now tell me what's new in the investigation. I'm hearing some strange stories about Nat Cardenas."

I wasn't about to spread rumors, at least not until I got half-blitzed on rum eggnog. "Milo talked to him," I said, then found a perfect opening to change the subject. "Did you call the sheriff's office to let them know about Victor's departure?"

Paula sat down on a Second Empire chair that may or may not have been the real thing. Outside, I could hear the wind stirring the bare branches of the cottonwood trees. "Yes," Paula replied. "I talked to Dwight Gould. He said Dodge wouldn't be happy."

The news didn't surprise me. Then I wondered when Milo had been happy about anything. Was it when we were still together? Struck with guilt, I took a big swig of eggnog.

And another. "Paula, are we friends?"

"What?" She gave me a goofy grin. "Of course. Why do you ask?"

"I don't know," I said slowly. "Maybe this is the time of year when we take some personal inventory."

Paula shrugged, creating ripples of silver in her caftan. "I suppose it is. But I don't even have time for that. I've still got some projects to grade, and then I have to finish a bathroom window divider for a couple in Sultan who are giving it to each other for Christmas. It's so hectic. I've never been a big fan of the holiday season."

I didn't agree, so I kept my mouth shut. Rain began to spatter the tall, beautiful windows that ran from floor to ceiling.

Paula snapped her fingers and stood up. "We need snacks. How about some Brie? Or salmon mousse? I've got a terrific Gouda in here someplace."

"Any of those will do," I said, watching the cats sniff around Paula's hem. "Didn't Victor eat you out of house and home?"

"He tried," Paula said as she set out both kinds of cheese, opened a box of crackers, and tossed some kitty treats at the Siamese cats, who had somehow assumed pathetic expressions. "But he complained about everything, including the Brie."

I offered Paula an ironic smile. "It must make you wonder what you ever saw in him."

She dropped a cracker, which broke in two on the floor. "What do you mean?"

"Come on, Paula," I said, still smiling. "When we first met a few years ago, you told me about your past, which included an affair with a tuba player. Did you think I'd forgotten?"

"There are a hell of a lot of tuba players," Paula retorted. "What makes you think it was Victor Dimitroff?"

I leaned on the counter across from her. "It's a little much to be a coincidence, isn't it? Besides, you knew he lived in the Ansonia, and you knew it had an elevator. I have to assume that either you visited Victor there, or you lived there, too. It's famous for artists of every type who've been residents over the years. Besides," I added with a little shrug, "why not Victor? I can see that he must have been rather attractive before he fell in love with himself. Or," I added, catching my breath, "did he fall in love with Crystal?"

Paula uttered a fractured sort of laugh. "I don't think so. He used her. Typical of men."

"So they were lovers?" I munched on a chunk of Gouda and noticed that the rain was coming down harder, heavy drops that beat a prelude to snow against the glass.

"I doubt it." Paula bit off the words, then finished fixing the crackers, cheese, and mousse. "Let's sit down. You seem to be full of odd little ideas."

We resumed our places, but not before Rheims and Rouen had to be evicted from the chair in which I'd been sitting. In a sulk, they left the living room and disappeared.

"You must admit I have good reasons for thinking odd thoughts," I said. "I've been trying to figure out what's going on with the murder investigation. So far, I've lost a front window, my beloved car, and most of my reputation."

"That was a shame about your Jag," Paula said. "I loved that car, too. Is it totaled?"

"I guess." But the Jag wasn't uppermost in my mind. "So why did Victor really come here if he and Crystal weren't lovers?"

"He wanted a change of pace, a winter retreat," Paula explained. "He'd gotten to a point in his *Vichy* composition where he really needed to concentrate. I gathered he'd made arrangements to stay with Crystal, but by the time he arrived, Aaron had shown up. Victor tried to get some work done at the ski lodge, and kept hoping Aaron would bail out. But after a couple of days, he realized that wasn't going to happen, and he made plans to leave. Of course Aaron wasn't at Crystal's the whole time—he was in jail for a few days, and before that, he'd met up with some old pals and bunked with them. But Crystal could never be sure when he'd turn up again as long as he was in the vicinity. Victor, as you may have noticed, is not a patient man."

Finding the eggnog not only delicious, but comforting, I took a couple of quick swallows. "Victor strikes me as someone who doesn't like waiting for anything, including international renown," I said. "Yet he called on Crystal. We know he did, at least the night she was killed. Did that bother you since you and he had once been so close?"

Paula frowned at me. "What is this, girlfriend? You're probing my psyche?"

"I'm curious," I replied, drinking more eggnog. "I'm trying to sort through everything in my mind, including all the players. Maybe I'm tired of being 'it.' "

"Understandable," Paula commented in an offhand manner.

"For instance," I went on, "did you know that Aaron thought someone was trying to break into Crystal's cabin this morning?"

Paula's eyes widened. "No. Did he actually see someone or did he imagine two-headed bugs crawling up the walls?"

"Who knows? But he called the sheriff," I said as Rheims and Rouen padded back into view. Actually, there were four cats, or maybe six. My eyes didn't seem quite focused. "The more I think about it, the more I figure that Aaron wouldn't want any contact with the law unless he really thought he needed some help."

"Checking on a prowler beats getting busted," Paula said. "Hey, how about another nog?"

"Why not?" I tried to give Paula my mug, but we bobbled the handoff. It bounced off the braided rug, undamaged. We both giggled as we proceeded back to the counter bar. I was still giggling as she did a hit-and-miss job of replenishing our drinks.

"I shouldn't do this," I finally said. "It's beginning to snow, and I've borrowed a car, Ed Bronsky's expensive Bummer. I mean, *Beamer*. I might as well cap off the holiday season by driving it off the bridge at Deception Falls."

"Ed." Paula sighed. "Talk about an impossible male. I've always wondered how you dealt with him when he was at *The Advocate*."

The wind was moaning in the eaves of the converted farmhouse and the cats were uttering surreal little cries. Maybe they wanted to go out. I thought cats had more sense when it came to comfort.

As we meandered back to our chairs, Paula gave the cats a cross-eyed glance, then looked at me with a curious expression. "Did you come here tonight just to ask about Victor and me and our long-ago romance? How come, Emma? You've never pried into my love life before."

That was true. It wasn't my style. In any event, Paula was open, if casual, about her past relationships. "As I said, I'm trying to sort things out. Clearing my name," I added, gulping down more nog.

Paula laughed, the familiar gusty sound that was one of the things that had always endeared her to me. "In other words, you're trying to eliminate Victor as a suspect. Or," she continued, no longer laughing, "you're trying to figure out if I'm on the list." She blinked at me. "Am I?"

"Who ishn't? I mean, *isn't*." I started to giggle again. "I sure am."

"Am I?" Paula repeated, then frowned. "Did I already

say that? My lapse seems to be having a brain. I mean . . ." she began, and threw up her hands. "Have another cracker," she offered, holding the plate out to me. Three crackers slid to the floor. "Don't eat those. Take a clean one. I'd better eat a couple myself." She gave me a lop-sided grin.

"Thanks," I said, taking two and jiggling my eggnog mug. "You're right. This is much better than Crystal's poisoned punch."

"I can make more," Paula said.

I looked outside. The trees were now blurred by snow. Or maybe it was my eyes. I definitely felt blurry. "In a minute," I said. "Maybe." Then, on teetering legs, I stood up. "Excuse me, Paula," I said with an apologetic smile, "I need to use the bathroom. Okay?"

"Sure," she responded. "Just don't let the cats in. They like to swim in the toilet bowl."

Picking up my purse, I laughed. "I like cats. Maybe someday I'll get one."

"Keep the cats out," she murmured. "They like to jump in the toilet bowl."

"So you said. Sounds like fun. Maybe I'll let them."

Proving Paula's point—or points, as long as she was re-peating herself—Rheims and Rouen followed me to the bathroom door. It took some doing, but I finally man-aged to get myself on the inside while they stayed on the outside.

I emerged five minutes later to find Paula mixing an-other batch of eggnog. At least that's what it looked like she was doing. For all I could tell, she was stirring up a pot of bats, toads, and eye of newt.

"Love's a good motive," I said, propping myself against the counter bar. "How about Victor? I crossed him off my list earlier because I thought he was too"—I fumbled for the right word— "impetuous. Then I got to thinking that you can't compose music and be totally impetuous, right? And you have to have patience to play in a symphony orchestra. 'Course, maybe that's why he quit. What do you think, old buddy?"

Paula refilled both our mugs. "Not Victor," she said, shaking her head. "Victor has affairs. I doubt he's ever been in love with anybody but himself." She looked at me and we both giggled.

"Love," I said in a voice that didn't sound at all like me. "What a crock. How do people get together and stay together?"

"Don't ask me," said Paula, drinking deeply. "My parents were miserable together."

"That's sad," I said, with a wobbly shake of my head. "My parents stayed together, but they were killed in a car crash when they were in their early fifties."

"Maybe they were lucky," Paula said in a melancholy voice. "Maybe they were still happy."

"That's the trouble," I said, my voice dropping a few notches. "Women are always looking for happy endings. Men are just looking."

"And then running." Paula sighed. "Everybody runs, I guess. Sooner or later."

"A toast," I said, raising my mug. "To love, and the six or seven people who've been lucky enough to find it and keep it."

Paula didn't join the toast. "Love sucks," she said, also leaning against the counter. "It makes us do some crazy things. I hate love. It made me crazy."

It made me crazy. The past tense. I don't know how that phrase managed to sink into my befuddled brain, but it did, right there alongside my nutty little idea.

I reached out and clapped Paula on the shoulder. "Oh,

hell!" I gasped, between giggles and gurgles. "You *did* do it, didn't you?"

Paula slumped against me. "Yep, I did. I killed, killed, killed Crystal Bird. Crazy, huh?"

Chapter Eighteen

THERE WAS SILENCE in the room, though the storm had begun to gather force. I felt sick, and full of self-loathing. Sometimes it was wrong to be right. Or at least horribly painful.

Paula just stood there, staring at me with a moronic grin on her face. Maybe, once she got over the shock of her admission, she would scream denials or even attack me. But for the moment, she hugged me and I hugged her back. I wished Paula would say something, anything to break the tension. And where was Milo? Fifteen minutes ago while I was in the bathroom, I'd called him on my new cell phone. Had I imagined the call had gone through? Had I followed the instructions correctly? My vision had been so blurry that I'd had trouble reading the pamphlet and great difficulty pushing the tiny buttons.

"You were jealous of Crystal," I said, my mouth suddenly dry. "Maybe not just about Victor. Maybe you saw her and *Crystal Clear* as some kind of threat. Goodness knows, I did."

Paula leaned against me, her ample body a dead-weight. "Jealousy is a powerful motive," she said, her voice hoarse. "Ugly. Very ugly emotion."

"True," I agreed, wishing she'd move. "I didn't want to think it was you, I tried not to believe it. But you said that love had made you crazy, as if you were referring to something specific—like Crystal's murder. You also mentioned the rum punch Crystal served me when I called on her the night that she was murdered. I don't remember telling you about that. And then it dawned on me that it tasted so bitter because there were already a dozen or so sleeping pills—my pills—in the drink. In fact, I felt slightly sick the next morning. It was you who arranged the meeting between Crystal and me, it was you who stole my pills. You set me up, and I ought to be damned furious about it. But I'm not. I'm just sad."

Finally releasing me, Paula half staggered to the Second Empire chair. Rheims and Rouen jumped into her lap. "You're wrong, Emma."

I had also sat down, and tensed in the chair. "In what way?" I asked.

Paula stroked each of the cats with shaking hands. "I wasn't jealous of Crystal and Victor. How could I be? Crystal wasn't in love with Victor. And vice versa, for all I could see."

"Interesting," I murmured, wondering how long Paula would remain calm. The wind was howling and the rain was swiftly turning to snow. Maybe Milo had been held up at the higher elevations. "Still," I remarked, "you must have been pretty fed up with men. You haven't had a lot of luck. Neither had Crystal."

"Men!" Paula made a slashing gesture with one hand, which sent Rheims and Rouen leaping off of her lap. "They're a useless sex. Why did I ever bother myself?"

"It's true," I said, not without sympathy. "Men can be a pain. Why do you think I never married?"

Paula's expression was ironic. "Because you're a romantic. You've told me your sad story, about a married man—the worst kind—and how you had his child even though you knew he wouldn't leave his nutty wife. I've never figured that one out. Haven't you ever heard of an abortion?"

"I had," I said quietly. "It was legal when I got pregnant with Adam. I didn't choose to take advantage of what was handed down then by twelve old men."

"Well, I did. Twice." Paula's voice sharpened. "Why not? Both of the men ran out on me, and yes, one of them was married."

I actually managed a laugh. "So you let a bunch of old farts on the Supreme Court manipulate you. What's the difference between them and the men who took off? I don't get it, and it's not just because I'm Catholic."

"The Supremes didn't knock me up."

"But you developed a hatred of men," I said. "You got gypped, as well as manipulated. So what are you trying to tell me?"

Paula also laughed, but without mirth. "What you, apparently, didn't figure out."

But I had. "That you became a lesbian?"

Paula clapped both hands to her head. "You don't *become* a lesbian. That's what you are, how you're born. It simply took me a long time to figure it out and admit who I was. Am. As it did with Crystal."

Deep down, that's what I expected to hear. But it wasn't enough. "I don't think it's always that simple," I said. "Sometimes, I think it's a form of rebellion. Look— I can't say as I blame you. As of today, I was about ready to give up on men myself. Maybe I will. I might even find a woman who can fill a void in my life. But I won't *become* a lesbian." I put the emphasis on the verb and looked Paula straight in the eye. "But I think with you, it cut both ways. You were jealous of Crystal, and you were physically attracted. She not only didn't reciprocate your romantic feelings, she'd been involved with a man you once cared for very deeply. And that's why you killed her, and you tried to pin it on me because ... I don't know. Why, Paula? As I said before, I thought we were friends."

Paula's shoulders slumped, and somehow the silver threads in the caftan seemed to turn a dull gray. "We *were* friends. We had so much in common." She paused, then stood up. "I think we need another drink."

I started to protest but this was no time for side arguments. I remained in the chair as Paula went behind the counter bar.

"You told me about Tom," she continued, getting more eggs and milk out of the refrigerator, "and how you had Adam even though his father wouldn't marry you. At first, I felt you'd been a fool. Then I met Adam. He's a wonderful young man. And I thought—not for the first time, but with an altered perception—of what would have happened if I hadn't had those abortions. I began to envy you, resent you, even hate you. Unfortunately, all these things overwhelmed me about the same time I met Crystal." Paula stopped speaking as she emptied the rum bottle into the mixture, then reached under the counter, presumably for the nutmeg.

"It was bad enough discovering that she'd had an affair with Victor in Portland," Paula said, her voice gone dull, though her hands were busily mixing the eggnog. "It was even worse when I learned she'd sworn off men and was attracted to women. It wasn't a real revelation for her. She'd always known, but had been in denial. Then she came out of the closet when she moved back here. I not only admired her courage, her causes, her ruthless determination, but I had other, physical feelings for her. She rebuffed me. I couldn't stand any more rejection, especially from my own sex. I guess I snapped." Paula gave me a strange, sad look. "I set you up because before there was Crystal, there was you. I fell for you from the start, even though I knew it was hopeless."

The shock sobered me as if someone had poured ice-cold water over my head. "Oh, Paula," I gasped, "I'm so sorry!"

"Then let's drink to us," she said, with a melancholy little smile. "To what might have been."

I suddenly realized that Paula had stirred the eggnog after putting in the nutmeg. But the nutmeg went on top, as a garnish. She had added something else to the mixture. I still had my mug. Involuntarily, I covered it with my hand.

"No more for me, Paula," I said, my voice sounding unnatural. "I really should . . ."

Paula drained her mug in four big gulps. "This batch wasn't for you." She staggered a bit against the counter, the mug falling from her hand. "I thought about it, but I couldn't." She lurched between the counter and the refrigerator. "Sorry, Emma," she muttered, and fell to the floor.

Rheims and Rouen raced to Paula's lifeless body. The stained-glass windows seemed to weep.

That damned Milo had been listening outside for the past ten minutes. I could have killed him.

"Hey," he said, after Paula had been taken away in an ambulance that was in no hurry to reach its destination, "when do I get to hear a confession like that? I mean, with women being a triangle? It was kind of hot."

Men. "What were you doing out there in the snow?" I snapped. "Jacking off ?"

"Emma!" The sheriff looked shocked. We were in his office, where I'd gone to give my statement.

"You might have stopped her," I retorted, firmly closing the pet carrier where Rheims and Rouen were complaining about their transport. "You might have saved her life."

"That's dubious," Milo said, though he looked a bit shaken. "She didn't want her life saved. That's why she drank the poisoned eggnog."

I leaned back in the visitor's chair, and tried to ignore the smell of stale cigarettes, which about now tickled my nostrils like some Babylonian elixir. "It's my fault," I said in a tired voice. "This has been one hell of a December. Now I've not only lost a friend, I've caused her death. What a miserable Advent."

Milo frowned. "Sometime you'll have to explain this Advent deal to me. I don't think Congregationalists had that when I was going to Sunday school."

"Maybe not." I reached out a hand. "Give me a cigarette or I'll have to hurt you."

"I thought you already did." The words had slipped out of Milo's mouth, and I could tell by the look on his face that he regretted them.

"God, Milo, I thought we were past that. I really did." It didn't work that way, of course. What was the difference between my dumping of Milo and my correctly perceived rejection of Paula? Neither of them had been able to revert to a real friendship.

The sheriff leaned across the desk to light my cigarette. "I thought I was pretty much over it until Cavanaugh showed up."

"You think that didn't have an effect on me?" I shot back.

"A good one, though," Milo said.

"That's debatable."

"Huh?"

I heaved a heavy sigh. "Let's say it was fun while it lasted." Then I explained about Tom and Kelsey and my mixed feelings toward the man I was beginning to call The Phantom.

"That's weird," Milo said when I'd finished.

I shook my head. "It's not at all weird. It's Tom. He needs to be needed, and always by someone who is weaker, more troubled, and beset with problems he thinks he can solve. I don't qualify. I'm too damned normal."

"That's weird," Milo repeated.

I gave up trying to explain and started to stand up, then stopped. "Do you want to sleep with me tonight?"

Milo's long jaw dropped. "Are you kidding?"

"No. I need a friend. I need a lover. I need a *man*. You're it, cowboy."

But the sheriff hesitated. "Are you still drunk? You seemed to be able to drive Ed's car okay."

"I'm completely sober. Come on, Dodge, give me the courtesy of a prompt reply."

Typically, Milo needed to mull. Then he shook his head. "I don't think so, Emma. Sorry."

I gaped at him. "You're turning me down?"

He gave a nod. "It wouldn't be right. It isn't your style. It's not mine, either."

Milo was right, of course. I avoided his gaze, then stood up. "I guess it was a bad idea. Blame it on Crystal Bird. She's cost me plenty in the last week or two."

"No problem," Milo said, also getting to his feet.

I glanced down at the pet carrier and gave the sheriff a wry little smile. "After all, I have the cats."

But I still didn't have a car, which dawned on me once more as I left Milo's office. It was after ten, it was snowing, and I wondered if Ed would mind if I kept the Beamer until morning.

I decided he wouldn't. Ed would have to drive me home after I delivered his car. Knowing how lazy he was, and genuinely concerned about disturbing his comfort so late at night, I drove the BMW to my log house.

Again, someone was waiting for me. This time, however, I readily identified my visitor. Vida was sitting in her Buick, which was parked by my mailbox.

"Good grief," she cried as she got out of her car, "is that one of Ed's collection?"

"I borrowed it," I called back.

Vida trudged up to the front porch. "Why does he keep buying German cars? Why can't he get himself a big Cadillac if he wants to show off?"

"Ed thought he was buying an English automobile when he got that one," I said, nodding at the Beamer. "He was sure that BMW stood for British Majesty Wheels."

"He's almost as demented as you are," Vida retorted as I let us into the house. "Now you tell me how you deduced that Paula was the killer and why you didn't let me know what you were up to. And yes, I would definitely enjoy a cup of hot tea. I've been waiting twenty minutes in front of your house. I'd no idea you'd take so long at the sheriff's. Not to mention that that wretched nephew of mine didn't call me until almost ten to let me know what had happened."

Poor Billy. He was definitely getting coal in his Christmas stocking this year. "Come into the kitchen," I said, after putting our coats in the closet. "I'll tell you all about it."

"Start with why you didn't tell me in the first place," Vida demanded, pulling out a chair at the kitchen table.

I glanced over my shoulder as I turned the heat on under the teakettle. "I thought I might be wrong. I hoped that I was wrong. It was all sort of intuitive. When Tom left me that note today, I raved and ranted about giving up on men," I continued, joining Vida at the table. "Then I had a sudden thought. Some women *do* give up. Most of them simply go on with their lives, get a hobby, volunteer, whatever. But occasionally, a rejected woman will form an attachment with another woman. I'd remembered that when I first met Paula, she'd given me a brief rundown on her previous lovers. One of them was a tuba player. I guessed that Victor was that long-lost love. He'd come to see Crystal, not Paula. I gathered that Victor and Crystal had also been lovers, apparently while she was still in Portland. Everything began to fall into place."

I stopped as the teakettle whistled. "Somewhere in the early stages of the investigation, I mentioned that Paula, among others, had had the opportunity to swipe my sleeping pills. But I dismissed the idea, because I couldn't see a motive then, I couldn't imagine her trying to frame me, and most of all, I didn't want her to be the guilty party. She was my friend."

Vida harrumphed. "Some friend. Didn't I always tell you I didn't think much of Paula Rubens?"

I bit my tongue. Had Paula been a saint with a heavenly crown, Vida still wouldn't have warmed to her. Thus, I would never tell Vida that Paula had been attracted to me. Her reaction would be extreme, and very negative.

"So Paula was secretly in love with you?" Vida said as I handed her a mug of tea.

I slumped into my chair. "How'd you guess?"

"I'm just putting it all together," she said in an amazingly matter-of-fact voice. "Why else would Paula try to set you up as the killer? Goodness, it's a wonder she wasn't after Marisa Foxx, too. But then we don't know about Marisa, do we?"

I had to admit that the thought had crossed my mind. Maybe Crystal had been attracted to Marisa. Maybe Marisa had rejected *her*. Hell, for all I knew, Marisa was in love with Milo. I've learned not to make hasty judgments about people, having been wrong so often.

"Anyway," I went on, "here's how I figured it. Paula showed up at Crystal's around seven. She helped Crystal make the rum punch. That's when she slipped my sleeping pills into the mix. She came back later, to make sure Crystal was dead. As an afterthought, she slashed Crystal's wrists with a razor she'd found in her own house when she first moved in. She admitted that, and I realized that Victor had said nothing about seeing Crystal's wrists cut. Also, Paula had to remove the love letters she'd written to Crystal. She took a chance, but figured that no one would show up so late, unless it was Aaron, and he'd be stoned anyway."

Vida was silent for a few moments. "I can't believe Paula actually confessed."

"She was drunk," I said, but was unwilling to admit that I was, too.

"Still . . ." Vida drew circles on my vinyl table covering. "I suppose it was rather brave of her. To be so honest, I mean. Though suicide is a cowardly act."

"Paula couldn't face the humiliation, not to mention the ultimate rejection by the people, which translates as the law," I said. "But she did have courage. It's one of the things I admired about her. She and Crystal had that much in common."

"My, my." Vida looked unusually thoughtful. "Love *is* strange, isn't it?"

"It crosses all boundaries," I said, "and makes human beings do foolish things, regardless of race, religion, or sexual preference. We all operate from the same wellspring of human emotions. The heart is a very delicate thing."

"Perhaps it does rule us," Vida murmured. "After Ernest died, I used to think my head ruled me. But . . ." Her voice trailed off.

My eyes widened as I leaned across the table. "Vida, are you and Buck . . . serious?"

Vida reeled in the chair. "Goodness! You smell like a distillery! Have you been drinking, too?"

"A little," I admitted. "Now tell me about—"

"There's nothing to tell. Yet." She gave me her owlish expression.

I assumed that if Vida and Buck Bardeen, her companion of the past few years, had an announcement to make, I'd be the first to know. Thus, I let the subject drop.

"So Nat and Aaron and even Dean Ramsey and the Eriks clan were not involved," she mused. "I wonder what Aaron will do now."

"My guess is that he'll sell the cabin," I said, pouring more tea. "The real-estate market's good right now, and it'd still make an excellent summer or winter vacation home."

"Yes," Vida agreed. "Though it would be nice to think that Aaron wouldn't fritter away the money on drugs and such."

"Who knows?" I replied. "Aaron needs to get his head straightened out. Having his estranged wife get murdered might have done that, but so far, I don't see any signs of it happening."

"Was it Paula who was at the cabin this morning?" Vida asked, adding ample amounts of sugar and milk to her tea.

"I don't think so," I said. "She seemed genuinely surprised when I mentioned that Aaron had called the sheriff."

"Hmm." Again, Vida grew silent. "I wonder."

"What?"

She gave herself a shake. "Nothing. It's late, I'm rather tired, and my mind is wandering."

"Mine wandered in the right direction, for once," I

said. "Looking back, there were so many hints about Crystal's state of mind, and Paula's, too. When I went to the glass exhibit at the college, Paula had a piece—a wonderful, luminous glass panel—that depicted Hera, queen of the Greek gods and goddesses. If I remember correctly from my college mythology class, Hera was famous for being jealous. She held a grudge and could be cruelly vindictive. In some vague way, I wondered why Paula was drawn to the subject. Now I think I know."

"Stained glass," Vida remarked. "Whatever is the point, except in churches? You can't really see through it, so why bother?"

I ignored the comment, and continued. "Then there were the men in Crystal's life. They spoke of her as if she'd cut them off in more ways than one. She hadn't bothered to divorce Aaron. I considered the friendship between Crystal and Paula as odd, it struck a false note." After the funeral, it wasn't Victor whom Aaron was yelling at—it was Paula, who was next to him. In some weird way, Aaron may have blamed Paula for Crystal's anti-man stance. I grimaced. "I feel really awful about Paula. I liked her a lot. Maybe I've regained my reputation, but I've lost a friend."

Vida had finished her tea and was standing up. She patted my shoulder. "You still have me." She gave me another pat. "And I don't find you the least bit attractive."

That weekend, the fourth and last Sunday in Advent, Ben called to say that he and Adam wouldn't arrive until Christmas Eve day. It seemed that my brother had talked to Tom, who had had to revise his schedule because of Kelsey's near miscarriage. He couldn't get together with Ben and Adam until the twenty-third.

I had cussed and ranted when Ben relayed the news.

"Though hundreds of miles away," I raged, "Tom has still managed to screw up my holidays. This is about the worst Advent ever."

"Hey," my brother said, "at least you give a damn about the reason for the season. Hang in there, Adam and I are bringing a boxload of cheap gifts and some of the best tequila you ever poured down your throat through a funnel."

"I hate tequila," I retorted, then wished I'd kept my mouth shut. "Okay, okay," I grumbled, "but you know you'll get to Alpine really late. Your flight will be delayed in San Francisco, the airport will be jammed in Seattle, you'll have to wait forever to get a rental car, and then we'll have another blizzard up here and they'll close Highway 2."

"Sounds like fun," Ben said in his most aggravatingly cheerful voice. "Got to go. It's seventy-eight degrees in Tuba City, and time for my dip in the pool."

There was no pool at Ben's rectory, but I didn't doubt that it was seventy-eight degrees. I would have hated that. Heat and sun aren't my style, especially at Christmas.

Which reminded me, I was once again behind in putting up my Advent figures. I took the last two Wise Men out of the carton in the closet and set them up on the mantel. Then I tried to pray, but my thoughts kept straying to Paula. I prayed for her, for Crystal, too, but my heart was still heavy, my soul a wasteland.

I was right about my brother and son's trip from San Francisco. Adam called three times on the twenty-fourth, first to say that they were fogged in. Then he phoned from Sea-Tac, telling me that the baggage machinery had malfunctioned and they'd be late leaving the airport. The third and last call had come from Monroe at seven P.M. Ben and Adam were starving, so they'd stopped for something to eat. They hoped to arrive by nine. Naturally, around eight o'clock, it started to snow.

Half an hour later I was covering the potato-roll dough, made from a recipe that had been passed down through four generations of Alpiners by the Clemans family. As I placed the bowl in the refrigerator, I heard someone at the door. Through the peephole, I could see a woman I didn't recognize. She had something in her arms.

Cautiously, I opened the door. "Yes?"

A girl in her twenties stood on the porch with a baby wrapped in a blue blanket. Her face, which was red from the cold, looked pinched, and snow-covered wisps of blonde hair stuck out through the crocheted scarf she had tied around her head.

"Are you Ms. Lord?" she asked in a hoarse voice.

"Yes," I said. "I'm Emma Lord."

"Could I come in, just for a minute?" She was shivering, and held the baby so close to her chest that I was afraid she might smother it.

"Sure," I said, stepping aside. "I'm sorry, I didn't catch your name."

"I didn't give it," she replied, breathing heavily and examining the baby. "Poor Danny. He keeps throwing off his little mittens."

"Sit down. Please." I ushered her and the baby to the sofa. Concern as well as a sense of wariness overcame me. Was this some kind of scam? *While pitiful mother and tiny child distract homeowner, male accomplice steals everything not bolted down.* I could see the headlines in next week's *Advocate*. "Now tell me your name," I said, sounding rather stern.

The young mother removed the heavy diaper bag from her shoulder. "I'm Amber Ramsey," she said. "Does that mean anything to you?"

* * *

At first, it didn't. Then I thought of Dean Ramsey and Crystal and the daughter who had run away. "Good Lord," I whispered.

"I thought my dad would be here," she said, ignoring my shocked expression. "I mean, here in Alpine. But they told me at the sheriff's office that he'd gone back to Oregon to spend Christmas with his new family. I'd tried to get hold of him before, a week or so ago, after I heard my mom had been killed. Dad was out on a job, so I didn't see or talk to him, but I found out that my mom had lived in a cabin down the road. I went there and I saw my stepdad through the window. I didn't want anything to do with him. He's a creep."

So that was who had been at Crystal's cabin the morning that Aaron had called the sheriff. "Is it because of Aaron that you ran away?" I asked, still shaken by Amber's arrival.

She nodded. "He kept coming on to me. I couldn't tell my mother. They were having problems even then. I was ashamed to go to my dad. He was doing real good with his new wife and kids. So I just kept going. That was six years ago." Her shoulders sagged under the worn car coat, and her weary expression seemed to hold every mile and every day that she had been on the run.

"Are you married?" I asked as Rheims and Rouen padded into the living room and began sniffing Amber's boots.

Amber shook her head. "I got raped." Her eyes avoided mine. "In Vegas."

"I'm so sorry." I put out a hand to touch her sleeve. "How old is the baby?"

"Danny?" She brightened, and I could see that she was probably pretty when she wasn't half-frozen and near exhaustion. "Five weeks. Isn't he precious?"

He was. Now that the hood of his bunting had slipped

off, I could see blond hair, soft as duck down. He yawned and made tiny fists.

"How come you came to see me?" I asked, discouraging Rheims and Rouen from jumping onto the sofa.

Again, Amber avoided my gaze. "My car broke down. Nobody can fix it until after Christmas. When I went to ask the sheriff's office about who had killed my mom and where my dad was, they told me to talk to you. I walked up here. I didn't realize these hills are so steep."

"Let me get you something to eat," I said. "Do you have formula for the baby, or are you nursing?"

"I'm nursing," she responded. "It's cheaper." Now she did look at me, and there was a faint spark of irony in her blue eyes.

I smiled. "What would you like? I have ham, cheese, cookies—tons of stuff."

"Um . . ." She unzipped her car coat and started unbuttoning her flannel shirt. "Anything, I guess. I don't suppose I could stay here tonight? The motels are all full with visitors and skiers, and anyway, I'm kind of running out of money. . . ."

My face fell. "Oh, Amber, I'm so sorry. My brother and my son are due any minute. I only have two bedrooms. I'm afraid we're full up, too."

"Oh." She turned away, then put the baby to her breast. "That's okay. We can sleep in the car."

"But the car's all the way down Alpine Way, isn't it?" I'd stood up, on my way to the kitchen.

"It's at that Texaco station," she said, her face fixed on little Danny.

I shifted from one foot to the other. Then my eyes drifted to the mantel. I made a face. In the rush to get the presents wrapped and the cookies baked and the house decorated, I'd neglected to add the last two figures to the Nativity scene. Mary and Baby Jesus.

I took a step toward Amber. "You can stay here," I said, and was surprised to find that my voice was trembling with emotion. "Take my room. Please."

Amber looked up. "Oh, no. I couldn't do that."

"Yes, you could." I glanced at the mantel again. "You have to. For me."

"What?"

"Come on, say you'll stay. Please."

Amber looked faintly bewildered, but she finally nodded. "Okay. But I hate to be a bother."

I shook my head. "You're no bother. In fact," I added with a wry little smile, "you might say you're my salvation."

I gave the mantel a final look before heading for the kitchen.

My Nativity set was complete.

In Alpine, murder always seems to occur in alphabetical order—and you can be sure Emma Lord, editor and publisher of *The Alpine Advocate*, is there to report every detail.

Don't miss any of the Emma Lord mysteries, beginning with

THE ALPINE ADVOCATE

As editor-publisher of *The Alpine Advocate*, Emma Lord is always in search of a good story. But when Mark Doukas—heir to the richest old man in town—is murdered, Emma gets more than she bargained for.

THE ALPINE BETRAYAL

Dani Marsh—former Alpine resident, now Hollywood star—returns to Alpine for some location shooting in the Cascade Mountains only to become embroiled in the murder of her ex-husband. Once again, Emma Lord has to do some heavy investigating to get to the bottom of the story.

THE ALPINE CHRISTMAS

It's Christmastime in Alpine, and that means snow, carolers, Christmas trees . . . and murder. The discovery of one woman's leg and another woman's nude, half-frozen body in the lake leads Emma Lord and her House & Home editor, Vida, into a deadly holiday.

THE ALPINE DECOY

The arrival of a young African-American nurse in Alpine is news enough in this predominantly white community. When a second newcomer—a young black man—is found dead, Emma Lord suspects that something sinister is afoot.

THE ALPINE ESCAPE

When Emma Lord decides to take a few days off, she expects some time alone to do some soul-searching. Instead, she is caught up in a century-old mystery: Her friends have found the skeleton of an unknown young woman in their basement. . . .

THE ALPINE FURY

The Bank of Alpine has been a fixture in Alpine for generations, but suddenly something fishy seems to be going on. Emma Lord decides to investigate—and finds the bank's sexy blonde bookkeeper strangled to death at a local motel.

THE ALPINE GAMBLE

The year's biggest news story is the development of a luxury spa around Alpine's mineral springs—and the controversy surrounding it. But even those who predicted that the spa would bring sleaze and "Californicators" didn't expect to be confronted with murder.

THE ALPINE HERO

In the facial room of Stella's Styling Salon, Emma Lord stumbles across the body of a woman, anonymous under a mud pack, throat slashed. As rumors begin to fly, shady strangers turn up in town, and a young woman disappears—making Emma more determined than ever to scoop this story.

THE ALPINE ICON

Glamorous Ursula Randall returns to Alpine to marry her third husband—only to be murdered, her body dumped facedown in the river. As Emma Lord hunts for a stop-press story, a snake-in-the-grass killer, unappeased by one murder, slithers unnoticed through the shadows. . . .

THE ALPINE JOURNEY

Emma Lord journeys to Oregon for a reunion with a former colleague. While visiting nearby Cannon Beach in the off-season, Emma soon discovers that there's no off-season for murder.

THE ALPINE KINDRED

When a local philanthropist is brutally stabbed in the old logging town of Alpine, Emma Lord can scarcely pry a word out of the victim's reclusive relatives. But that doesn't stop Emma, who is hot after a story that is fueled by rumor, malice, and the deadly antics of a maniac. . . .

by Mary Daheim

Published by The Ballantine Publishing Group.
Available at your local bookstore.